Hoax AND Kisses

ELODIE COLLIARD

This novel is entirely a work of fiction. The names, characters and incidents portrayed in it are the work of the author's imagination. Any resemblance to actual persons, living or dead, events or localities is entirely coincidental.

First edition

Editing by Beth Lawton.
Book cover and design by Leni Kauffman.

ISBN 9781778137938

By this author

It's Always Been You series
The Last Encore
From Paris, in Love
Unbearably Yours

Author's Note

Reading is political. Let's start with that.

But these days, reading almost feels like an act of defiance in itself, doesn't it? Especially when you read about diversity, mental health, or something as fundamental as empathy.

Writing about autism in this current political context felt just like that—an act of resistance. Like I was giving a big middle finger to the clown in charge of the Health Department. Representation in books has always mattered, but it is especially crucial right now. When public discourse is hostile or dismissive toward marginalized communities, simply telling the truth becomes a radical act. In a climate where those in power often devalue or erase neurodivergent voices, asserting that reality through literature is necessary.

Several sensitivity readers have read HOAX AND KISSES to help me portray autism as authentically as possible. But autism is a spectrum, and Daphne's experience will not be anyone else's. As with all other kinds of neurodivergence, which are deeply subjective, I ask readers to approach their reflections with empathy, understanding, and kindness. God knows we need it these days.

With love, always,
Elodie

For those who dare to be their true selves around the people who are supposed to uplift them, only to be met with silence, judgment, or rejection.

Your worth is not defined by others' inability to understand you. You deserve to be seen, accepted, and celebrated just as you are.

And for my mom, who has stood by me through every choice I've made. Even when I moved 4,200 miles away from her at nineteen. I love you.

Prologue

Zoey

Six months earlier

The door slams, startling me from my deep study of the latest blueprints for the new Alberta resort.

Blinking, I glance at the clock. One a.m.

Shit.

Jake appears, shuffling into the kitchen, and tosses his keys on the counter.

"How was dinner?"

"Fine." It's all I get from him in response.

I quirk a brow, my focus drifting back to my screen. "Just fine? How were Sarah and Tom? Lauren was there too?"

"It was Tom's birthday. Of course she was. Everybody was there. Well. Not *everybody*, obviously."

I peel my attention away from my computer and set it on Jake. His shirt is unbuttoned at the top, his black hair tousled. His eyes are glossy, like he's had a drink or two too many.

Unease curls in my stomach.

"Corey sent me the plans tonight," I say. "I had to approve them for tomorrow."

He drags a hand down his face, jaw tightening. "Tomorrow's Saturday."

"I know. But my dad's breathing down my neck about this new expansion in Calgary, and the team is waiting for me to—"

I snap my mouth shut. It's pointless to explain. Nothing I could say would excuse my absence. Again.

With a sigh, I rub at my temples. I haven't been the best girlfriend these past few months. Work's been stressful, consuming my days and nights, and sometimes my weekends.

But in my defense, Jake knew what he signed up for when we started dating two years ago.

"I'm sorry I missed dinner," I say softly. "You know I can't just say 'fuck it' when something urgent comes up. Even if it means missing out on a night with your friends."

He lets out a sharp laugh, running a hand through his hair. "Yeah, god forbid you actually show interest in the people I care about."

Ouch. I reel back a fraction. "What does *that* mean?"

"You're never here!" he explodes, his voice punching through the room. "How many times have we talked about this? Nothing is changing, Zoey. You just… You work and work, and you miss everything. Dinners. Dates. But you never miss *me*. I'm tired of this shit."

The words pummel me like physical blows. I hold his gaze, and he doesn't let go either, as if the first one to look away will lose the fight.

"I'm tired of arguing over this." I work to keep my voice steady. "We've been doing this for months. But I'm here right now. I'm listening. I'm present."

He shakes his head, his shoulders slumping, his arms falling limp at his sides.

My hands twitch toward him. I want to get up, wrap them around his waist, and tell him he *does* matter to me. But his gaze catches the motion, and he takes a deliberate step back. Swallowing hard, I dig my nails into my palms and keep my feet rooted to the floor.

"You're not, though," he says, his glassy eyes throwing daggers at me. "You're not *present*, and you haven't been for a long time. I've been trying to make this work, but most days, you barely listen to me. You nod and hum, but you're not paying attention. When was the last time you asked me a question about my day or what's going on in my life?"

Heart squeezing, I press my lips together. I've got nothing. Absolutely nothing.

"I can't keep doing this," he throws, exasperated. "I can't pretend like this is enough. That what you're willing to give me is enough."

Another punch. It takes everything I have in me, years of PR training and honing my public persona, to keep from showing how easily he hit his target. And that's sad, isn't it? That I won't let him see my softer side. As if he'd find some twisted satisfaction in my vulnerability. Sticks and stones never broke my bones, but emotional cracks will, and I can't have that.

"I've never lied to you about the importance of my job." I keep my emotions tightly wrapped up, my tone sharp and dry. "Don't act like you didn't know what you were getting yourself into. You used to find my ambition and drive *sooo* sexy."

"Yeah," he scoffs. "When you still made time for me. For the two of us. When was the last time we went out? When was the last time we—"

He cuts himself off, the words dying on his tongue as he looks away. But his silence is loaded with what he doesn't say. *When was the last time you touched me? When was the last time we had sex?*

It's the same conversation over and over, the same accusations.

I'm exhausted. And yes, our sex life has been... well, nonexistent lately, but isn't that how it goes for everyone once the honeymoon phase is over?

"You're not being fair. I know our relationship hasn't been perfect, but it's a rougher patch. If you could just—"

"It's never been great, and you know it," he says before I have a chance to, what? Beg him to give us more time?

"I've always felt like I'm the only one who craved intimacy," he continues. "It's been a one-way street from the start. You don't even know what I like." He takes a step closer, and I shrink back. "What turns me on, Zoey, huh? Are you even capable of answering that question? No, how about this. Do you at least know what turns *you* on?" His cruel laughter echoes in every corner of my brain. "Of course you don't. You'd have to think about what brings you pleasure outside of your work to figure that one out."

"Wow, Jake. Very classy." I swallow, the knot in my chest tightening with each breath. I need to pull myself together. So I straighten and lift my chin. "I'm not the only one who's stopped trying. You think it's only me shutting you out, but what about you?" I arch a brow. "What about all the times I've initiated conversation, intimacy, any of it, and you were mentally checked out? Always on your phone, texting god knows who."

His eyes flick wide, and a wave of dread washes over me. He smooths his expression quickly, but it's too late. The truth is out, and I've just nailed it.

The air shifts, like a subtle crack in the tension that's been simmering between us since he walked through the door.

I cross my arms. "Who have you been texting?"

Jake scoffs, sliding his hands into his pockets. "I haven't been—"

"Please don't insult me further," I cut.

He leans against the wall behind him and sighs. "Lauren."

Lauren.

Nausea rises at the sound of my best friend's name on his lips. It lands on my chest with a thud, closing my throat another notch.

I swallow down the bitter taste, every muscle in my body strung tight. For a split second, I'm certain I misheard him.

But his contrite expression tells me I didn't.

"Lauren?" My voice is too steady, too calm for the fire blazing inside me. "Really? You're cheating on me with my *best friend?*"

Jake exhales, slow and long, almost like he's… *exasperated?* "She's my colleague too. And it's not like that. It's not what you think."

Hackles rising, I pin him with my gaze. "Oh, yeah? Then please enlighten me. What *is* it like?"

I cross my legs and plant an elbow on the table, resting my chin on my knuckles. There. He's got all my attention.

He glances away, fidgeting with something in his pocket. "It's… we're…" Finally, he looks at me, an apology in his eyes. "She's been there for me. She knows what it's like to…" He swallows, his throat bobbing. "To be with you."

"Wow." The word escapes me along with all the air in my lungs. Two breakups, then. "How long has this been going on for?"

Jake scrapes his fingers over his jaw. "Six months."

I can't stop the quick exhale that leaves me, or the tiny cracks that fissure at the edges of my heart. "Six months."

The double betrayal is a sharp, deep cut, slicing through any hope I had left. I don't know which one hurts more.

"Zoey, I'm so—"

I raise my hand. "You need to leave."

Eyes widening, he takes a step forward. "It's not like I'm—I didn't—" He breaks off, as if his mind is swirling as out of control as mine is.

Though I doubt his thoughts are anywhere near the ones plaguing me. As I survey him, my brain reorganizes the pieces of our lives, molding a new reality, dismantling the past six months in search of a logical explanation to this fucking mess.

His shoulders sag. "I didn't mean for it to go as far as it did. It just… happened."

I let out a small, humorless laugh. "Seriously? That's what you're going with? And what exactly *happened*, Jake?"

"I'm in love with her."

The words reverberate in my skull like an echo that refuses to fade.

In love with her. Is that a fucking joke?

He takes another step toward me and puts his hands on my arms.

I hate that I let him. I hate that I don't pull away.

"I didn't—I didn't plan for this. I never meant for it to—"

"You didn't plan for it? Six months, Jake. Six months of lying, of sneaking around, of betraying my trust. Betraying me. And you think you can stand there and say you *didn't mean for it to happen*? That you *didn't plan for it*?"

His face falls, but an instant later, anger flares behind his eyes. "You're right. I have no excuse. But I won't let you belittle me as if you're a saint with no fault. We've had problems since the day we met, but you refused to address them because, oh, surprise, you were too busy *working*. None of this would have happened if you had just—"

My heart plummets in my chest and I free myself from his touch. "Oh, don't you dare go there. Don't you *dare* put your cowardice on me."

Silence stretches between us. I replay the last two years, recalling all the times his head was buried in his phone, every smile he directed at his screen. I want to fucking throw up.

Jake doesn't speak. Doesn't move. I've known him long enough to know I won't get an apology out of him, and honestly, I don't want one. What's the point?

I take a step back, cold and empty.

"Zoey…"

"I'm done. We're done. I want you to leave." The words are like stones in my mouth, but I force them out anyway.

With a shake of his head, he snatches his jacket from the chair. "Yeah, we *are* done. Good luck, Zoey. I hope you find someone worth your time one day."

I don't look at him as he walks out. I refuse to give him that satisfaction. Only when the door closes after him do I let the tears roll down my cheeks.

The man I loved is gone. My best friend betrayed me. And all I'm left with is the wreckage of those relationships.

But if my father has taught me anything, it's that our hardest moments only make us stronger. And nothing is ever torn down completely.

So I'll take the night to be sad, to mourn those losses. To break his stuff and burn his clothes.

But tomorrow? Tomorrow, I'll rebuild.

Chapter One

Zoey

Have you ever felt as though the person you are now is nothing like the one you wanted to be when you were younger? That at some point, something went horribly wrong and the path that was so clearly mapped out in your mind dissolved into a future that, in hindsight, was inevitable?

My shift was so brutal that I can't even remember who I pictured myself becoming all those years ago. What my childhood aspirations were.

It's as if one day, I just—poof—grew up and forgot all the hopes that once filled me with wonder and made my heart pound in my chest. The dreams I once thought would come true (because how could they not?) remained just that: dreams.

And as time went by, they faded into mirages that made me question whether they ever existed at all.

It takes strength and stubbornness to keep from being sucked into the gloom of adult life.

And though I may possess those qualities in theory, they failed to rescue me from the vortex. And these days, the gloom of adult life is where I thrive.

Thirty-two years on this earth, and everything I know boils down to my nine-to-five (well, to seven or eight most of the time). Passion? None. Hobbies? Nonexistent. Relationships? Married to my job. Some say I have my shit together. I agree, if shit means my back is fucked from sitting behind a desk all day and I wear anti-fatigue glasses because my life revolves around my phone and my computer. If that's the case, then yeah, I'm crushing this. Big time.

"It's me!" I throw my keys on the small table in the foyer and ease the door closed behind me.

Gustav is already here, waiting for me. "Good evening, miss. Can I help you with your bags?"

"Yes, thank you." I give him my purse, then my tote bag. "Is my dad here?"

He cracks a knowing smile that makes the skin around his eyes crinkle and nods. "In his usual spot."

My lips quirk up, too. "Figured."

I unbuckle the straps of my heels, slip my feet into comfier shoes, and follow Gustav through the maze that is my dad's house.

When I was little, I would often get lost in this behemoth of a home. I never stayed with my dad for too long, only on odd weekends and for a week or two during the summer. Mom didn't like leaving me here. Probably because she knew I'd spend most of the visit by myself. My dad worked all the time, and me being with him a few days a month didn't change that. But I was never truly alone, because Gustav kept me company.

He helped me with my homework and taught me how to ride a bike, swim, and flip a pancake. And this gigantic, mostly empty house in West Vancouver was the perfect place to play hide-and-seek with him. A couple of rounds could stretch into hours. I'd always wander too deep, caught in the labyrinth of endless corridors.

When we get to the main room, my dad is sitting on a large cream-colored L-shaped couch, his glasses perched on the bridge of his nose, his brows furrowed as he pores over a document. The French doors are open, the soft summer breeze ruffling the hem of my dress and strands of his graying, slicked-back hair.

Oscar Marchiatto is a creature of habit. His schedule is meticulously planned out by his assistant. Not one second goes to waste. And at seven p.m. on the dot, he catches up on executive tasks he couldn't get to throughout the day.

I round the back of the couch and pat his shoulder, dropping a quick kiss on his cheek. "Hey, Dad."

He glances up for a fraction of a second, then returns his attention to the document. "Hi, princess. How was work?"

"The usual. Putting out fires before they get a chance to start." I sit on one end of the couch, eyeing the half-full bowl of what looks like stew on the coffee table. "We launched the new hotel chain today. You know, our affordable line?"

"I heard. Did it go smoothly?"

"Of course it did." I can't help the smug satisfaction that bubbles up inside me. "You know me. I wouldn't have had it any other way."

Dad looks up again, a small smile tugging at his lips. "I know, princess. You learned from the best."

I did. I spent years shadowing him, memorizing all aspects of the family business, drinking in information greedily, until I knew every facet of it like the back of my hand. I was relentless in my quest to become the perfect daughter. To deserve the status of heir to his empire. I let him shape me into his image so I'd be ready to take over once he retired.

He and I weren't close when I was a kid. That changed, though, the moment he saw potential in me. I don't exactly remember what I did that caught his attention, but I do remember the shift in his demeanor. Suddenly, I was worthy of his time, of his interest. No longer a useless child he didn't know what to do with.

I don't blame him for it. For tying my worth to my skills. For not showing up until he discovered a reason that served him. The world is full of greedy, selfish people, and my dad is no exception. When I came to terms with that truth, my life got so much easier.

"Lisa dropped off dinner again?" I nod at his plate.

"She says all the junk food I order will kill me," Oscar grumbles. "As if it won't be the job that ends me first. If she weren't the only nice person in this damn neighborhood, I'd have told her to fuck off a long time ago." He waves at the kitchen. "There's some left if you want it."

"Oh, perfect," I say as I get up. "I haven't eaten all day."

In the kitchen, I grab a bowl from the cabinet and fill it with her homemade beef stew. "I like Lisa," I call over my shoulder. "She keeps tabs on you when I can't. And she's not wrong. At your age, you gotta be careful with your cholesterol and blood pressure."

He waves me off as I come back. "Bunch of nonsense. What difference does it make? I'll die anyway. If I can't enjoy the things that make me happy, shoot me now."

"Don't have to, old geezer." I settle back on the couch. "The deep-fried chicken will take care of it for me."

Mumbling, he goes back to reading, ignoring the TV playing softly in the background.

"What's got you so focused over there?" I ask.

"My retirement plan strategy. Devon sent it to me today. I have to approve it." He raises one eyebrow. "Which is why I wanted you to stop by. We need to talk."

The words grip me like a hand at the throat.

I'm no stranger to the look he's giving me. *Are you finally ready? Can I pass you the torch?*

We've been doing the same dance for a few years now, and each time he's broached the subject of his retirement, I've backed away, insisting I need a couple more months. Those months have turned into years, and here we are again.

He's tired. It's etched in every line on his face. He's been a hungry businessman his whole life, but the spark that kept him going has been missing for a few years now.

Knowing he's still hanging on to the job because of me makes my stomach twist.

But am I ready? I want to be. I think. I've been the head of our business development team for years. Carrying the weight of the entire company on *my* shoulders, though? That's a terrifying thought. Taking up the mantle is a big commitment.

"I know I promised you the job," he says, the words startling me. "But things have changed. Evolved, if you will. Some shareholders have voiced their... doubts." His brows are crunched low, a hint of pity threading through his expression.

I frown, taken aback. "Doubts? Doubts about what?"

An awkward silence stretches between us. It's strange, Dad sitting through it like this. He rarely tolerates hesitation.

"Your reluctance to take my place has been heavily noted, princess," he finally says, his tone flat. "You know the business well—you're my daughter, after all. But sharing my DNA isn't enough. You can't lead a hotel group as large as Imperial Excellence if you don't want it. If you're not hungry for it." He taps his fingers against his belly. "Some shareholders aren't convinced you still do. At the last board meeting, they decided to start looking for an outside hire."

An outside—

"You'd never let them do that," I say, my pulse picking up.

Dad shrugs. "I've put it off as long as I could, but it's out of my control now. Of course, you can imagine how disappointed I'd be if my legacy were to be thrown away because you couldn't muster the courage to show them that you want to take over. All these years I've spent building this company for it to go to someone else?" He shakes his head, his shoulders deflating. "What a shame."

I swallow hard, my cheeks flaming. I can't let my dad down. Can't give him more reasons to second-guess me. To be ashamed of his own daughter.

He knows exactly what to say to make me forget my fears and doubts. I should hate him for it, but instead, my competitive side takes over, thoughts whirling in my mind.

Do I *really* want this? I don't know, and maybe that's why I've been pushing this discussion for so long. But who cares? An entire group of balding shithead men—the kind who send emails with the whole text in the subject line—think I'm not fit for the job. That alone is enough to make me crave it. Even if every bone in my body is telling me to slow down. To consider. To think.

I can't. There's no time. My back is against the wall.

I'm about to respond when the image on the screen snags my attention. It's a documentary on the Wild Planet channel. A woman talks to the camera like she's sharing the most exciting secret with her best friend, and in a matter of seconds, I'm completely drawn in. She's surrounded by gigantic pine trees, standing next to a river while rain pours, soaking her hiking gear and her shoulder-length auburn hair. She's drenched, but the elements don't deter her in the slightest. Her eyes are bright, her voice steady, as if the storm only makes her more alive.

In the background, two white bears, what looks to be a mom and a cub, stand in the water, catching their dinner.

Tuning out the topic my dad broached, I grab the remote and turn the volume up.

"I've been doing this for a while now, and let me tell you, nothing comes close to the beauty of this place. There aren't a lot of rainforests left on earth, so to explore the one in British Columbia is a privilege. We must protect it at all costs. An entire wildlife ecosystem relies on us to make things right. The spirit bears you see behind me are some of the rarest creatures on this planet. And for the next two hours, I'll take you on a journey to meet them."

She goes on about the history of the forest and the native communities still predominantly inhabiting the lands. It's enthralling enough that I'm *this close* to packing my bags and driving there. And that's saying a lot, since I've never worn hiking boots in my life, let alone spent more than a single day surrounded by trees and wild animals.

"This place is beautiful," I say, lost in my thoughts.

My dad grunts, pulling me from my stupor.

Frowning, I drag my attention away from the screen. "What?"

He zeroes in on the woman on the TV, his lips turning up in a sneer. "I know her. She's the bitch who tanked the deal in Pine Falls."

Whoa, there. I bite back a grimace. Dad has been skipping the annual HR seminars his employees are required to attend, and it shows. "A bitch, huh? Because she disagreed with you?" I *tsk*. "Which deal?"

"Two years ago," he huffs in his usual way. His vocabulary consists mainly of grunts, mumbled words, and wildly inappropriate cursing. "When I was trying to close on a project north of Vancouver. Lakeside Resort planned to open a complex there. The area attracts a large number of tourists due to its location. We were set to make big bucks. I had the mayor so deep in my pocket he was tickling my balls. But the deal got tanked." He points to the TV, spitting his next words. "And she's the one who convinced the mayor to cancel it. Cost me millions. Pissed off shareholders and investors for months."

I cringe, sitting a little straighter. "Oh, I remember this. I didn't know it was such a big loss for you, though. What did she do to get the mayor to side with her?"

"It doesn't matter now," he mumbles. Though he steers clear of the details, he continues to rant about how he got screwed over.

While he grouses, an idea takes root in my mind. It'd be risky, but... If I conduct thorough market research and surround myself with the right people... High risk, high reward, right?

"Let me try," I cut in.

The glint in his eye as he focuses on me turns my insides queasy. "You think you can do better than me?"

Oh, the old man pride.

I draw my shoulders back. "I do, actually." The words are laced with far more courage than I feel. "You came in guns blazing with grand plans and schematics of your luxury hotels, scaring off small-town folks who are probably very protective of their way of life. If you'd involved me in that project, I would have told you what a bad idea it was. When I first launched my lodge line, you were so sure I'd fail, and yet here we are. That line is now among the top three most lucrative revenue streams for the entire group. Let me go and see if there's anything up for sale."

He studies me for a beat, the challenge still flashing in his eyes. I know my father well. His ego is bigger than his bank account. Insinuating I can be better at something? On a project he's already failed at? Oof. I better put my money where my mouth is.

"And then what?" he asks.

I pick a piece of lint off my dress and smooth the fabric on my lap. "Then I close the deal and build a hotel that will make sense there. Maybe the lodge line, actually. Still high-end, but with structures that blend well with that sort of background." Licking my lips, I steel my spine for this next part. "Succeeding where you fell short... Would that be enough to convince your shareholders that I can run the company?"

Though he's silent for a beat, his eyes never leave mine. "I suppose so." He looks at the TV screen, where the woman moves through the forest. The man accompanying her is also decked out in hiking gear. He's tall, his brown hair falling over his forehead when he dips to avoid a tree branch. "You have a month, princess."

My heart lurches. "*One* month? No. That's not enough."

"Take it or leave it." He cocks a brow. "If you can't seal the deal in one month, I can't help your case with the board. They're already eager to begin their search for an outside hire."

I wince. I've never heard my father use the words "outside hire" before, yet he's spoken them twice in ten minutes. This company is his family's legacy. He's bluffing, but I'm too scared to call him out on it.

With a deep inhale, I lift my chin. "One month, one hotel in Pine Falls, and the job is mine?"

He holds out his hand and winks. "That's the deal, princess."

I shake it, hoping he doesn't notice the tremor in mine. Time to finish what he started.

Chapter Two

Matt

"Hey, it's me!"

As usual, the first to (un)welcome me to my parents' house is Mom's creepy three-legged creature—some might call it a cat. Unsurprisingly, it stands at the end of the hallway, back arched, and hisses.

Little satanic devil.

I thought cats had a life expectancy of roughly fifteen years, but Freddy is blowing off every prediction. Twenty-one years old and still the meanest motherfucker in the house. Last week, when I walked past him, he growled and played Tarzan on my leg, biting so hard that his lone tooth pierced the fabric of my jeans and left a bloody mark on my calf.

"Mom, come get your thing out of the way!" I yell from the doorway.

Freddy hisses again, low and deep, and maybe it's my sleep-deprived brain, but his pupils almost seem like they're glowing.

"You're so dramatic." Mom appears, scooping up her abomination, who proceeds to rub its face on hers and *purr.* "Who could he possibly harm? Huh, Freddy? Who? Tell me, who?" she says in a baby voice, holding the cat in front of her face.

When she nuzzles into his gray fur, I swear he watches me and smirks. Twisted two-faced asshole.

I take off my boots and grab the flowers I brought, keeping him in my peripheral vision as I skirt past them, half-expecting a paw to come swinging.

In the kitchen, Dad is making his usual Sunday roast. Daphne sits on one of the stools, deeply engrossed in her coloring book.

"Hey, Daph."

My sister doesn't look up. Her tongue is stuck between her teeth while she outlines a rose with a red crayon.

"Daph. Daphne."

"Can't hear you, bud." Dad taps his ear and nods at her. "She has it on to the max."

I crane my neck, and sure enough, I spot the AirPods hiding under her long blond mane. So I round the counter, then lower my face to its surface and wave.

When she catches sight of me, she breaks into a big, toothy smile. "Matt!"

She jumps off her chair, darts over to me, and pulls me down for a hug. "Hey, Daph." I circle one arm around her and lift her off the ground, holding her as tightly as she clings to me.

"You let your hair down today," she says. "I like it better this way. It looks like mine."

"It does." With a kiss to her cheek, I set her on her feet. "What were you listening to?"

"My nature sounds playlist." With one hand on her hip, she glares at the man beside me. "Dad was cooking very loudly."

He only smirks in return. "I might have dropped a pan."

"Anyway, it was perfect because I'm working on coloring this rose, and with those sounds, I could almost believe I was in a field full of flowers—oh, except roses grow on bushes and they have so many thorns. A field of rose bushes wouldn't be very comfortable. I don't think I'd like it. I wouldn't want to accidentally hold a rose too close to my body and get my heart pierced like the nightingale."

I smile, amused. "I doubt the thorn would be long enough to get to your heart, Daph."

"You never know." With a shrug, she settles on her stool again. She picks up her crayon, tucking her hair behind her ears, and watches me expectantly. "What bouquet did you make today?"

"Someone ordered flowers for a Barbie-themed party, so I made a total of forty using zinnias, snapdragons, echinacea, strawflower, yarrow, lisianthus, and apple mint."

Her eyes grow wide. "Your store must have been *so* pink."

"It really was. I took photos for you." I fish my phone from my pocket and swipe the screen to unlock it. "Look."

As I open the photo of the forty completed bouquets inside the store, she gasps. "They take up the whole store! And you even used pink tissue paper. Did they like it? Can I keep the photo?"

"Yes, they did. And yes, I'll send it to you later. But I can do you one better."

With a flourish, I whip out a small pink bouquet from behind my back.

Daphne squeals, the sound ear-splitting. "This is *gorgeous*. Can I have it?"

God, I love her. "Of course, silly. It's for you."

She plunges her nose into the zinnias and inhales deeply. "They smell *so* dreamy. Thank you, Matt. I'm gonna put them in a vase in my bedroom."

Without waiting for a response, she darts down the hallway and up the stairs to her room.

"You just made her day," Dad says as he slides the roast into the oven. "I take it business is going well?"

"It is, yeah." I rough a hand through my hair. "I have an important meeting with a venture capital firm next week. Thinking about expanding."

"Already?" Mom chimes in as she joins us—sans Freddy, thank god. "It's been, what, five years since you opened the store? And you've been working so hard. Why not take it easy for a bit? Focus on something else for a while. Maybe *someone*."

A groan threatens to escape me, but I lock it up tight. Here we go again. *When will my eligible son find someone to spend his life with? Will I ever have grandkids? You know, I'm not getting any younger. Are you not interested in girls, is that it?* I've heard them all, and Mom is barely fifty. She's not going anywhere anytime soon.

I exhale sharply, biting back a retort. "It's my business, Mom, not a hobby. I can't just 'focus on something else.' And I don't want to pass on this opportunity. It could be huge."

With a sigh, she deflates. "As long as you're happy, sweetie, and not burning yourself out. You know how much I hate it when you put too much on your plate. I hardly get to see you."

"You see me every Sunday." I arch a brow, giving her a pointed stare. "And besides, Daphne's here. Spend time with her."

Mom waves me off. "You know how she gets. It's hard to do anything with her."

I grit my teeth, tamping down my irritation. "Mom."

"What? I've tried so many things, Matt, and she's not getting any better. Last time I took her to the mall for back-to-school shopping, she freaked out thirty minutes in and we had to leave."

"You know the mall is too crowded, and you brought her there anyway?" I pinch the bridge of my nose and sigh. That must have been hell for my sister. Guilt sinks in my gut. If I'd been with her, I could have protected her. I was probably busy with the store, and the thought makes me sick. "The mall overstimulates her. Did she at least have her headphones to cancel out the noise?"

Mom lets her arms fall to her sides with a huff. "I don't know, Matt. I can't keep up with all her little quirks. Why can't she be more like you? You've always been so easy-going, even when you were a kid. I'm telling you, it's a phase. She'll grow out of it."

I clench my jaw and groan. "It's not a *phase*, Mom. Daphne's autistic. It's not something she can get rid of."

Mom frowns. "You shouldn't call her autistic. Barbara at work says it's 'people with autism.'"

I drag a hand down my face. "We've been over this already. Daphne's autistic. Saying 'with autism' makes it sound like she's sick or something. She's not. It's just how her brain works. And since when do you care what Barbara thinks anyway?"

Bouncing my knee, I glance at my dad, who stays focused on cleaning the kitchen, pointedly ignoring the conversation. It's always been like this—this weird dynamic between the two of them.

Dad understands Daphne. He went to every one of her specialist appointments, joined parents' information sessions, and carved out time in his schedule to take her to activities with other autistic teenagers. Ever since her official diagnosis, he's done all he can to support her. Except shut my mom down in situations like this, I guess.

But Mom? She's a different story. She isn't a bad mother, despite some of the shit that comes out of her mouth. Her love for her kids is beyond any measure. But with Daphne, it's like she's hit a wall of ignorance and has no idea how to move around it.

Her generation was raised with hands of steel. The only wounds that mattered were physical. All other slights, hurts, and disappointments could be fixed with a bit of hard work and perseverance. Dad's upbringing was less traditional in that regard, I suppose.

Mom really does try with Daph, but she often falls short, and then, they both end up miserable.

And I'm caught in the middle. Being my sister's most fervent protector while trying to live up to Mom's perfect image of me.

Dad moves behind Mom and cups her arms, dropping a kiss in her hair. "She's doing her best, honey. Matt, can you get your sister? Dinner's ready."

I study Mom for a second, noting her frown, and sigh. "Sure."

Upstairs, Daphne is locked in her room, with a "You shall not pass" sign hanging on her door.

I snort and tap my usual pattern on the wood: three knocks, a pause, two knocks. "Dinner time, Daph."

"Coming."

There's a thump, and an instant later, the door flies open and my sister stands proudly on the other side, a sprig of echinacea in her hair.

"That's very pretty," I say.

"Thanks." She pats the flower. "I want to stare at the flowers all the time, but that might be hard. So this way, I can have a piece of the bouquet with me. Then, if I want to, I can take it out and look at it."

"That's very true. Come on, Mom and Dad are waiting."

As I hit the bottom step with Daphne on my heels, Dad's voice carries all the way to us. "Maybe we can still cancel it."

"Cancel what?" I say as I slide into my usual seat at the dinner table.

"Well, sweetie—"

"Deborah." My dad presses his lips together, his attention drifting to Daphne.

I follow his line of sight, then look at him, frowning. "What's going on?"

With a sigh, Mom sets her napkin on the table. "It's not a big deal, sweetie. You know our thirtieth anniversary is coming up. And, well, we booked a month-long cruise for the occasion. The reservation was made months and months ago. We're leaving next week."

Dread curls in my gut. "Daphne's first day at her new school is next week. You can't leave."

Dad clears his throat.

"Oh, she'll be fine." Mom waves like she's batting at a fly. "We can't cancel it. It's a nonrefundable trip." She looks at Dad, then at me. "We were hoping you would take care of Daphne while we're away."

I rein in the "absolutely not" that tries to push its way out of my mouth. Even if Daphne is only half listening to this conversation, she shouldn't be subjected to yet another instance where someone makes her feel unwanted. She wouldn't understand all the reasons behind my initial reaction. I love her to death. I'd do anything for her. But the timing couldn't be worse, and on such short notice…

I sit forward, forearms on the table. "Can't you reschedule? Go next month, maybe?"

"We could probably look into it, Deb," Dad replies.

"It's not ideal," she quickly retorts, shooting him a glare. "According to the cruise website, the weather in both Alaska and Hawaii is perfect in September." Mom sniffs. "You'll be fine, Matt. The two of you love spending time together."

"We do, but I'm in the middle of clinching a huge investment opportunity. I can't take care—" I glance at Daph, only to find her chomping on a hunk of Dad's roast, her focus fixed on me.

"You can't take care of me?" she asks, mouth full.

"Of course I can," I rush to say. "But next week would be difficult. I'm very busy with work. I don't know if I could drive you to your new school and make sure you're doing okay on your first day."

Mom places a hand on my forearm, as if her touch might appease the annoyance forming inside me. It does not. "I wouldn't ask if we could change our plans, sweetie. I'm afraid we don't have an alternative."

I stare at her, fork frozen in midair. Of course there's an alternative. Canceling. Canceling the damn cruise. And *ask*? She's not really *asking*.

"We deserve a break." Her attention drifts to Daphne. "You could have your meeting once when we come back, couldn't you?"

Anger claws at my throat, but I swallow it down for my sister's sake.

She's not a bad mother, she's not a bad mother. She's just stressed and ignorant. Be patient.

Eventually, my irritation fades. But so do the high hopes I had for this meeting next week.

It was a friend of a friend of a friend situation. An accountant James knows through his job put me in contact with his brother-in-law. The guy works for a venture capital firm looking to invest in fast-growing start-ups in rural areas. I fit the bill to a T. My business is booming, and I've won several prizes for my creations, but I don't have the resources to maintain my current workload. I need money. To hire, to expand. But mainly to help my dad pay for Daphne's private school. The one my mom refuses to contribute to.

I don't know whether I'll ever have another opportunity like this again. And there's a good chance they won't agree to wait a week for me. Business is a fast-moving train. If I miss it, then there's no telling when the next one will show up. *If* it'll show up at all.

I've poured my heart and soul into Daphne's Wildflowers, but at the end of the day, family comes first. My sister always comes first.

"Looks like it's going to be you and me for a whole month, Daph."

She shrieks, her voice full of glee.

I laugh in response, but the sound is hollow, empty. Much like the brighter future of my store I've just closed the door on.

Chapter Three

Zoey

My Louboutin sinks into the soggy grass of Pine Falls with a squishy sound, tipping me sideways. I flail, catching myself on the car door handle just before my bag slides off my shoulder. I glance down at the heels now covered in so much brown sludge, there's not a trace of the iconic red sole visible.

Great. Now they're ruined.

Somewhere between packing and closing a deal this morning, I made two crucial mistakes.

1- Not getting the precise location of the cabin I'm renting. Instead, I told my dad's chauffeur to drop me "anywhere in town," thinking it couldn't be *that* hard to find my way in such a small place.

2- Not checking the weather app before leaving. When I said I wasn't a nature girly, I wasn't kidding, but in *these* shoes with *this* weather, I downright come across as unprepared. Not off to a great start.

I adjust the coat I've draped over my head as the rain doubles down, then wrench my heel out of the hole it was sinking into. Back on solid ground, wind whipping at the hem of my dress, I run across the street to find shelter.

"Miss!" Andrew calls from the car. "What about your luggage?"

"Uh? Leave it in the trunk!"

Smile falling, he stammers, "I h-have to get back to the city before five to drive your dad to his charity event. I'm sorry, miss."

Fuck, fuck, fuck.

"Give me a minute," I yell back.

How far can this cabin be? I fumble in my pocket, digging out my phone. I unlock it, and that's when I notice my third mistake.

"Great. Perfect. Amazing." Should have checked whether I had coverage in this town lost in the middle of fucking nowhere.

Eyes fixed on the screen, I turn back to join Andrew by the car again. I've barely taken a step when a truck roars by, sending a wave of cold, gritty mud splattering across my legs and skirt.

Yelping, I jump back. "Hey!" I flail my arms. "Asshole!"

The truck comes to an abrupt halt.

Uh-oh.

The door flies open, and a man straight out of Lumberjack Magazine steps out. Big shoulders, big thighs, big boots.

"What did you say?" he asks, marching toward me.

I plant my feet, refusing to back down. "You drove right in front of me, and now my clothes are wet and ruined. You could have *killed* me."

"Maybe," he snaps, nostrils flaring, "if you didn't have your face buried in your stupid phone, you'd have seen there was a vehicle coming." He gives me a long look, from my head all the way to my shoes, where he scoffs. "And who dresses like that with a storm rolling in? Ridiculous."

"I didn't check the weather before I left!" I yell like a frustrated kid. I don't know why I'm telling him this. Why am I even arguing with this man who clearly doesn't have any manners?

The stranger pushes a strand of dark blond hair from his face and tucks it haphazardly into his bun.

My gaze snags on the movement. Big hands too.

He gives me another slow once-over. "Next time, watch where you're going, lady. And get yourself some warm clothes. It's not fashion week."

"Next time, don't barrel down the street like a maniac and drench innocent people in with filthy gutter water," I bite back.

I whirl around and storm toward Andrew. There's no way I'll let this ass have the last word.

The truck's door slams, and a split second later, the vehicle speeds away. *Good fucking god.* I was told the people in this town were welcoming and friendly.

"Are you okay, miss?"

"I'm fine." I yank on the handle of one suitcase, sliding it from the car. "Thanks, Andrew."

Once I've set the second one beside it, I sling my tote over my shoulder, then drag my luggage across the street.

"Come…on…" I grunt, hoisting the bags onto the sidewalk.

As I wipe my hair from my face, I spot a small café on the corner of the street, and my lungs deflate. There has to be *somebody* who can help me find this damn cabin.

I stalk that way and push through the door. A bell rings as I step in, drawing the attention of the woman behind the counter.

She gives me a long look up and down and smirks. "Can I help you?"

"Yes, *please.*" I drag my belongings behind me and plop my ass on the closest stool. "I just arrived in Pine Falls and—"

The woman snorts. "You don't say."

I narrow my eyes. "What's that supposed to mean?"

"Take a look around." She nods at the dining area.

Slowly, I shift on the stool and scan the space.

Okay, yeah. I understand her point. The patrons of the café are decked out in leggings and jeans, many wearing boots similar to the kind that rude guy had on. Backpacks are draped over chairs or set on the floor beside them. Beneath the scent of coffee, the air is tinged with hints of damp wood and insect repellent.

I definitely stand out in a cherry-red dress, matching purse, and the Dior perfume I spritzed on when I left this morning.

It's fine. I'm used to not blending in. It's never fazed me before, and it won't start affecting me now. I think that's what makes people tick. What forces them to give me their attention when I'm not even seeking it. As if my lack of discomfort breaks some unspoken universal rule that leaves them outraged.

I turn back to the woman—Rosie, according to her nametag—who's still watching me, her lips twitching in amusement. She seems to be about my age, with purple streaks slashing her black hair.

"Got it. It's obvious I just arrived. Do you know where I can find this cabin?"

I take my phone out of my tote bag and open the photo album app, fishing for the confirmation email I had screenshotted before I left Vancouver.

"Oh, sure," she says, leaning over the counter. "You're a bit far out. Oliver lives on the outskirts of town, about a kilometer from here."

I arch an eyebrow. "Who's Oliver?" The listing didn't mention an Oliver. Only that the rental was the perfect place to enjoy "the true essence of Pine Falls."

"The owner of the cabin," Rosie says. "And of Oli's, the restaurant a few streets up." She points vaguely out the front windows. "Can't miss it. It's always packed. If the house is available, he must be away on a trip with Charlee."

This woman talks to me like I've been living in this town forever and would know who these people are, yet only moments ago, she was making sure I understood how obviously I don't belong here.

"Who's Charlee?" I ask, locking my phone screen.

Rosie's brows shoot up. "Charlee Fletcher? You don't know who Charlee Fletcher is?"

I make a face. "The only reason I know the name is because you've said it twice in the span of five seconds."

With a roll of her eyes, she throws the towel she was holding onto her shoulder and snatches her phone next to the register. She extends it to me, a video playing on her screen.

I watch, and it hits me immediately.

"Oh, I know her." I look up, sliding the phone back to Rosie. "I saw her documentary on a forest around here last week."

"She's our national treasure," Rosie says proudly. "And Oliver's girlfriend. When she's shooting, and as long as his schedule allows, Oliver follows along. That might be why his cabin is available." Her gaze lingers on my wet hair. "Do you maybe want a cup of coffee or tea? Something hot?"

My damp clothes cling to my skin, and cold sinks into my bones. I should probably find a way to get to my lodgings and change, but Rosie is smiling at me with a warmth I've rarely encountered, and weirdly, it makes me want to stay.

I straighten on my stool. "A grande cappuccino with cold foam, please."

She snorts again. "Who do you think I am, Starbucks?" She lets out a huff. "I don't complain when you tourists steal all our parking spots in the summer, but I draw the line at cold foam. I'll make you a cappuccino in a bowl."

"Will you mock me if I ask for oat milk?"

She shakes her head, her purple hair bouncing. "I wish, but Pine Falls gets a lot of tourists throughout the year, and with them come all sorts of ridiculous requests like hazelnut syrup and cinnamon sprinkles. Gotta meet the demand." She locks the portafilter in place beneath the coffee bean grinder. "What brings you here, clearly not dressed for the storm coming in?"

Fidgeting with my fingers, I weigh my answer. I did a little research on Pine Falls, and Dad talked my ears off about how vehemently the townsfolk opposed his resort concept. Though when I went through our archives for more information, I didn't find any traces of that failed deal. It's strange, since our company's policy is to keep everything. I meant to ask Dad about it but didn't have time to connect with him again before this trip.

Based on the digging I did, I've gathered that one available plot of land will be discussed during the next town hall. If they're already a sensitive bunch, I can't go around saying I'm here to build a hotel. I can't mess it up before I have the chance to present the project. They need to get on board, even if it means giving them the illusion of a choice. The process will be much smoother if they believe it was their idea all along. You know, *marketing*.

"I wanted a break from the city." It isn't a complete lie. Charlee's documentary has overtaken my thoughts. As if it awakened something in me, and it's been stirring relentlessly ever since.

"Ah." Rosie places the bowl in front of me. "The classic city girl in need of a nature escape."

With a whispered thanks, I take a sip, relishing the warmth already settling around my fingertips. "If I fall for a small-town man next, I'll be a cliché Hallmark movie."

"Who knows?" She shrugs. "Pine Falls has a couple of eligible single men."

"The only guy I've met so far almost ran me down and splashed water all over me. Not off to a great start."

Her eyes dance. "*Yeah*, we have a few grumpy ones too."

I tap on my phone screen, zooming in on the photo of the cabin, searching for landmarks that may help me find it. "So what's the easiest route to get to Oliver's?"

Rosie looks at my bags, then at me, and grimaces. "I'm sure someone around here can give you a ride. You can't walk all the way there with those torture devices on your feet while dragging your entire closet behind you."

Grunting, I drop my head to the counter with a thud. "I really wish I had checked the location beforehand."

"That would've been smart." Rosie nods to the windows on the right side of the café. "There's a bookstore just up the street called One Last Chapter. The owner knows Oliver well. She may be able to drive you there."

I glance up. "Now, *that's* an idea."

While Rosie goes back to work, chatting with patrons and refilling coffees, I drink the rest of my cappuccino. Once the bowl is empty, I gather my things.

"Thank you for the warm welcome, Rosie," I say, leaving a ten-dollar bill on the counter.

"Hope you get to your cabin safe!"

Outside, the rain has slowed to a soft pitter-patter. Loaded down with all my belongings, I step out into it and cross the street.

As I approach the bookstore a few shops down, I take a deep breath. "Please, please, please bring me to my cabin."

Inside, a woman with long black hair and tattoos swirling around her right arm turns to me, a smile lighting her whole face.

Next to her, a man leans on the counter, his elbows propped up casually. He glances over, curious. But the moment he catches sight of me, the expression falls.

Fantastic.

Of course I'd bump into the guy who almost ran me over.

Chapter Four

Matt

"It's gonna be an adjustment." I slump against the counter. "I've never taken care of her for this long. I'm scared I'll mess something up."

Lola glances up from the register. "You won't, come on. You and Daphne are so close, and she adores you."

I rub my beard. "But she's still a teenage girl who needs extra care, and I'm not all that fluent in that department."

"You know how to take care of your sister, Matt." She gives me a pointed look. "You've been doing it since she was born."

"It's just—"

The door of Lola's bookstore bursts open, and instinctively, we turn toward the commotion.

Standing in the doorway is the stranger I nearly ran over.

She's just as beautiful as she was when I rolled by her, despite her wet clothes and the obvious tiredness on her face. All long legs and smooth curves that made me do a double take when I got out of my truck an hour ago. It's those damn heels—the ones she shouldn't be wearing in Pine Falls, the ones that define the muscles of her calves perfectly and give her a few more inches—that keep my rapt attention. She's ridiculously underdressed for this weather, but still, I can't bring myself to look away.

At the threshold, she's frozen in place, still clinging to the door handle, her focus fixed on me.

"Can I help you?" Lola asks.

The sound of Lola's voice startles her, and she tears her gaze away from me. "I didn't realize Pine Falls was *this* small."

"Huh?"

"Must be your lucky day," I shoot back.

Lola frowns at me and whispers, "Do you know her?"

"She jumped in front of my truck earlier."

The stranger scoffs. "I did not *jump* in front of your truck."

Lola lets out a low whistle, her brows rising high, side-eyeing me.

"*You*," the woman says, pointing at me, "almost ran me over."

I hold my hands up. "Let's agree to disagree and call it a day."

Her expression hardens, and she presses her lips together in a thin line. She's been here for thirty seconds, and she's already riled up. I shouldn't like it. But seeing how easily I can spark a reaction out of her is entertaining. I've never witnessed someone getting this bothered by a little taunting.

She moves closer, dragging her heavy luggage behind her. "I've had a long day, and I could use a bath and a bottle of wine right about now, so if you could help me, I'd be willing to forget that you almost killed me."

She fumbles in the pocket of a coat that looks more expensive than my house and pulls out her phone. With a series of taps on the screen, she turns the device to Lola. "Rosie at the café mentioned that you know the owner of the cabin I'm renting. She thought maybe you could drive me there."

I glance over Lola's shoulder. "You're staying at Oliver's?"

The stranger stares at me. "You know him too?"

"He's our best friend." Lola offers her a warm smile. "I can give you a ride, but…" She checks her watch. "It's just me today, and I can't close the store before I get my delivery at three."

The woman's eyes swim with despair. She's shivering, partly because of me. Her hair is plastered to her face, her expression drawn, like she's at her wit's end. She could use a little sympathy, even if she came barging in here like an entitled city jerk.

I sigh. Fine. "I'll drive you."

She whips her head in my direction, her shoulders tensing. "You will?"

I shrug. "Yeah, why not."

"Oh. O-okay then." Voice pitched high, she darts her gaze around, as if she's looking for the suitcases parked beside her. "Now?"

"Yeah, give me a minute, okay?" I slip my keys from my pocket and hit the unlock button on the fob, nodding toward my truck. "You can climb in if you want. I'll be right over."

"Yeah, okay. Uh… thanks." She turns around, her movements wooden, as if my offer throws her off.

Come on, I'm not *that* mean. Actually, I'm not mean at all. She's the one who called me an asshole.

"Hey!" Lola adds as the woman pulls the door open. "I didn't catch your name."

"Zoey," she says.

Zoey. The sound of her name is like a soft brush of her lips against the shell of my ear.

"Nice to meet you. I'm Lola, and this is Matt."

Zoey nods and dips her chin. "I'll go wait in the truck."

"You remember which one it is, right?" I wink, and her cheeks turn pink.

After she's stepped out and the door has closed behind her, Lola gently pushes me. "Behave."

"It's just a little fun teasing." I press a kiss to her hair and back away. "Thank you for the pep talk. You should stop by to say hi to Daph before school starts."

"Will do."

I head out to my truck. "Sorry for keeping you waiting," I say to Zoey as I approach. She's standing next to the passenger door, watching me.

Why didn't she get in? It's warm and dry, and she wouldn't look so… puppy-like.

"Are you?" she volleys back.

"Not really." I load her suitcases in the bed, then climb in and crank the heat for her. As I shift into reverse, my finger grazes her thigh, and the cool softness of her skin sparks a tingling sensation that works all the way up my arm.

"Sorry." Despite my best effort, the word still came out strangled.

I back out, a hand behind her headrest. "So, what are you in town for?"

"Ah, you know... I needed to get away from the city and connect with nature."

Her tone is detached, her expression flat. There's no way that's why she's here. It's none of my business, though. I'm just trying to make polite conversation.

"If you want to connect with nature," I glance down at her shoes, "maybe you should lose the heels for the rest of your stay."

I shift into fourth, and my finger brushes against her thigh again. And for a split second, I swear she presses her leg further into my touch.

I release the stick and grip the steering wheel.

"Noted," Zoey says, her voice tight. "I'll buy some more appropriate footwear tomorrow."

A handful of minutes later, we approach Oliver's cabin, and I slow.

Zoey leans closer to the windshield, and for the first time since I met her, her eyes sparkle, her whole face lighting up with it.

"Oh, I can work with that," she says as the log cabin comes into view, snugged between the forest and a lake.

I hum. "Wait until you see inside. The place is gorgeous. Oliver and his grandpa built it. They used trees from this forest and spent hours in the woodshed putting it together." I point to the small outbuilding just visible behind the house, then drag my finger over to the dock. "Oli added this later. Great diving into the lake from there."

"It's like I'm cutting myself off from civilization," she says, inspecting the pointed roof.

With a huff of a laugh, I park next to Charlee's car, twigs snapping under the tires. I slide out and pull her suitcases from the bed, and as I round the truck with her luggage, I spot her still struggling to climb out of the passenger side.

I smirk and hold my hand out. "Would it be mean if I said I wish I could follow you around just to witness how you 'connect with nature'?"

Groaning, she swats it away. And without help, she jumps down, though not without almost twisting her ankle when her heels make contact with the uneven ground.

"I may be from the city, but that doesn't mean I can't handle myself in Sticksville."

I let out a bitter laugh. "Sticksville? Really?" I scoff, stalking toward the cabin. "Unbelievable."

"Hey! Wait!"

Without slowing, I climb the couple of stairs that lead to the front porch and drop the suitcases onto the wooden decking.

This is why I stay in my small town, surrounded by people I know and trust. It's why I don't mingle with the city folks. I can do without their judgments and arrogant attitudes. I've already had a go at it once. Been there, done that. Four years later, I still think about the time in my life that took so much from me. It was nothing but a blip in *hers*, I'm sure. I should have known better.

I've made plenty of mistakes in my thirty years of existence, but that one taught me more than any other in the last decade.

Zoey climbs the stairs behind me. "I'm sorry," she says, voice dripping with sarcasm. "I didn't realize you're one of those people who tie their worth to where they live."

Annoyance builds in my gut. "I didn't realize you're one of those people who tie their worth to their expensive shoes," I shoot back.

She holds my gaze, and I don't budge. The seconds tick by, but eventually, she looks away. "You know what? Thanks for the lukewarm welcome to town, but I'm exhausted and cranky. I could use a shower and some sleep."

"Here." I dig my keys out of my pocket, find the one for Oli's place, and slide it into the lock. "Welcome to your home," I bite out as I open the door.

Zoey blinks at the door standing ajar. She opens her mouth, then closes it. This happens once or twice more before she finally blurts, "*You* have a key to the house I'm staying in?"

"You're staying at my best friend's place. Of course I have a key. But I won't use it while you're here. It's for emergencies only."

She narrows her eyes at me, unconvinced.

I shrug, a smirk tugging at my lips. "I swear on your shoes."

With a tired exhale, she walks past me. "Thank you for the ride." She puts one hand on the door, her attention darting from me to it and back again.

Message received.

I take one last look at her—her eyes, her mouth, the tips of her dark hair curling on her shoulders, her tight dress, her sculpted legs—and allow myself to feel the physical attraction. But I leave it at that, a physical thing, and back away.

Though as heat colors her cheeks, I can't help but grin. "Enjoy your stay in Sticksville, city girl."

Chapter Five

Zoey

The minute the door closes, I slump against it and slide to the floor with a heavy sigh.

Did the guy who almost ran me over seriously just check me out?

Yes, he certainly did.

And something is wrong with me, because I enjoyed it. For a second, I forgot I was in the presence of a perfect stranger, and I let the weight of his attention lull me into a spell. It was as if the longer his gaze lingered on my body, the more eagerly I invited him to take his fill, to indulge himself.

I can't recall the last time a man looked at me with such hunger. I can't recall the last time it had such an effect on me.

It's been years since anything but my job has given me that rush.

I gave up on men a long time ago. Even before Jake, if I'm honest with myself. I don't have the time or the interest needed to sift through the ocean of liars, cheats, and boys who refuse to grow up. We had a good run, my love life and I, but finding out Jake spent his Saturdays with his tongue down my best friend's throat was the nail in her coffin.

I push myself up and shed my damp coat. Once I've hung it in the entryway, I begin my exploration of the house.

"Not too shabby," I murmur as I walk into the main space. The living room is open to the kitchen and dining room, every inch wrapped in warm wood. Huge windows line one wall, as though the forest is branching inside. On the opposite side, tall bookshelves stretch from the floor to the exposed beams, crammed with colorful spines, photos and other memorabilia.

"That must be Oliver," I say as I shuffle over to the shelves. In one photo, Charlee and a man stand at the top of a cliff, his arms lovingly encircling her waist. Next to it, another frame holds a bunch of folded letters addressed to Charlee.

Against the farthest wall, I spot a fireplace, and a shiver rushes through my body. Time to ditch these wet clothes and get warm.

If only I knew how to make a fire. I can picture it perfectly: me, swaddled in flannel, lounging by the crackling logs, wine in hand, casually flipping through a novel I plucked off the shelf like I do this sort of thing all the time. But let's be honest. I'd look up a tutorial, fail, and possibly set off the smoke alarm. The furnace will have to do.

I scour every inch of the main space for the thermostat, even behind the books and the frames hanging on the wall. But still, nothing.

"Don't tell me there's no other way to heat this house..." I groan.

I glance behind the couch and under the windows for vents that hint at the presence of a furnace, but the more I search, the more defeat sinks in my stomach.

That's it. This is how I'm gonna die. Not even a day out of Vancouver, and I'm already screwed. Doomed to slowly slip into hypothermia because I don't know how to start a fire.

I pull out my phone and connect to the house Wi-Fi. In the browser, I tap on the first "fire-making for dummies" video I find.

I watch it, brows creased. "What the fuck is a kindling?"

Surveying the room, I spot logs neatly stacked next to the hearth and a box of matches. No weird white cube that's supposed to help me light a fire. No convenient bundle of twigs either.

"Yeah, no. I'm not going outside at this hour to frolic in the dark woods for sticks. I have *some* survival instincts."

I breathe in deeply and close my eyes, willing the emotions climbing up my throat to stay the fuck down. "One thing at a time, Zoey. You're just tired," I tell myself, hoping the reminder will keep the tears from flowing. Though since I'm now talking to myself out loud, I'm not so sure there's a lot of rationality left in my body.

Am I going delirious from the cold? Is that a thing?

It's fine. I'll figure out the fire. If worse comes to worst, I'll search the place for a warm hoodie to borrow until I can pop into a store tomorrow and buy a few essentials. Because the clothing I packed is not going to cut it. I obviously underestimated how cool the nights are here, on top of forgetting to check the heating system of the rental. And the weather app.

"It's okay," I say. Out loud. Again. "I'm a resourceful woman."

If there's no solution to your problem in sight, create one. My dad burned this into my brain even before I was old enough to understand what a problem was.

Forcing the tears to abate, I grasp the handle of one suitcase and haul it up the stairs leading to the mezzanine where the ad said the bedroom is. When I get to the top, the solution is standing right in front of me.

"Oh, I can absolutely work with that." With more pep in my step, I stride straight past the gigantic bed to the pristine clawfoot bathtub on the other side. I run a finger alongside the edge and take in the breathtaking view of the lake through the large window.

Maybe my rustic evening fantasy isn't dead yet.

I turn on the faucet and adjust the temperature, then shed my damp clothes. The goose bumps already covering my body form their own goose bumps when the cool air of the room meets my skin.

When the water level rests just below the overflow drain, I dip a toe and groan with a pleasure bordering on orgasm as the warmth hits me. Without hesitation, I submerge myself, leaving only my head above the steaming surface.

Three weeks.

I spent the first week of the month my dad gave me planning the trip to Pine Falls. So I only have three weeks to endure this place. And in that time, I have to secure the plot of land that's for sale, convince the people of Pine Falls that their town needs this hotel, and coordinate with the construction and operations teams. Then I'll be gone as quickly as I arrived.

Easy. Sort of.

Three weeks.

Why did I think fresh air and an escape into nature would do me any good? Selfishly, when I saw Pine Falls on TV, I thought it could give me a break from my exhausting routine. I figured I'd carve out some time to discover what exists outside of my nine-to-five, which I haven't done in… I don't know, almost ten years?

But now what? In a town where I have no reception, where I don't know anyone, where I have no bearings, what do I do?

I have nothing to do but… wait. Wait for the town hall that's scheduled a few days from now to discuss the land. Wait to talk to the mayor. Wait for authorization to acquire the plot. *Wait, wait, wait.*

Ugh.

Maybe it wouldn't be so bleak if I wasn't alone in the middle of nowhere, surrounded by total silence. Not a sound in the house. No creaks, no hums. Only my screaming thoughts. And the wind outside, howling like a wounded animal.

It's unsettling. Almost eerie. It's *too* quiet.

I don't like it.

I sink beneath the surface, and when I come up again, there's no way to tell the bath water from my hot tears.

Building the hotel here would give me the key to my father's legacy. But if I'm really honest with myself, the only reason I'm doing this is to convince my dad and his shareholders that I'm more than just a nepo baby. That I'm capable of running the business, of taking over.

But is it truly what I want? I've never had the chance to sit down and think about the type of future I'd envisioned for myself. My dad hardly gave me much agency in that regard, and most of the time, I'm okay with it. I'm not miserable. I love my job. I make good money, I have a killer apartment, and I always get invited to the best dinners in the city.

I'm thriving.

Am I?

Now that I've got five minutes to myself, now that there's no noise to pull me away from my thoughts, now that I'm *bored*, I don't even know what I'd do if I had the freedom to choose.

My brain has gone blank. Crickets. Tumbleweeds rolling with the wind in the desert.

I'm paralyzed. Frightened, really, to earnestly think about that answer and its consequences. To pull the curtain back on what might be awaiting me on the other side. The quiet has stripped away the security blanket I've clung to since joining my dad's company, and now, with nothing left to distract me, the mere possibility of a different path grips my throat.

Head resting against the edge of the tub, I close my eyes, trying in vain to stop the tears.

What am I doing with my life?

Despite how hard I work to make it look like I have my shit together, I'm a mess. I'm falling apart. And it didn't even take twenty-four hours.

I lie in the bath until the water turns cold, until I'm shaking again and the silence screams too loud.

Gathering what's left of my mental strength, I pull myself up. I've just made it to my feet when three sharp knocks sound on the front door.

My heart slams against my chest and my ass hits the bottom of the tub with a splash.

"What the fuck?"

I take it back. I like silence.

The knocking starts again, this time harder.

Maybe I should call 911. Yes, that's exactly what I should do. I stand and wrap a towel around my body. My fingers are inches from my phone when a voice comes through the door, loud and powerful.

"Zoey, it's Matt." *Bang. Bang. Bang.* "You forgot your sunglasses in my truck. Open up!"

"For fuck's sake," I seethe.

What do I do? I turn in a circle and catch a glimpse of my reflection in the bathroom mirror. Panic sweeps over me. My hair is a wet, tangled mess, my eyes are red and puffy from crying, I'm still dripping water from the bath, and I'm wearing nothing but a flimsy towel.

"Zoey, are you in there? Are you okay?"

I grunt. "Yes, yes. I'm coming!"

This is just my luck.

Fuck it. I make sure the towel is secured around me, then trudge down the stairs.

On the last step, my wet foot slips on the wood, and I throw my arms out for balance. I catch myself on the kitchen chair. The move sends my towel tumbling to the floor, leaving me stark naked.

"Are you okay?" Matt says from behind the door.

"Yes, I'm coming, two seconds," I croak, thanking my lucky stars that the front door is solid wood and not glass.

Once I've secured the towel again, I cross the room, steadying my breath along the way.

I open the front door to find Matt standing there, smiling. "Hi," I say, forcing a cheeriness I don't feel.

Inch by inch, his eyes travel down my body, lingering where my towel clings to my upper thighs.

Every place his gaze caresses bursts into flames.

He curses under his breath and looks away.

Yeah, I really didn't think that one through, did I? How worked up and turned on his scrutiny could make me.

"You, uh… I… I'm bringing…" He holds out my sunglasses, clearing his throat. "You forgot them in my truck."

"Thank you." I take them and put them on the bench behind me. When he doesn't move, eyes stuck to the porch, I say, "You need anything else?"

"No, nope, that's all. All good." He hikes a thumb over his shoulder, exhaling sharply. "Better get back, huh? Cool. Bye."

At last, he looks up at me. His face is flushed, his pupils blown, but a frown crosses his features.

"Were you crying?"

"Huh? *Uhhh*, no. I mean, why?" I press my palms to my cheeks. "Okay, yes. I was. But it was nothing."

Perfect. Now he knows that in a matter of hours, Sticksville has broken me.

His frown deepens. "Are you okay?"

I tighten the towel around my body, and his gaze slides to where my breasts are pushed together.

My heart rate picks up. "Yeah, I'm fine. A bit tired." I force a smile, but his attention hasn't returned to my face. It's now stuck on my thighs… "Uh… Matt?"

He snaps his head up, his cheeks turning pink beneath his beard. "I'm sorry. Sorry, I, uh… There was a drop of water going d—" He exhales sharply. "Fuck. I wasn't expecting to find myself in front of a half-naked woman."

I laugh, but the sound is hollow. It's stuck in my throat, caught somewhere between embarrassment and horniness.

"You were rather insistent with the knocking, and I was getting out of the bath."

Sulking and crying over my loneliness and life.

His gaze softens, as if he sees right through me. The expression changes his whole face. Like this, he reminds me of a big teddy bear. His features are gentle and smooth, framed by long strands of dark blond hair, and the crinkles at the corners of his eyes make me want to reach out and brush my fingers over them.

Would he be gentle with me too? Would his large hands be soft on my skin? Or would they be rough and callused?

The thought sparks another, and I pause.

Maybe, *maybe*, I don't have to spend the rest of this miserable evening alone, drinking the cheapest bottle of wine I found in the cabinet, then crying myself to sleep. Maybe I can have a wild one-night stand with a perfect—and hot—stranger. Maybe I can let loose for once in my life. Let my hair down and live a little, without worrying about the *appropriate* thing to do. Oh, there's not a single appropriate thought running through my mind right now. And the man standing in front of me, drinking me in, doesn't look like he'd turn me down if I made a move.

Suddenly, I'm consumed by a need to know if I'm right. If he's that perfect mix of sweet and spicy his demeanor gives off.

"Well…" He clears his throat again, snapping me out of my thoughts. "Good night, then."

I run my hand not holding the towel, through my hair and sweep it neatly to one side, exposing my shoulder. "Yeah, thanks. You too."

Neither of us moves. Neither of us speaks. Chills race across my skin, and Matt's gaze follows the trail with razor-sharp focus.

I want his mouth to trace the same path.

Lip caught between my teeth, I tilt my head. "You're not leaving?" I ask, a bit breathless.

"Do you want me to?"

Easy answer. "No."

He swallows hard, his Adam's apple bobbing with the motion. When he speaks, his voice dips two octaves. "And what exactly do you want, Zoey?"

Maybe that's why I'm here in Sticksville. To give myself a peek at what it'd be like to live a life completely different from mine.

To see what happens when I don't act like myself. When I don't have to be careful or responsible or perfect. When I focus on *my* needs, for once.

I inhale slowly. "You."

Chapter Six

Matt

*Y*ou.

The word shakes me. But it's more than that. It's the low tone in which she says it. It's sure, unafraid, like she's inviting me to follow whatever reckless thought is popping into my mind. No hesitation, no second-guessing. Just pure *want*.

I swallow, my throat like sandpaper.

Okay, deep breath.

I could do this. One night, before my parents leave. Before I'm left to take care of Daphne for a full month. One night of careless, meaningless fun with a beautiful stranger.

People do this kind of thing all the time. Why would I say no? I could use a good fuck, to be honest. I can't even remember the last time I felt a woman's touch. The thought of it makes my body pull tight. Over the past couple of years, I've been consumed by growing my business. I haven't really found the time to care about anything else. Or anyone else.

There's a stunning woman standing in front of me, wearing nothing but a ridiculously tiny towel, who says she wants me.

And the truth is… I need a little distraction. To release some of the tension that's been building, to take my mind off my problems… so, why not?

One night. That's all.

She studies me, waiting, the weight of her gaze palpable.

Hoping she's only interested in a night of filthy fun too, I move closer. She retreats a step, giving me the space to come in. Slowly, I close the door behind me, only glancing away for an instant. But when I zero in on her again, her breath hitches. Her eyes flick to my lips, then back up to mine, daring me, tempting me to take what I want.

Fuck it.

I reach out, grazing the side of her neck. It's the barest of touches, but it's enough to elicit a soft sound from her.

God, she's stunning.

"I'm not looking for anything serious," I tell her.

She doesn't move away. No, she leans into me, and the fabric of the towel rubs against my shirt.

"Me neither," she says, breathless. "I could never see you again, and I'd be perfectly fine with that. I don't even like you."

A low chuckle escapes me. "Good, good. The feeling's mutual." With a hand on her waist, I pin her to me. "Just a one-time thing, then."

Zoey nods and slips her fingers to the back of my neck. "I should warn you, though. It's been a while for me. I don't…" She bites her lip, her attention darting away. "I'm not sure if I'm any good at… this. My ex and I didn't have a lot of… chemistry."

I press my thumb to her bottom lip, gently brushing over the light marks left by her teeth. "I'd say you're handling yourself pretty well so far," I whisper.

A hint of relief flashes on her face. "Are you gonna kiss me now?"

Grinning, I lean in.

The kiss is sloppy. Messy. Nothing about it is tender or sweet, but it makes me hungry for more. Her mouth moves easily over mine, her hands clinging to the back of my neck as my tongue slides in, tasting her better.

"Hang tight," I say against her lips.

She obeys, literally grasping the hair at my nape.

Groaning, stars dancing in my vision, I take her ass in my grip and lift her. Her towel rides up as she loops her legs around my waist.

Fuck. If I weren't already fucking hard, the warmth of her bare pussy filtering through the fabric of my jeans would do the trick.

Zoey shifts gently, rubbing against the rough material, and lets out a tiny sound, but loud enough to send my balls into a tizzy.

"Fuck."

I back us up, then spin, wedging her between my body and the wall. My hand travels down the column of her neck and stops at the edge of her towel. "Can I take this off?"

She nods, the movement jerky. "Please."

The towel falls to the floor, dragging the rest of my restraint with it. Her hesitation evaporates too. Fingers fumbling, she gets to work with my shirt, her movements frenzied, and a second later, it joins the discarded towel.

Her chest heaves as she stares up at me, her hard nipples brushing against my skin.

"Let me touch you," I rasp.

She wiggles to give me better access, and that's all the answer I need. Loosening my hold on her, I slide her down the length of my body.

"Just for a moment," I murmur against the shell of her ear, "but then I want you back up there."

With my gaze steady on her face, I lick two fingers. And I don't look away as I ease one into her and sweep the other over her clit.

Instantly, her pupils blow wide, and she drops her head back against the wall.

"So smooth," I breathe against her lips.

Moaning, she pulls me down, kissing me with the same intensity as earlier. I kiss her back, pumping into her with that one finger, relishing the way it drips with her arousal. When I feel her ready for more, I add another digit and pick up the pace. Again and again, I repeat the motion until her breathy little noises float around us, punctuated by the sound of my fingers dipping into her wetness.

Soon enough, her legs start to shake, and a breath later, my hand is soaked, her release gushing down my arm and onto the floor.

"Oh my god," she pants, her knees buckling. Instinctively, I wrap a hand around her waist and steady her to keep her from collapsing.

"Did I just… *squirt?*" she blurts, eyes wide, cheeks flushed.

I slide my fingers out of her tight channel, fighting the urge to lick them clean. "Yeah, you did."

Fuck, I'd forgotten how much I like sex. Watching someone come apart under my touch while I hold their pleasure in my hands is one of my favorite kinks. To get them off or edge them until they beg for release. Shit, how long has it been since I had this much fun?

"Do you have a condom?" she asks, planting her palm on my chest.

I shudder. Fuck, fuck, fuck. It's been way too long.

Get a grip.

"Yes." I swipe my shirt from the floor and wipe my hands with it, then fetch my wallet. "Wanna help me with it?"

She nods, takes the wallet from me, and retrieves the condom.

Her eyes dart between mine, then drift to my waistband. "Do you want to…"

Brow quirked, I smirk. "Oh no, please. Go ahead."

Her blush darkens, but she gets to work unzipping my jeans. I keep my focus on her face, the curve of her cheek, the way her mouth parts, anywhere but lower. If I'm not careful, I'll come before I'm buried inside her.

In seconds, the cool air of the cabin hits me, and I suck in a breath at the thought of what's next.

She takes me out and wraps her fingers around me, and by the way her eyes widen, I think she likes what she sees. I grit my teeth, all the blood that hasn't already pooled in my cock rushing to where she touches me.

"Is this okay? Or is it too tight? I mean, my pressure. The way I hold... it." She lets out a hushed groan, her next words trailing off. Finally, she looks up, though her gaze lingers somewhere near my Adam's apple. "I'm sorry. I'm not used to this.
My ex—"

I lift her chin with my index finger and exhale sharply. "Forget about your ex tonight, beautiful. You're doing so well. *Trust* me."

Her lips part and a soft *oh* comes out.

Ah, I hit the right target, I see. Praise it is.

I jerk my chin at the condom. "Slide it on me."

With a nod, she ducks her head again and gets to work.

When she's done, I dip in for a quick kiss. "Keep your arms tight around my neck, okay?"

"Why?" she asks, even as she does what I told her to.

"Because I want both of us to experience as much pleasure as possible."

Bending, I lift her again. With her back pressed to the wall, I slide my forearms under her knees, tilting her to me.

"Perfect," I whisper, gazing down at her pussy on full display.

I rub myself against her, coating the condom in her wetness, and she squirms, guiding me to exactly where she wants me.

I give her what she asks for. I notch my length at her entrance, then push inside her, inch by inch, letting her adjust to me, giving myself time to breathe as I sink into her tight heat.

"God, you feel so good," I say as I pick up the pace.

"Yes, just like that." She lets go of my neck and clutches my biceps instead, her nails digging into my skin.

The sudden sting sends a bolt of need straight to my balls. Jaw clenched tight, I zero in on where my cock moves in and out of her, relishing the way it disappears with each drive of my hips. Tension starts to coil at the base of my spine, but I inhale sharply and will it to stay put. Not yet. I can't come already.

I thrust deeper, using my grasp on her ass to slide her over me, tilting myself until her breathing hitches, telling me I've hit the right spot.

"Are you close?" she pants hard against my neck.

"*Yeah*," I gasp, my vision going hazy. "You?"

"Almost."

Heat curls low and tight, threatening to snap. I grit my teeth, teetering on the edge. Not yet. Not until she falls apart first. So I bring my thumb to her clit and draw small circles until it swells and her legs shake.

"That's it, Zoey. You're taking me so well. So pretty like that."

Her breath hitches again, and her pussy grips me harder, spasming rhythmically, leaving me no choice but to tumble over the edge with her. My release takes me by storm, fast and powerful, roaring through every nerve in my body until it spills into the condom.

"Shit, that was good." My forehead falls gently to hers, my chest lifting hard. "You okay?"

Her mouth stretches upward. "Yeah, I'm great." She flicks back a few strands of hair that cling to my face. "Amazing, actually."

With a grin, I flex my fingers into her flesh. "Don't move."

I crouch, and when her feet touch the ground and I'm sure she's steady, I release her, then slide the condom off. "Here." I snag the towel from the floor and hold it out to her.

"Thanks." She takes it and quickly wraps it around her body. "So, um… do you… do you want a drink or something?"

I check the time. "I hate to be that guy, but I actually need to get going. I'm sorry."

"No, no. It's okay. Don't worry," she says, dismissing it with a slight wave, her expression unbothered. "I was being polite. I don't even like you, remember?"

Her lips quirk up an inch and so do mine. "Feeling's mutual, in case you forgot."

Truth is, I would have loved to spend the rest of the evening here. Sip a few drinks and maybe go for round two. Get a peek of what's beneath that bougie exterior. But we agreed to just once, and I'm more than fine with that. Sure, she was a great fuck, but that doesn't mean I should hang out and get to know her, especially when she's passing through. I'm not going to have a minute to myself for the next month anyway. It's better this way.

I slip my shirt back on and button my jeans. "For what it's worth, your ex is a clueless dipshit. Respectfully."

Zoey laughs, light and soft. "You don't have to be respectful. God knows he wasn't."

The vague response piques my curiosity, but I fight the urge to quench it.

Just a casual one-time thing, Matt.

I rough a hand through my tangled hair and dip my chin. "I'd better go, then."

"Yeah, of course." She stands there, wrapped in nothing but that towel, her body so damn tempting, so inviting.

I take a step and lean forward, dropping a soft kiss on her cheek. "Thank you for tonight," I whisper. "It's been a long time since I had this much fun."

When I straighten, the pink hue that stains her chest from exertion has darkened and crept up her neck. "M-me too."

At the door, I glance back at her one last time. "Welcome to Pine Falls, Zoey."

Chapter Seven

Zoey

I park my car on Main Street, not too far from Rosie's café.

I've been in Pine Falls for four days, consulting with my team virtually in preparation for tomorrow's town hall meeting, as well as uncovering all there is to know about the town and its population. I got a rental car and cell coverage, spent some time with Rosie at the coffee shop, and took a trip out to the lot we're considering purchasing. But I have yet to explore the town properly.

So today, I'm in tourist mode. I've got Rosie's recommendation list in my pocket, with all the places I can't miss for the full "Pine Falls experience."

And this time, I'm prepared. Yesterday, I bought a pair of cute boots, some leggings, wool sweaters, more technical clothes (ew), and a hat in case—god forbid—it snows.

The good news is that I officially blend in perfectly with this outdoorsy town, dressed in nothing but hiking gear, looking like a Patagonia Ambassador.

The bad news is that I miss my designer clothes and my heels.

But let's be real: I'd never get a slice of approval from the locals in the outfits I love. I'd be branded as a spoiled, rich city girl, blitzing through the town, salivating over the prospect of owning it.

Can't have that.

On top of that, the streets of Pine Falls are mostly made of cobblestone. Sure, it gives the town its charm, but it's also the mortal enemy of every shoe in my expansive collection.

If only my dad could see me now. Maybe I'll snap a picture and send it to him later. It's strangely satisfying, the thought of him grumbling and scolding me about wearing "sloppy clothes" to a work function.

But like this, I don't feel so much like an outsider anymore.

And all the self-doubts that consumed me in the tub that first night have melted away. I've put my focus on what I do best: work.

Well. Almost. Like 95 percent work. The other 5 percent is dedicated to a tall, long-haired man.

Fine. Eighty-twenty.

… Sixty-forty. But not more.

Every time I moved through the hallway this week, my body heated, and memories from that night rushed back to me. The way he held me against the wall, so strong and sure of himself. Hard in all the right places, yet with the gentlest touch. Precisely how I thought he'd be.

I can't recall the last time I let myself be so vulnerable with a man. Probably because I never have. I guess, without trying, Matt made trusting him easy. Like I was in good hands (literally) and could shut my brain off for a while. It was nice.

More than nice.

Damn, he knew what he was doing. Wet kisses and raking fingers all over my body. A few times this week, when I closed my eyes at night, I imagined his hands warming my skin, roaming my curves with the same intensity. And if I thought about it hard enough, I could almost trace where his touch had been.

Okay, maybe I've been obsessing over it a little. Nothing too wild, but enough that I sometimes catch myself daydreaming, in the middle of a work meeting, about long dirty-blond hair in a bun and a sweaty chest.

Sooo, yeah. Definitely fifty-fifty.

"Tourist mode today, Zoey. Enough."

Standing beside my rental, I fish the piece of paper with Rosie's handwriting from my jacket.

"Start your day on the most famous pedestrian street in British Columbia, Moss Street," I read out loud. "Your first stop is Oli's for lunch. It was originally called Jerry's, but was renamed when Jerry's grandson, Oliver, your host, reopened it after a fire damaged the building. The restaurant gave our little town its reputation, and the food there is to die for. I recommend the duck grilled cheese. Ask for a table on the terrace. You'll have a fantastic view of the lake that borders the structure."

I cock an eyebrow. Damn, I didn't know Oliver was such a big deal around here.

"Then," I read silently, "make your way up the street to the romance bookstore you've already been to, One Last Chapter. If you're in the mood for a steamy story, I suggest talking to Lola; she always has great recommendations. Last but not least, Daphne's Wildflowers. The florist shop is very popular with tourists and locals alike."

Rosie proceeds to name a few hiking trails for beginners right outside Pine Falls, ending her list with a stop at her café, where she promises a cappuccino will be waiting for me.

Smiling, I tuck the note back into my pocket. It's nice to have a friend in a place I've just set foot in. In a town where I know no one.

Almost no one.

I stroll down the sidewalk, passing in front of antique shops, my mind wandering back to Rosie's mention of the flower boutique.

At home, there are always fresh flowers in a vase somewhere, courtesy of my mother. When I was little, every room in the house was filled with arrangements. Most of my childhood memories are scented with jasmine, lilac, rose, and lavender. Now that I have my place, Mom brings bouquets with her every time she comes over. It never fails to whisk me back to a simpler time, when all I had to worry about was what film to choose for our Saturday movie nights.

I frown, despite the warmth seeping through me at the memories. When was the last time we had some mother-daughter quality time? Seems like decades ago. The thought stays with me as I make a mental note to pick up flowers at that boutique on the way home.

At Oli's, I get the duck grilled cheese and a plate of homemade fries, per Rosie's instruction. And honestly, I'm gonna make it a daily stop, because this might be the best food I've ever tasted.

After lunch, I make my way up the street, wandering in the direction of One Last Chapter Bookstore. It's easy to see why tourists love Pine Falls. Moss Street stretches through the heart of the town, its cobblestone surface, while not welcoming to specific footwear, gives the area a quaint charm. Dozens of shops line each side, waiting to greet tourists and locals alike. The crisp air carries the scent of the trees that give the town its name, fresh and musky. Or maybe it comes from the houses nearby, all made of wood and stone.

The wind ruffles my dark hair, and I tighten the lapel of my coat around me. Life here is so different from life in Vancouver. I've never pictured the city as a particularly bustling place, but compared to this town?

Not a person I see is in a rush. There are two women over by the pet store, sitting on a bench chatting, coffees clutched in their hands, while their kids play in a patch of grass next to them. An older couple on the other side of the street is out for a lazy afternoon stroll, stopping to admire a bed of dahlias.

The pace is unhurried, life slow but steady. Time seems to pause, to stretch, allowing for moments of connection and quiet enjoyment of simpler pleasures.

It's such a foreign concept to me, living in slow motion like this. I'm always on the go, so to even take a walk on a Monday during business hours? Can't say I've ever done it.

When I get to the bookstore, the wooden sign above the door swings gently in the breeze. The shop's windows are crammed with neatly stacked books—some new and some old, but all stories of lust and love. A bell chimes softly as I step in, and I'm immediately greeted by a woman with black hair who's perched on a ladder, tattoos covering her right arm.

"Hi! Welcome to One Last Chapter." She tilts her head, assessing me for a moment. "Wait, Zoey, right? The woman who rents Oli's house?"

I smile warmly. I need every ally I can get if I want to succeed in building this hotel, so I have to make a good impression. Just have to remember her name first.

Fuck.

It's Laura… no. Lydia. Shit, that's not it. Looo… Lola!

Mental high-five.

"Hey, Lola! Yep, that's me. Thanks to your friend, I finally found the place. Not my finest moment, I have to say."

She places a stack of books on the shelf and comes down. "Ah, don't worry. I get it." Quickly, she gives me a once-over. "I see you're starting to get the vibe around here."

I peer down at my sweater and the leggings tucked into my boots. "Quite the change from last week, huh?"

She chuckles. "It fits you well. How's your stay in Pine Falls so far? Matt didn't scare you too much?"

Cheeks heating, I do a half turn, fidgeting with the spines of several books on a nearby shelf and hoping like hell she can't see how red my face is. "Scared? N-no, not at all. Quite the opposite, actually. I mean…" I clamp my mouth shut.

What the fuck is wrong with me?

I take a breath and add, "Turns out he was very helpful, that's all."

"That's our Matt," she says.

That little affirmation pulls on an invisible thread, tugging at my curiosity. What does she mean by that? What kind of guy is he? All I know is he likes sarcasm and is very good with his hands.

Sigh. I'll never forget that, will I?

"Rosie told me you had amazing recommendations," I say, determined *not* to think about him. "So I thought I'd stop by."

Lola's face lights up like I just mentioned I'm giving her ten puppies. "Of course she did. Because I sneak her books when she sends people my way. Are you into romance at all?"

"Can't say I've read a lot in the past several years. Unless it's related to work." I grimace. "Don't really have time."

"Well, now that you're in Pine Falls, you can unwind a bit." She rounds the table nearby and motions for me to follow her.

The first time I came in, drenched, freezing, and tired, I didn't pay attention to anything but Matt and her. Now? Damn, the place is cozy. The store isn't big, but it's warm and welcoming, with fluffy pink couches scattered throughout the sage-colored space. A few readers are tucked into their own little worlds in the comfy armchairs, while others browse the shelves in search of their perfect find, their soft murmurs blending with the rustle of pages.

Lola stops in front of a collection of colorful spines. "What's your spice level?"

I open my mouth, but quickly snap it shut. Finally, I say, "My what?"

"Spice level. I'm sorry, you might not be familiar with that term. Are you comfortable reading sex scenes?"

"Oh." Cue the warming cheeks again. "Um… I've never thought about that before, but I guess, yes."

Lola's lips curve upward. "I've got just the thing to get you started," she says, her voice barely above a whisper, while she rummages through the shelves. "There." She pulls out a thick book with a half-naked man on the cover.

I blink at it, then gape at her. "You want me to read *this*?"

She pats my shoulder, her expression sparkling with mischief. "You'll thank me later. This one's got the perfect balance of steam and plot. You'll laugh, you'll cry, and…" She leans in and cups a hand to her mouth. "You'll *definitely* need a fan and charged batteries."

Winking, she presses the book into my hands.

"Let me know what you think when you're done." She's already striding to the counter. "Or when you want to talk about the scene in chapter fourteen."

I stare after her, the book hanging from my hand.

And then I laugh.

The genuine sound catches me off guard. It's been a while since I've felt the serotonin boost that comes with it. "I'll keep you updated."

Did Rosie really send me here for a book rec, or could she have magically known that Lola would be exactly what I needed today?

"Any other plans for this afternoon?" Lola asks, settling behind the counter.

I drop the book on it and dig my wallet out of my purse.

Just as I slide my card out, she lays her palm gently over mine.

"Don't worry about it. It's on me."

I frown, still holding the card. "Are you sure? I can pay."

Smiling, she waves it off. "I know you can. It's not about that. Consider it a welcome-to-town gift and your official introduction to smut."

Bewildered by her generosity, I tuck my wallet back into my purse. Guilt stirs in my chest, and I rub the spot where it settles, easing the discomfort. Bonding with the locals has been surprisingly effortless. Once they learn the real reason I'm here, I doubt they'll still think the same of me.

"Thank you," I say, pushing the feeling away. "I'm strolling around town today, following the list Rosie made for me. I can't believe how nice everyone has been so far. Well, minus when I first arrived."

Although Matt definitely made up for it.

"Pine Falls is magic like that," Lola says softly. "That's why it's always packed during tourist season. It has a way of pulling you in and forcing you to take a break from your life." She places the book in a tote bag and holds it out to me. "And who wouldn't want to escape for a bit, huh?"

With a grateful nod, I take it. "I guess you're right."

Maybe it's the town, or maybe it's Lola's easy confidence, but this moment feels important. I just can't put my finger on why.

"Thanks for the book and the chat," I say as I head for the door. "*And* for introducing me to a new genre."

Lola grins. "Oh, sweetie. You have no idea what you're getting yourself into."

Something stirs in my gut, as if her lighthearted comment struck true. She doesn't know the half of it.

My last stop of the day, according to Rosie's list, is Daphne's Wildflowers. When I pause in front of it, I suck in a breath. It's beautiful.

The expansive windows built into the lavender-painted wood façade are decorated with dozens of carefully arranged flowers. The shop's name is written on one of the windows in cursive lettering, partially covered by a waterfall of ivy.

Outside, in front of the entrance on the cobblestone street, there's a chalkboard sign with a neatly handwritten message.

Bouquet of the day: Wildflower Daze.

Phone out, I snap a photo of the store with the chalkboard sign and send it to Mom.

Zoey

> Seems like a store right up your alley.

She reacts to the photo with exclamation points.

Mom

> You have to send me the address! I'll stop by when I get home from Norway.

> Leaving tonight for my research seminar and won't be reachable for the next few weeks. Hope your dad isn't being too hard on you. Love you, honey.

I send her a heart and lock my phone. At fifty-five, my mom still strives to learn more about her passions. I admire her so much for it. To be honest, I wish I were more like her in that department.

When I push the boutique's door open, I'm greeted by the soft ambient music playing and a multitude of scents wafting through the space. But the sight in front of me is what stops me in my tracks. With his back to me, working on a bouquet at a table behind the counter, a leather apron wrapped around his waist, is a tall man with dark blond hair tied into a bun.

Oh, god. I'd recognize that hair anywhere.

I freeze for a moment, my heart racing against my ribs, my throat dry. Then I finally croak, "Matt?"

He snaps upright and spins around, his mouth hanging open. "Zoey? Wh-what are you doing here?"

"Taking a stroll. What are *you* doing here? Do you work at the store?"

He removes his gloves, sets them on the table, and I'm definitely not staring at the way his sleeves are rolled up at his forearms. Or how his hands grip the edge of the counter when he comes to stand in front of me. Seeing them in person after dreaming about them for the past week is hitting me harder than I expected. Damn it.

"This is my store."

I snap my attention to his face. "You *own* Daphne's Wildflowers?"

A glint of amusement dances in his irises. "I do. Are you surprised?"

My chest tightens a fraction. "Yeah. I don't know. I thought you were more the cutting-wood-in-the-forest type or that you built stuff with your…" I lower my focus to where he's still gripping the counter, heat rushing to my cheeks. I clear my throat. "Hands."

Matt follows my gaze. "I get that a lot. But yes, this is my shop, and I'm the florist." He nods at the flowers on the table. "Would you like a bouquet? I don't usually take same-day orders, but I'll make an exception for you." He punctuates that sentence with a wink, and my pulse skips.

I have a hard time maintaining my composure around him, and it's becoming an actual problem.

I've really misjudged him, haven't I? This man keeps shedding layers, and the more he does, the more I want to stick around to discover what's hiding beneath the next one.

"I did come in to get flowers, but I didn't know you were that busy. You don't have to bend your rules for me."

He gestures toward another table where a variety of fresh flowers are already set out. "I'd love to create something for you. What do you need right now?"

I blink. "Need?"

His lips curve into a ghost of a smile. "Flowers have meanings. They're not just pretty things to look at. Some are for love, others for healing. Depends on what you're after."

I've never viewed flowers that way. I rarely paid much attention to how they made me feel or what they meant, except for the fact that I've always associated them with my mother.

So I suppose they bring me peace.

"Why don't you surprise me?" I finally say. "What do you think I need?"

He arches an eyebrow, a smirk tugging at his mouth. "I'm scared this is gonna backfire on me, Zoey."

Shivers spread across my skin, prickling down my spine. The way he says my name, like he's taking his time to taste it on his tongue, makes my knees wobble.

I'm weak. I'm so weak.

"Promise it won't."

"Okay, then." He moves around the space with ease, plucking stems from vases. He pauses for a moment, his gaze flicking between two sorts of flowers like he's deciding which ones would suit me the best. Finally, he grabs a handful of pink and white lilies, then some lavender. The rest I don't recognize.

When his selection is made, he lays the flowers in the middle of the table and arranges them. Watching him work is mesmerizing. His fingers shift with grace and care, as if this is second nature for him and he could do it in his sleep.

Wow. Not gonna lie. This is doing it for me.

"I see you found your way to more comfortable clothes," he says, focused on his task.

I frown. "My clothes are comfortable."

That makes him pause. He looks at me like he's calling bullshit.

"Okay, yes," I sigh. "This is definitely a better option for here."

That pulls a chuckle from him. Then he's back to work. "It looks good on you." He keeps his attention riveted on the stems, as if I shouldn't take his words as a compliment.

Even so, my pulse kicks up a notch.

He wraps twine around the bundle of flowers, then holds it out to me. "Voilà."

I take it and turn it from side to side, admiring his work. The foliage woven together with flowers in shades of pink reminds me of summer mornings. "It's beautiful, Matt. Thank you."

His gaze on me is a physical caress. I keep mine on the bouquet, giving him time to take whatever he needs from me.

"What kind of vibe did you go for, then?" I ask eventually.

"Why don't you tell me?" He nods to the bouquet. "How do you feel?"

I bury my nose in the flowers and inhale the multitude of scents until my muscles loosen and the knot in my throat—one I didn't realize even existed—dissolves.

"Relaxed."

Finally, I look up, finding Matt watching me. An emotion flits over his face, but I'm not fast enough to decipher it before it's gone.

"Lavender and freesias for calm when your days get too intense; lilies for confidence, when you need that extra boost; and alstroemeria for support when you feel alone," he says, his voice soft.

His words land too close. My stomach knots, and I look away before he can realize how true they've hit. How did he see the feelings I've been working so hard to keep at bay?

"Zoey?"

I meet his gaze. "How did you know?"

He shrugs, his mouth ticking up a fraction. "I'm good at my job."

He says this like it's every florist's job to know exactly who their clients are and what they need, but the reality is that this man pays attention.

The bouquet turns heavy in my grip, so I set it down.

Matt's eyes follow the movement, his expression dulling. "It backfired, didn't it?"

"No, no. It's just…" I rack my brain for a way to explain my spiraling thoughts that won't make him follow up with a hundred more questions.

I feel too exposed, too vulnerable. Nobody has put me in this position in the last twenty years. Alarms blare in every corner of my body. So I do what I do best when the emergency response has been triggered. I play it cool. I brush it off. "I didn't know I was giving off this vibe. But thanks. It's beautiful."

Matt cocks one eyebrow. Dammit. For a moment, I brace for his usual wit and quick retort. But his expression smooths out, and he simply says, "I'm glad you like it."

Thank god. I'm not ready for this level of scrutiny, especially from a man I know nothing about and didn't expect to see again after…

He clears his throat. "I was about to grab a coffee. Do you maybe want to—"

His question is interrupted by a shrill ringing. On autopilot, I fumble for my phone. As I register my dad's name on the screen, a loud *clink* resonates through the store.

I startle, eyes darting toward the sound.

Matt is already bending down, retrieving a pair of scissors.

When he straightens and sets them on the table, his face is unreadable, his mouth pressed into a firm, unforgiving line.

"Sorry, I need to take this." I shoot him an apologetic smile and shuffle a few steps away. "Hey, what's up?"

"Hello, princess," Dad booms. "How's the trip going so far?"

My focus flicks to Matt. "Good, good. Been settling in before diving into work."

"Any updates?"

"None for now. I can't do anything until…" I glance at the man hovering nearby again and lower my voice. "The town hall. But I've been doing the rounds, chatting with locals and trying to get a good sense of the town."

"Don't get too comfortable with these people, Zoey. They look after their own. They wouldn't know good business if it slapped them in the face. If they don't get their tourism activity under control soon, their town will be a complete circus in no time. Trust me."

A pang of guilt pokes at me. "I won't. Don't worry. Can I call you back?"

"You have more urgent matters to attend to? If you're waiting for the assembly, I doubt you've got anything better to do than strategize with me."

"I'm in a store," I say, lowering my voice even more. "I can't talk right now."

There's a pause on the line, followed by a sigh. "Don't disappoint me, princess. I met with the shareholders this week. My retirement has been discussed, as well as my replacement. They'll be considering your ability to take over at the next meeting two months from now. The hotel deal in Pine Falls needs to be done by then."

"Dad, I'll call you back."

I hang up before he can add anything else and walk back to Matt, who's arranging another bouquet. "Sorry about that," I say, forcing a smile. "Overbearing parent."

He hums, his focus glued to his work. "No problem."

"You were going to say something?" I hedge, a flicker of hope that I have no business feeling rising in my chest. "Before my dad called?"

"Nope," he says, still avoiding my gaze. Then, "Actually, yes." Finally, his eyes meet mine. They're full of an anger I don't understand. "Next time, maybe don't pick up your phone while you're in the middle of a conversation. It's fucking rude."

I gape, blinking.

"You think I'm the rude one? Yeah, okay." I snatch a hundred-dollar bill from my purse, drop it on the counter, and grab the bouquet. "Thanks again."

"You got it."

I close the door behind me and inhale deeply, willing the fresh air to clear out the confusion swirling in my mind. What the fuck is his deal?

The wind has picked up, and the sun is setting, the temperature slipping into chilly territory.

I peer into the store, where Matt is working away, not giving me a second thought. Back to being an asshole, I see.

At least it'll make it easier to focus on what I came here to do.

No more distractions.

Chapter Eight

Matt

"Did you brush your teeth?" I ask from downstairs.

Daphne appears at the top of the stairs, frowning. "You bought the wrong toothpaste. I don't like this one."

I pinch the bridge of my nose, drawing an uneven breath. It's not yet seven a.m., and the day has gone to hell. I barely slept. My flower supplier canceled today's delivery. And Daphne is being particularly demanding this morning. Her shirt didn't feel right, she couldn't find the daisy backpack she loves, and the scrambled eggs were overcooked.

"What's wrong with the toothpaste?"

"It tastes bad and hurts my tongue. Dad gets me the strawberry one because it's sweet. Mint burns my mouth."

I let out a frustrated sigh. "Okay, I'll buy the one you want after work. Sounds good?"

She gives me a toothy smile. "Yes!"

Shoulders slumping, I rub my beard. Guilt settles firmly in my chest like a brick. I shouldn't be this exhausted. I've been taking care of my sister since she was born, but having her here with me twenty-four seven is another ball game. And because I'm functioning on coffee and a couple of hours of broken sleep per night, my patience is running thin.

But then she gives me the biggest, sweetest smile, and I feel like a jerk for letting my temper get the best of me.

I shake out my hair, then twist it into a tight bun. Coffee in hand and jacket thrown over my arm, I open the door. "Daph, ready to go? School starts soon and we don't want to be late."

I'm still waiting for her to barrel down the stairs when my phone chimes. I dig it out of my pocket, and when I see the venture firm's name on the email notification, my heart leaps.

"Dear Mr. Becker," I mumble, staring down at the device. "We regret to inform you that we are not able to postpone our meeting planned for this week. We've been presented with several opportunities and will be moving forward with those that are still in the running for this year. Thank you for..."

I lock my phone and close my eyes.

Fuck. I knew rescheduling was a long shot, but I clung to that thread of hope anyway. Now, it's well and truly over, and I don't know how the hell I'm gonna grow my business and pay for my sister's school.

The noose around my neck tightens uncomfortably.

Daphne runs down the stairs, her backpack slung firmly over her shoulders and her blond hair tied up in pigtails by elastic bands decorated with daisies.

"Hey, Daph," I croak when she throws her arms around me for a tight hug. Time to put a lid on my worries for now. "You look great. Ready for your first day at your new school?"

Face alight and eyes sparkling, she pulls back, her body vibrating with excitement. "*Yes.*"

"That's a big yes." I chuckle. "I spoke with your teacher last week. She's very happy to meet you too. I think you'll love her. And you're gonna make so many new friends."

This is such an important milestone for her, and I'm excited too. She's finally getting the help she needs at this new private school. After two years on her public school's waiting list for that extra support, I lost my patience. The change was long overdue, honestly, after the bullying she's been subjected to. I had enough of seeing her come home sad and hurt. Girls can be pretty fucking mean in those early teen years.

I fought long and hard with Mom to get her to agree to move Daphne to that school.

At first, it was "*It's too expensive,*" and "*Do you really expect me to make the drive all the way there every day?*"

She nitpicked everything, every little detail.

Until one night, she broke down in tears in front of me, and we had an honest talk. It wasn't only about the money or the drive. She didn't want her daughter to be seen as different. Not "normal," as if my sister was supposed to conform to some rigid idea instead of defining it for herself.

We went back and forth for hours.

"*You're labeling your sister,*" she said. "*Shielding her isn't the solution.*"

At the end of the day, we compromised. Dad will handle the drop-offs and pickups, and I'll pay for the school.

Shit. That tuition fee, though.

The thought alone gives me a headache. It's not fucking cheap. But I'd do anything for Daph, and the school is worth every penny. Sure, bullying can happen anywhere, but our tour of the facility put me at ease. The robust mechanisms they have to support neurodivergent kids are impressive, and I was instantly relieved when I noted the openness of the teaching staff and the welcoming atmosphere in general.

I toss my jacket and bag onto the back seat and drag myself behind the wheel. I'll figure it out. I always do.

As I turn the key in the ignition, I throw a glance at my sister. "All fastened?"

With a nod, she slips her headphones into place. "Ready!"

I can't help but stew in my frustration as I drive away.

Even on Daphne's first day, Mom couldn't be bothered to be here. My sister doesn't notice Mom's lack of involvement, her disappointment. I hope she never will. At least Dad called this morning to wish her a great day.

Forty minutes later, I pull into a parking spot and touch Daphne's arm with a soft press. When she looks up, I say, "We're here."

She removes her headphones and surveys the bright yellow and orange building in front of us. At the entrance, Ms. Claris, Daphne's teacher, is welcoming the students who are trickling in with a genuinely cheerful expression.

At the sight of her new school, Daphne bounces around in the back seat, flapping her hands and arms.

I wait while she stims, familiar with her reaction when she gets excited. After a moment, she calms down and peers out the window again.

"Do you want me to come with you?" I ask.

Her mouth tugs down. "Will people make fun of me?"

The question guts me. "Not at all. It's your first day."

She pulls on her fingers, one at a time, over and over, the way she does when she's apprehensive.

"It's normal to be a little scared," I say, my tone gentle. "Come on, I'll take you."

As we approach the building, hand in hand, Ms. Claris gives us a warm smile.

"Welcome, Daphne," she says. "I'm Ms. Claris, your new teacher. How do you want us to say hello today?" She points to a sign with drawings of three options: a wave, a high five, or a hug.

Daphne contemplates her choices with a hum. And then, her face lights up. She breaks into a smile, rocking back on her heels. "A high five, please."

Ms. Claris holds her hand up. "You got it."

With her lip caught between her teeth, Daph taps her hand.

"You can go inside whenever you're ready," her new teacher informs her.

Following Daphne's repeated requests, Ms. Claris grants me permission to walk my sister to the door of her classroom.

When we get there, she turns to me. "I'll see you later."

I open my arms and give her a quick, tight hug. "Have an awesome day."

She strides in, finds the desk labeled with her name, and settles in with ease. Patiently waiting for the other children to take their seats, she studies the space, admiring the walls lined with art projects. At the sight of a drawing of daffodils, her face brightens, and she turns to me, as if to make sure I didn't miss her significant discovery.

I nod in recognition, but her attention is quickly snagged by a girl with red hair who approaches her desk. After exchanging names and sharing what they're passionate about, Daph grabs her flower book from her backpack. The other girl's eyes sparkle as she pulls her chair closer.

My nose stings. Before I get choked up, I turn and stride for the front doors.

"Mr. Becker!" Ms. Claris jogs to me with a paper in her hand. "I forgot to give you this."

I take it, my gaze immediately catching on the number in bold at the bottom. Twenty-five *thousand* dollars.

"This is Daphne's tuition bill for the year. It was due before school started, but if you need some time, we can grant you an extension till the end of the year."

End of the year.

As in three months.

"Th-thanks." Gut twisting, I fold the paper and stuff it into my back pocket. "I'll make sure it's paid by then."

Though I have no idea how I'll get all that money in three months.

And the noose tightens a little more.

By the time I'm back in Pine Falls, it's almost nine.

I need to get the morning routine down faster. Even if it's bringing her to school thirty minutes early, it would make a huge difference.

I can't afford to start work so late, not with the number of arrangements waiting for me every day. But today was bound to be an ordeal. And I promised I'd drop her off and pick her up all week. But next week, we'll have no choice but to utilize the school bus. Otherwise, I'll drown. Thank fuck James has opened the store for me since my parents left town and Daph has been with me. He's been a lifesaver.

"Hey, man," I say when I step inside.

James is sitting on the stool behind the counter, his glasses perched on the bridge of his nose as he frowns at his computer.

"Hey," he mumbles distantly.

I stroll over and clap his back, narrowing my eyes to the screen when I catch a glimpse of an Excel sheet. It's all gibberish to me. "Accounting stuff?"

"Yeah, an issue with a client's tax return."

With a hum, I step away and check the list of orders for today. Thirty-seven, and they all need to be done by three p.m. so I can pick Daphne up and make it back to the town hall meeting in time.

I roll my sleeves. It's gonna be a fucking day.

"Thanks for today, man. I don't know how I would have done it without you."

James glances up for a quick second before returning his focus to the computer. "It's fine. Don't worry. It's a nice place to work, really. With the flowers and the natural light."

"You can stay as long as you want," I offer.

"Thanks," he mumbles, leaning in, brows creased.

I've never understood what James finds so fascinating about doing people's taxes or spending all day swimming in math problems. But I won't complain, since he does a fantastic job keeping the books for Daphne's Wildflowers.

"Anybody stopped in before I got here?"

"Three customers picked up their orders. I noted them over there." He waves a hand vaguely. "And one woman asked to see you. Didn't recognize her. I told her to come back around lunchtime. I'm not sure she will, though. Seemed like she was in a rush."

My heart skips a beat. "What did she look like?"

James studies me, curiosity glinting in his gaze as he pushes his glasses up. "Tallish, in her thirties, medium-length dark brown hair." He narrows his eyes. "Why? You know her?"

Fuck. She's the last person I want to see.

With a long exhale, I get to work setting out my supplies. "Her name is Zoey. She's from Vancouver. She arrived in Pine Falls about a week ago." My tone is flat. I can't help it. "I almost ran her over when she crossed the street without looking. She had ridiculously high heels. I bet she would have face-planted a second later with those on anyway. And then we had sex the same night."

James sucks in a breath. "You wh—"

I hold both hands up. "There's more. She came in here yesterday, and I made her a bouquet. And then…" I swallow thickly, irritation bubbling in my gut. "She got a call. You'll never guess from whom."

I almost choked on my saliva when I saw the name.

"Who?"

"Oscar."

Honestly, who the hell saves their dad's number with his first and last name? "Oscar…" His eyes go wide. "*That* Oscar?"

"The very same. Oscar Marchiatto."

His jaw practically unhinges.

I can count on one hand the number of times I've seen that reaction out of him. Usually, he just nods, maybe raises an eyebrow—never much more. He's the type who chews on information in silence, waiting until he has something useful to contribute, if at all.

"You slept with—"

"Please don't say it out loud." I wince. "I'm upset enough with myself. I didn't know who she was when it happened."

I've been trying so hard not to think about it since his name flashed on her screen. Since I overheard her conversation. That fucking idiot's voice was so loud, I could hear it even after she stepped a few feet away.

What game is he playing? Sending his daughter to woo us? Not a fucking chance.

Says the guy who already slept with her.

I shut my eyes tight.

"So what does she want with you?" James asks, visibly confused.

"With me? Nothing. She wants to buy Emile's land."

His brows lift so high they disappear under his shaggy hair. "What for?"

"From what I gleaned from her conversation yesterday, she wants to build a fucking hotel."

Anxiety flares, heat crawling up my neck. When will they leave our town alone? When will they understand that we do not want to become a mega complex with Targets and Walmarts and resorts packed with rich assholes who couldn't care less about the damage they'd do to a small town like Pine Falls? They're not here for the nature, our history, or our "quaint" streets. Their only true interest lies in gentrifying another corner of this world. It's about ownership. Power.

For years, we've fought off these assholes. And I damn sure still have some fight in me. I'll gladly go against one more corporation trying to dictate what they swear is best for us, when their only goal is to line their pockets.

I was *so* close to asking Zoey out yesterday.

What was I thinking? With Daphne at home right now, with the shop busier than ever and in dire need of a cash influx... Maybe it's a good thing that she turned out to be the exact kind of person I imagined during our first encounter. A deceitful, spoiled city girl.

No more second-guessing my gut, that's for sure.

"That's unfortunate," James says, cutting through my thoughts.

"What? Why?"

He shrugs. "It's been a while since I've seen you this interested in someone."

"I'm not—"

He gives me a stern look.

"Fine." I sigh, deflating. "She got intriguing for a second, but that's all."

"Sorry, man." He mindlessly pushes the hair off his forehead, only for it to immediately fall back into place. "It would've been nice for you to meet somebody new."

I'm grateful for what he doesn't say, even if the message is clear. Four years later, and it still hurts to hear her name. Hell, just thinking about her still makes my chest ache like there's a tight fist around my heart. Because I wasn't enough. Pine Falls wasn't enough. And my family was too complicated for her.

That last part brings with it a bolt of anger. Nobody—*nobody*—will ever be more important to me than my sister is. If she couldn't accept that, couldn't deal with the fact that a good chunk of my time will always be devoted to Daph, then I wasn't the guy for her.

Even if I had all of it mapped out for us. A slow, mellow life in this small town. The traveling, the kids. But it was growing old by her side that I looked forward to the most. Seeing the gray in our hair and the wrinkles on our skin.

I thought she was *it* for me. So much so that I—

With a sigh, I push the memory aside. No need to rehash the past or dwell on it. It's never done me any good. It doesn't matter. None of this matters. And Zoey will never matter now.

"It is what it is," I reply flatly, picking up my shears. "Are you going to the town meeting tonight?"

"I was planning to. Lola is joining us there."

"Good. That's good." I use the back of my forearm to wipe a stray strand of hair from my face. "There's no way in hell I'm letting this project go through. That's not what Emile would have wanted."

James snorts. "What *would* that old bastard have wanted, except for the whole town to grunt and frown till the very end the way he did?"

I chuckle. He's not wrong. The old man gave us shit every day.

"Remember the time he took our soccer ball away when we were playing *in a park* because his car was down the street?"

James snorts. "Or when he gatekept Oli's mail for years because he was convinced he got food poisoning after eating at his grandparents' restaurant?"

I laugh, shaking my head as I continue to peel the damaged petals from roses. "I thought Oli was about to strangle him. But you can't say the guy didn't love this town. He was a mean one, but he cared for Pine Falls the most."

"Yeah. I'll give him that." James nods, his attention on his work again.

I devote the rest of the morning to processing orders, creating bouquets, cleaning vases, watering pots, and cutting stems to preserve flowers. I adjust the window display to include fall accents, change the name of the week's bouquet on the chalkboard outside, and check in with my supplier about the next delivery.

Throughout the day, and even on the way to pick up Daphne from school, a single thought consumes my mind.

Tonight, Zoey is going down.

Chapter Nine

Zoey

The space is bursting with loud chatter when I arrive, the buzzing sound reverberating against the bare walls.

I weave my way through the crowd. At the back of the room, pastries and half-full pitchers of lemonade are displayed on a long table. As I burrow deeper, furtive glances shift in my direction, and whispers grow louder, more insistent.

"Are you sure you heard right?"

"Her? Really?"

"Not again."

I shut it all out, focusing solely on what I need to do tonight. This is not the time to spiral over things I can't control.

Near the front, I spot the mayor—with the same gray hair from his headshot on the town's website—speaking with another man.

"Mr. Mayor," I say when I get to him. "Zoey Delacroix." Shoulders pulled back, I extend a hand. "Nice to officially meet you."

He studies me, not a single flicker of expression betraying his thoughts. For a second, I worry my judgment was off and tonight's outfit choice was a mistake. I kept it rather professional but still left the heels behind, opting for a silk blouse tucked in fitted black pants and leather ankle boots. My hair is twisted and held in place with a clip, and I went for a very natural makeup style. It's an approachable look, right? I really toned it down.

Unease threads through me as the silence stretches. I'm racking my brain for a way to stray away from the awkwardness when he breaks into a wide smile and finally shakes my hand.

"Robert Denison. But everybody calls me Rob. Welcome, Ms. Delacroix. Your father and I worked together a few years back. But then, everything went down and—"

He closes his mouth, leaving the rest of his sentence hanging.

That unease blossoms into a hint of discomfort. *What* went down?

Whatever it was, I push the thought aside. "Call me Zoey, please." I pause, my mind backtracking on his words. "Wait. How did you know about my dad? I didn't mention—we don't have the same last name. I don't—"

He pats my arm. "It's a small town. Information travels fast."

My stomach lurches. Fuck. *Fuck, fuck, fuck.* When did it even *get out?* At what—

Matt. It has to be him. After my dad called the other day, his whole attitude changed. I'm pretty sure he was about to ask me out, and then… he dropped his scissors just as my phone rang. Did he see his name on my screen? Did he overhear the conversation?

Fuck.

Visibly tired of watching me gape, Rob starts to turn back to the man he was speaking to when I interrupted. But I clear my throat, stopping him, and wipe my sweaty hands on my pants. I have one shot at this.

"I've read the agenda for tonight, and I'd like to submit a project for the land that's up for sale. I wonder if you'll be kind enough to give me the floor for a few minutes."

He frowns. "The land isn't open for submission yet, and the decision won't be made before the next meeting." He pauses, scrutinizing me with narrowed eyes. Then, voice lowered, he asks, "What kind of project are we talking about?"

I can smell interest when I see it. Rob worked with my dad till the very end. That alone tells me he might not be as close-minded as most of his constituents. If I play this right, I can sway him in my favor.

"A hotel."

His eyes widen in alarm.

Dammit. "*Not* your conventional hotel," I rush to add.

Poor guy must have really gone through the wringer with that failed deal.

"I'm not talking about a resort or anything luxurious, and I'm not asking for you to endorse my project. Let me present my case. That's all I want. If people don't like the proposal, they'll be free to express it, and we can go from there."

He presses his lips together and hums. Eventually, he pushes a hand through his gray hair and says, "People won't be happy about this."

I shrug. "I don't need them to be. What I'm offering is working. I would rather avoid protests, but as long as you're on board, that's what matters."

He looks at the pile of documents next to him. "I wouldn't be so sure about that."

What does *that* mean?

I clear my throat again and lift my chin. "I only ask for a chance to speak, that's all."

Rob holds my gaze for a long moment. Finally, he sighs. "Okay. I'll go over the testament, and you can take it from there."

"Thank you."

On my way to an empty seat, a tall, broad frame appears in the doorway at the back of the room.

When I meet Matt's eyes, my breath hitches. His jaw locks, his expression dripping with hostility.

Well, that confirms my suspicion. It's a good thing he wasn't there when I stopped by this morning, then. If he had looked at me like that while it was just the two of us, I would have lost it.

Disappointment rises up inside me. Why should I care what he thinks anyway? *I shouldn't*, and yet I freaking do, and I don't know why. It's making this thing ten times more complicated than it needs to be.

It was one fuck, Zoey, my brain screams at me.

But it was such a good one. That's definitely not my brain talking.

Matt looks away first. With a shake of his head, he lumbers to a chair in the back of the room and sits, his leg sticking out in the aisle. Next to him, a teenage girl wearing headphones is deeply focused on the notebook she's drawing in. On her right, Lola leans over to the man I saw at the flower shop this morning.

I take a seat and flip through my notes, barely registering the words I've jotted down. A dull ache prickles in my chest as I wait for the meeting to start, and I absently rub at the tight spot. I've given a lot of presentations in my career. In front of investors, CEOs, and industry titans. But somehow, this one feels monumental. Like a turning point. What if I fail? What happens then?

You don't have a choice. You don't have the first clue what you'd do with your life if you weren't Daddy's little helper.

I let out a bitter chuckle. Mom was smart to get out while she could. Now what's left for me to do? Start from scratch? And go where? Do what? I'm trapped as long as my father is still around.

"If you'd all take a seat, we'll get started," Rob says, the mic releasing an ear-piercing squeal.

I cover my ears, and so do just about all the people around me.

"Sorry about that, folks," he continues. "The purpose of tonight's town hall is to discuss the testament of our beloved Pine Falls resident, Emile Roland, who served this town as its postman for almost fifty years."

There are a few sniffles, some mumbles. The crowd has mixed feelings about him, I see. Maybe I can use that tidbit to my advantage.

"Emile, as peculiar as he was, left the town with a parting gift." Rob places his glasses on his nose and reads from the document in front of him. "It is no secret that I loved my town very much. I may have pissed off at least half of you, but everything I did was with Pine Falls in mind. Except when I dumped your mail in the shredder, Marty. You deserved every bit of it, you fucking old bastard."

A burst of laughter threatens to escape me. I clamp a hand over my mouth.

"Hum…" Rob says. "Sorry about that, Marty."

The old man with a cane who sits two rows in front of me scoffs and flips the mayor off.

"Whoa. Okay, Marty. These aren't my words." Rob tilts his chin down again, scanning the paper, his lips moving as he goes through it. "Okay, folks." He sets his glasses on the table, then links his fingers on top of the testament. "His wishes are fairly straightforward. Our dear Emile is leaving his land to the town, on the condition that we use it for the common good of Pine Falls. A proposal must be presented to the town, and the one that receives a majority vote will be approved."

Rumblings erupt all over the room.

A *majority vote*? That wasn't part of the plan. At all.

I wanted the residents' approval, yes, but I didn't think I'd need their *actual* approval to secure the land. I figured I'd work my magic and get people on board with the concept of the project. But I fully intended to go forward with it regardless of their blessings.

Fuck. Now that they seem to know who my father is, how am I gonna convince these people that I'm not here to build a disgusting concrete hotel for billionaires? That I'd rather offer a full experience for adventurous tourists while maintaining the charm of this picturesque town? That I want to do it with the help of the local businesses?

"Please, everyone, let's calm down," Rob says into the mic.

The room quiets slowly, and people return to their seats. In my periphery, Matt is up, leaning against the wall, his arms crossed over his chest, eyes on me.

I dart mine to my lap.

"I'm sure we'll find something we can all agree on in time. Speaking of, we have a guest with us tonight who's ready to present the first idea for the lot. Zoey?"

Rob moves away from the podium.

As I stand, whispers grow and carry me to the stage as the weight of the stares settles heavily on me.

Matt, still leaning against the wall, is watching me intently as I step up behind the podium and square my shoulders with a shuddering breath. I tune him out, pushing him out of my mind. I've done this a million times. I could do it in my sleep.

"Thank you, Rob." I nod to the mayor. "Good evening, ladies and gentlemen. My name is Zoey Delacroix, and I couldn't be more excited to be with you tonight."

I offer the crowd a broad smile, but I'm met with nothing but cold, dead silence. Okay, it's fine. They need a minute to warm up. I get it.

In the front row, Rosie leans forward, giving me all her attention. Her brows pinch together, as if she's trying to figure out what I'm doing up here, addressing them.

"I first came across Pine Falls in a documentary and instantly fell in love with the place. As I learned more about the town—its values and its people—my appreciation only grew stronger. And the more I discovered, the more I realized that your economic environment is missing a vital element." I clear my throat, scanning the blank faces in the audience. "You see," I go on, keeping my tone upbeat, "whether you like it or not, you're the gateway to wilderness tourism. Every year, thousands of people stop in Pine Falls before beginning their epic journey away from their modern lives. But every year, it's the same story. The streets and shops are too crowded, too crammed. You're suffocating. It's obvious that your blind spot is your lack of infrastructure to accommodate the influx that takes over your town each season."

I pause, taking in the now inquisitive looks. I've piqued their curiosity, related to their issue, and empathized with their needs. I've got this in the bag.

"What I'm offering isn't just a way to handle your problem. It's an experience. A path to make space for tourists while partnering with *your* businesses and helping them thrive. You'll be at the core of it all. Because I'll always ask myself, 'How can this project serve your needs?' and 'How can we blend your expertise with mine?'"

"So," a deep voice interrupts, "what you're really doing is using fancy words to bullshit us into building an all-inclusive fucking hotel, is that it?"

I snap toward Matt, who pins me with a cold stare, not a hint of friendliness left on his face.

Gripping the podium, I pull myself straighter.

He thinks he's the first man ever to try to intimidate me? In this line of work? Think again.

"It's not an all-inclusive h—"

"What is it then?"

"It's an experience that, yes, includes accommodation, but it's so much more than that."

One brow arches. "Will there be bedrooms available for guests to rent?"

"Yes."

"Will there be a place where they can eat?"

"What's your point?"

He lifts one shoulder. "It's a yes or no question."

I lean closer to the mic. "There will be dining options—"

"Then it's an all-inclusive hotel."

The crowd stirs, people exchanging concerned and even angry glances.

"It's a clever use of Pine Falls unlike anything that's been done before. You'll no longer be a stopover town, but a destination."

Matt scoffs, pushing off the wall. "A clever *use*?"

My stomach plummets. "That wasn't the right choice—"

"On that, we agree. Pine Falls isn't a tool to be used to whatever end you have in mind. And if you had done your *research* properly like you said you did, you'd know that this town is already a destination."

"That's right!" a man shouts from one side of the room.

"We run successful businesses, and we work our asses off year-round to welcome visitors and to ensure they're treated like our most esteemed guests. Since you've been playing the tourist for the past week, you should know that better than anyone." Matt's focus is unwavering, every one of his words sharp as a blade. "The last thing we need is your *hotel*."

Murmurs of agreement rise, mutters of "yeah" and "he's right" coming from all directions.

Heart racing and throat dry, I glance at Rosie. I'm desperate for one friendly face, somebody who can understand I wasn't trying to be deceitful. But her seat is empty. *Shit.*

"That's exactly what I want too. I want to help your businesses thrive. All I'm asking is for a chance to present what we have in mind for this land," I plead into the microphone, my grip on the podium tightening until my knuckles turn white.

"One more question, Miss Delacroix, before you go." He cocks a brow, a smirk on his lips. "Is it true that your father is Oscar Marchiatto? The very same businessman who wanted to build his monstrosity of a resort in our town two years ago?"

A quiet gasp spreads through the crowd.

I close my eyes. "Yes. But that doesn't have anything to do w—"

"We don't want your hotel!" a woman says in the back.

Next to her, another adds, "This town is not for sale!"

The locals rile each other up, and a second later, the whole room is screaming and shouting their opposition to the hotel's construction.

Flushed, I stagger a step back. How could everything have gone so wrong, so fast?

Rob is at my side in no time, steadying me with a grip on my elbow. "Are you okay?"

I gently ease out of his hold and smooth out the creases in my pants with shaking fingers. "I'm fine, I'm fine. I think I'm gonna go."

The minute it takes me to get to my chair and grab my bag stretches into an eternity. My chest tightens, and no matter how deeply I try to breathe, the pressure only sharpens, pushing and pushing against my lungs, crushing my ribs.

Without looking up, I move through the crowd, shoving a chair aside as I sprint for the door, barely glancing at Matt when I pass in front of him.

Even so, his attention weighs on me, as if he can sense the panic and irritation pouring out of me.

I don't need pity. Especially not from him. I raise my chin and push forward, and the second I'm outside, I gasp, sucking in the fresh evening air.

I let out a frustrated groan. "What an ignorant, tone-deaf, closed-minded, rude *asshole*!" I shout into the peaceful night.

Can't even let me finish explaining what I have in mind for his precious town. Oh, no. He wouldn't know what's good for this place if it slapped him in the face. These people are so fucking *stubborn*, so entrenched in their own outdated ways, that they won't even take five seconds to consider something new.

Ridiculous.

I could turn their little town upside down in the best way possible. But no. He'd rather deal with the overcrowding every high season. I haven't been here long, and it's already getting tight in the streets.

Matt really fucked me over, in every way. Scratch all the thoughts I had about him, how I let myself believe he was someone worth trusting. He's worse than I ever could've imagined.

I storm to my car, my hands still shaking, my lungs burning, and yank the door open. I slam it shut with a force that leaves my palms stinging.

"*Ughhh.*" The sound rips out of me, so sharp, so high-pitched, that it reverberates through the car. My head falls against the wheel, my hair spilling around my face, draping over my frustration like a curtain.

I knew it would be hard. I knew my association with my dad could be an issue. But I didn't think it would go sideways before I had a chance to plead my case. Show them that I'm nothing like Oscar Marchiatto. I'm clever, I listen, and I actually *care* about the people my work affects. And still, they wouldn't give me the time of day.

Now I'm no longer climbing a hill. It's a fucking mountain. And my father's expectations, his impossibly high standards, are like weights around my ankles. If I can't prove that I can do it, that I'm fit for the job, then what's left for me to do?

All those years of busting my ass at work, sacrificing everything—my friends, my life, my relationships, my own damn happiness—all to get to this point, only to fail at the finish line?

Hell to the fucking no.

Zoey Delacroix does *not* quit.

Tonight was a tough blow. I have no clue how the hell I'll turn this around, but I will. I'll find a way. I always do. I've come too far to back down now.

I start the engine, my hands gripping the wheel as if I'm holding on to my future.

I'll get this hotel built if it's the last thing I do.

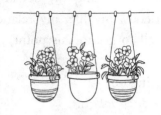

Chapter Ten

Matt

*O*h, I fucked up. I *really* fucked up.

Guilt rushes through me faster than a torrent mid-hurricane.

I could have been a tad nicer, and maybe not started a riot. To be fair, people got angry *very* easily.

I suppose, in a sense, that's good. Now I won't have to work to convince anybody to vote against that shitty hotel.

But damn, I wouldn't have wanted to be in her shoes up there. She didn't deserve the level of ire thrown her way, regardless of what she came here to do. She went through the wringer, and yeah, yeah, I know, I started it. I'm the one to blame.

I always tell Daphne to lead with kindness and expect the same of the people in her life, and yet there I went, pulling a stunt like that *in front of my sister*. I'm gonna have some explaining to do later, because, of course, I taught her about accountability too.

Shit.

I glance at the doors Zoey bolted through a minute ago. Maybe I can still catch up with her and apologize. There's a good chance she'll rip my head off, but it's probably worth the risk, right?

Would it be weird if I drove to Oli's and knocked on her door? Again? Flashes of her sweaty skin under my fingertips pop into my mind, but I shove them away quickly. Not the place, not the time. Not anymore.

I push through the exit doors just as she backs out of her parking spot.

"Zoey, hey." I jog into the road and stand in front of her car.

When she realizes it's me, her entire face closes off. "Move," she mouths through the windshield.

Bravely—stupidly?—I set both hands on the hood and lean down, meeting her eyes. "Can you give me a minute?"

Damn. The steering wheel is getting an aggressive treatment. The way she's gripping it? Pretty sure her fingers will leave a permanent imprint.

After an eternity, during which her eyes narrow more than once, as if she's considering the pros and cons of running me over, Zoey kills the engine and lowers her window. "I'm feeling benevolent. You have thirty seconds."

I walk around the car and rest my forearm on the frame, leaning in. "I'm really sorry about what happened in there. You have every right to be mad at me."

"Thank you for your approval," she says, derision dripping all over her tone. "Is that all?"

"I messed up. I'm sorry." I drag a hand down my face. "You have to understand—"

"Oh, I *have* to understand. Do I, now? After you couldn't give me that same courtesy in front of the whole town? What else do you have to teach me, Matt, huh?"

I deserve it. No denying that. "All I'm saying is that nothing I mentioned in there was personal."

She exhales loudly. "Oh, okay. Now I'm relieved. Thanks for clearing that up."

She glares out the windshield, though when she peers back at me through her lashes, the pretense has been dropped. There isn't a trace of sarcasm left on her face. No mask, no fake smile. Just Zoey and the hurt I caused.

"I didn't even have time to present my idea. You jumped on me like a starving hyena as soon as I opened my mouth. What if I actually had something good to say? Maybe, *just maybe*, I don't have any ill intention when it comes to this town. Is it so unbelievable that I could have thought long and hard about finding the best solution to your problem?"

She turns the engine back on, my sign that my seconds are numbered.

"I'm sorry. I shouldn't have interrupted you." My shoulders sink, the weight of shame pulling me down. "We're a sensitive bunch when it comes to our town, Zoey. It doesn't excuse my behavior, but I meant it when I said it wasn't personal."

I don't expect her to understand. Belonging to a community and caring for the well-being of others isn't something people who live in big cities are very familiar with. But still. I need her to know it's bigger than her. It's about our town's identity at its very core.

Her grip around the wheel relaxes an inch. I have no idea whether my explanation resonated, but I'll take it.

"Noted," she says. "Good night."

Facing forward again, she presses the button that raises her window, and I have just enough time to retreat a step before she drives away.

"Who's up for a hot cocoa?" I turn the key and the lock clicks open, Daphne squealing next to me.

"Do you have something stronger?" Lola asks, following my sister inside.

James raises a six-pack. "Don't worry. After that shit show, I stopped at Sue's."

"Thank god," I mumble. "Okay, Daph. Go hop in the shower while I get the cocoa ready, please."

My sister takes the stairs two at a time and slams the bathroom door shut.

"Someone's excited." With a chuckle, Lola sits at the kitchen table. "You don't seem too out of your depth here, Matty."

Side-eyeing her, I pull mugs and glasses from the cabinet. "Glad I make it look easy."

"You're putting too much pressure on yourself. Daph told me earlier that she loves spending time with you."

I open the fridge and grab the gallon of milk. "The feeling is mutual, but I don't think I am. It *is* a lot of pressure. I'm not a parent, and suddenly I'm in charge of her education and her well-being, and I also have to make sure I don't fuck her up while she's staying with me. And after tonight, I'm not off to a great start."

Lola throws me a pointed look. "You mean the first week with you is worse than living with a mother who can't even accept that she has an autistic daughter?"

Sighing, I place the saucepan half full of milk on the stove. "At least she has my dad."

"And she has you." James opens a beer and offers it to me, then sits next to Lola. "Tonight was nothing. Daphne probably didn't even notice. She had her headphones on the whole time."

"She notices everything." Even if she didn't say a word on the way back, I could see the wheels turning. Once James and Lola leave, the questions will come pouring in.

I dump two spoonfuls of cocoa into a mug, then take a swig of the beer. "What a shit show. People really went at her."

"To be fair." Lola drags out the words with the same careful tone she uses when she's about to drop a truth bomb that nobody wants to hear. "You were *kinda* leading the charge."

"The little she was able to say made sense," James adds.

The muscles in my shoulders tense, and I turn away from the stove. "Okay, whoa. Did you guys consult before ganging up on me? I know I screwed up. I apologized to her afterward, but she was having none of it."

"You *did* humiliate her in front of the whole town not even an hour ago," Lola says. "I think it'll be a few days before she can entertain the idea of hearing you out." With a shrug, she snags a beer for herself. "Why do you care anyway? It wasn't your finest moment, but she'll probably move on to something else. Saved her some time."

"They slept together," James whispers.

Lola's eyes nearly pop out of their sockets. "*What?*"

I breathe in through my nose, bracing myself, and nod. "We did."

Lola whips her head back and forth, studying James, then me. "*When?*"

"The night she arrived." I take a small sip of beer and wipe my mouth with the back of my hand. "It's not a big deal. It was a one-night kind of thing, that's all."

Lola bursts out laughing. "You? A one-night stand? Please. Since *when?*"

I pour the hot milk over the cocoa powder and stir. "Since I'm tired of being alone. Since I've officially realized that over-complicating everything has not brought me a lot of success."

Lola's face softens, but she doesn't say anything else.

Next to her, James is quiet, scrolling his phone, as if he's been mulling something over. I don't like Analytical James. He makes me queasy. I'm not great with silence or thinking everything through. But when James gets super into his thoughts, he can stay like this for hours and not say a word about what's going on in his brain.

As I add a generous amount of whipped cream to Daph's cocoa, Lola moves behind me and clasps my shoulder. Before I can set the can down, she snatches it from my fingers.

"Hey, leave some for Daph," I say. "She loves that shit."

She gives me a thumbs-up with the bottle already turned upside down in the direction of her mouth, then presses on the plastic tip.

James finally glances up from his phone, his gaze hazy, like he just woke up from a fever dream. "Did you look Zoey up online?"

I frown. "No." Should I have? The less time I spend on social media and company, the better. "Did you?"

He nods and holds up his phone, her LinkedIn profile pulled up on the screen. "She's the business development head for Oscar's group, Imperial Excellence. They have chains all over the world."

"Not surprised," I scoff as Lola peers over my shoulder. "Exactly who I thought she was."

"But if you look closer at what she does," James continues, his voice steady, "it says here: 'Zoey Delacroix is better known for her work founding the Traveler's Lodge chain, an affordable eco-friendly accommodation experience that's been revolutionizing the hotel industry. These lodges partner with businesses in their area, from coffee suppliers to exclusive activities, and give them much-needed economic boosts.'"

A pit forms in my stomach. Okay, so she's had one great idea. Doesn't make up for the fact that she works for a massive conglomerate that is no doubt responsible for the disappearance of hundreds of small businesses, the wildlife essential to maintaining our ecosystems, and the spread of tourism to the detriment of local communities.

So what if she's helped a few of them along the way? I'm sure I can easily find disgruntled companies and towns that would have a lot to say. One single article doesn't mean shit to me. It doesn't tell me how the people of those communities felt when her organization came in and took over.

"She also created an independent mentorship program. Look." He clicks on another link, which opens a page titled Leading the Future. "Seems like she's selecting a handful of promising start-ups in BC every year and investing in their growth."

"That's a lot of work," Lola says.

"*Leading the future*," I scoff. "Gotta love how humble she is."

Lola rolls her eyes while James types her name into the search bar. When he hits Enter, hundreds of articles populate. One after another, they describe the projects she's led since joining the company, and not only in BC. Thailand, Indonesia, Morocco. She's been everywhere.

"Wait, scroll back," I say.

He does, and one article in particular grabs my attention.

I lean in closer, squinting at the small print. "I didn't know her dad was nearing retirement. Do you think she'll take over?"

"She's briefly mentioned here, but the journalist is floating other names as well. Hard to say. But she's family. It would make sense."

I hum. So she could be in the running to take over for her dad. And, conveniently, that's happening at the same time she's trying to get her project off the ground here. It's just all... too coincidental.

"Looks like she got a degree in social science," Lola says. "Wonder how that led her to what she does now."

"Okay, fine." I pick up the saucepan and take it to the sink. "She might not be as terrible as I originally thought, but I'm still not sold on her intentions in Pine Falls."

Lola whirls around, brows furrowed. "But—"

"*However*," I cut her off. "I'll admit that it's hard to be sold on something when I don't know what that something is. And it's my fault we don't have the details. She deserves to be heard." The guilt is back, a dull ache in my chest. "But I don't know how to go about it now that the whole town hates her guts."

James clears his throat. "There might be a way that could also benefit you."

Before I can ask him what he means, Daphne bursts into the kitchen, dressed in her flower-covered pajamas. "Did you make my hot cocoa?"

I slide the mug to her. "Here you go. Extra whipped cream."

"Thank you." She wraps her fingers around it and takes a sip. When she puts it down, a little white mustache spreads over her upper lip. "Lola, do you want Matt to make you one too?"

"Thanks, Daph." She jiggles her beer. "Already set with mine."

"Okay." Without another word, my sister takes her hot chocolate to the couch. A second later, the faint sound of the TV reaches us.

"HGTV?" Lola cocks an eyebrow.

"That's all she watches. Gardening shows every night." I take another sip of my beer and turn to James. "You were saying?"

"Factually speaking," he starts, pushing his glasses up, "you're a pillar of our community. Your store is thriving, and everyone knows and loves you. You're very respected. You could… help Zoey get a second chance to advocate for her project by using your positive influence on the people of Pine Falls."

"Okay… And how do you suggest I do that? I can't force people to listen, and I won't go around trying to convince them like I'm some kind of spokesperson. I won't do the work for her."

"No, but you can show them that *you've* changed your mind."

"How?"

James stares at me, unblinking.

I'm growing impatient, ready to tell him to get to the point, when Lola sucks in a breath. "Oh, *yes.*"

He shrugs. "It'd work."

"It could *absolutely* work," she agrees. "I can't believe you were the one to come up with the idea."

Annoyance rolls through me. "Can someone fill me in? *Please.*"

Lola gestures for James to go ahead.

He draws a slow sip from his beer, taking his sweet-ass time. Eventually, he sets it down and narrows his focus on me. "You could pretend the two of you are dating."

My stomach lurches. "Absolutely not."

"Why not?" Lola exclaims. "As a romance bookstore owner, I'm an expert in the subject, and if I say it works, then it works."

"Actually, Matt, it could benefit you as well," James says, more pragmatic. He tips the bottle to his mouth. "Maybe she'd accept you into her mentorship program. I'm sure she gets hundreds of applications every year. There's no way she can go through all of them herself. Request an in-person interview at their office. Bypass the pre-selection process but still plead your case. This could be exactly what you need now that you've lost your investment opportunity."

This is what I meant when I said James thinks about everything. He's always ten steps ahead of the rest of us. I don't love this plan, but it's hard to deny that it makes sense.

I retrieve the school invoice from my back pocket and drop it on the table. "I got the bill for Daph's tuition fees today."

Lola unfolds the paper and winces. "Ouch."

"Yeah." I blow out a breath. "Three months to settle it."

"That's a lot of money, man." James exchanges a look with Lola, then snaps his fingers. "Hey, you know who could help? Zoey."

"She'll never get on board." Not after tonight.

Lola shakes her head. "I disagree. And it's the two of us against one. That means you have to try. Group rules."

My chest tightens. "I can't *fake date* that woman."

Can I? The pressure of my precarious situation is forcing me to consider it. But is making it happen worth putting my integrity in question? Worth fooling the people I love? Could I get close to her and live with myself, knowing who she is?

I suppose I wouldn't be bound to anything. Neither would she. And I already know the chemistry is there. It wouldn't be hard to sell it, though I'd need time to work past the mental hurdle that comes with the knowledge that she's Oscar's daughter.

We'd need to set clear boundaries. No crossing any personal ones, and Daphne is obviously one of them.

Fuck. I'm actually considering it. As if I need something else to make my already overcommitted days more complicated.

Before I entertain the idea of lying to the folks of this town, I have to know what Zoey's plans are for Emile's land. But other than that?

If being seen with me is enough to change people's minds, if I have this much sway and influence, if her project really would benefit Pine Falls, then why the hell not? If it means securing the future of Daphne's Wildflowers, thus allowing me to pay for my sister's tuition, what do I have to lose?

"I don't think it'll be the solution to my problems." I smooth back strands of hair that have escaped my bun. "But I don't have any other grand ideas for how to come up with the money, so might as well run it by her."

"It may not be a solution," James counters. "But it's definitely an opportunity for the store and for you."

I look at the price of Daph's tuition again. It's an inescapable reminder that I don't get to be picky. "Chances that she'll agree are as high as the likelihood of the Cleveland Browns going to the playoffs."

Lola tilts the whipped cream bottle to her lips again. "I don't know what that means."

I huff a laugh. "Nonexistent."

Chapter Eleven

Zoey

"I'll do it."

Matt, who's just taken a sip of coffee, chokes and sputters, hot liquid dribbling down his chin. "W-what?"

I've been up all night, going over every strategy I can think of that would help me gain the trust of the locals after yesterday's meeting. But nothing stood out.

"I'll do it," I repeat.

His face remains etched with disbelief.

It's okay. He probably didn't expect to get this particular response from me. Our interaction last night didn't exactly hint at the two of us pairing up easily. But desperate times call for desperate measures, and let's face it: I'm up against the wall.

I hate to admit it, and I hate to even consider this, but I have no other choice. It's success or corporate death.

And if Matt can help me achieve that success, if he has as much sway as he claims, then I'll swallow my pride and anger, and I'll roll with whatever he's suggesting.

By the way he rallied the whole town against me last night, it's hard not to have at least a little faith in him.

"I'm sorry." He shakes his head, his unbound hair following the movement.

Here's something I'm learning about myself: Men with long hair that belong in shampoo commercials? Hot.

"I was half convinced you weren't gonna show up this morning, and if you did, I thought there was a high probability of violence, so I need a second to process."

I dig my fork into my pancake and take a bite. "You said free breakfast. I'm easy to please."

And maybe finding a bouquet of petunias when I got back from my run, along with a sticky note that not only held an invitation to breakfast at Rosie's café but also a heartfelt apology, stirred something in the dark pits of my chest.

I might have shoved the bouquet into the trash before I saw the note, but he doesn't have to know that. Not that I need to spare his feelings after what he put me through last night.

"I haven't even told you what I want out of the deal," he says, one eyebrow raised. "Don't you want to know what you're getting yourself into before you agree?"

"Tell me the scandalous offer you want to make me." I sink into the cushy seat and survey him. What does this man so desperately need that he cannot get from anybody but me?

Matt leans in, threading his fingers together on the table. "I looked you up online."

I stop chewing. Oh fuck. What did he find? I school my features. "You looked me up? Is that something you should be confessing? That plus the note and bouquet combo this morning is giving obsessed bordering on stalking."

He scoffs. "No. I assure you, it's none of that." The faint color tinting his cheeks underneath that beard gives away more than he'd like. "I noticed your role inside your father's company. You have power. As his daughter, for starters, but also as the head of business development. And I stumbled upon your mentorship program for small businesses." He clears his throat and sits a little straighter. "I've had my store for five years now, and I'm looking for new opportunities. If you can facilitate an interview to get me into the program, and as long as your vision for Pine Falls doesn't go against everything I stand for, then I'll help you convince the rest of the town to hear you out." He pauses, assessing me, as if considering his next words carefully. Finally, with a sigh, he adds, "And if your project is really worthwhile, I'll do what I can to make it happen."

Well, well, well. Isn't this gruff man full of surprises this morning?

"So that's it?" I ask. "That's what you want?"

He nods once. "Yes."

"Okay, done. I'll see what I can do and who you can meet."

A brief flicker of surprise crosses his face, but he quickly regains his composure. "Yeah, that works for me," he says, smoothing out his beard. "So, tell me, before we actually commit to this, what's so special about Emile's land? Why do you want to build a hotel there so badly?"

I press my lips together. How much do I want to reveal? I don't owe him any explanation. He doesn't need to know that this is my one and only chance to show my dad what I can do. To prove to him that I'm a worthy successor.

It's not really a lie, just an omission. Still, a small pang of guilt seeps into my chest.

Realistically, if I want his help, then I should at least show some cooperation. Give him the main lines.

"I'd never heard of Pine Falls until I saw the documentary on TV. I don't know how to explain it, but I felt drawn to it, like it was calling me. Emile's land is in a prime spot, and it's one of the rare plots of land available in the area. Perfect for nature lovers." I shrug. "You have a need, and I saw an opportunity."

Matt's eyes narrow, his brow furrowing. His skepticism is palpable in his posture, the way he leans back in his chair as if he's trying to solve a puzzle with missing pieces.

"An opportunity," he repeats. "For whom?"

"I get it." I stab another slice of pancake. "You probably think I'm just your typical corporate asshole looking to cash in on a small town. But I'm not. I'm not here to insult your home or turn it into the next Atlantic City." I drag the square of pancake through the syrup on my plate. "I'm not gonna pretend I'm doing this out of the goodness of my heart either. It's a huge move for the rest of my career. And there's money to be made. But not just for Imperial Excellence. I see the potential. This town could flourish with the right push. The local businesses too."

He shakes his head. "Potential, huh? You're talking about it like we're numbers on a marketing sheet. I've lived here for half my life and know Pine Falls beyond any potential you might see. We're flourishing pretty well on our own. We don't need a cookie-cutter hotel."

Irritation swirls in my stomach, threatening to kill my appetite. "That's not what I'm offering, and maybe you'd know that if you hadn't been such a jerk last night." The words slip out before I can stop them.

I slide a folder in front of him, the one that contains a detailed description of the project, and sit back.

"Why don't you go over it and come back to me with your notes? From there, we'll see what we can do about it."

Matt studies me for a long moment, his brow furrowed. "I'll give it a read, but if I catch you in the slightest lie, we're done. Deal or no deal. This place is my home, Zoey. It's not some project to me."

I meet his eyes. I can't tell if his words are a warning or a challenge. Maybe they're both. And they spark something deep in my stomach, something resembling respect for this man who seems to care so profoundly about this place.

I lean forward, holding his gaze. "I'm not my father. I always make sure our projects benefit all parties involved. I want to build something that lasts. Something that fits in with the community and generates profits. And I can't get there if the whole freaking town hates me. I need the chance to talk to them, to show them what I'm bringing to the table. But as things stand, I'm useless on my own. You're my way in."

For a moment, it feels like we're standing on the edge of our fates, dangerously teetering between trust and doubt.

Then he lets out a breath and grabs the folder. "All right. I'll take a look. If everything checks out, we'll, uh, fake date. And in return, you'll introduce me to the right people. But if this thing turns into some sort of mega resort complex at any point, I'm out."

With a nod, I stick my hand out. "Deal."

He slides his hand along mine and squeezes, the move firm but gentle. The moment stretches, the air growing charged around us as we stay that way longer than we should.

His fingers move almost imperceptibly, but it's enough to make my breath hitch. Swallowing thickly, I slip my hand out of his grip and rest it on my lap.

"I want to apologize again for last night." He pushes his hair back. "It was out of character for me. I was just… triggered, I guess. But hurting you like that didn't sit well with me. I'm sorry for putting you through it."

Without my permission, my stomach swoops. A man who takes accountability for his actions? Maybe this town *is* special.

"I accept your apology. Plus, you're trying to rectify it by offering this fake dating stuff. You must have a lot of faith in your charming abilities if you think it'll be enough to convince people to give me another chance."

He takes a sip of coffee, his gaze never leaving me. "You tell me. How am I doing?"

I keep my expression flat. "Eh. Okay, I guess."

He laughs, the sound so deep and rich it drips down my body like honey. "Might need to work on that before we go out on dates, then."

On dates. Going out with this man. Go out and… do what? Oh fuck. Dread washes over the warm, sticky sensation, my pulse hammering with it. What did I just say yes to? What will I have to do to make the locals believe in this charade?

"We should go over what this fake dating includes and what we're comfortable with," Matt adds, as if reading my thoughts. "This will work better if we hash things out before we go out in public."

I nod vigorously. "Agreed."

Smiling, he brings his mug to his mouth. As he sets the coffee down, he flips over the bill the server left next to his plate and pulls a pen from his jacket. "Tell me your nonnegotiables. Stuff you don't want to do. Your limits."

He looks up, brows arched expectantly, his pen hovering above the crumpled paper.

I gape at him. Is he really about to take notes using a coffee shop bill?

Fine.

"No kissing," I say, raising one finger. "Obviously."

"Obviously," he repeats, a smirk on his face as he scribbles on the piece of paper.

"No sex." I tick on another one.

I need to give this project all my focus if I want to pull it off, and god knows the memories of sleeping with him are already seared into my eyelids. Who *wouldn't* want a surprise midnight rerun of the best sex of their life: lumberjack edition? Night after night, it's as if my brain says, "You know what'll help you sleep? A very detailed scene-by-scene of the one night you're trying to forget."

My heart rate picks up like a drum in my chest, but I will it to calm down.

No. Safer this way. Plus, we all know mixing business and pleasure never ends well.

"I think we can manage to convince people without it," he agrees. He's still wearing that smirk, but the rasp in his tone gives it another edge.

Is my face on fire? I really feel like it is. It's these damn sweaters I bought. I'm not used to being stuffed into woolens and scarves and leg warmers. And I'm definitely not used to talking about my dating life this way.

Pretend dating life.

Which, really, isn't all that different from the actual thing.

"How much public display of affection is necessary?" I ask, lifting my chin, desperate to regain a little composure.

"We can keep it to a minimum." Matt sets the pen down, as if his answer requires all his focus. "I don't think we should force it too much, but we also need people to believe we're together. When we're in public, we should get physical to some degree. Holding hands and light touches, like a soft press on your back or your arm. Do you think you can manage that?"

I nod. I can't trust myself to speak right now. Not when his words are conjuring images of his rough hands on my bare back and all the things he did afterward.

Gosh, before Matt, when was the last time I had honestly good sex? Carefree, unbridled, addictive sex? Our night together might have been intense and rushed, but I can't think of any other moments in my life where I felt so in tune with someone else's body.

"Zoey?" Matt watches me like he's waiting for something. "Does that sound good to you?"

Does what sound good to me? Fuck. This one-night stand will haunt me forever, won't it?

"Yes," I reply without asking him to repeat himself. I'm sure his request was perfectly reasonable.

He keeps his focus fixed on me for a second, and my cheeks grow hotter. But then he looks back at the paper and reads.

"No kissing, no sex. Touching is okay. We'll attend every town event together to make the relationship believable, and we'll talk up your project when it feels appropriate. Did I miss anything?"

"Nope, you covered everything."

He scans the small paper. "Ah. I forgot to add my nonnegotiables. No personal questions, and family is off-limits."

I frown. This firm, unbending tone is so at odds with the playful banter from a few seconds ago. It immediately puts me on guard. What is he protecting so fiercely?

"Shouldn't we go over at least the basic personal stuff so, you know, we pass for a real couple? What if someone asks me when your birthday is or how many siblings you have? This is info I need to have."

Not that I've ever fake dated before. I don't actually know the requisites for a successful fake dating experience, but getting to know one's fake boyfriend seems like a fundamental first step to me.

"Okay," Matt says, bracing his elbows on the table. "I'm the oldest of two, and my parents have been married for thirty years and are still together. I'm closer to my father. My relationship with my mother isn't bad, just complicated. Daphne's Wildflowers is named after my sister, who's thirteen. I've had the store for five years, and before that, I worked in landscaping for the town of Pine Falls. I spent most of my childhood in Nova Scotia. We moved here because of my father's job when I was seventeen, and I haven't left since. No college degree, and Lola, James, Oliver, and Charlee are like my family. I've had one serious relationship in my life, and it didn't end well. That's all you need to know." He settles back in his chair. "You want to share?"

My mind is reeling. He's thrown all kinds of information at me, yet none of it contains any real substance. A thousand and one questions race through my brain, curiosity prickling my skin like an itch I desperately need to scratch. But from the way his arms are crossed over his chest and the bluntness of his delivery, it's clear the subject is closed. I'm not going to get anything out of him.

At least not right now.

"I'm an only child," I say, taking his lead. "My parents are divorced, so I've never really known them together. My mother spends her days in her garden, which is why I've always loved flowers. My father has been working tirelessly all his life. I get along with both of them well, but our dynamics are very different. I was born and raised in Vancouver. Six months ago, my relationship ended, and as you know, he didn't have very nice things to say about me."

I'm painfully aware of how little I have to say. Even if I hadn't condensed my life to the briefest of points, virtually nothing would stand out. It's all work, work, work. And I can't share a big part of myself with Matt without alienating him. He already hates my father. No need to rub it in his face.

But if I could, I'd tell him that I started working here and there for my father when I was sixteen. I'd tell him that changed my relationship with him forever. That my dad traded in his role as a father for one of a corporate executive. That I initially followed in my mother's footsteps and studied pediatric nursing, but that my father's influence was inevitable and lethal to my development. That I don't even remember the woman I was before he sank his claws into me.

"All right, then." Matt splays his hands on the table, his voice startling me from my thoughts. "I think that covers the personal questions segment."

"You know," I say, "if we want to pull this off, you're gonna need to act like you actually like me."

He sighs. "It's not that I don't like you. It's—" He runs a hand down his beard. "It's going to take a minute for me to trust you, Zoey. Your father... he really scarred us. For a while, we thought we'd lose Pine Falls. So forgive me if I'm a tad wary of his precious daughter."

I scoff. "You didn't have an issue the first night when you fucked me into the wall."

Wow, I felt brave for a moment there, but now that he's practically pinning me to the chair with his gaze, I'm regretting the level of spunk I poured into that answer.

"Hard to think straight when a beautiful woman opens the door for you wearing nothing but a towel. And, in my defense, I didn't know who you were then."

If I had, I wouldn't have done it, is the subtext there.

I arch an eyebrow, ignoring the last part, and focus on the first half of his comment. "So I'm beautiful?"

"It's hardly a secret, Zoey, but that's beside the point." He looks away, peering out the window, his brows lowered.

I can't help but study him. What is he thinking about? Is he avoiding eye contact because he revealed more than he meant to? Or is he replaying that night in his head like I've been driving myself out of my mind doing?

But then he looks at me again, his gaze softening as his brow relaxes. "You're right. If we want our deal to work, I need to put this whole thing behind me and start fresh."

I thrust my hand out, wearing a smile that makes my cheeks ache. "Hi, I'm Zoey, and I'm new to town."

Matt takes my fingers in his, flipping them so my palm faces down. Before I can put two and two together, he brings them to his lips and drops a kiss there. "Nice to meet you, Zoey. I'm Matt."

His touch sends an electric pulse down my arm, heat radiating from where his lips were a second ago. Still hovering above my hand, his beard caressing my skin, he looks up at me from beneath thick lashes, his attention setting my face on fire.

Oh, this man is trouble. Big, big trouble.

As if he hasn't done enough, he straightens and winks. "Might as well get started on our ruse now," he whispers.

And sure enough, when I glance around us, a few patrons are looking our way, expressions full of surprise, several murmuring to the people sitting next to them.

Matt sets my hand gently on the table. "Meet me Friday after work. We can discuss the specifics then."

He stands, removes his jacket from where it hangs off his chair, and rounds the table. I'm frozen in place as he sidles up beside me and places a kiss on my hair.

"I'll see you Friday."

And just like that, he's out the door. And I'm left swamped with a swirling tide of emotions, wondering whether I've just made the worst or best deal of my life.

Chapter Twelve

Matt

*I*t's been two days, and whiffs of mint and rosemary still tickle my nose. It was a single kiss to her head, quick and short, and yet the smell of her shampoo has lulled me to sleep both nights since I saw her last. More than once, I've jolted awake, the scent so vivid I swore someone was beside me. But it was all in my mind.

She's been on my mind.

Ever since our deal, she's been a constant thought. A constant worry. Did I make the right choice? How is this going to work? Can I actually pull this off? If so, at what cost?

I was so focused on the opportunity to grow my business and earn enough to pay for Daphne's school that I didn't stop to think about the implications of spending this much time with Zoey. Holding her hand, getting close to her, pretending she means something to me in front of the people who've known me since I was a teenager. Giving them a feeling of déjà vu.

A pinch of guilt twists in my stomach. It's gonna take some heavy convincing. The number of women I've been serious with can be counted on the fingers of one hand. And suddenly I'm parading through town with a stranger who's been here for a week, acting like she's the love of my life, fully ignoring that, in their minds (thanks to yours truly), she wants to turn our town into one giant Walmart?

Yeah, solid plan, Matt. They'll totally buy into that.

I need to find the angle. What's the catch? What is it about her that could make me fold so easily?

It's been a while since I've seen you this interested in someone.

James's words echo in my head. She intrigued me at the beginning, yes. I couldn't help but want to know more about her. Discover why she seemed so desperately alone and miserable, and work out why I felt the need to fill that void for a brief moment.

But that was before I knew who she was and why she's here.

"So what do you think?" I ask.

Lola closes the folder, then slips her glasses off and sets them on the counter. "I hate to say it, but this is impressive." She exhales. "I like that the focus is to connect people to nature and take them on excursions in the area. The small individual cabins are also a nice touch. They'd be much more fitting here than a luxury resort. I don't know, Matt. She thought of everything."

"Hmm." I prop my elbows on the counter and lean against it.

My hope was that Lola would go over the documents and find glaring reasons why this project wouldn't work for Pine Falls. But no. Her take is similar to mine. It's almost too good to be true, coming from Oscar's daughter, and that's what makes her so unreliable. Like father, like daughter, right?

But when I sat down to read it last night, I was struck by the level of detail and care she put into her proposal.

Which, I know, I know, makes me an even bigger jerk. She's on the town's most-hated list because of me. The least I can do is help her get off it.

Lola flips through the pages again, stopping at the section on services offered. "The core focus of her plan is teaming up with small businesses. From coffee suppliers to construction crews. She even noted Carl's company as a potential partner for her nature excursions. She really did her research."

A lump forms in my throat. "Do you trust her?"

"Not sure. I don't know her like you do," she says with a teasing smile. "But I'd be open to hearing her out."

I hide my face in the crook of my elbow and groan. "Please don't remind me I slept with Oscar's daughter."

Even if I can't stop going back to that night in my mind.

Lola pats my head lightly. "There, there. It's gonna be okay. There are worse things in the world."

"She's coming to the store in an hour so we can strategize the best way to do this dating thing."

"Oh, how romantic," Lola rests her palm above her heart. "They say chivalry is dead, but look at you. A true modern Romeo."

I huff. "Please, don't start. This is embarrassing enough."

"It's not." She leans in, brow arched. "Your sister is your priority, and without you, she can't get the education she needs. Your heart is in the right place, Matty. I just hope you won't get lost in this make-believe and end up breaking it again."

"Not a chance," I scoff, pushing off the counter. "I've learned my lesson. I know better than to get tangled up with city folks. This is a professional agreement, nothing more, and I'll treat it as such."

"Sure you will." Lola gives me a stern look. "Still, be careful, okay?"

"You don't have to worry, Lols." I round the counter and pull her into a bear hug. "She and I will never happen."

Never happen *again*, that is.

All morning, I muddle through the day's orders mechanically, cutting flowers, wrapping bouquets in tissue paper, and slipping personalized notes inside. It's a routine after all this time, but today my mind is elsewhere. I fidget more than usual. I dropped a vase, then spent far too long cleaning up the pieces scattered across the floor. And at the faintest sound, my eyes keep darting to the door, thinking she's finally here.

She's late. Over an hour late. Damn, I hate it when people waste my time.

Just as I'm ready to move to my office to start on the day's paperwork, the bells above the door jingle and Zoey bursts in.

"I am *so* sorry," she says, chest heaving. "I got held up in a meeting and couldn't get out of it. I rushed here as soon as it was over."

It's warm today, and the sight of her in more casual clothes—a snug black top that reveals her collarbone, tucked into a suede skirt that stops mid-thigh—sets my blood pounding. I force my focus away from her legs, from her sheer black tights and high leather boots. The last time I lingered there too long, I ended up fucking her against a wall, and nobody wants a repeat of that. Sort of.

"I thought you'd bailed on me." I swallow thickly, fixing my attention on her face.

"Oh, no. I wouldn't." Her eyes drift to the folder next to the register. "Did you take a look?"

"I did. Last night."

She pops a hip to one side, placing her hand on it, smug. "And?"

I crack a smile. She knows she nailed it. Doesn't erase who she is or who she works for, but I'll give her that. I was an asshole for jumping the gun.

"Wildly different from what your dad had in mind when he came here a few years ago."

Her lips twitch. "That's because I want to build lodging that belongs in the community, not just a fancy block of concrete."

Eyes narrowed, I scan her face for any signs that would betray her words. But I don't know her well enough to pick up on them.

"It shouldn't be too hard to sway the town once they get past the initial 'she's Oscar's daughter' shock. We're a stubborn, protective bunch. But that's where I come into play, right?"

Her gaze flicks to my mouth. "Right."

A loaded silence falls between us, thick with understanding. We both know *how* I come into play, and neither of us has any idea how to navigate that.

I clear my throat. "Should we go into my office?"

Her eyes widen, and she takes a step back.

"Not like that," I blurt out. "I meant so we can discuss our game plan for the upcoming weeks."

"Oh," she says softly, a rosiness coloring her cheeks. "Of course. Lead the way."

Once inside, I close the door and sit behind my desk.

She stands in the middle of the room, taking it in. It's not a grand space. Four walls without windows, a table and two chairs, and an old leather couch for the countless all-nighters I pulled during the first year of business.

It's simple, but it gets the job done.

"Lola has been begging me to decorate the office," I tell Zoey as her attention continues to wander across every object and piece of furniture.

"You should let her do it." She looks at the second chair warily before she eases into it. "It's a bit... bland and old."

I cock an eyebrow, suppressing my amusement. "Way to earn my favor."

"Well..." She crosses her legs, tugging at her skirt, which hiked up with the movement. "At least you can note 'honesty' as a very strong personality trait of mine."

"We'll see about that."

I open the top drawer of my desk and take out a notebook.

"First, we should exchange phone numbers. Then I'll text you my address, just in case. This is information you should know as my fake... person."

She holds back a laugh, pressing her lips together. "Person? Yes, okay, sure."

"I made a list of the people we should hit on our fake dating tour if we want to secure the deal," I say, ignoring her mocking remark. "People who have influence and respect." I flip to the first page. "And I've made another one for the events we should attend together."

Zoey nods, leaning in, wearing an impressed frown. "You put a lot of thought into it."

"Not a *lot*," I retort. "I prefer to stay organized. If I don't write stuff down on paper, I tend to forget."

I don't like the way she's observing me, as if she's just cracked a minuscule piece of the *Who's Matt?* code. I didn't think such a small detail would spark so much curiosity in her. I've always been like this, so I long ago found a system that works for me, and it's nothing even remotely groundbreaking.

"That makes sense," she finally says. "What do you have?"

I turn the notebook so she has a clear view of the outline I created. "In two weeks, we'll all meet and vote on your proposal for Emile's land," I say. "I suggest we build this relationship gradually if we don't want to arouse suspicions."

"Smart," she cuts in.

"However, with only two weeks to do so, it'll be tricky," I continue. "So gradual but effective. We'll start tonight with the last movie-in-the-park of the season. The whole town will be there."

Except Lola and Daph, since my sister hates being outside when it's chilly, and the evening temperatures have dipped in the past few days. Lola offered to keep her company so I could have my night free. They plan to watch the same movie we'll be watching in the park, *Pretty Woman*, with a big bowl of sweet popcorn, Daph's favorite.

"Is a movie the best place to *talk* with people? That's the goal, right?" She cocks an eyebrow, mouth curled slightly.

The sarcasm in her voice is undeniable, but I ignore it. "You're not going to win them over if you immediately start babbling about your hotel project. The key is for them to see us together first."

She leans back in her chair with a sigh. "Fine. What's next?"

I scan the page in front of me. "The weekly farmers' market on Wednesday. We should also make an appearance at Cooper's microbrewery fundraiser party tomorrow. He and I go way back, and I told him I'd help set up the place and supply the flowers. You should help too."

"Cooper," she says as she taps on her phone screen, taking notes. "One of the bros."

"What are you doing?"

"Noting names of the people I need to remember, along with who they are to you," she says. "I assume I'm gonna meet several, so I might as well have a cheat sheet."

"Smart," I reply.

She smiles easily, but it doesn't reach her eyes. She does that a lot. During most of our encounters, she's been stressed or nervous, but she's still managed to force her lips to stretch into this thin, practiced curve. As if she's smiling because that's what's expected.

It bothers me.

Daphne did the same thing when she was younger. Responding according to people's expectations because she was scared they'd get angry if she didn't react "correctly."

I want Zoey to feel like she can be herself around me, smiling when she wants, not because she thinks she should.

She tilts her head. "Anything else?"

"Yes, sorry." I lower my gaze and focus on the list again. *How long was I staring?* "Once a month, the kids from the local school go on a wilderness trip with Carl. Oliver usually accompanies them, but when he's not here, I step in."

One more task to add to my never-ending pile of things to do. Poor kids, stuck with me when they could get all the fun facts from Oli.

"Oh, I've heard about Carl." She taps away again. "When I researched the town, his business came up a lot."

I nod. "He's very popular around here. Probably smart to pay him a visit. His vote will be important. Patty, who owns Roots and Tresses, and Sue at Willowbrook Market are also very influential in town. Add them to your must-talk-to list. Though Patty is very good friends with Ruth, who owns the only hotel in Pine Falls, the Butterfly Inn, so she'll be a tough sell. You're directly challenging Ruth with that project."

Zoey nods over and over as she takes notes. "Look at us, talking about people like they're swing states in the next US election."

I stiffen. The joke lands flat, even if she didn't mean it that way. I hate having to strategize how to handle the people of my town, but if she has any chance of succeeding, Zoey needs to know who to win over.

"These people matter to me," I say, a bit harsher than I intended. "They're not pawns in this game, nor will I force them to agree to anything. It's all on you. You have to do the work."

"And yet here you are," she retorts, her tone just as sharp. "Ready to deceive them."

It's funny how the mood can change so suddenly. A minute ago, I could taste the careful tension between us on the tip of my tongue. Now, her gaze is loaded with defiance, guns pointed at me, ready to ride into battle.

One step forward, three steps back.

Part of me wants to get to know her. To peel back the layers shaped by years of abandonment and loneliness, the kind I can only imagine she endured growing up with a man like Oscar. But, fuck, she doesn't make it easy. And other times, I can't help myself. She's her father's daughter, and my brain refuses to let that go.

"Fuck." I sigh, passing a hand over my face. "I'm sorry. That was uncalled for."

Surprise shines in her eyes, but she recovers quickly. "You're fine. I'm the one who's, um…" She clears her throat. "Sorry. I shouldn't have made the joke."

She smiles, but again, it barely stretches to her cheeks.

"The movie is at seven p.m. tonight. I'll pick you up around six thirty so we can arrive together. Work for you?"

Zoey gets up and gathers her things. "Yes. Starting slow, right?"

With a nod, I flip my notebook closed. "I would never do anything you're not comfortable with." I make my voice as gentle as I can. "You can trust me, I promise."

"I do." She turns and shuffles for the door.

"Oh, and Zoey?" I say as she reaches for the knob.

She looks over her shoulder, waiting.

"Wear something warm. I'll bring blankets, but it'll be a bit chilly."

"No towel, then."

Instantly, heat licks at my skin. "Exactly." My voice comes out hoarse.

"Noted," she replies, amusement coating the word. "See you tonight, *honey*."

Chapter Thirteen

Zoey

"See? Improvement from the last time I opened the door, no?"

Matt stands in the doorway, surveying my leggings and oversized turtleneck sweater.

He cleaned up nicely tonight. A canvas jacket over a flannel button-up shirt, along with a simple pair of jeans and boots. But it's his unbound hair, some strands still wet from the shower, that holds all my attention. I want to run my fingers through it, see if it's as soft and thick as I remember.

"I don't know about improvement," he says under his breath as he steps back so I can exit the house, "but definitely weather appropriate."

I blush, hopeful that the color rising in my cheeks isn't visible beneath the faint glow of the moon, and close the door behind me.

Neither of us speaks on the ride to the park, though his knee won't stop bouncing. The man is nervous. It's endearing and honestly, understandable. I've spent most of today working and then went out for a run to take my mind off what the two of us are doing. To keep from thinking about what will happen if I don't secure the lot. Dad was pissed when I called him with the news that the meeting went sideways. "Deception after deception," I believe were his exact words.

As we roll up to the park, Matt navigates into what seems like the last available space.

"You weren't lying when you said it was popular," I muse, looking around.

Dozens of people sit on blankets spread out over the grass, bundled up against each other in front of the big screen at the far end of the green.

"Nope. Nobody wants to miss the last one of the season." He unlocks his phone and taps at the screen quickly, then puts it away. "Ready?"

I smile weakly, my heartbeat speeding up like a hummingbird taking flight. "Let's go."

As I climb out of the vehicle, the gentle air soothes my heated skin. The scents of buttery popcorn and cotton candy waft from a grouping of food trucks lit up by strings of lights hanging from nearby trees.

"Can you help me out?" Matt asks in the back.

"Coming." I circle the truck and find him snagging blankets from the bed.

"Take these two. I'll get the rest," he says, holding them out.

I obey, tucking them under my arm while he picks up the what's left, along with a small basket.

"Do you always come this prepared?"

"Only when I have someone to impress." He winks.

I steady myself on the frame of the truck.

Oh, okay, so we've started pretending. Shit, it's gonna take some getting used to.

I tuck a strand of hair behind my ear. "Well. It's working."

Matt stares at me, silent for the space of two heartbeats, before nodding toward the gathering. "Let's find a spot."

We walk side by side, closer than friends should. All along, his arm brushes mine over and over, lingering long enough to make it look intentional. I catch his eyes on me several times, hiding smiles and stealing glances as if he can't help himself.

God, he's good at this.

As we move through the crowd, the attention on us grows heavier, more and more frowns appearing on questioning, concerned faces. The mayor, Rob, and his wife, are set up in a pair of camping chairs. He nods at me in greeting, and I nod back. In the distance, Rosie sits with a group of friends. She shoots me a deadly glare before turning back to the conversation going on around her.

My shoulders drop. I itch to walk over to her and explain myself, but something tells me she would rather spend a month being violently sick than speak to me ever again.

"Here okay?" Matt asks when we reach an empty spot in the middle of the park.

"That's perfect."

He sets the basket on the ground and spreads one blanket out, then adds a second on top. When he takes the two I've been holding, his fingers brush and linger against mine.

A shiver rolls down my spine.

"Are you cold?"

I fold my arms in front of me and rub them. "A little."

The lie slips out. I promised I would be honest from now on, but there's no way I'll admit to how easily he affects me. So instead, I turn toward the food trucks, cataloging the options.

Matt rests his palm on my back. "We could grab something warm to eat, and a hot chocolate if you want. My treat," he adds.

"That sounds nice." His hand on me pulls my focus completely and I lose my train of thought. It's a simple touch, but still, my body temperature rises several degrees, and suddenly, I'm not so cold anymore.

All the way to the food trucks, his hand is a steady presence, grazing at times, more pressing at others, burning an irrevocable mark into my skin.

People nod at him and stop to say a quick "hi" or a "how have you been?" Everybody we meet knows and loves him. With each greeting, envy grows inside me. Because he's still a stranger to me, and already, it's clear he's someone worth knowing.

"That's Mia." Matt jerks his chin at a young woman behind the counter of a food truck. Her brown hair falls to her shoulders, her long bangs hanging over her eyes. "She owns the only bakery in Pine Falls. She makes the best pastries. The whole town loves her, so you'll want her to like you too."

I swallow. "Noted."

When the couple in front of us is served and we step forward, Mia's face lights up.

"Hey, Matt!" she chirps. "Long time no see." Her eyes flick to me, and then she does a double take and blinks. "Oh, um... Zoey, right? The woman who wants to build that fancy resort on Emile's land?"

"Not a—"

"The one and only." Matt tightens his grip around my waist and brings me closer to him. "That town hall was something, huh?"

I am *so* confused right now. What's happening? Shouldn't he be singing my praises?

Mia releases an awkward chuckle. "True. It got a little out of control toward the end." She shoots me a sympathetic look. "Nothing against you, but we have to protect our people and our town. Especially after the stunt your dad pulled."

I get it. My dad's approach two years ago hit a nerve. But I'm not him, am I?

I force my lips to tip up in a smile, summoning all the friendliness I can muster. I'm used to dealing with corporate bros and business moguls rather than actual people, and it shows.

"I get it. I'd do the same thing if I were in your shoes."

Matt slides his hand from my waist up to my arm and wraps me in a side hug. "Actually, the whole evening was my fault," he says to Mia. "I was so pissed when I found out Zoey was Oscar's daughter that I lost it. But since then…"

He pauses, his gaze melting into mine before slowly drifting to my mouth.

It's only a few seconds, but the heat in his stare coaxes my lips apart.

With an uneven breath, he drags his focus back to Mia, who hasn't missed a beat of the show he's just put on.

"Since then," he continues, his voice husky, "I've gotten to know Zoey and her project, and… she's got something special here."

He gives me a quick squeeze, and I lean into him on instinct.

"Oh, wow. I didn't know you two had spent so much time together," Mia says, eyes wide.

Matt shrugs. "After the meeting, I wanted to apologize for my behavior. One thing led to another, and… Let's just say I no longer judge a book by its cover. Right, beautiful?"

I flush hard at the sound of the endearing nickname he's given me. He's called me that once before. Against a wall. And I couldn't stop thinking about it for days.

"Right," I say with a strangled laugh, patting his chest. "We both had some groveling to do."

He leans in and buries his face in my hair, murmuring, "That's a nice visual."

I cough, my cheeks flaming.

"Well," Mia says, dusting her fingers on her apron. "That certainly wasn't on my bingo card for tonight. Anything I can get you two before the movie starts?"

"What do you want, Zoey?" Matt's voice is barely a whisper, so quiet I don't think Mia heard the question. Like it was meant only for me.

He holds my gaze, and for a moment, I get lost in his. I forget that he's waiting for my answer. I forget that Mia is waiting for our order. I forget that the movie is starting in a minute.

It's impossible to think clearly when he's looking at me like he can't believe his luck.

Fuck. Scratch him being good at this. He's lethal.

I glance at the counter full of pastries, at the list of at least a dozen types of hot chocolate and other warm drinks. I'm lost. There are too many options, and I'm suddenly sweating over sweet treats. I don't usually do this, and as pathetic as it sounds, cookies and hot chocolate aren't exactly on the menu at investor happy hours or fundraising galas. "I don't know." I peer up at Matt. "You choose."

Brows knitted together, he searches my face. "You sure?"

"Yeah," I say with a faint stretch of my lips.

With a sigh, like he's still not convinced but he isn't going to argue in front of Mia, he scans the display. "Two brownies and two hot chocolates with marshmallows and extra whipped cream, please."

Mia perks up and snags a pastry box from a stack beside her. "Coming right up."

She boxes our order and pours the drinks while Matt pays.

"There you go." She hands me the box, and Matt takes the hot chocolates. The smell is so rich and sweet, it makes my mouth water.

"Thanks, Mia," Matt says. "See you around."

Just as we're turning, Mia calls out. "Oh, Zoey! You should stop by when you have a chance. I'd love to hear more about your plans."

I raise my eyebrows. "Really?"

"Yeah." She grins. "Do you know how hard it is to change this guy's mind? If you've done it, then I'm intrigued."

"You haven't seen anything yet," Matt says to Mia, then to me. "Come on. The movie is starting."

I wave to Mia and follow Matt to our spot. "That went well, I think."

He sets the hot chocolates down on the blanket. "Yeah. She's sweet, though. That was an easy win for you."

He bunches up the blankets to create a bit of cushioning, then gestures for me to sit.

"Thank you." I settle down and pick up one hot chocolate while Matt gets busy unpacking the basket. "Will you be upset if I take a sip before you join me? It smells so good."

He turns to me, his lips kicked up on one side. "Not at all. Go ahead while it's still hot."

I press my mouth to the plastic lid and tilt the cup slowly. The moment the sweetness of the chocolate registers, a moan rumbles out of me.

"Oh god, this is good."

I take a second sip, savoring the rich flavor, unable to hold back another embarrassing noise.

When was the last time I had hot chocolate? Probably when I was five or six, maybe? Back when it was still considered "age appropriate," as my dad liked to say. I can't believe I gave up something so simple, so ridiculously comforting, all on my own.

A lump forms in my throat, my eyes stinging as I bring the cup to my lips again.

A freaking hot chocolate.

And for what? For work? To please my father?

Matt exhales a chuckle as he rifles through the basket. "We said we'd take it slow. If you continue making those sounds, people will—"

He turns to me and stops cold. In a heartbeat, he's next to me, his fingers pressing on my arms. "Hey, Zoey, what's wrong?"

"It's nothing," I say, half crying, half laughing. If he didn't think I was crazy before, he definitely does now.

He cups my cheeks, forcing me to look at him as he wipes away a tear.

"Tell me," he whispers, unruffled by the yo-yo of my emotions.

"It's silly." Fingers tightening around the plastic cup, I shake my head. "You're going to laugh at me."

"I would never do that."

Gosh, this is mortifying. Crying in front of my mom is embarrassing enough, but in front of a man I just met? Is the deal really worth more than my dignity? I didn't even know I could cry like that anymore.

Vision blurry, I lift my chin and steady my voice the best I can. "I can't remember the last time I drank hot chocolate." I sniffle. "If I can't recall something as simple as that, what else have I erased from my life? What else have I missed out on? I couldn't even order for myself back there because I don't know what I like. I got overwhelmed by the possibilities and the unknown."

I exhale harshly. *Get it together. You're a fucking grown woman, not a child.*

"Sorry," I say. "That was a lot. I'm not doing well with our 'no getting personal' rule, am I?"

"Don't apologize." His thumb draws circles on my cheek in a soothing pattern, the warmth of it lingering like soft aftershocks. "There's nothing wrong with feeling overwhelmed. I feel that way all the time."

"You're very good at hiding it," I murmur.

He laughs, low and deep. "I'm not. But the goal shouldn't be to hide what we feel. If a hot chocolate leads to an eye-opening moment for you, that's okay. It doesn't matter what brought that realization to your mind. All that matters is what you learn from it and what you choose to do next with that knowledge."

I'm too stunned to reply. I wish somebody had said that to younger Zoey, when she was fighting back tears for fear of being yelled at because "women will never be taken seriously if they're always crying or showing emotions."

Matt lowers his hand to his lap.

"Thank you," I say, pushing the words past the knot in my throat as I dry my tears.

"Nothing to thank me for." He tilts his head toward the screen where the movie has started. "Should we watch?"

"Yes, great idea." I take a deep breath, centering myself.

He settles next to me and drapes a blanket over my shoulders.

I grasp the edges and tighten it around me. "Thank you."

"Have you ever seen *Pretty Woman?*"

"Never," I say after another hit of hot chocolate that calms my frayed nerves.

"That makes it all the more special, then." He slides his arm around my waist and pulls me to him, all bundled up in my blanket.

I lean into him willingly, his warmth soothing the last of my anxiety. His firewood and daisies scent swirls around me in a dangerously tempting blend. I want to lift my face and press my nose to the hollow of his neck, inhaling until he's all I can breathe.

My brain screams at me that none of this is true, but I ignore it. Let me pretend a little longer. Just for the rest of the night.

The sky is dark now, except for the stars twinkling above us. The film plays, and I curl further into his side, his body solid and steady beside mine. The whole time, his arm stays draped around my waist, his legs stretched casually in front of him.

Without giving it a second thought, I rest my head on his shoulder. I don't move or say anything when he leans into me in return.

Chapter Fourteen

Matt

My arm is falling asleep, but I can't bring myself to move out of Zoey's hold or push her away.

She's finally relaxed against me, and I wouldn't take her peace away from her for anything. Especially not after she had a mini existential crisis that left me with the furious urge to help her reclaim her life.

By the time her hot tears had dried on my fingers, my mind was made up. This won't be your average fake dating situation. From now on, I'm going to make it my mission to turn every moment we share into an opportunity for her to experience the things she seems to have been missing out on.

"He's really trying to woo her," Zoey says, her attention riveted on the screen. "A private jet to go to an opera show? Who does that?"

I chuckle. "Has nobody ever been romantic with you?"

Jesus Christ. One day. One day, and we've already broken the rule about staying out of each other's personal lives. I can't help it. The questions burn my tongue.

"I don't do romance," she mutters, her body instinctively curling in on itself.

She's so predictable.

"Nonsense." I flick at a strand of hair that's slipped from behind her ear and is tickling my chin. "Everybody craves romance. You've just never met anyone who knew exactly the kind you needed."

She lifts her head, her face so close that the sweetness of her breath is like a ghost of a touch hovering over my lips. My gaze trips to her mouth, and for a second, I imagine what it'd be like to kiss her again. Soft and slow this time. Tasting her with care and dedication, until the motion becomes muscle memory.

"You're a natural at this," she whispers as her eyes follow the same downward path as mine.

"At what?" I whisper back.

"Making it look like you want me."

I frown. "It's not—"

My thoughts are cut short when a familiar silhouette appears behind Zoey, a daisy backpack on her shoulders.

"What—"

I scramble up, putting distance between Zoey and me. When she stomps close enough that I can make out her red-rimmed eyes, I rush to Daphne. In three strides, I'm next to her. "What are you doing here? Are you okay?"

Lola runs up behind her and comes to a sharp stop when she reaches us, heaving breaths. "Sorry, give me a second."

I look frantically between the two of them. "Daph, what's going on?"

"I wanted you," she sniffles, her voice cracking. "I wanted to see you, but Lola said it wasn't a good idea because of the noise. But I didn't want to stay home. *I wanted to see you.*"

Fuck.

I bring her into my chest and hold her tightly, brushing her hair back. "You're okay. I'm here."

She buries her face deeper, looping her arms around my waist.

"Didn't you get my texts?" Lola pants.

"What? No." I fish out my phone with one hand, the other still cradling Daph snug against me. Already, her overstimulated body softens in my arms.

Sure enough, my screen is filled with close to a dozen messages from Lola.

Lola

> Daphne wants to see you. Is the movie almost over?

> I don't know if it's a good idea, but she's being really insistent.

> I think she's about to have a meltdown. Can you pick up?

> We're on our way. Hope you see these before we arrive.

> Just parked. Can you let me know where you guys are?

I scrub a hand over my face, panic settling deep into my bones. "Lols, I'm so sorry. My phone must have been on silent."

She peers over my shoulder. "It's okay. We're fine. It's not the first time, and it won't be the last." She nods to Daph, who's still clinging to me. "She's okay."

I release a breath that shatters into the air. Yeah, she's okay.

But.

She needed me and I wasn't there.

That's what happens when I get sucked in.

One night. That's all it took for my focus to slip.

Fuck.

Daphne is my priority. She always will be. What if she'd been hurt and I had no idea because I was too busy pretending to be infatuated with someone I barely know?

I won't make the same mistake twice. I have to show up when my sister needs me. I'll just have to make time for Zoey when—

Shit. Zoey.

Hands braced on my sister's arms, I crouch down and meet her eyes. "Wait for me at the car with Lola. I'll be there in two minutes."

"Sorry," Lola whispers, glancing nervously behind me.

"It's okay, Lols. You did good bringing her here."

I wait until Lola and Daphne are several yards away before I jog over to Zoey. "I'm sorry. I have to go. Something came up."

Her brows shoot up so high they nearly disappear into her hairline. "What do you mean you have to go? What about the movie?"

I drop my head and sigh. "I have to take care of something. I'm sorry to leave you like this, but I don't have a choice."

She peers around the park. "You're... not driving me home?"

A few people nearby turn in our direction at the sound of her voice.

Stomach twisting, I dig my keys out of my pocket and hold them out. "I promise you, I'd never do this to you if it weren't important."

After what she shared with me tonight... shit, I'm such a jerk.

We may have broken a rule, delving into details of her life, but I can't let her into mine. Not when it comes to Daphne. My priority is taking care of her, and tonight, I utterly failed in that department.

Zoey yanks the keys from my grasp, making sure her fingers don't touch mine. She looks away, her face unreadable.

"I'll call you tomorrow, okay?" I rub my beard. "I'll swing by and pick up my truck."

She doesn't answer, keeping her focus locked on the movie instead.

My lungs deflate. Time to go, then. "I'm really sorry. Enjoy the rest of the movie," I say as I back away.

No answer.

"You guys have a deal. She won't back down," Lola says when we step into my house. "She needs you way more than you need her."

"Thanks for taking care of Daphne tonight," I say, ignoring the Band-Aid she's trying to slap on my guilt. "I'm gonna finish the movie with her if you want to stay."

Lola shakes her head. "I have to go home. Freddy's waiting for me."

I shudder. I can't believe she's looking after that satanic monstrosity while my parents are away.

I give her a quick hug. "Thank you again."

She pats my sides. "Don't sweat it."

Once she's gone, Daphne and I settle on the couch with our popcorn and hit play.

"Better?" I ask

Snuggled in with her favorite heavy blanket, she pops a piece of popcorn into her mouth. "Yes."

I sink deeper into the cushions. "Good."

The pressure in my chest eases a notch, but there's a hitch there, a kernel of discomfort that won't go away. It only flares more painfully when thoughts of Zoey all alone in the park plague me.

I dig my phone from my pocket and send her a text.

Matt

Are you still at the park?

My nerves wear thin as the minutes crawl by, and when my phone finally vibrates, I startle, and the device clatters to the floor.

"Are you okay?" Daphne asks, peering at me out of the corner of her eye.

"All good," I say as I retrieve it. "Watch the movie."

Zoey

Just got home.

A knot loosens in my chest. She's home safe. She's replying to me. There might be hope.

Matt

I didn't mean to leave like I did. I'm sorry again. I had to take care of something.

Three dots in a bubble dance on the screen before her message appears.

Zoey

> You don't owe me anything. We
> have a business deal and that's all.
> Though I would have appreciated
> a little help putting all the stuff
> back in your truck.

"Fuck." I didn't even think about the piles of blankets and the basket I prepared.

Daph gives me a side-eye.

"Sorry."

"Five dollars in the swear jar. And you're distracting me. Are you watching the movie or not?"

"Yes, yes, sorry," I say. "Give me a minute to wrap up something on my phone and then I'll put it away."

Matt

> Tell me how I can make it up to you. I
> feel awful. You said nobody had
> ever made a romantic gesture, and
> now I made things ten times worse.

This time, she responds instantly.

Zoey

> Don't waste my time like
> that again.

Yeah, she's furious. And honestly? If I were in her shoes, I'd be livid too. I scrub my beard, thinking.

I owe her an explanation, but without dragging Daphne into it, that'll be tricky.

My fingers hover above the keyboard. I type out a sentence. Delete. Start again. Delete.

With a sharp exhale, I drag a hand down my face and stare up at the ceiling. Everything I've been juggling seems like it's about to fall to the ground. I'm out of my depth—with my sister, with Zoey.

With all of it.

Finally, I type. And hit send.

Matt

> I can't guarantee that. My parents are out of town this month, and I'm taking care of my sister while they're away. She wasn't supposed to come tonight, but she did.

> Can I stop by tomorrow morning and bring you breakfast? I want a chance to apologize in person.

> Please?

My pulse climbs, thick and tight in my throat, as I wait for her reply. I typed the word *autistic* next to *sister* half a dozen times but deleted every one of them.

I glance at Daphne, half expecting her to hit me with another snarky comment, but she's too into the movie to bother with me, absorbed in a way only she can achieve.

The tightness in my chest loosens at the sight. Never again will I expose her to someone who doesn't accept her for who she is. Zoey's only passing through our lives. Daphne doesn't need to know her.

But now you're hiding her.

I close my eyes, rubbing my temples.

I'm not *hiding* her. I'm shielding her until I'm sure she won't be made to feel less than she is.

I'll never be ashamed of Daphne. She's perfect the way she is. And I'm proud of her and how far she's come, even if the world doesn't always make it easy for her.

The issue is me. My own trauma. Selfishly, I don't want to find myself in a place where someone I'm close to makes snarky or disgusting comments about people on the spectrum. I get enough of that with our mother as it is.

And what if Zoey uses my sister for her own gains? What if she thinks she can buy herself some sort of sympathy with the rest of the town if she's seen with her?

No. That's a clear line I'm drawing. In any other situation, with strangers, *anyone else*, I wouldn't care one bit. I would proudly declare that Daph is autistic only so I can revel in the discomfort they feel when faced with their stupidity.

But I don't know if I can trust Zoey yet, and there's no way I'll put myself or Daph through that. For now, ignorance is my best friend, especially if I want to see this deal to the end. Because if Zoey knew that Daphne is autistic and she said *anything* that would even remotely piss me off, I'd be out before she finished the thought.

I'm still trying to figure out how to make the next few weeks go smoothly. I've got enough to worry about without allowing someone else to meddle and screw it all up.

I stare at my phone. Nothing.

Come on, Zoey. Please don't leave me hanging here.

When the screen lights up, a relieved sigh escapes me.

Zoey

> You're a good brother. I hope she's okay. Forget about breakfast. I'm sure your plate is full enough without having to worry about me.

The last of the lump in my throat dissolves.

Matt

> Good night, Zoey. I'll see you at Cooper's tomorrow. Wear casual clothes for setup, but bring something to change into for the evening.

> For once, nobody will tease you for wearing something nice.

When she reacts to the text with a heart, I toss my phone onto the cushion.

"Got room for one more?" I scoot toward Daphne, who only has her head peeking out from beneath the blanket.

"No. I don't want your beard scratching my face."

Chuckling, I fold my arms behind my head and stretch my legs out on the sectional. "Fine. I'll make myself comfortable here, then."

"Shh."

I snort, and when she shushes me again, I fall silent. Rather than paying attention to the movie, I watch the way the light from the TV dances on her face as she laughs along with the characters and frowns when dramatic music comes on.

Eventually, my gaze shifts to the screen, my thoughts drifting to Zoey.

I will make it up to her. I don't know how or when, but I will. And hopefully, it'll be enough to make her forget what a supreme asshole I was tonight.

Chapter Fifteen

Zoey

Outside Mia's bakery, I pull my phone from my pocket and check the time. 7:27. Three more minutes until the place opens.

I'm freezing. Tired. In a crappy mood.

Why, oh why, did I feel the selfless need to drag myself out of bed at the crack of dawn to pick up breakfast for Matt and his sister?

I could have done a million other things. Like sleep. Go for a run. Get a jump on today's to-do list. Sleep. Sort out my emails. *Sleep*.

I tug my coat tighter and bounce on my toes, but it does little to combat the cold that's already burrowing deep into my bones. I glance up at the bakery's windows, still dark and uninviting. The silver lining this morning? I can chat with Mia again and check in after our talk last night. See how she feels about me now.

Though when I walked past Rosie's café on my way here, a heavy weight settled in my chest. I'm such a coward. I've been avoiding her since the disaster of the town meeting, too petrified that if I walk in, she'll downright refuse to serve me. I don't think I could handle it if the first person in town to show me kindness now hated my guts.

Inside the bakery, the lights flicker on and a silhouette appears at the door, flipping around the sign that now reads *We're open!*

The knob rattles as Mia turns the lock, then the door swings open. When her eyes land on me, they widen comically.

"Zoey! What are you doing here this early?"

"I'm asking myself the same question," I mumble, burrowing deeper in my coat. "Can I..." I motion behind her, toward the cozy interior, desperate for more of the warmth seeping out through the doorway.

"Yes, of course." She shuffles out of the way. "Come in, come in. It's toasty inside."

"Thank you."

It's not just the inviting temperature that welcomes me when I step in; it's also the buttery smell of freshly baked croissants, bread still warm from the oven, and the spice of cinnamon sprinkled on apple muffins.

Okay, now I regret my decision a little less.

"How do you get through your days here without eating everything?" I ask, salivating over the stack of croissants like Pavlov's dog over a treat.

"Lots of discipline." She ties an apron behind her back. "Keeping my business afloat for one, along with the promise of high cholesterol."

A chuckle bubbles past my lips. "That'll do it."

She smiles politely. "What can I get you this morning?"

"Hum…" I survey the display. "Do you know what Matt and his sister like? I want to drop off a little treat before they start their day."

For the second time in five minutes, Mia's eyes widen in surprise. "You're bringing Matt breakfast?"

"Attempting."

With the tongs, she snags two croissants and an apple turnover and slips them into the bag.

Holding the goods out, she beams. "The croissants for Matt, the turnover for Daphne."

"I didn't know Matt had a go-to order," I say, retrieving the bag.

"Oh, everyone in Pine Falls does. That's just how it is in a small town. We all know each other's routines and quirks. That's why it's nice when someone new shows up. Fresh faces keep things interesting. And don't worry," she adds with a wink, "Everybody is welcome here, hiking skills or not."

I grimace. "Not *everybody*."

She presses her lips into a thin line. "There may be a few exceptions, but they're typically reserved for those whose motives we're concerned about."

"My only motive is to help visitors enjoy nature and everything Pine Falls has to offer." I scan the mouthwatering array of pastries. "You know, the lodge could use a supplier who'd curate thoughtful breakfast baskets for the guests."

She quirks a brow. "You'd work with businesses around here?"

"My father really did a number on you guys, didn't he?" I sigh. "I'm sorry. I know how difficult he can be. But I'm not my father, Mia. The way he does business is not the way *I* do business. Plus, the lodge—I prefer that term to hotel—isn't part of the offshoot of the company he was pitching for a few years ago. We're a big corporation, but that doesn't mean we can't work with locals and build accommodation that makes sense for the community."

"I see." Mia stares off in space, as if processing my words. Eventually, she focuses on me again, a glint in her eyes. "It's been a rough year for the bakery. Peak season is always busy, but when the foot traffic slows, I often struggle. It's a shame, because the nature here has so much to offer all year round." She bites her lip. "Next time you stop in, bring your proposal with you. I'd like to take a quick look."

Yes.

Though I want to jump up and down, I stick with smiling warmly as I sidestep to the register and slip my credit card out. "I can absolutely do that."

"So, you and Matt, huh?" Mia asks as she inputs my purchases.

"Me and Matt? Oh n—"

Mia narrows her eyes, her expression going wary.

Fuck, fuck, fuck. *Yes*, me and Matt. *You dufus.*

"—othing too serious so far." I swallow. "It's very new."

The lines on her face smooth out. "I'm glad to see him back to his happy self. He hasn't been the same since Andie left."

Andie. Am I supposed to know who that is? Would Matt tell a new girlfriend who Andie is?

I tap my card on top of the reader, and as I put it back in my pocket, I decide to reply with the truth. Isn't that how the best lies begin? Stay as close to reality as possible? "He's been a nice change for me too. Unexpected."

"Unexpected always makes for the strongest relationships." She nods like she uttered a well-known tidbit of wisdom that has been passed down from generation to generation.

I put the receipt in my jacket, the word sticking with me. Last night felt just like that. Unexpected. Everything about him was. The gentleness in his voice, his soothing touches, the solid weight of his body against mine. I could have stayed like that for another three or four movies, not bothered—for probably the first time in my life—about the clock or keeping myself together. I *cried*, for god's sake. That, too, was unexpected.

I flash a half smile at Mia, who's still watching me intently.

"Thank you for breakfast," I tell her as I step away from the counter. "I'll stop by tomorrow with the proposal."

Back at my car, I slump behind the wheel, dropping the bag on the passenger seat, and stare through the windshield.

He hasn't been the same since Andie left.

Mia's statement pokes at me, prodding questions that are practically burning a hole in my tongue.

Who is Andie? Is she the ex with whom things ended badly? What did she do to you? What happened? Are you okay now?

Would he answer if I asked? Probably not. He's been insistent when it comes to that absurd rule.

I can't help but want to know more, and though I try to shake it, the strange feeling stays with me all the way to Matt's place.

When I get there, the porch lights are off. I lean against the wheel, peering up at the closed curtains.

Are they still sleeping? Did I wake up early for *nothing*?

Ugh.

I'm here now, so I have to at least knock. I kill the engine, climb out, and stride to the front door, burying myself in my coat again.

I rap my knuckles on the solid wood and wait. If nobody answers after two minutes, I'll drop the bag and leave.

Twenty seconds later, there's a click, and the door opens.

On the other side, Matt's eyes widen. "Zoey?" he scrubs at his face, his hair a wild mess. "W-what are you doing here?" He peers over his shoulder, then takes a step forward—*barefoot*—and pulls the door mostly shut behind him.

Okay, so he just woke up. No big deal. Nothing to get all worked up about, even though it feels like I've intruded on a very private moment of his life. Sleep still clings to his lashes, softening his face despite the marks left by his sheets. A well-worn white shirt hangs loosely on his chest and falls over a pair of gray sweatpants that do *nothing*—or the lord's work, depending on the point of view—to hide that he's not wearing anything underneath.

I swallow, forcing my eyes up, and with my best smile plastered to my face, I jiggle the bag in my hand. "Breakfast is served?"

"You brought b—"

The sound of footsteps rushing down the stairs stops him. He mutters under his breath, turning toward the inside of the house. As the door flies open, his body goes rigid.

A girl wearing rose-print pajamas with hair as bright as the sun appears at Matt's side. She looks to be about twelve, maybe thirteen. His sister, then.

Matt is rooted to the spot, a shadow of tension falling across his face. He drapes an arm over the girl's shoulders and draws her close.

Damn. I'm only bringing breakfast, not weapons.

His sister inspects me from head to toe. "Your sweater is so pretty, but your shoes are ugly."

A huff of a laugh escapes me as Matt coughs into his fist.

"Daphne," he chides gently, "we don't say that to people we just met."

"It's fine," I cut in, still chuckling. "You're right. My shoes are ugly. I have prettier ones at home, but I can't wear them here."

I give Matt a cheeky wink, a strange thrill zipping through me as his panic morphs into confusion.

"Why not?" she asks.

"Because they're not very… practical. Right, Matt?"

"Right," he rasps, still watching me like I'm from another planet.

"What's in there?" his sister nods to the bag.

"I brought breakfast for you guys." I hold it out.

She lets out a little gasp, her hands fluttering at her sides. "Are you eating with us?"

"I have to get back to work, but it would've been lovely."

It really would have been, but I have a feeling one person in this group wouldn't be so comfortable with the idea.

"Daph, go put on socks. I'll be inside in a minute, okay?"

"Okay. Bye! Thanks for breakfast."

"You're welcome!" I wave, but she's already disappeared behind her brother.

"I'm sorry." Matt rakes his fingers through his long hair. "That's my sister. She doesn't mean to be rude. She's autistic."

"I figured," I say, a faint smile tugging at my lips. "I didn't think she was rude at all. Honestly, she was kind of funny."

Matt's frown deepens. "You figured that she was autistic?"

"Yeah. She was very blunt, and when she got excited, her hands flapped a little. Both are pretty typical signs, though I didn't want to assume."

He exhales a quiet *oh*, then goes silent, like his brain is still catching up.

"Anyway," I say as I backtrack to my car. "I'll leave you to your morning. Enjoy breakfast, and I'll see you at Cooper's this afternoon, right?"

He swallows, his eyes finally coming back into focus. "Yes. And Zoey?"

I pause with my hand on the car door. "Yes?"

"Thank you."

My heart gives a small, unexpected thud. "Of course."

There's a weight to those two words, as if the simple thanks is for more than just the breakfast.

"Have you secured it yet?"

"I'm working on it, Dad," I say, trying my best to keep my tone even. "I've hit a few bumps in the road, but nothing I can't fix."

"Ah."

The single syllable hangs heavy in the air. No rant, no questions. Just that quiet, clipped sound. My grip on the phone tightens. My father has never yelled at me in his life. He doesn't need to. His silence is so much worse.

"It won't be a problem," I try.

The effort is pointless, really. He's already made up his mind about how poorly he thinks I'm handling this problem. And there's no way I'll tell him that I'm handling said problem by fake dating the town's most eligible bachelor to earn the favor of the locals.

I swallow the nervous laughter that bubbles up in my throat.

Jesus, what would he think of me if he knew? He wouldn't recognize me, that's for sure. I don't even recognize myself. It's been a week, and so far, I've been humiliated and screamed at. I cried and discovered that life can actually have meaning outside of work if you make time for it.

What a weird concept, right?

"Though the locals seem to hold a grudge against you," I continue. "What the hell happened when the deal fell through?"

"We weren't a good fit, that's all." His tone is dismissive, condescending. "Too many unhappy voices. It wasn't good for business, so we went somewhere we were wanted. But that has nothing to do with now, princess. The board meeting is in less than two months. You have to give me something before then."

"I will," I say, throat tight.

Oscar hums on the other end of the line. "This company is my life's work and your legacy, princess. Don't force them to look for an outside hire."

Before I can respond, the three tones signaling that he's disconnected the call ring in my ear.

I sigh. He's brought this up twice before, and I'm starting to think he's not bluffing. Though this time around, my stomach didn't sink. And that dreadful pang in my chest that reminds me I'm failing my father and all he's worked so hard for doesn't come.

I spend the rest of the morning sending emails and confirming the speakers at our upcoming annual cocktail party, and at two p.m., I close my laptop.

It's strange. And exhilarating, really. Who am I, finishing work this early on a Saturday?

Getting ready to leave, I slip into my new favorite pair of leggings, high socks, leg warmers, and an oversized shirt. When I snag my purse from where it's tipped on its side, something falls out and hits the floor with a thud.

I scoop up the book Lola gave me. I'd forgotten all about it. I tuck it back in, pick up the change of clothes I set out for tonight, and head out.

When I get to Cooper's microbrewery, I park next to Matt's truck in the driveway. The facility looks a lot like a farm, with a massive wooden warehouse and a silo that probably stores grain for the beer. It's dripping with the typical rustic charm you'd expect from a small town like Pine Falls. Tourists must eat this up.

Through my windshield, I spot Matt and a clean-shaven man with a backward hat carrying a heavy-looking board.

I climb out, and as I close the car door, Matt turns, and a wide smile settles on his face. "You came!" he shouts.

I frown. Of course I came. Did he doubt that I would?

Tugging at the strap of my bag, I flash him a grin.

My pulse quickens as I cross the gravel driveway, a little flustered by the smile he so easily broke into at the sight of me. "Need a hand with that?" I ask, nodding toward the board.

Matt tsks, the grin still firmly in place. "Nah, we're good. We've already moved two others. At least we're getting our arm workout in."

My attention drifts to his biceps, taut with the effort. He's only wearing a T-shirt, a light sheen of sweat coating his skin, despite the crisp afternoon temperature.

I don't know how long I stare or if there's a puddle of drool at my feet, but when my gaze shifts back to his face, Matt's grin widens with smug satisfaction.

Busted.

At this point, I'm not even being subtle about it, so I don't bother hiding the flush creeping into my cheeks.

"Give us a second to put this down, and I'll be right over."

He and the man I assume is Cooper haul the board to the building and set it on two sawhorses with a *thud*, sending dirt flying around them.

Matt dusts off his hands on his pants, then walks to me.

"Hi," he says as he steps up close. He leans in and drops a sweaty kiss on my cheek, lingering there a bit too long. For theatrics, I'm sure. "I'm glad you came," he adds, like he's genuinely happy that I came. For him.

I don't understand why he's surprised enough to mention it twice when the whole point of this charade is to get in the town's good graces.

Behind him, his friend clears his throat.

"Right." Matt laughs, moving out of the way. "Coop, this is Zoey Delacroix. Zoey, this is Cooper Darfield."

Cooper holds out his hand and smiles, his eyes creasing at the corners. "Hey, Zoey. I heard you made quite the first impression."

"Unfortunately." Cringing, I shake his hand. "You weren't there?"

"Oh no, those kinds of meetings are not for me. I like the folks here, but not all at once." He shudders, as if the mere thought is terrifying.

Matt leans in so close that the heat rolling off him warms my skin. "He's a bit of a hermit."

"I heard that." Cooper gathers two chairs in each arm and carries them inside.

I shoot Matt a glare. "I thought we were supposed to convince people with *influence*."

"Who do you think people turn to when they want a drink? Who do you think listens to them talk about their problems and can easily offer his opinion in return?" He nods in Cooper's direction, who is bent over, picking up a drill off the floor.

"Plus..." Matt adds, his lips grazing the lobe of my ear.

A treacherous shiver shoots straight to my core, and I curse myself for being so weak. Then, his voice drops, rough and smoky, and the sound rolls down my spine like the drag of his finger. "He's a good friend."

My breath quickens, but I shake off the haze of lust that's fallen over me and step away. I need distance. Space. Or I'll spend the whole afternoon looking like a horny idiot.

"You didn't miss much," I say to Cooper when he returns, forcing my focus on him. "Except a lot of name-calling and finger-pointing."

"And yet you've managed to bag this one," he says, hiking his thumb toward Matt, who swats him lightly. "He's been talking my ear off about you all morning."

"Has he, now?" My heart flips, but I keep my expression steady and smirk.

"Okay, okay, we've got work to do," Matt cuts in, looping an arm around my shoulders and bringing me to his side.

My body relaxes, like a marshmallow melting over a campfire.

Being pressed up against a sweaty dude like this should make me want to run to the nearest shower, and yet... I don't want to move. Worse. *I like it*. Discreetly, I lay my palm to my forehead. No, no fever. I'm not delirious.

"I'm not very good with manual labor." I study the faded wood of the barn, the boards and chairs. This is a recipe for splinters, bloodied fingers, and chipped nails. "Do you *really* need my help? I can confidently say I'll be more of a nuisance than anything."

Matt chuckles, the sound vibrating through me. "I'll make sure you don't hurt yourself."

I pout.

Yes, I'm fully aware that I'm acting like a brat, but I couldn't care less. Some people love to get their hands dirty. I am not one of those people. I am the complete opposite of those people.

"What happens if I don't do it?"

He tsks. "Then you miss out on the reward. We're testing a few new beers before we serve them tonight, and Cooper's got a special batch brewing for us as a thank-you for helping. But we can't try it out until we're done setting up."

He nods to the chairs spread throughout the space and the sawhorses waiting for their boards.

"Okay, now you've got me interested," I say, following him inside. "But I'm gonna need a pair of gloves."

The space is huge—open and airy, with a long wooden counter lined with bottles and barrels on the far end. The air is thick with the smell of hops and malt, making me want to sit at the bar and crack open an IPA instead of carrying chairs and tables all afternoon.

"Here." Cooper holds out a pair of bright yellow gloves.

I stare at them, keeping my arms crossed over my chest. They look like they've gone through the shredder and haven't been washed in years.

"I'd do a better job at cheering you guys on, I swear."

I glance at Matt, who watches me with gleeful amusement and nods to the gloves. "Put them on."

Reluctantly, I take them from Cooper and slide them on. I don't know how much protection they'll offer, but I guess it's better than nothing. Unless I contract an infectious disease from them and die.

"All right." Cooper gestures to the chairs he hauled in, which are now stacked next to the bar. "Zoey, maybe you can arrange the chairs in rows to face here." He points at the wall behind us. "Matt and I will continue setting up tables for food. Leave some space in the front," he adds. "We're gonna build a stage there."

I give him a single nod. "Got it."

For the next two hours, I move back and forth, placing the chairs in neat rows while Matt and Cooper haul the wooden planks onto the sawhorses set up against the wall. I don't know how many chairs I carry, but the number is far more than my arms were built for. The temperature in here is still brisk, but I'm sweating, and flakes of dirt stick to my skin. I've never been this gross in my life. God, I'm sure I smell.

"Bend your knees," Matt calls as I lean over, legs straight, to pick up two chairs stacked on top of each other. "You'll hurt your back if you don't."

"I know how to lift things," I shout back.

I don't. My lower back is already screaming at me.

Once the guys are done, Cooper heads outside, and Matt waves me over.

"Where is Cooper going?"

"I brought flowers to add a bit more warmth to the place for tonight. He's getting them from my truck," Matt says. "Here, come help me with this."

He positions two pieces of wood to make a forty-five-degree angle. Then nods to the hammer sitting on the table near us.

Wincing, I pick it up. "*Uhhh*, what do you want me to do with this?"

He holds a nail to the top of the boards, point side down. "Hit it. We're going to build a makeshift stage for the fundraiser."

I adjust my grip. "I want to preface by saying I've never held a hammer in my life."

"It's not rocket science, Zoey. Come on, drop it on the nail."

I stare at the nail, then his fingers.

"What is this fundraiser anyway?" I ask.

"Remember Carl and his once-a-month trips to the forest with the kids?" He nods at the pieces of wood. "Go ahead."

Giving in, I lower the hammer and hit the wood right next to the nail, only millimeters from Matt's fingers.

"Okay." He exhales sharply. "Careful, all right? I'd like to keep all my fingers if I can."

"I'm so sorry." Panic washes over me, and I drop the tool onto the table, hands shaking. "I told you I've never done that. Are you okay?"

His expression softens and his lips stretch into a reassuring smile. "It's fine, Zoey, breathe." He puts the nail down and takes my gloved hands in his, bending to meet my gaze. "I'm fine, see?"

I nod. "Okay, yeah."

With a quick squeeze of my fingers, he releases me. "Lower the hammer slowly onto the nail first, to make sure you're lined up with it. Then give it a sharp blow. Like this."

He picks it up and shows me. When the nail is halfway in, he moves his fingers away and hits it again.

Smiling easily, he hands it over. "You're good?"

"Yeah, I think so," I say, tensing up as I take the tool and follow his instructions. This time, I drive the nail straight in.

"You were mentioning that Carl is involved with the fundraiser?" I ask as he sets up another one.

Matt dips his chin. "He's planning a week-long expedition this year, with the help of Oliver and his girlfriend, Charlee. They're taking the ninth graders from Pine Falls' school on a scientific research trip to investigate soil quality in the Great Bear Rainforest. They'll study how climate change is impacting the habitat of many species there. Coop offered to host the fundraiser for the trip here."

"It's gonna be a great night," Cooper chimes in from where he's setting a floral arrangement on a table. "We're gonna raise a ton of money. You know," he says, waggling his brows at Matt, "Patty is excited about it."

Matt responds with a groan.

Frowning, I hammer the next nail. "Patty?"

"The lady who owns the hair salon."

"Oh." I straighten, still confused. "Why would she be excited?"

Matt pinches the bridge of his nose and huffs. "No reason."

"You're gonna have some competition tonight, Zoey," Cooper says. "Hope you don't mind a little fight."

I whirl on him. "What? Why?"

"I'll fill you in later," Matt grumbles.

I drop the subject at the sound of his annoyed voice, and we continue to work on the stage.

"Thanks again for breakfast this morning," he says, glancing at me as Cooper disappears toward the truck to retrieve another arrangement.

And once more, it feels like he's saying thank you for more than just the pastries.

"Don't worry about it." I focus my attention on the next nail, ignoring the warmth that spreads through me. "I had to talk to Mia anyway. Figured I'd drop off a little treat for you guys on my way back."

It's not a complete lie. I did need to see Mia. But yeah, part of me wanted to do something nice for him, but showing him I care makes me want to barf.

He hums. "It was still a sweet gesture. Thank you."

"It's nothing." I look back down at the nail and hit it with the hammer.

Once we finish the stage, the venue is finally ready. Cooper gets the beers out, and for a moment, we're quiet, each of us taking a well-deserved swig.

"Oh, this is good." Matt tilts the bottle to his mouth again.

Cooper chuckles and follows his lead. "Figured a blonde would be the perfect choice after all that sweating. But hey, seems like brunettes might be more your style."

I flush and quickly change the subject. "I can't believe we did all this." I wipe my forehead with the back of my hand, taking in all our hard work.

Cooper even strung lights along the wooden walls, adding a cozy touch to the atmosphere.

"You did great." Matt surveys me, a flicker of pride shining in his eyes. His gaze drifts up to my forehead and the corner of his mouth lifts. "You and I need a good shower if we're going to look presentable tonight."

"I brought a change of clothes, but I didn't think I'd need a shower." I scrunch up my nose. "Do we have time to go back to the cabin?"

Matt pulls out his phone and checks the time. "Shit. Doesn't seem like it. The event starts in an hour."

My shoulders slump a little. Oh well. Surely there's a sink around here somewhere. I can at least wash my face and rinse my armpits. Though seeing how catastrophic my first impression on the town was, it would've been nice to freshen up properly so I could redeem myself.

"You guys can use my bathroom," Cooper says. "There's only one, but it shouldn't be an issue, right?"

Matt and I exchange a silent look. We have no good excuse to say no.

But the mere idea of being locked in a small room with this man while he showers on the other side of a flimsy curtain is doing things to long-dormant corners of my body. Corners I'd rather not wake up, *thankyouverymuch*.

I don't want to think about him naked, lathering up— while the shower stream drenches his long hair and rinses the dirt off his body—but I also can't *not* think about it. And by the way Matt's pupils have dilated, I'd say his mind has wandered in a similar direction.

Well, one of us needs to respond to Cooper, and my gut is telling me Matt isn't keen on making the decision for me. That thought triggers entirely different emotions that bubble up inside me, but I push them aside for now.

Clearing my throat, I paste on a smile. "Thanks, Cooper. That would be amazing."

Matt's swallow is audible, but he nods and holds out his hand to me. "Come on, we don't want to be late."

Chapter Sixteen

Matt

I'm walking straight into my own personal hell.

We drift through the microbrewery, weaving between the fermentation and brewing tanks, Zoey's hand firmly tucked in mine.

Touching her is ridiculously easy. Soothing and invigorating at the same time. Her skin is soft against my callused fingers, her body delicate when I bring her to my side.

Which is why being alone in confined spaces with her is such a bad idea. I remember all too well what happened the last time I saw her in nothing but a towel.

But we're "dating," so how could we have said no?

"Crossing through the microbrewery is faster than going around," Cooper tells Zoey.

Her fingers flex against mine. I brush my thumb along her skin in small circles, trying with each stroke to sweep her nervousness away.

"Have you ever thought of offering tours?" she asks as she surveys the tanks on either side of us.

"I have," Cooper says. "But I haven't had time to look into it too deeply. I'm not sure I have the capacity to operate a microbrewery while also spending several hours a day doing tours and handling all the logistics."

"I could help with that," she says. "If we build the hotel, I mean. Our staff could organize them and keep a schedule that'd work for you. It'd be a nice additional stream of revenue."

I peer down at Zoey, impressed.

It's becoming a trend. It's only been a couple of days, but at every turn, she surprises me.

She thinks of everything, plans every detail. I have no doubt that she's spent hours working on this proposal.

She's so different from her father. She cares.

Even if she doesn't want me to see it. Even if she hides behind a professional façade. This morning is a perfect example. I know very well that she went out of her way to drop off breakfast for Daph and me.

And her interaction with my sister?

God, I spent hours afterward replaying that moment. How she casually brushed over my sister being autistic. Like it was just…I don't know, just a fact. Not a big deal. I'm not used to that. When Daph blurts things out like she did this morning, I always rush to apologize, explain, justify.

But not with Zoey. Zoey looked at Daph like she was nothing less and nothing more, and the anxiety that had been coiling in my chest eased and bloomed into relief when I realized that my sister could be herself around her.

Plus, she got our order exactly right.

She doesn't strike me as the type to make small gestures like that. It threw me more than it should have—the breakfast, her casual attitude with Daph—and I haven't stopped turning it over since.

What went so wrong in her life that she's putting on this rigid, closed-off mask?

Though in only a matter of days, that mask is already beginning to crumble under the influence of our little town and its people. With any luck, she'll shed it completely before she leaves.

This hotel project is becoming so much more than what it was supposed to be. And I like it more than I'm willing to admit.

"That could be an idea, yeah," Cooper says, interrupting my thoughts. "Could be nice to show visitors how we make our famous sourdough beer."

He pushes the back door open, and we walk across the field toward his house. Once inside, he retrieves two towels from a closet and sets them on his bed.

"Make yourselves at home. I'll be in the kitchen if you need me."

"Thanks, man."

The instant the door clicks shut behind him, the air in the room grows thicker.

Zoey drops my hand and lets out a nervous laugh, tucking a strand of dark hair behind her ear. "Well, this is awkward."

"Trust me, I know." I smooth my beard, glancing at the open bathroom behind her. Of *fucking* course there's no door.

"Uh… you can go first. I'll just…" I scan the space, searching for the farthest spot from the shower. "Stay in the chair over there. I promise I won't look."

She blushes a faint shade of pink. "O-okay, thanks. I'll be quick."

I sink into the armchair and swivel so I'm facing the wall, blocking the flashes of Zoey's clothes falling softly to the floor from entering my mind. I squeeze my eyes shut, inhaling as much air as my lungs will hold.

When the tap opens, I release a shaky exhale and pull out my phone. Daphne answers on the second ring.

"Hi." Her voice brings me instant peace.

"Are you having fun with Emily?"

"Yes. We spent all afternoon at the botanical garden studying the flowers, and tonight she's going to show me her favorite documentary about safaris in Africa."

"That's great, Daph. Don't go to bed too late, okay? I'm picking you up early tomorrow."

"I won't," she mumbles. "Emily's mom always says staying up after ten puts us in a bad mood."

"Emily's mom is right," I smile into the phone. She's been hosting Daphne every week since the two girls met in an autism development group. "Be good. If you need me, call me and I'll be right over, okay?"

Daphne sighs on the other end. "Yes, Matt. But I'm fine. I stay at Emily's every Saturday."

"I know, I know. But if you need me, I'm here."

"It's time for dinner. I gotta go. Bye, Matt!"

She hangs up before I can tell her I love her.

"Did you say something?" Zoey calls from the shower, and all my newfound peace evaporates.

"N—" I clear my throat. "No. Just on the phone with my sister." I grip the chair to keep myself from crossing the room and meeting her under the stream.

"I'll be done in a minute. Can you—uh, can you look away?"

"Already am."

I tune out the sounds of the bath towel rubbing along her body, the elastic of her underwear snapping against her skin, the lotion being spread on her long legs.

"All done!" she calls from the bathroom. "Your turn."

I stand and spin around. "Perf—" The word dies in my throat. Black lingerie. Why is she wearing black lacy lingerie *in front of me*? It barely covers her breasts, straining against the fabric like they're begging to be freed.

"Matt?" She tilts her head.

"What-*uh*…" The noise comes out hoarsely. I clear my throat again. "Where's your shirt?"

With a frown, she looks down. "Here?" She tugs on the very tight fabric of her *lingerie*. "It's called a bustier. You don't like it? I thought it would go well with my black pants."

"That is not a shirt," I say, shaking my head. "You can't go out like that."

Scoffing, she crosses her arms over her chest. The move makes everything so much worse. "And why's that?"

"Because…"

Because I can't think straight when you look like that. Because I'm gonna be staring at you like a creep all night and people are gonna ask what's wrong with me. Because if anybody looks at you for a second too long, they might not have anything else to look at ever again.

"Because?"

I scrub a hand over my face. "Because I'm gonna have a hard time focusing if you wear this all night."

Her lips twitch. "I didn't peg you for a lingerie type of guy."

The lump in my throat makes it tough to swallow. "Something like that, yeah."

She watches me, hunger flickering in her eyes. It's the same emotion I saw there when Cooper suggested we use his shower.

She's looking at me like I'm the starter, main, and dessert, and she doesn't know where to begin.

And the worst part is, if I thought she'd act on her urges, I'd stand still for hours, allowing her to make up her mind. I'd be her toy, hers to command and use as she pleased.

A jolt of electricity runs down my spine at the thought, and I shudder with pleasure.

She's dangerous for me. Too dangerous.

She makes me forget all the reasons I don't want to get attached. The nights I lay awake hoping Andie would come back and accept me and my family for all we are fade into a distant memory when I'm caught in her spell.

Actually, Zoey hasn't made me forget those reasons. Instead, she keeps proving at every turn, with every action, that she's different. And in some ways, that's almost scarier. Because then, how do I protect myself?

"Why do you need to focus anyway?"

"Uh?"

Zoey smirks, the expression a little wicked. "Tonight. You said you needed to focus. Why?"

Ah, yes. The fundraiser. And *how* we'll be raising the money.

I take a deep breath. "We're holding a bachelor auction. Folks will bid on…" I cringe. "Pine Falls bachelors for dates, activities, and all kinds of other stuff."

She snorts out a laugh, clapping a hand over her mouth. "Whose idea was this? Wait." She sobers up. "Are you… are you going to be on the auction block?"

"Cooper's idea, and yes." I squeeze the back of my neck. "Unfortunately. Didn't have a choice."

All because I lost a bet with Lola this summer. I wagered I'd kick her ass at the annual Pine Falls Triathlon. I didn't. She wiped the floor with me.

Zoey sits on the bed. "And what are you offering to the lucky winner?"

"Flowers and dinner. And the 'lucky winner' won't just be anybody." I give her a pointed look.

Her eyes go wide. "You want me to—"

"Yes." I nod sharply.

"Because we're—"

"Yes."

"And if I don't—"

"Our cover is blown," I finish, then force a cheerful tone. "Congrats, you're the lucky winner."

She bites her lip, her leg bouncing. "Do I need to think of a strategy? How much should I bid? Do you want me to—"

"It's not a big deal, don't worry," I cut in gently. "Just top whatever the highest amount is, and it'll be fine. You can strategize while I shower." I get up, standing in front of her. "But Zoey?"

She glances up, her eyes bright.

"If you look at me the way you were five minutes ago, we won't have too much trouble selling it."

As a flush creeps up her cheeks, I sidestep her and head for the shower.

When I emerge from the steamed-up bathroom ten minutes later, Zoey is nestled into the armchair, her back to me and a book propped up on her knees. I narrow my eyes on the shirtless man on the cover and smirk. That has Lola written all over it.

She turns the page, so absorbed by what she's reading that she hasn't noticed me.

Slowly, I close in on her, only stopping when I'm at her side. I bring my mouth to her ear.

"What are you reading?"

She startles, jumping several inches off the chair. "Nothing."

Before she can slam the book shut, I slide my finger in it, marking her place.

I pluck it from her hands and survey the cover. "*The Charmer Next Door*. Is it good?"

"Y-yeah, it's okay. I mean, I don't really know." She tucks a strand of hair behind her ear. "I've never read romance. Can I have it back, please?"

I grin, relishing her flustered state. God, I love teasing her. Now she's got me even more curious.

Moving away, I open the book to the page I marked.

> *He twisted a loose strand of her hair around his index finger, and Delia gasped. If that touch alone made her lose her mind, what would it be like once he had his hand between her legs?*
>
> *"Jason, please," she begged.*
>
> *His lips grazed the thin skin below her ear, his warm breath causing ripples of need through her, heading straight for her already throbbing core. Softly, too softly, he brushed his mouth there.*
>
> *Delia's eyes rolled back in her head. She couldn't help herself. She turned her face toward him, giving him no time to toy with her further. Her lips found his, eager and hot, her tongue sliding against his in flawless rhythm. She clutched at his shirt as he ran his fingers possessively down her chest, her hips, until he reached her ass and pressed her against his hard—*

Zoey snatches the book out of my grasp. "Give me that."

"Interesting read," I say, my grin widening. "Very informative. Don't you want to know what happens next? We can stay a bit if you want to finish." I press my lips together, trying in vain to school my features. "The *scene*, of course."

She rolls her eyes and plants her hand on her hip, popping it for good measure. "And where will you be while I do that?"

"I-I… not… Obviously, I wouldn't…"

She throws the book onto the bed with a satisfied smirk and drapes a jacket over her shoulders. "Let's go. I don't want to be late."

As we step into the venue, the mood has completely shifted from this afternoon. The microbrewery hums with soft chatter, and even though the whole town is crammed into five hundred square feet, the dimmed tinsel lights lend the space a kind of atmospheric intimacy.

"Mission accomplished." Zoey surveys the room for a long moment before fixing her attention on me. "You look very handsome."

She settles a hand on one suspender, sliding a finger between it and the white shirt beneath it. Though she's not touching my skin, my body sizzles in response. "I've never seen you in anything but jeans, boots, and plaid shirts. It's a nice change."

She's right. I don't often trade in my lumberjack clothes, as Oliver calls them, for clean pants and a white shirt. But I wanted to make an effort tonight. For her. Because I knew she'd bring her A game too.

I brush the hair off her shoulder, exposing her collarbone, and cup my hand around the back of her neck, my thumb stroking her skin there. "I appreciate the compliment, beautiful." I lean in, my lips grazing her ear. "But you're the one who's stealing the show tonight." When I pull away, I nod subtly at the crowd, noting how many people glance her way.

If there's one thing we are not in this town, it's discreet. And right now, all eyes are on her.

"They're probably wondering what you're doing with me."

I splay my other hand over the curve of her hip and turn her to me. "They're staring because you're a goddamn vision. And I'm the luckiest bastard in the whole town." I offer her my elbow. "Let's get a drink, shall we?"

A few folks stop us to say hello on our way to the bar. Rob compliments Zoey on her project, explaining that he finally got a chance to read it, his voice loud enough for a few eavesdroppers to hear. Mia welcomes us with a warm smile. Zoey listens attentively while Carl and his wife, Laura, talk about the bear encounter they had today, and the money they're hoping we'll raise tonight.

By the time we reach the bar, I'm having a hard time differentiating between what's real and what's not.

For a moment, I honestly believed I was here with my girl, chatting away with our neighbors and friends. She fits into this life so well, and I don't think even she realizes it.

"What can I get for you two lovebirds?" Coop asks from behind the bar.

Zoey rests her elbow on the counter. "I'll take a lager if you have one." She glances at me. "What do you want?"

I wrap my arm around her waist. "I'll have the blonde we tried this afternoon. Thanks, man."

Beer in hand, she turns and taps it against mine. "Cheers."

She twists around and leans against the bar, tilting the bottle to her lips while she watches the crowd. "Even with all the research I did, I could never have gotten it right."

I follow her line of sight, cocking a brow. "Why?"

"You have something rare in this town. I can't even begin to explain it, but I've never experienced it before."

I bump her shoulder softly. "Community?"

"Maybe," she murmurs a little absently.

"I'm surprised your dad didn't brief you on that ahead of your trip," I say with a chuckle. "It's the folks here who brought his ridiculous luxury hotel down. Group effort."

"My dad and I have very different ways of doing business. It's hard to make him see reason sometimes. That's why I usually prefer to mind my portfolio and leave him to handle shareholders and investors. He's not a bad guy," she says with a sigh. "Just very stubborn."

"Oh, so *that's* where it comes from."

She rolls her eyes, fighting a smile. "I'm the *very* diluted version."

I hum. She's not that bad.

From the corner of my eye, I spot Carl's kids running in our direction, playing tag. I press myself up against Zoey to keep her from being trampled.

"If it's so difficult to work with him, and if you don't like the way he handles things," I say, "then why are you staying in the business?"

She flinches, averting her attention to the crowd. I swear her body curves in on itself a fraction.

"Because it's all I've ever known. I went to college fully aware my dad disapproved of my path. He was already showing me the ropes then. I'm his only kid, and he had big dreams for me. Dreams that didn't align with the ones I had for myself."

"So you got roped into the business," I say.

Zoey nods, her face blank. "At sixteen. He didn't force it on me. It just… happened. I didn't officially work for him till after college, but being the boss's daughter, I was always at his office. I followed him everywhere. To meetings, to visit sites. He liked having me around."

I cock an eyebrow. "Don't you think he was grooming you to work for him later on?"

"Oh, he definitely was," she says matter-of-factly.

The lack of anger in her voice triples mine. Who uses their kids like that, to serve their own agenda, feed their own ego?

"After I finished my undergrad," Zoey continues, "my dad decided enough was enough and refused to invest more in my pediatric nursing program. I got more involved, and eventually, he insisted I take over the business development department. I couldn't say no. Like, Matt, I *physically* couldn't say no." Her voice wavers, her words imprinted with the kind of pain that leaves indelible scars. "I wanted to make him proud so badly, and I knew that's what he wanted. And…" She shrugs. "I figured that my dad would always do what's best for me."

She takes a sip of her beer, her expression turning pensive, like something's brewing in her brain. Does she question her dad's intentions now?

"Sometimes," she continues, her voice quieter, a little more guarded, "you don't walk away from a career you've spent years building, no matter how much you disagree with the people involved. Sometimes, you stay because you hope you can do something different and change things from the inside. You just... keep going. Even if you're not sure this is what you want anymore."

"Zoey..." I clench my fists, my chest tightening just as hard.

Completely wrong. My assumptions about her were *completely* wrong.

Her father is a very lucky man not to be standing in front of me right now.

I turn to her and hook a finger under her chin, tilting her head up so she's forced to look at me.

"I know what you're doing, okay? I *know*. You're trying to show your dad that you can take over when he retires, and I have to be real fucking honest—I don't know *why* you do that. Based on what I'm hearing, you've spent years grinding at work, growing the business, doing really groundbreaking shit, if my research is correct. Yet he still can't see how capable you are. Maybe he just doesn't want to. And that makes it worse. But either way, the result is the same. You feel like you're not enough, like you should be doing more to prove yourself to him, like you are not worthy. That drives me absolutely out of my fucking mind."

"You know?" she exhales, stuck on the first part of my rant, her breath shallow as her face drains of color.

"I do," I say softly. "Since before we started to pretend to date. I had an inkling. I read a few articles about your dad. Figured it wasn't a coincidence that while he's talking about retirement, you're here, working on a project he couldn't nail down himself. I was giving you the time to tell me yourself, but after all you've just shared, after what you had to put up with all these years..." I inhale deeply. "I couldn't keep it in any longer."

"Are you mad?"

I brush my thumb over her cheek. "Yes, I am. At how your dad's been treating you. The rest doesn't matter."

"I'm sorry I didn't tell you sooner," she says, meeting my gaze without flinching. "I don't know why I so badly want to please him. It's like a vicious cycle that I can't get out of. That I didn't want to get out of until I—"

She shakes her head, swallowing back the rest of her words.

Until she what? Until she came here? Until she met me? Until what?

"No one has the right to tell you who you should be or what you should do with your life. Not even your father. You're allowed to leave. If that's what you want, go ahead. Slam the door if it means you can finally find out who you are." I press my hand to her chest, right above her heart. "Who you really are in here."

Carl's kids race past us again, laughing and shouting.

Zoey watches them with a half smile that doesn't quite reach her eyes. Eventually, she dips her chin, picking around her nails.

I slide my hand in hers, stopping the nervous habit, and stroke her skin. She needs to know she's not alone.

"For so long, this company has been my whole life," she says. "I don't know who I am without it. That's all I've done, day and night. For over a decade. Work, work, work." She shakes her head, a bitter laugh escaping her. "I'm not even close to forty yet, and I'm having a full-blown existential crisis in the middle of a fundraiser."

Cupping her jaw, I meet her eyes again. "It's okay. You don't have to put on a happy face all the time." I don't tell her she's pretty terrible at faking it anyway. "It's a fucking lot to put on your shoulders. Have all the crises you want, anywhere you want. I'll be right here next to you, holding you up so you can break down."

Her eyes glint in the soft lights, and for a second, I worry she's about to cry. "What's it like?" she whispers. "Knowing you have people who will always be there for you?"

A heavy ache settles in my chest. Nobody deserves to be this alone.

"It's like constantly having a safety net beneath you. It's being able to fuck up and knowing your people won't define you based on your mistakes. It's being accepted for who you are. And you, Zoey, are so much more than your dad's version of you."

How is it that some parents can't accept their kids as they are? Why do so many of us feel pressured into being a version that fits their expectations? The parallels between Zoey and her dad and Daph and Mom make me want to share everything with her. Show her that I understand what she's going through.

But this is not the place or time.

Later.

When we're alone and I have a moment to breathe, I'll crack open the door to my personal life and talk to Zoey about Daphne, tell her how the world has treated my sister.

She trusted me with this part of her tonight, and I want to give her a piece of me too. Even if I'm terrified to bare myself to a woman again.

I stroke her cheek, and her eyes flutter shut. My gaze drifts to her lips, and for a second, I have this wild urge to kiss her. For real.

Gently, I trace her cheek again, my thumb trailing the flush down to her bottom lip. Her soft inhale brushes the tip of my finger, sending an electric current through me.

I press deeper, only stopping when her lips part.

The world narrows to her.

"I don't know what I'm doing," I whisper. The words shouldn't be loud enough for her to hear, and yet she does.

"Don't think. Do it."

I lean in, so close her breath blends with mine. I can almost taste the pillowy softness of her lips on mine, but just before they meet mine, I'm yanked back.

A loud squeal in my ear makes me wince. "Matt! Finally. I've been trying to find you all night. Look at the two of you, all cozied up at the bar."

The bubble bursts, and with a record scratch, the whole room resumes its normal pace.

I drop the hand still cupping Zoey's face, and when I tear my gaze away from her, I'm met with a mass of frizzy blond curls.

"Patty, hi," I say flatly. "How's it going?"

She squeezes my arm too tightly, her long, sharp nails poking uncomfortably against my shirt. "Better now that you're here," she purrs. Her eyes flick from me to Zoey. "Hi, I'm Patty."

"Zoey. Nice to meet you," she replies in a polite tone.

"Ah, right." Patty snaps her fingers. "The hotel girl, right?"

"She's the head of development for her company," I say, pulling her to my side and looking into her eyes. "And my date for tonight."

"Oh." Patty's face falls for a second, but she quickly breaks into a phony smile, her pupils gleaming in a way that makes my insides twist. "Are you still participating in the bachelor auction?"

I dip my chin. "I am."

"I'll see you later for my reward, then, Matty." She drawls my name and winks, whirling around as she leaves.

"That's... Patty?" Zoey asks, following the woman as she sashays through the crowd.

Hand at the back of my neck, I blow out a breath. "Yeah."

She hums. "She's younger than I expected. You didn't mention she has a huge crush on you."

I quirk a brow, my lips stretching into a smirk. "Jealous?"

"Why would I be jealous?"

I shrug. "I don't know. You tell me."

"I'm not," she retorts quickly, this time avoiding my gaze.

Hands lifted in surrender, I give her my most winning smile. "Okay, then. But if you were, know that you'd have no reason to be. Patty literally crushes on anything that moves and breathes. I'm not that special."

On the stage, Cooper taps the mic a few times. "Hello, hello, folks. Grab your paddles and take a seat. The auction will start in a few minutes."

I turn to Zoey. "I should get going. You'll be okay on your own?"

"Yes, I'll be fine." She pushes onto her tiptoes and laces her arms around my neck. "I'll see you when I come to claim my prize," she says, then drops a quick kiss on my cheek.

The truth is, I don't want anyone but Zoey to bid on me tonight. And that thought scares the shit out of me.

Chapter Seventeen

Zoey

I sit in the front row, paddle in my grasp, and wait for the show to start. The night has taken a turn I didn't expect. Matt was going to kiss me, and I don't know what to do with that. Or with the fact that he didn't run away when I trauma dumped on him while we were surrounded by the entire town. This whole night has gotten away from me, and now I'm about to bid on my fake boyfriend during a fake date to win a fake romantic dinner with him. Yep. Just your average, run-of-the-mill Saturday evening.

I'm not even sure why I'm doing this anymore. For the hotel, my career, my father, yeah, yeah, I know. But tonight, it felt like I was doing it for another reason too. One I can't quite explain to myself.

My thoughts are interrupted when Cooper jumps on stage, and the music in the room dies down.

"Well, folks, here we are," he says, grinning. "The most highly anticipated moment of the night. That's right! The bachelor auction."

All around me, people clap and shout.

Carl whistles with two fingers and his wife lightly swats him on the arm.

"I know, I know." Cooper lifts both arms, palms down, motioning for the crowd to settle. "We're all excited to see the most eligible men in all Pine Falls—me included—shake what nature gave them on the stage. But first, a reminder that all proceeds will help Carl finance a week-long excursion in the Great Bear Rainforest for the freshman class. So don't be shy. Show these guys how much they're worth, yeah?"

"Show us the men!" a woman shouts from a few rows behind me, followed by a "Yeah!" and a round of catcalls sprinkled with laughter.

A few seats down, I spot Rosie. She smiles in my direction—small and tentative, but it's there—and something in me twists in relief. I wave, then focus on the stage, unable to keep my own lips from curling up. I'm starting to find allies in this town, allies that sometimes feel more like friends.

The thought warms a part of me that's been out in the cold for far too long.

None of my "friends" from home have checked up on me since I've been here. Not that I expected them to, since we haven't hung out in months. I've been too busy to join them on trips and birthday weekends, and invitations are getting scarce these days. It doesn't help that Jake has slithered his way into my friend group by dating my ex–best friend. They made their choice, and I've been pushed out.

"All right, all right." Laughing, Cooper glances behind him. "Our first bachelor up for auction tonight is Austin. Austin, come on out."

A man in his early twenties steps onto the stage, flashing his dimples to the crowd.

"As you all know, Austin is a firefighter," Cooper says, clapping the man's shoulder. "He's offering one lucky winner a picnic date, followed by a movie. We're starting the bids at fifty dollars."

Music blasts from the speakers as a handful of paddles lift. When the bidding is done, the date goes to a young woman in the back of the room for a hundred and fifty.

"Next up, we've got everybody's favorite florist. Matt, step on the stage, please."

Matt comes into view, and my heart stutters and races all at once. The minute his gaze finds mine, his resting bitch face—resting grump face?—morphs into the most adorable golden retriever expression I've ever seen. He walks to Cooper, a little bounce in his steps, as he keeps his bright eyes on me, wearing a goofy but genuine smile that sends my heart pumping even more.

Just as I get my pulse under control, the music plays once more, and Matt starts to move.

He works the crowd, all effortless swagger, pulling at his suspenders with his thumbs, swaying his hips in a way that makes my insides coil tight and brings hot flashes of memories to the forefront of my mind.

My thigh muscles tense instinctively. My body betrays me, my breaths growing choppy as I shift in my seat, desperate to relieve the pressure building inside me. While people cheer and whistle, I'm over here, unraveling in slow motion.

I hate how much he affects me.

"All right, Matt," Cooper says, his tone playful. "After *that* performance, I'm expecting a bidding war any minute now. Matt is offering a romantic dinner and a bouquet. Bids start at seventy dollars."

I lift my paddle so fast. "Eighty."

Grinning, Cooper points to someone behind me. "One hundred."

I frown and turn.

Patty flashes me a smug smile. Oh, so I'm making enemies as well as friends. It wasn't on the to-do list, but if that's how she wants to go about it, then I can play this game all night.

"One-fifty," I say, holding my paddle high.

"One-sixty," Patty adds before I'm even done speaking.

"Looks like I was right. Let the bidding war commence," Cooper says with a smirk. "How do you feel about that?" He points the mic in Matt's direction.

Matt ducks, his expression wicked. "May the best woman win."

While the entire room breaks into laughter, he doesn't look away from me.

Oh. By 'best woman,' he means me. I'm his—*the* woman.

Okay, then.

I raise my paddle. "Six hundred dollars."

The room goes dead silent.

"That's ridiculous!" Patty yells into the quiet.

"What?" I shrug, scanning the crowd. "It's for a good cause, isn't it?"

On stage, Matt and Cooper wear matching wide-eyed expressions.

"Just to be clear," Cooper says into the mic. "You're bidding six hundred dollars for a bouquet and a dinner with this gentleman? The same one who's already dating you for free?"

I smile. That proclamation in front of all Pine Falls is yet another win for me. "Absolutely."

"Then at this price, you'd better get up here and collect your prize," he calls.

Well, fuck.

"Oh, no. I'm fine, thanks," I stammer, my heart pounding for a different reason now.

"Come on. Come get your man. Everybody, let's give it up for Zoey," Cooper cheers.

The whole room follows his lead, clapping, whistling, and stomping so loudly it rattles the floorboards.

On stage, Matt looks like he'd rather run into traffic than spend another minute up there.

But nobody's paying attention to him. All eyes are on me, waiting to see if I'll step forward and claim my fake boyfriend.

And you know what? Why not? I paid for it. Might as well go get my prize.

I square my shoulders and stand, earning a roar of approval from the crowd that rings in my ears as I make my way to the stage with an assured step.

When I reach Matt, his gaze locks on mine, hesitant, almost guilt-ridden. It's as if he's silently apologizing for putting me in this situation, which is completely absurd, since I'm the one who bid a ridiculous amount on him.

But still, he draws me in. His focus on me is magnetic, and I'm pulled into his gravitational force. The noise of the crowd, the lights, the overwhelming heat of the room—it all disappears as I take him in, standing on the stage, waiting for me. And for that brief second, I forget that we're pretending. And I can picture it, walking toward him like he's mine and I'm his. Hugging him when I'm close enough. Letting him kiss me in front of everybody.

Matt watches me intently, like he can read the thoughts crossing my mind, and you know what? Let him. Let him see how much I wish we weren't faking it right now. How much I'd like him to stop playing the game.

"Let's hear it for Zoey, folks." Cooper's voice is muffled, barely there.

The crowd's cheer never stops, but the sound is distant too, like I'm underwater. All I can concentrate on is the tension crackling in the air.

Him waiting for me, a few feet away.

It takes everything in me to tear my attention away.

Focus.

Like a rubber band snapping, the noise returns to full volume.

I take a deep breath, empowered by the atmosphere soaring through the microbrewery, and climb the small step.

"Zoey," Cooper says, "thanks to your incredible donation, Carl's trip is 80 percent funded."

Matt's eyes stay firmly on me as I approach, making my stomach flutter.

"Hi," I whisper once I'm next to him.

"Hi back." His voice is just as low, the sound traveling through every part of my body. "I'm sorry."

I brush my fingers against his. "Don't be. I'm having fun."

"All right, Zoey." Cooper slides an arm around my shoulder. "Looks like you got your man. How about a kiss to seal the deal?"

Anticipation floods my veins and swirls deep in my belly. Without missing a beat, I snag the mic from his hold. "I think that's only fair for the price I'm paying," I say, the words loud and clear.

Matt's face flushes as the crowd breaks into raucous applause.

He closes his eyes for an instant, but when he opens them again, I'm taken aback by the fire blazing in his irises.

Grasping my wrist, he pulls me closer and splays his hands high on my hips. There's no hesitation in his touch. No second thought. He's touching me like he knows exactly what he's gonna do with me, the same way he touched me on my first night in his town. But this time, there's a weight to it. A history there that fortifies my belief that he knows precisely how to handle me. And that thought sets me on fire.

"Only fair, huh?" he rasps.

My throat is so thick, no words come out. So I settle for a single nod.

His gaze dips to my mouth. "Can't argue with that logic."

He brings me to him with ease, only stopping when my breasts are pressed firmly against his chest.

A gasp escapes me, heat pooling low between my legs.

"Is that what the guy in your book did before kissing the girl?" he asks, his voice dangerously low.

My pulse pounds in my ears. "What?"

He twists a loose strand of my hair around his index finger, like he's testing the texture, and suddenly, his words sink in. *The page he read earlier. The kiss that was leading to—*

"Do you expect me to beg for it, then?" I say, popped up on my toes, my lips inches from his.

He leans in, his mouth grazing the shell of my ear, his warm breath causing my skin to erupt into thousands of shivers that head straight to my core.

"I think I'll kiss you regardless of whether you beg," he whispers.

He moves back up, his focus locked on my mouth. For a moment, time stretches between us.

My heart hammers, and beneath the hand I've pressed to his chest to steady myself, his follows the same rhythm. When he finally closes the gap, when his lips brush mine in the lightest of touches, everything goes dark.

The kiss is brief. Too brief. A touch, a flash of heat that makes my head spin. His breath melds with mine, and on instinct, my lips part, ready for more.

But it never comes.

With a sharp inhale, he steps back. The loss of his closeness is immediate. I'm left with the ghost of his lips, the scent of firewood and daisies clinging to my skin as if he's still grasping my waist.

And then, just like that, the crowd goes wild. But I don't care. All I can think about is the way Matt's mouth felt against mine, the way his fingers dug into my bustier as if he was trying to tether himself.

How that kiss wasn't *entirely* a lie.

"Give it up for Zoey and Matt." Cooper snaps me back to reality.

I laugh, but it comes out too fast, too nervous.

"Steep rate for a five-second kiss," I tell Matt, trying to play it off.

He arches a brow. "Gotta save some for that date."

Swallowing, I nod. "Right."

I'm not fooling him, let alone myself. Truth is, I'd give anything to kiss Matt Becker again.

"I don't think I made a friend in Patty tonight," I say, sinking lower in the car seat.

Matt offered to drive me home, and at this point, my willpower is hanging by a thread.

"It's okay. You can't win them all. Your donation alone will help sway the community. It showed that you care."

"I think… I do."

I've always cared, but not in the way I do now. It's always mattered to me that the project fit into the community and respect the town. That it gets accepted and off the ground.

But now?

I care about the people. I want Carl to take the kids into the forest. I want Mia to survive through this tougher year. I want Cooper to boost his sales and make a name for himself. I want Matt to expand his business.

Speaking of.

"Are you free next weekend?" I ask. "My company is holding its annual shareholders' gala. That'd be a great time for me to introduce you to the team behind my start-up program."

He glances at me. "In Vancouver?"

"Yes. Is that an issue?"

"It's tricky for me to get away now that my sister is staying with me." He sighs. "I don't think I can ask Lola or James to look after her again. Daphne would hate me if I did anyway."

I shrug. "Would she like to come with you?"

Matt gives me a thoughtful frown. "You wouldn't mind?"

"Not at all. We'll book a room for the two of you at the hotel where we're holding the cocktail party. Then Daphne can enjoy all the room service she wants while you're networking."

Lips pressed together, he keeps his focus on the dirt road ahead. Finally, he says, "I'll have to ask her. See if she's comfortable with it."

"She can put a movie on and do nothing all day," I continue. "That's the perfect weekend. I can even book an appointment at the spa if she likes massages."

Matt parks the car in front of my place and kills the engine. His hands fall to the bottom of the wheel and his head follows the same pattern, drooping forward between his shoulders.

My stomach sinks. Did I say something wrong?

"If that's not her thing, she can absolutely do something else," I rush to add. "We can coordinate with the hotel to make sure she's comfortable and has everything she needs."

"No, no, it's not that." He releases a shaky sigh. "I'm just... protective of her and mindful of the people in her life. Maybe I go overboard a little, but I've learned the hard way that not everyone is open to understanding others' differences."

He smooths his beard, peering over at me.

"All that makes it hard to trust people with the person I love most, you know? Autistic people are often all or nothing, and that applies to who they let in too. Once Daph likes you, she'll like you forever. She'll constantly ask how you are and when you're coming by." He worries his lip, once again staring out the windshield. "I don't want her to end up hurt when you're done with the project and leave. Even if my gut tells me you'd be great with her. So yeah... I'm a bit mind-fucked."

"I understand," I murmur, angling my body toward him.

He lets out a soft chuckle. "I've been taking care of my sister while our parents are away, but really, I've been doing it my whole life. It's been me and her since the day she came into this world. I'd love to bring her to Vancouver with us, but I need to think it through. Make sure I'm okay with the two of you spending time together. And I want to talk to her first. She isn't always great with unfamiliar places, but raising the possibility first might help."

"Of course."

He's right—I'm not here to stay. So why does my chest tighten like I'm being pushed away from something I was never meant to be part of?

"It makes a lot of sense, and please know that I would never hurt your sister on purpose. Is there anything I can do to make her more comfortable? Maybe I can show her photos of the hotel? And you could prepare a bag with some of her favorite snacks and books. That could help her stay grounded while we're in Vancouver."

What else? I delve into the hazy memories of my college days. It seems like a lifetime ago, back when I was a completely different woman.

Though maybe that's not entirely true anymore. Lately, I feel closer to that version of myself than I have in years. I'd almost forgotten she existed, that woman who used to go out with friends after an exam and lose track of time in some dimly lit bar. Who danced until her feet ached and her cheeks hurt from smiling. Who spent sleepless nights bent over textbooks, learning everything she could about what she loved. Now I find myself reaching for her, dusting her off like an old coat in the back of a closet I've kept shut for years.

"We can map out an itinerary and a rough schedule as well," I add. "To give her a better idea of what we'll be doing and what she can expect."

Matt blinks.

"What?"

"How do... How do you know all this? What to do?"

"Oh." I glance down and hide a smile. "Before my dad got his claws into me, I studied pediatric nursing and worked with a lot of autistic kids during clinicals. It's a bit foggy, but the more I think about it, the more it's coming back."

His surprise morphs into something else, something I can't quite pin down. But the way he watches me makes the blood in my veins pump more fiercely.

I reach across the gearshift and lay my hand on his.

"All her life, Daphne has been surrounded by people who don't understand her," he says, as if empowered by my touch. "My ex couldn't stand how much time I spent with her or the space she takes up in my life. So, now, I'm a bit overly cautious about who I introduce her to. I promised myself that if you weren't okay with her, then our deal would be over. No hesitation. When you brought us breakfast, I was ready to fight. I was so worried you'd say something offensive."

He lets out a soft laugh, and I echo it.

"But I didn't," I murmur.

"No," he says, matching my tone. "You didn't."

Silence stretches, the air in the truck cab shifting to accommodate the growing chemistry between us.

The relief on his face is mostly for his sister, but part of me can't help feeling that he's also relieved he didn't have to let me go.

"Your ex... Andie, right?"

He studies me. "How do you know?"

"Mia mentioned her this morning."

"Right." He gives a dry, bitter chuckle. "The whole town remembers because I didn't come out of my house for months after she left. I think they all grieved her departure right alongside me. She became family for a lot of people around here. I wasn't the only one who was hurt when she decided she was done."

"Including Daphne," I breathe, my gaze fixed on the horizon. I try not to let envy distract me from what's important, but that doesn't stop it from stinging just beneath my skin.

"Including Daphne," Matt repeats. "She doesn't really grasp all the facets of what a relationship is, but after spending so much time with Andie, she became obsessed with the idea of love. Relationships. She wanted to find her own person and kept asking me how she could go on dates."

A tightness builds in my throat. "The breakup must have been tough on her."

Who breaks up with someone because of their autistic sister? She must have been something special if Matt fell in love with her. Then again, maybe she was just good at hiding her true colors at first.

I can only imagine how easy it was for Daphne to grow attached to Andie, with her soft heart. The loss must have been unfathomable.

"Yeah, it was." Matt sinks his fingers into his hair. "She loved Andie so much. She asked me for months and months where she was and why she wasn't coming back. That wrecked me even more than the breakup itself. And the worst part is that I had to lie to her over the reason she left. I couldn't tell her the truth. It would have crushed her, and I wasn't about to hurt her even more. She has enough to deal with my mom already."

I frown. "Your mom is having a hard time with your sister?"

"I wouldn't call it a hard time. But she refuses to accept that Daphne has needs different from most girls her age."

I rub my thumb over his hand. "Weird family dynamics is a language I understand. Your mom might need a bit more time to adjust."

"Maybe..." He raises his eyes to mine, soft and heavy, like he's been carrying the weight of the world on his shoulders. Juggling so much—his work, caring for his sister, the issues with his mom—must be tough on him. "You don't mind letting her come to Vancouver, then?"

My smile spreads easily. "Absolutely not. We'll make sure she has the best time. Promise."

"As long as it's okay with Daph, I'm in."

"Talk to her and let me know. I'll confirm our presence once we know she's on board." I peer through the windshield at the cottage. "I should get going. It's late."

"Thank you for tonight," he says. "I owe you a bouquet and a romantic dinner."

I search for sarcasm in his voice but don't detect any. As if he really is looking forward to the idea.

"As long as the romantic dinner doesn't end up with me being left by myself in the middle of a park," I say, opening the passenger door.

He laughs, the sound carrying me outside.

I collect my small bag and lean on the doorframe. "Bye."

"Bye, Zoey. Sleep well."

I head for the cabin, Matt's gaze a phantom caress on my back the whole way. Is it wrong that I wish he'd walk me to the door? And even follow me inside? He's nothing like I thought he'd be, and the more I learn about him, the more difficult it is to walk away. Day by day, all this time alone becomes more challenging.

My step falters.

I don't even know what I want from him.

Sometimes, I think that simply having him by my side would fill the empty space in my chest that aches with loneliness. That everyday space where doing mundane things with someone is the best part of your day.

I wouldn't know what it's like. I've only read about it and seen it in the movies.

Jake and I never built a life together in my apartment. He moved in after a year, and even then, our schedules rarely lined up. I'd come home to the uncomfortable silence, him already fast asleep. Most mornings, I was out before he could stir awake.

What would it be like return from work to a house full of light? To push open the door and be greeted by the familiar sound of the person who makes that house a little warmer? The smell of a meal already in the making?

I want to know. I want to find out.

I've been alone all my life, and for the most part, I've been comfortable that way. I talked myself into believing that I didn't need anyone to be whole, that loneliness was an inevitable consequence of the life I'd chosen, that I couldn't have it all.

Work or love.

Success or a relationship.

Then Matt waltzed in, and I'm not so sure anymore. He makes me question so many of the beliefs that have been deeply rooted in me for years.

The hardest part of all is realizing that the solitude that once felt familiar has become unbearable.

When I glance back, I find him watching me through the windshield, his chin resting on top of his knuckles.

I give him a wave and slide the key into the lock. Only after the door closes and I let out a sigh does he pull away, his engine a low rumble in the night.

Chapter Eighteen

Matt

I haven't seen Zoey in four days, but she hasn't left my mind for a second during our time apart. Even through hectic mornings with Daph, frantic days at the store, and my new routine in the evening that keeps me busy until ten, there hasn't been a moment when I haven't thought about her.

I woke up early this morning, unable to wipe the grin off my face. Even Daph called me out on it when I dropped her off at before-school care, saying I was acting weird.

I'm not. I always like Wednesdays because it's the Pine Falls weekly market, and this week, it just so happens that Zoey will be there to help me mind the stand. Pure coincidence. Not at all related.

Plus, I've been looking forward to a relaxing day at the market and catching up with my regulars.

I'm sure Zoey's never done this before, and the idea of sharing that moment with her makes my body shiver with anticipation.

I load the flowers in the van, overcome with more joy than I have any business feeling over something as trivial as this, when a familiar voice breaks through the quiet hum of the morning.

"Do you need help?"

I turn, and there she is.

Zoey rounds the front of my delivery van, and once again, I'm grinning like a fool, far too excited at the sight of her. It's been four days, and I—well, I really fucking missed her.

My fingers flex around the flowers I'm holding. The low sun catches her hair, turning it a warm chocolate brown. In that soft morning light, she looks a little brighter than the rest of the world, and something inside me whispers that I've never known anything more true.

She leans against the van with an easy smile, crossing one ankle over the other.

Did she feel my absence as much as I felt hers? Did the four days we were apart stretch like weeks for her too?

I drop the flowers in the cargo area of the van and close the distance between us. The second I'm within reach, I wrap my arm around her waist, lifting her against me. "Good morning, beautiful."

She buries her face in the crook of my neck, draping her arms over my shoulders and melting further into me. "Morning."

Her voice is so soft, so content, it makes me want to keep her nestled here forever. There's no one around, no one watching, but even if there were, I wouldn't be pretending. I couldn't fake this if I tried. I just need her near. And her eager response? It's like she's forgotten about it too.

My heart hammers so hard against my ribs I'm sure she can feel it. But does she realize that she's the reason why?

Pressing my nose into her hair, I breathe her in. "Ready to sell some flowers and mingle with the town?"

"I guess so." She sighs, and the puff of air warms my skin. "Even if you made me get up super early."

Laughing, I stroke her hair. "I warned you when we agreed to fake date, remember? You said you had no problem with it."

"I don't think I was listening at that moment," she mumbles.

I untangle myself from her, setting her back on her feet. As we step apart, the blinds of the grocery store a few doors down roll up and Sue appears in the window. She waves to me, and I return the greeting. Zoey turns, and when she spots her, a quiet *oh* slips from her lips, her shoulders dropping an inch. When she looks back at me, her eyes have lost a bit of the spark they had a few seconds ago.

I place my hands on her arms. "Everything okay?"

"Absolutely," she says, flashing me one of her famous fake-ass smiles. "Do you need more help?"

The switch in her attitude gives me whiplash. I want to go back to when she had her arms around my neck and it felt like I was dreaming with my eyes open.

I rock back on my heels. "I have a couple more crates to load, and we'll be on our way."

With a nod, she backs away. "I'll wait for you in the van."

Ten minutes later, we're on our way.

"It's called the Pine Falls Market," I say as I head for Brookhaven, "but we hold it in a nearby town. It's a more convenient location for all the hamlets in the area. Kind of like a community market."

"You do this often?" she asks, shifting in her seat to face me, her expression glinting with curiosity.

I nod. "Every week. It's very popular, so it's good business for me."

When we get there, the square is already buzzing with the early morning energy. All around, local merchants set up their stands, chatting and hauling their wares.

"Anything I should focus on today? Anybody I should charm?" Zoey asks, her tone playful.

"The usual suspects," I say as I unlock the bed. "Justin—he owns a construction company—usually picks up lunch at Mia's stand. He'd be a good ally." With a hand on the van handle, I turn to Zoey. "Just be yourself. You've been doing great so far. From the snippets I've gleaned here and there, the lodge is on everybody's mind. Continue what you've been doing today. All I ask is that you don't sell more flowers than me."

Cheeks pink, she breathes a soft laugh. The sound lights me up from the inside. I worry I've become addicted to it.

"I can't promise that." She drags the folding table from the bed and hauls it over to our spot. "I've never sold flowers," she calls back, "but if you do it, how hard can it be?"

"Actually," I argue lightly, "it's—you know what? Let's see how easy it is, then. Are you up for some friendly competition?"

She quirks a brow, studying me with a mix of amusement and suspicion. "Depends. Are you a sore loser?"

I grin at her. "I wouldn't know. Can't say I've ever experienced the feeling before."

Her lips twitch. "Guess you're about to learn something, then."

How could I expect anything less from a woman who's at the top of her game? She hasn't gotten where she is by tiptoeing around work and following orders. I'm a laid-back kind of guy, but I'll play along. Just to see how far she'll take it.

"Careful," I warn. "I have a soft spot for cocky women."

She crosses her arms and gives me a look. "What are the rules?"

"The person who sells the most flowers has bragging rights for life."

Head tilted, she asks, "Quantity or dollars spent?"

Oh, she's getting technical. I love it. "Quantity. I need to know if you're a better salesperson than I am."

Without hesitation, she thrusts her hand out. "Deal."

I take her hand and give it a firm shake. Though when it's time to let go, I don't. Instead, I drag my thumb over her skin, then twist gently and graze her palm, savoring her warmth.

"You're distracting me." She swallows audibly, her delicate throat working.

"Am I?" I ask, voice low.

She slips out of my hold, her gaze flitting to the ground. "Shouldn't we set up your stand before the market opens?"

"Look at you, willing to do the dirty work all of a sudden. Who are you and what have you done with Zoey Delacroix?"

She chuckles. "I know, right? And it's not even nine a.m. Ew."

I laugh and her smile widens, more genuine than the last one she gave me. I like that I can pull it out of her.

We get to work, unloading the van and carrying the crates of flowers and vases to the table. Zoey moves quickly, her focus sharp. We fall into an easy rhythm, one that feels more familiar than it should, and thirty minutes later, we're all set.

Standing beside me, Zoey shoots me a sly grin. "Ready to lose?"

"It's good you're used to dirt now, city girl, 'cause you're about to eat some."

She's way better at this than I thought she'd be.

So far, I'm still in the lead, but she's not that behind. And I've been working my ass off all morning.

The market is buzzing now, and Zoey's surrounded by customers, chatting away like she's done this all her life. She's a natural, hooking people with her charm and sharp wit and that easy energy that tells you there's nowhere else she'd rather be.

"Not bad." I move behind her and grab a few roses for the elderly woman waiting on my side of the stand.

"Thanks," Zoey replies quickly, her attention set on wrapping a bouquet for a customer of her own. "Hey, where did the sun go? It's getting chilly."

I lean forward, glancing at the sky. It's not supposed to rain, but the heavy clouds moving in don't bode well at all.

"Do you want me to run to the van and get my jacket for you?"

She ties the bouquet and hands it to the customer in front of her. "And give you an excuse to say you let me win? Not a chance."

I roll my eyes, but then I catch sight of the spreadsheet we're using to tally sales, and my plan to check the weather app slips my mind.

Dammit, she's getting close to taking the lead. And I *know* most of these people, which makes the fact that they're coming to her and not me even more impressive.

I glance over at her, a sudden rush of warmth flooding me. She's talking to a young dad with a stroller, effortlessly making him laugh.

Her hair is tossed into a messy bun, but a few strands have fallen free, teasing the curve of her neck.

Does she notice how much she affects me? The way she stands, the way she moves—every little detail draws me in, pulls at something inside me I don't want to acknowledge. It travels to my hands, through my chest, in my jaw. It's a tension that won't shake loose. I'm just standing here, wanting, aching, wishing I could do something… anything.

Okay, yeah. I've been doing that a lot. Getting lost in my thoughts while watching her, instead of selling flowers. And it's clearly costing me this game.

Focus, Matt.

I turn to the next customer, a guy in his mid-thirties. "How can I help you today, sir?" I ask, flashing a grin.

In the distance, the sky rumbles.

"I'd like to buy a bouquet for my wife."

"Of course. Do you know what you're looking for?"

He presses his lips into a thin line. "Something that says, 'I'm sorry'?"

"Ah." I chuckle. "I have the perfect one for that." I glance at Zoey, who's handing out an arrangement of sunflowers.

"Do you know about our promotion today? If you buy two, the second is 30 percent off. Any other lucky lady in your life? A sister, or a mom maybe?"

By the time he walks away, he's purchased two bouquets.

As I add them to my tally, Zoey sighs dramatically and bumps me with her hip on her way back to her spot.

"I swear you could sell weeds and people would throw their money at you."

I'm about to retort when Justin steps up to the stand.

"Hey, man." I check the time, surprised he's stopping by so early, only to realize lunch break is already over.

"Just dropping by to say hi before I get back to work." He leans in, giving me a conspiratorial grin, and nods toward Zoey. "Heard through the grapevine that you had company today."

"Of course you did. Let me introduce you." Time for our second game of the day. "Hey, Zoey."

Hands in a crate of daisies, she peers back at me. "Yeah? Oh." She straightens, brushing the dirt off her fingers, then steps closer. "Hi," she says, sliding her hands casually into her back pockets. "Justin, right?"

Justin raises an eyebrow, a hint of amusement tugging at his lips. "How come you know my name when all I've heard about you is that Matt found his dream girl?"

I sputter, nearly choking on my saliva.

"Wow," she says with a laugh, unfazed. "Gossip sure moves quickly around here. But between you and me," she adds, leaning in. "Your van gave you away." She nods toward Justin's construction van parked down the street, the one with his name and face plastered on the side.

"You gotta get rid of that thing, dude." I let out a chuckle. "I don't think it's bringing you the kind of publicity you think it is."

Justin shrugs. "I don't know, man. Business is going pretty well. And it doesn't hurt that it gets the ladies' attention too." He winks at Zoey.

She snorts in response, her eyes dancing.

"I'm right here," I mutter, wrapping an arm around Zoey's waist, pulling her to my side like a jealous asshole. I have to play my part, right?

"Calm down. I'm joking." He holds both hands up.

"I'm calm," I grumble.

I glance at Zoey, but her focus is stuck on Justin's van. "So business is good, huh?"

"Yeah." Justin shrugs again. "Can't complain. Things are running pretty well."

She narrows her eyes. "But could be doing better, am I wrong?"

I frown. What is she up to?

"Yeah. Well, you know." He smooths his hair. "You always need more money when you're your own boss."

Zoey nods, her voice leaking confidence. "Absolutely. Especially when you have employees to take care of and raises to hand out every year. Not to mention the costs of material these days." She scoffs. "Hello inflation, am I right?"

I hold back a snort. She's brilliant. She carefully weaves a web until her target can no longer escape. Then she goes for the final blow.

"There may be a new lodge in the area soon," she continues, her voice low, as if she's spilling her secrets. "That would be a whole lot of work for your company."

Justin narrows his eyes. "I've heard about it. I thought it got turned down."

"Nope. And if it gets the green light, then you and I could talk about what it'd mean for your construction business."

Justin chuckles awkwardly, his attention drifting to me. He shifts his weight like he's ready to bolt.

"What's the catch?"

"Thought you'd never ask," she grins. "All I need is your vote at the next town meeting. Simple as that."

I can see the wheels turning in Justin's head as he considers his options. Finally, he lets out a long sigh. "All right. You've got me intrigued. I'll think about it."

She smiles, keeping the expression tame, but the way her leg shakes against mine betrays her excitement. "That's all I ask."

Once Justin is out of earshot, I turn and grasp her upper arms.

"You were fantastic." I breathe. "The way you got him exactly where you wanted him? A master class."

I don't realize I'm jiggling her with each word until she laughs. The rich, spontaneous sound stops me cold.

She tilts her head back, and it's like my whole world tilts with her.

"What?" she asks, her laugh fading in the breeze.

I swallow, my breath hitching in my throat. "Do it again," I whisper, steadying her.

She searches my face, her brows pulled low in question. "Do what?"

"I want to hear you laugh again."

Her frown deepens, her smile faltering. "I laugh all the time."

I trace my thumb gently across her cheek, soaking in the heat of her skin. "Not like this. Not with your whole heart."

Her expression shifts, a flicker of vulnerability peeking out from beneath the layers of her usual confidence.

Give me more, I want to tell her. *I* want *more*.

"No one has ever noticed that before," she says thickly.

I lean closer, my chest pounding, and stroke her cheek again, as if this small touch could somehow coax her closer. "I do. I notice everything about you."

She wraps her fingers around my wrist, holding on to me like she's afraid I'll slip away if she lets go.

Her eyes take a pleading edge. "Are we still pretending?"

I scoff, locked in on her completely. "Look around, Zoey. There's nobody watching us." Fingers threading through her hair, I tilt her face up. "I haven't had to pretend for a while now," I say, throat dry.

The truth is laid bare between us, pulsing in the thick tension we're shrouded in. My heart slams against my ribs as the silence stretches.

How could I ever have believed she wanted to take advantage of our town the way her father wanted to? But behind that question come ten others. What if I'm wrong? What if she's still stuck in her father's shadow? *What if she's not ready?* What if this is a repeat of what happened with Andie?

The silence is unbearable. Thankfully, she breaks it before my thoughts consume me, her voice barely above a whisper. "How about when we kissed on stage last weekend? Was that real too?"

"It—"

I'm cut off by a drop of water landing on her cheek. I chuckle, brushing it away with my thumb, but before I can blink, another one falls, and then another, each one coming faster than the last. A low rumble of thunder rolls overhead, and then, as if on cue, the sky breaks open.

"What the *hell*?" I shout, my words barely audible over the roar of the rain, my laughter bubbling up despite the chaos unfolding around us.

Wind howls through the market, lashing the rain against our skin like needles. Within moments, we're drenched, our clothes clinging to our body, water streaming down our faces.

"The flowers!" Zoey's voice cracks through the din.

I turn, and my stomach drops. Dammit. The storm is already hammering the petals. "Shit, we have to get them in the van."

I rush to the roses, hauling several pots, shielding them from the worst of the downpour as much as possible. Zoey's already scooped up the daisies and dahlias, her feet slipping in the puddles as she bolts for the van.

"Matt, the tarp!" Her voice rises above the clamor, her eyes wide and fixed on something over my head.

I catch the tarp as it tears free of the ropes, snapping at me like a whip. I yank it into my grip, barely able to keep hold of the slippery material, and scramble to tie it to the pole.

"We have to pack everything up," I shout. "You finish covering the flowers, and I'll take care of the stand."

"Got it."

"Oh, and Zoey."

She halts mid-step, looking back at me, drenched to the bone, her hands shielding her face from the torrential downpour.

"My jacket is on the back seat. Put it on."

An amused smile stretches on her lips. "Thanks, but have you seen me?" With the soaked wool of her cardigan pinched between her fingers, she laughs. "A little late for that, I think."

It takes ten minutes to pack everything into the van and dismantle our stand. All around us, the market is a frenzy of rushing vendors and drenched customers darting for cover.

"Let's find shelter," I tell Zoey once we've salvaged all we can.

"Where?" she shouts over the pounding rain.

I point to a spot down the street where the shops are all tucked under alcoves, then hold out my hand. "Over there. Ready?"

Without hesitation, she slips her palm against mine. Her freezing skin sends a small jolt up my arm.

"Three. Two. One. Go," I shout.

We bolt for the street, laughing as we dodge puddles, rain pelting us the whole way.

"This weather is *crazy*," she shrieks between spurts of laughter.

I can't hear much beyond the rush of water, but I don't need to. Her face says it all. Her eyes squinted from the deluge, her mouth wide open in a laugh that's more wild and free than I ever imagined it could be. Her wet hair clings to her cheeks the way her clothes cling to her body, but she's lit up brighter than I've ever seen her. She's running without a care in the world, and the sight will be burned into my memory for the rest of my life.

I don't know how it's possible, but time slows, as if the universe knows how desperately I want to savor this moment. For a few quiet beats, it's just Zoey. The real Zoey. A version of her I don't think she's ever realized exists. And I'm the lucky bastard who gets to experience her like this. It's enough to make my chest a little tight.

And just like that, time bends and snaps back to the present, and I'm running at full speed again, Zoey dragging me along, her fingers still tangled with mine.

When we finally reach the alcoves, out of breath, she doesn't let go of my hand. Her chest rises and falls, and mine follows the same pattern.

I can't tear my eyes away from her. I don't want to.

"You haven't answered me," she heaves, gulping down air.

With my free hand, I smooth the hair out of my face. "About what?"

She steps closer, the words heavy on her lips. "About our kiss. Was it real?"

I don't hesitate. "Yes."

My answer hangs between us, raw and electric, a spark so powerful it could set the whole world on fire.

She's so close to me.

I could bend down and kiss her.

Not like I'm about to fuck her into the wall. Not in front of a room full of people.

No. Kiss her like nobody's watching.

Like it's just the two of us.

My gaze drifts to her parted lips, and without a second thought, I grasp her waist, bringing her flush to me. "Can I kiss you for real now?"

Her breath hitches and she steadies herself by gripping my arms. She tilts her face up, her fingers roaming over my chest, then intertwining behind my neck. I shiver. "Yes."

I close the rest of the distance between us and finally kiss her like she was always meant to be kissed.

Slow and unhurried. Soft and lazy.

The first time I kissed Zoey, I didn't know anything about her, except how beautiful and stubborn she was. I was kissing a stranger that I thought I'd never see again. No connection behind the obvious physical attraction. Just a tangle of wet lips and instant gratification.

The second time I kissed Zoey, I wanted to do so much more, but my restraint kept me on a tight leash. I could tell behind that soft peck that she was hungry for more, but it didn't feel right to give in, knowing she didn't have any clarity regarding how much I truly wanted her that day.

Kissing Zoey now is a whole new experience. One I may never come back from. She tastes like rain and promises.

She's not a stranger anymore. I've spent the last two weeks peeling the layers off, stripping away the hard shell, and uncovering versions of her I've never met, ones that she had forgotten. And each one makes me want her even more.

Kissing Zoey now is kissing the woman she's always wanted to be.

There's no hesitation or second-guessing in the way she responds. She takes what she wants, as if I've denied her the possibility all along, and now she's starving for it.

She tightens her arms around my neck, pressing herself closer until there's not one inch where her body doesn't touch mine. I groan against her lips, sliding my fingers into her damp hair and tilting her head so I can savor her better. She lets out her own throaty whimper, and now, all I want to know is how to get her to make that sound again.

She deepens the connection, licking into my mouth, her hand curling around the back of my neck.

I jolt at the ice-cold sensation. "You're freezing."

"I d-don't care." She kisses me again.

"Zoey." I grasp her upper arms. "You're gonna catch a cold."

Her fingers rap against my ribcage, fisting my soaked shirt in her grip. "I don't c-care," she repeats.

"I do."

Her mouth is back on mine, and I forget what I was arguing about, losing myself in the abandoned way she clings to me.

But rational thought wins out after a moment.

"Wait." I pull myself away with the last shred of willpower I have left. "No more kissing until we get someplace warm and dry."

She pouts, her sigh almost impossible to hear over the rain still beating down. "F-f-fine."

I curse under my breath. If she wasn't trembling like a leaf, the blueish color of her lips would be a dead giveaway that she's freezing. "You're unbelievable. You're gonna die from pneumonia if you stay in these wet clothes in the fucking cold for one more second, and you're really pouting at me right now?"

She shrugs, her teeth clattering. "Wo-o-orth i-it."

My heart drums impatiently in my chest. We need to get warm, and fast. "Come on." I lace my fingers with hers. "Ready to run again?"

"C-can't we k-k-kiss inst-tead?"

I shake my head, unable to keep from smiling. I'm fucking soaked and cold. The wind bites at my skin, and my wet hair snaps at my cheeks like frozen whips. But I couldn't care less. The thought of Zoey wanting nothing more than to kiss me warms me more than any fire ever could.

Thumb brushing over her cold hand, I lean in. "Once you're dry and comfortable, we'll do whatever you want."

She gives me that look, the one that says she's not going to make this easy. So I tug her toward me, grazing my lips against hers quickly, just enough to make my pulse throb. "There," I say. "Now, let's go."

This time, I drag her into the rain before she has a chance to negotiate.

Chapter Nineteen

Zoey

"You and Matt gave us quite the show," Rosie muses as she froths milk. "Even through the rain, everybody could see you two eating each other's faces."

"Gross." I tighten the blanket she gave me around my shoulders. My clothes are still wet, but at least my teeth stopped chattering. "What are you doing here?" I ask as she moves behind the counter of the Brookhaven café where Matt and I took refuge.

It's the first real conversation we've had since the town hall, and… fuck, I can't believe she's actually talking to me. No awkwardness, no deadly glare. Just Rosie being her welcoming self.

"I own this place too," she says with a hint of pride in her voice. "I'm here every Wednesday to help my crew with the market rush."

My brows rise. "I didn't know you had more than one coffee shop. That's impressive." I envy her for having found something she's so deeply passionate about. "What is it that you like so much? Why coffee?"

"Hmm." She wipes down the frother with a rag. "It's less about coffee and more about helping people with their day, you know what I mean? I like that I'm the one they come to in order to feel better." She laughs, her cheeks flushing. "Wow, that makes it sound like I'm handing out blowjobs."

I raise my hands. "Hey, no judgment here."

"What I meant," she says, batting at stray hairs that have fallen into her face, "is that I make it my mission to ensure that the people who come in here, whether they're strangers or locals, leave happier than when they arrived." She frowns. "That still doesn't sound better."

"I get it." I chuckle. "You're very lucky to have found a career that pulls you out of bed every morning."

Her smile dims. "Haven't you?"

"It's… complicated." I glance over at Matt.

"Ah." Rosie scrutinizes me, sighing with a heaviness that screams understanding. "Does 'complicated' have another name?"

I fight a grin. "Maybe?"

"He came at you a bit hard at the town hall meeting last week. I was disappointed too, by the way. That you lied to me."

"Technically, I didn't *lie*," I say, though my heart sinks. "More like omitted the truth?"

She pins me with a look that makes my cheeks heat.

"It had nothing to do with you, I swear." I tighten my hold on my blanket again. "If I had been open on why I came to Pine Falls before I got a chance to explain, I wouldn't have gone very far. But..." I trace a finger along the countertop. "I felt awful about it. I was scared that I'd messed up our friendship before it could even properly start."

"I was mad, yes," she says. "But once I heard people talking about you and everything you've done for us in only a matter of days, I came around. I was just waiting for you to take the first step."

I reach across the counter and rest my hand on hers. "I'm sorry. I won't lie to you anymore. Promise."

Giving me a small nod, she steps away, grabbing two mugs from a shelf. "So, back to you and Matt. I was surprised to see you two at Cooper's last Saturday. And when I heard you were *dating*? It didn't make any sense. I almost thought you were using him to get to us. I was ready to fight." She laughs.

I laugh with her, in a "can you imagine?" way, but deep down, I'm freaking the fuck out.

You just said you wouldn't lie to her again. What the fuck is wrong with you?

Cups filled, she slides one in front of me. "I don't know what happened between you two since the town hall, but that chemistry outside?" she whistles. "That was piping hot. Can't fake that." Leaning against the counter, she nods to Matt. "You know, I never thought I'd see him this happy again. You're good for him."

"He's good for me too," I say without missing a beat.

Guilt swells inside me faster than the tiny speck of joy her words bring, and suddenly, the enormity of what we're doing hits me.

We've been lying to these people since day one. It didn't bother me much at first. I figured they liked him fine. That his business made him somewhat more influential than others, and that was the end of it.

But it's so much more than that.

They *adore* him. He's a pillar of this community. Their lives are tightly woven together, bound by a genuine care for one another.

And they're watching him "fall in love" again like he's their son or their brother. And they are *so* proud and relieved that he seems to have moved on from the hell Andie put him through.

I should have realized that before I let Matt rope me into this. Now, we're too far gone. When we inevitably "split," not only are they gonna think Matt is heartbroken, but they'll be heartbroken *for* him too.

Fuck.

"Keep it PG in here, okay?" Rosie says. "There are kids around."

Nose scrunched, I grab the coffees. "Guess I'll save the R-rated stuff for later, then."

"Tell Matt I'm terribly sorry," she throws out as I shuffle toward our table.

At the sight of him, his hair tousled from the rain, his shirt plastered to his chest, my pulse spikes, the same way it did when he kissed me senseless.

That kiss turned my world upside down. Reoriented my north to my south, tipped my sense of gravity toward his. Even weaving between the chairs of the café is a challenge, because my mind is still spinning.

It wasn't a casual kiss. I know it. He knows it. But now what?

"Rosie sends her apologies," I say when I set our coffees down.

Matt frowns as I settle into the booth across from him, his mug already at his lips. "Why?"

"She cockblocked you."

He chokes on his sip.

"Said our PDA was too graphic for the kids," I add, amused.

"I didn't think we had an audience."

"The whole café, apparently." I waggle my brows. Yes, I'm deflecting. If I don't, I'll spiral, replaying the admission he blurted out before he dove for my mouth.

That none of it has been pretend for him. It simply doesn't make sense.

Or maybe I'm not ready to accept that it does.

"Don't," he says, watching me.

"What?" I shoot back.

A shadow crosses his face, yet his gaze remains on me as he says, "Don't downplay this."

"Why?"

He raises a brow. "Why? Because there was nothing fake about that kiss, Zoey. Just so we're clear."

Why is it so hard for you to believe him? Why do you always self-sabotage?

And how does he read me so well?

"It doesn't make sense, though," I start. "I'm not... I mean, you saw what I—" I huff, scrambling to find the right words.

His attention doesn't falter.

Nothing remotely coherent is coming to me, so I give up. "It's just... why?"

With a soft chuckle, he sits back in his chair. But his expression sobers when he sees I'm being serious. "Why what?"

"Why would you want to have anything to do with me?" My voice cracks on the last word.

The moment the question leaves me, I glance down at my fingers wrapped around the mug, wishing I could take it back. That single sentence was loaded with way too much baggage.

"Are you on some sort of public-enemy list that would make me liking you a very questionable choice?" He gasps. "Am I attracted to a *criminal?*"

Liking you. Attracted.

He's throwing these out so casually, like they don't shake me to my core.

I keep reminding myself not to let my guard down, that at any moment, the other shoe *will* drop. But then he says stuff like that, and the idea of protecting my heart sounds like a joke I'm only playing on myself.

"No, no, of course not," I huff out. I try to regain my footing, but the floor is still wobbling under my feet.

Liking you. Attracted.

"Then why would it be so surprising that my feelings could be real?" he asks, his voice weakened by the vulnerability he's offering me.

"Maybe because the men in my life have always shown me that they're incapable of handling me," I blurt before I can think better of it.

So why should Matt be willing to?

Actually, no, why *would* he? Of his own free will?

Nah. I work my ass off and have very little time to give to others. It wasn't enough for Jake or any of the insecure men I dated before, so why would it be for Matt?

Though… In the last two weeks, I've hardly done any work. Come to think of it, the "work" I've done has consisted solely of spending time with Matt to get into the town's good graces. I can spin that any way I want, say I'm doing it to get the lodge off the ground, to convince my father I can take over, to woo the shareholders. The list goes on. I've got all the excuses in the world. But the reality is that being with Matt is effortless. It doesn't feel like work at all. And every morning, I wake up wondering what new things he'll show me and how I can make the most of this limited time with him.

I don't know whether this version of me has always been there, waiting to be coaxed out by him, or if it's who I've become around him, but either way, it's freeing. To expose another side of me, the side that exists outside my work. The side that's been muzzled for too long.

I hope you'll find someone worth your time one day.

The words Jake spat at me seconds before slamming the door behind him echo in my head. At that moment, I'd rolled my eyes, angry at his inability to recognize that he was the one who'd put us in this situation by cheating. But now, as I study Matt, who's still mulling over what I said, those words take on a new light.

"Is that what they made you believe? That you were too much to handle?" he asks, breaking the silence. The weight of his gaze makes me shift in my chair.

"I come with a lot of baggage, and by baggage, I mean my job. I barely have time for myself, let alone for a partner. They get tired of it."

"Did—" He gives a vague swirl of his hand. "All those men—by the way," he says too casually, "how many are we talking about? Ballpark."

The tightness in my chest eases a notch. His curiosity regarding how many men I've slept with gives me more satisfaction than it should. "Not that many. Less than a hundred."

"Oh." He clears his throat. "Okay. Well, that's cool, that's cool."

I can't contain the laugh that bubbles out of me. "I'll give you an A for your response, but you'd definitely fail acting class. I was joking. I had one serious relationship, a few situationships."

"It would have been fine either way," he says. Yet, the subtle drop in his shoulders tells me otherwise, almost like the thought of me with other men makes him... jealous. Which, again, doesn't make sense.

"Well, that guy you were serious with," he adds, "did he know how to get your mind off the job? Did he take care of you the way you needed?"

I have no idea how he does it, but time and again, he hits me right where I didn't know it would hurt. He's uncovering all my invisible wounds, one question after another. And I'm just standing here, clueless how to respond, trying to patch myself up before I bleed out on the floor.

"I mean, he was there, yeah. In some ways." My nose stings, but I refuse to cry. "It's my fault too. I missed so many… I wasn't the best… You know, it's not—"

He rests his hand on top of mine, and I snap my mouth shut. He's done this so many times in the past two weeks, and yet this touch feels different. It grounds me.

I fill my lungs with air and exhale. "I don't want to excuse my behavior by placing the blame on him. I was—*am*—busy. I did neglect him and our relationship."

"Sure," he concedes. "Maybe you could have been more present. But even after a few weeks of knowing you, I can't imagine a world where you wouldn't be involved in the life of the person you love."

He studies me too closely and for too long.

I feel like I'm under a microscope. I'm tempted to make a run for it, but outside, the rain is still coming down hard. Not to mention I'd look like a crazy person.

So instead, I sink deeper in my seat, hoping it'll somehow make me disappear.

"We weren't compatible, that's all," I finally say. "It's a poor explanation, but in hindsight, it's also the truest one.

"Let me guess," he chuckles half-heartedly. "He was the guy who said you weren't good at sex?"

Throat clogging, I nod.

Matt huffs out a bitter snarl. "A real winner, this one."

"I wish that was the worst of what he did." The whispered words are only meant for me, but, of course, this man listens to everything I say with a keen ear.

Matt's jaw works, his grip tightening mindlessly around his cup. "Why do I have an inkling of where this is going?"

I want to tell him all of it. Lay it all out—the hurt, the pain, the self-doubt.

I *want* to, but... instead, I freeze.

Where am I supposed to start? What am I supposed to say? I've never truly opened up to anyone before. Not about my life, my needs, my dreams. Certainly not about *this*. No one knows how broken and ashamed I was, except my therapist, who sat through entire sessions while I sobbed and hurled insults at my ex and former best friend. So putting this trauma into words, sharing the story with a man who hasn't been paid to help me unpack it, borders on impossible. Especially when the scars are still tender.

With a long sigh, I focus on the table in front of me and garner all the strength I have. "Jake and I were together for almost two years."

"Sorry," Matt cuts in. "You said Jake? Or Jerk?"

I smile, though I'm not sure he notices, given how tight the rest of my body is. "The last six months of our relationship, he cheated." I pause, swallowing as the memories of that night flood back in. "With my now ex–best friend."

Matt lets out a low whistle, sitting back in his chair. "Damn, Zoey. That's… that's cold. I'm so sorry."

"It's in the past now," I say with a shrug.

"Doesn't mean it hurts any less," he replies. The rasp in his voice carries everything he doesn't put into words. An understanding that only comes from someone who's known the same kind of heartbreak.

"True." I let out a shaky exhale. I lean in and take a sip of my coffee, the cup warming the still-cold tips of my fingers. "But I have to move on at some point… right?"

He nods, his eyes fixed somewhere beyond my shoulder, his fingers drumming a restless rhythm against his mug. Then he looks at me in a way my heart can't handle, his gaze slicing through my armor, as though it's nothing more than thin cotton, not years of fortified hurt.

"Sometimes it's a bit harder than flipping a switch, though, isn't it?" The softness he infuses in that statement stitches a piece of me back into place. Like he sees the *handle with care* warnings written all over me. "Even more so when the people who should've held you together are the ones who tore you apart."

He leans in, gently prying my fingers away from the cup and lacing them with his.

"I'm not those boys, Zoey. I can handle you. There's not a single side of you that scares me, that's too much or not enough."

I bite my cheek to stave off the tears welling up in my throat.

"Not even when I'm wearing my high heels and expensive clothes and threatening to slash your tires if you almost run me over again?"

I deflect. It's safer than letting my foolish heart get carried away.

"Not even then, beautiful." He cracks a devastating smile.

Good god, will I ever catch a break? If he's not finding the exact right words to mend my heart, he's flashing me those ridiculously cute dimples that melt it. I can't win.

He brushes his thumb against my skin absentmindedly as silence stretches.

"You say that," I finally force out, "but I don't think you'd have given me a second thought if you'd met me in Vancouver." I lower my gaze. "I'm… different here. You wouldn't have liked that other version of me."

He tsks, shaking his head. "Why do you keep referring to yourself as if you're multiple people? You think I don't see you? All the parts that make you whole?" He bends, searching for my eyes. "You refuse to let people past that hard, in-control exterior. But it's never worked with me. I see you for everything you are. Tough and soft. Funny and serious. Smart and goofy." He swipes at his bottom lip with his tongue and adds, "Full of confidence but just as scared."

My breath catches. "Scared of what?"

"Of being vulnerable with someone else."

"Aren't you?" I murmur, my palms suddenly sweaty.

Something flashes on his face, and for a second, I think he's going to change the subject. I wouldn't be offended. I'm not entitled to his answers. He's been very clear about that. Though some questions have been burning a hole in my tongue.

He leans into the chair, knuckles brushing his chin as he stares out the window. "I'm not scared of being vulnerable," he says, his chest rising and falling. "But I'm scared of trusting someone with my heart again. See?" He lets out a humorless chuckle. "We all have our demons."

I push my luck. "Because of Andie?"

Matt runs a hand through his hair. "Yeah," he says in one short exhale. "Because of Andie."

"You don't have to tell me if you don't want to," I offer.

"No, I do. Revisiting that part of my life is not something I particularly enjoy, that's all."

"I get that."

I'm here. You can tell me. I got you.

"I ran into Andie for the first time when she came to visit Pine Falls with a group of friends for a bachelorette weekend. I'd never met someone *so* vibrant. Just a ball of energy. She was only supposed to stay a week, but she fell in love with the town, and… well, with me."

He glances at me, eyes searching. I keep my face neutral, nodding to encourage him to continue.

"Things moved really fast. She only left once to pick up stuff at her place and bring it back to mine, and within two months, we were officially living together. The first few months were great. She got along with my friends, and they loved her. She fit into the cogs of my life effortlessly."

He swallows audibly and shifts in his seat.

"Looking back, I should have been more wary. I should have asked myself more questions. Relationships are never perfect. They aren't meant to be. But ours was, or so I thought. I didn't stop to consider why we never fought, why our lives wove so easily together, when she was a total stranger only a week before we became inseparable. I thought I had hit the jackpot. So much so that after six months, I asked her to marry me."

My heart sinks to my feet.

Marry him. He asked her to marry him.

It was serious, then. I knew it must have been, considering the way everybody and their mother wear pitying looks when they mention her. But I didn't think it was *that* serious. I-want-to-spend-the-rest-of-my-life-with-you serious.

I haven't known Matt for a long time, but still, he doesn't strike me as the kind of guy who'd make rash decisions. But then again, maybe he used to be. And then Andie happened.

"You're very silent," he says, watching me from beneath furrowed brows.

"I'm sorry. I'm processing all this information."

"Don't apologize." Once again, he's angling himself over the table, cradling my hands in his. I like this way better. "Sometimes, when I look back on it, I'm surprised too. I never thought I'd be *that* guy."

"What guy?"

"The guy who'd be reckless enough to ask a girl he's known for two minutes to marry him."

"You're being too hard on yourself," I say, squeezing his fingers. "You went with your gut, and it felt right back then.

Time holds no meaning when you love someone. It can be years or days; it doesn't matter."

I bite back a huff. Look at me rambling on love like I've got a PhD in romance. Like I've ever felt an ounce of what I'm describing.

His mouth quirks up slightly like he knows I'm full of shit.

That's the miserable truth when it comes to my own life. But that doesn't mean I've never witnessed it.

"My parents got married on a whim," I explain. "My mom is from Quebec, but she met my dad while on a business trip to Vancouver. They had the most cliché meet-cute ever. Both were attending conferences in the same hotel on the same day. Him on hotel development, her on cancer patients."

Matt raises a curious brow, but he doesn't interrupt.

"She's an oncology nurse. My father went into the wrong room, where my mother was giving a presentation on the emotional toll of chemo treatment on patients. He stayed until the end so he could buy her a drink after. The rest is history. Not even a year later, my mom was pregnant with me. She uprooted her whole life and moved to BC. They got married, they had me, and voilà."

"That's a sweet story. But I remember you saying they're not together anymore, right?"

I shake my head, brushing my thumb over his. "They're not. But I don't think it has anything to do with how quickly they got married or because they stopped loving each other. They were happy, for the most part, but marriage takes time and effort, and I think my dad loved his legacy more than he ever loved my mom. And at some point, he wasn't enough for her anymore."

"Is that why you're alone? You think you're bound to repeat your father's mistakes?"

Here he goes again, with questions that hit the bull's-eye. "Not by choice, but in the end, it's better this way. I'm not imposing this on anybody."

Matt gives me a lazy smile. "It's a job, Zoey. You're not part of a cult and demanding others join in."

"Kind of feels like one sometimes," I mutter.

"You're so dramatic." He chuckles, but the sound dies quickly, his smile fading as his expression darkens. "If I'm honest, I don't think what Andie and I had was remotely close to your parents' relationship."

"Why did you do it, then? Propose?" I gently rake my nails over the top of his hand.

His eyes flutter closed, and he inhales deeply.

"I don't know. I guess because I believed her. It felt nice to…" He pauses, attention darting away for a second, like he's tasting the word on his tongue. "Lean on someone. Allow her to share the weight I've been carrying by myself, the worries about my business, my parents, my sister. Andie was there. She listened to me. She was just as pissed when my mom took Daph to the movies, knowing she hates loud noises." His shoulders dip as he gives a slow, weary shake. "Rubbed my back after I'd worked late another night, searching for ways to keep my business open after I closed my first year in significant debt. I felt lighter than I had in years. And I think…" He scrubs a hand down his face. "Fuck, I can't believe I'm saying this out loud. I think, now that

I've made it to the other side, I might have liked the feeling more than anything."

Or *anyone*.

I hear the unspoken parts in the spaces between his words. Fragments of him are still scarred. Still healing. And if I wasn't such a chickenshit myself, I would tell him that I wouldn't mind being the one to mend his wounded pieces.

"Maybe she wasn't ready for the commitment," he adds. "But deep down, I don't think she truly loved it here. She liked the idea of living in a slow-moving town, but after a while, it wasn't what she imagined it'd be."

He shrugs, as if it doesn't matter that she quietly unraveled his heart when her rosy expectations didn't meet reality.

I can't help but loathe her for it. You don't get carried away like that with so much on the line. You think it through.

"And instead of being honest with herself and with me," he continues, "she looked for things that'd hurt me. That'd put distance between us."

"Like Daphne."

He nods, his eyes flicking down to where my fingers are still grazing his hand. "Sometimes," he starts, a carefulness in his voice, "I wonder what it'd be like to try again... to get back out there." He peers at me for the briefest moment before his gaze flits away. "I've been thinking about that a lot lately."

My heart picks up its pace, matching the tempo of the rain spattering on the café windows. "You have?"

He locks his eyes on mine, raw intensity smoldering in them and melting me from the inside. "More than I could ever admit. It petrifies me. Some days I want to say fuck it. Most days,

I remember how low I was after the breakup, and it's enough to pin me in place."

He reaches up and gently tucks a lock of damp hair behind my ear. It's such a simple touch, and yet my heart takes off in a way I'm not prepared for. "You're not the only one who's afraid, Zoey," he says, his voice steady.

I swallow, searching his face for any sign of doubt. All I find is the same brutal sincerity he's been offering me since the day we met. I want to believe him. I *need* to believe him.

Am I ready for this? To stand in front of my fears, to let go of the walls I've spent years building?

"I don't know how to do this. I don't know where to begin, how this," I wave a hand between us desperately, "could ever work."

He tightens his hold on my fingers, the warmth of his touch anchoring me. "We don't have to have it all figured out now. We still have time, right?"

The reminder of our looming deadline sends my stomach plummeting to the floor.

Do we? The vote is next week, and then what? If the locals approve my proposal, I'll be around for a while, in and out to oversee the progress. But after that? I'll be appointed CEO, and the sliver of free time I have now will be whittled down to nothing. If I don't get the hotel? Well, why would I stay?

How would any of that be sustainable for either of us? To entertain the possibility of a relationship would only feed our delusions of a positive outcome.

And yet I can't put an end to that possibility. I can't ignore the thread he's been weaving around my heart since I met him. Can't bring myself to sever it.

I peer outside, at the rain that's finally slowing, my mind racing in a hundred directions. But when I look back at him, there's nothing but raw hope in his eyes. And I'm too weak to fight that.

"One day at a time?"

Matt grins, wide and bright, dimples and all. "One day at a time."

Chapter Twenty

Matt

"You know I don't like when you pick me up in that," Daphne complains when she sees the shop van at the back of the school's parking lot. Her nose scrunches up. "It makes the road too bumpy."

"I know. I'm sorry." I wrap my arm around her shoulder. "But I was stuck in the rain all day and didn't have time to run home to get my truck."

She halts, frowning. "Why couldn't you get out of the rain?"

"What? No, I did."

Head tilted, she scrutinizes me in only the way she can. "You said you were *stuck* all day."

Oh. I chuckle. That brain of hers. "No, I meant because it rained so hard. I was at the market in Brookhaven, and I had to wait at Rosie's café until it stopped."

Her brow lifts slightly. "That's why you smell weird."

What? I give my shoulder a quick sniff. Okay, yeah. I stink like a wet dog.

"I didn't realize I smelled that bad," I say, rubbing her back the way she likes.

She wrinkles her nose again. "It's not *that* bad. But next time, could you please shower before you come get me? Now I have to sit next to you in the bumpy van while you smell like soggy cardboard."

Amusement courses through me. "I'll do my best to avoid every single raindrop. How was school today?"

"You can't avoid raindrops," she states, ignoring my question. "You're too big and there are too many. Maybe don't go outside next time."

"Thanks for the advice," I say with a laugh. "You didn't tell me how school was, though."

She groans, flipping her backpack over her shoulder. "Not so fun. We did a lot of math, and I hate math. I need help with my homework."

"Math, huh?" I tap a finger against my chin. "I think I remember how to add and subtract. Maybe even multiply, if you're lucky."

She rolls her eyes. "I know you can do all those things. You do math every day at the store."

Busted. But I love teasing her. "You're getting me confused with Uncle James, honey." I wink. "He's the math wizard."

"If I have to be stuck with you when you stink in your bumpy van for the next thirty minutes," she says, her tone brooking no argument, "you can help me with my homework later."

"Deal," I say, surrendering as we stride across the parking lot. "But only if you promise to stop telling me I stink."

"Fine. But you have to take a shower when we get home."

"It's a deal."

As I slip her backpack from her shoulders, Zoey pushes the passenger door open and steps out.

"Before you hop in my bumpy van," I hedge, "I need to tell you something."

"Did you get photos from Mom and Dad's vacation? Did Dad text you about the flower species he saw?"

I shake my head. Our parents have barely checked in all week. Though last weekend, Dad sent Daphne a photo of several tropical flowers he found. She's been obsessing over them ever since. "No, it's not about Mom and Dad. I brought a friend with me to pick you up today."

Her brows crunch in an adorable frown. "Who? Lola?"

"No, not Lola. Her name is Zoey. That's her." I point in her direction, and she waves. "She dropped pastries off for us the other day, remember? You told her you didn't like her shoes."

"Yes, I remember," Daph nods.

"She gave me a hand at the market today and is helping me out with the store. She's very nice," I add, my heart pounding. "And I believe she's good at math."

By the time the rain cleared, I had no choice but to bring Zoey along with me to pick up Daphne. It should have made me pause, but asking her felt terrifyingly natural. No churn in my stomach. No tension building in my chest like it always does when I introduce people to my sister.

Truth is, I didn't want to leave Zoey's side. Not after we'd poured our hearts out. I could have spent the whole evening talking to her. Or kissing her.

Fuck, that kiss.

My mind will forever recall The Day I Kissed Zoey Delacroix. Kind of like those pivotal events where, decades later, you still remember exactly what happened. A before and an after. A turning point where once you've tipped over to the other side, nothing can ever be the same again.

Kissing Zoey felt like that.

A defining moment in my life.

A permanent mark on my timeline.

I didn't want it to end.

I suppose I could have asked Rosie to take her home when she was done, but I didn't give that option a second's consideration.

For one, I didn't want to repeat my movie-night blunder.

But mostly because I wanted her with me. *Needed* her with me. I can't explain it. I don't understand the feeling myself, but it's too real to deny any longer.

So if we're going to do this right, she needs to meet my sister. We don't have to rush it. A small, no-pressure evening, just the three of us, feels like the perfect place to start.

"Okay," Daphne says. "Is she staying for dinner?"

My throat grows tight. "Only if you want her to."

"I don't mind." She shrugs. "Can I show her my flower encyclopedia?"

"You'll have to ask her, but I'm sure she'd be interested." With a deep breath, I close the space between us and Zoey.

"Hey, Daphne," Zoey says with a small wave. "Did you have a good day?"

My sister studies her, brows furrowed, attention catching on Zoey's damp hair. "Yes. Did you get wet too? Do you smell as bad as my brother?"

Whoa, why am I getting thrown under the bus like that?

Zoey's eyes widen for a second, though she replies quickly. "I did, yes. I think Matt smells worse than me, though, so maybe we should sit in the back together to avoid him."

Daphne giggles. "That would be better, yes."

Damn. It's gonna take my heart a minute to settle every time these two interact. Zoey has an ease I cannot put into words. She just… goes along with whatever my sister says. No overreaction, no outrage or frustration. Daph's comments glide over her as if she's stated she loves her perfume.

A warm flutter fills my chest. I'm not used to *not* having to fight for Daphne.

I grasp the handle of the sliding door and roll my eyes, though I can't help but chuckle. "Okay. Get in before it starts raining again."

Daph clambers into the van, but Zoey hesitates, smiling at me.

"You too." I nod at the open doorway.

"My shoes are ugly and now I smell?" she asks in a teasing whisper. "I'm not optimistic that I'll win your sister over."

I squeeze her hand. "Trust me, you're rocking it. She wouldn't have chosen to sit in the back with you if she wasn't comfortable."

Zoey gives a playful sniff in my direction. "Or you smell terrible."

Grinning, she slips into the back seat.

Bringing a woman home after the Andie nonsense, especially while Daphne is under the same roof, turns out to be more anxiety-inducing than I anticipated.

As soon as I slide the key in the door, my limbs freeze and my throat becomes as narrow as a straw.

Will Zoey care that the TV's on for the next hour? Daph's favorite show is coming up, and there's no way I'm turning it off. And what if Daph gets uncomfortable because Zoey chews with her mouth open? What if she has a meltdown because Zoey uses her heavy blanket on the couch or sits in the spot she's claimed for herself?

Maybe I should have gone over Daphne's main triggers before—

"Are we…. going in?" Daphne asks.

"Y-yes." I clear my throat, giving her a tight smile. "Yes, sorry. Go on."

I unlock the door, and Daphne darts inside, throwing her backpack on the bottom step and running up the stairs to her room. Before I can turn to Zoey, she interlaces her fingers with mine. "You okay?"

I nod. "I think so."

"Thank you for letting me into this part of your life. I know it's a big deal." She smiles, warm and soft. The combination is deadly for my heart, but her words ease my anxious thoughts.

"Come on in." I move out of the way, and as she passes me, I spot the state of the kitchen.

Fuck.

The counters are littered with bowls. A cereal box lies on its side, its contents splattered on the floor. Daph's schoolbooks are stacked beside her hairbrush and the pajamas she left behind this morning. And the sink is full of plates from the last few dinners.

I move around her and use my foot to nudge the cereal into a small pile before she can step in it.

"It's a bit messy. I'm sorry." I swipe two bowls up and send them clattering into the sink with the rest of the plates. "I haven't had time to clean this week."

Zoey puts her hand on my wrist, stopping me before I can go for another armload of dishes. "Matt, it's fine. I don't care."

I come to a halt, studying her face. "You don't?"

"No," she says, chuckling. "You think I expected you to be a neat freak? Please, I saw your office."

"My office is *old*, not dirty."

She pats my arm. "Whatever you want to call it." Her teasing smirk falls quickly. "I know you work all day, then come home and spend the evening taking care of your sister. It's a lot. Give yourself some grace, yeah?"

She scans the kitchen and the living room, where the sofa is buried under a mound of blankets and pillows.

"Daphne loves movie nights," I explain.

"I would too if I was bundled up in all these blankets."

Her words conjure images of the two of us curled up beneath them on an ordinary weeknight, her snug against me.

I exhale, pushing the thought aside.

She continues her curious exploration, and I follow behind her like a puppy, eager to know if she likes what she sees. *If she likes me.*

I want to know what's going through her mind as she gets a glimpse into my life. What makes her chuckle when she picks up the photo of Daph and me dressed as Tarzan and Turk on Halloween five years ago, or why she bites her lip to stifle a laugh when she sees my collection of random rooster memorabilia.

"I didn't peg you for a cock guy," Zoey says, examining a rooster-themed candle.

"I'm not. This is very much a joke between Lola and Charlee."

She turns to me, one brow arched.

I tip my face to the ceiling with a sigh. "When I was young, there was a lost rooster in our garden. I begged my mother to adopt it, but she refused because of her monstrosity."

"Her what?"

"Her cat." I shake my head. "Anyway. I cried for days, and when I told Lola the story, she wanted to make me feel better and got me those figurines in honor of George." I point to a pair on the shelf. "That was the name I gave him. From there, it became a bit of an inside joke between us. After a couple of years, it died down. And then Charlee happened."

Charlee, who thought it was *sooo* funny and teased me about it for weeks.

"Looks more like a cock shrine than a collection at this point," Zoey says as she surveys the second shelf of knickknacks, all "gifts" from Charlee.

"Cocklection," I say flatly, and regret it instantly.

Zoey spins around, eyes wide. Her hand flies to her mouth, shoulders shaking like she's about to explode. "*What?*"

I sigh, internally cursing myself. And Charlee.

"That's what Charlee calls it. My cocklection. All her doing, by the way. She travels so much, and I swear, she finds rooster coasters, salt-and-pepper shakers, and little glass figurines everywhere she goes."

This time, she can't hold it in. Head thrown back, she laughs, loud and bright. The sound, the vision, is like a power surge for my own heart.

"Why don't you… tell her …. to stop?" she asks between bouts of laughter.

"Because Daphne loves it." I shrug. And I secretly do too. Minus the name she's given it. Not that I'd ever admit it to Charlee. She'd never shut up about it. "It's her favorite part of the house."

"That's adorable." Zoey puts the candle down, a smile lingering on her lips, and continues to survey the shelves. "But they're arranged all wrong."

I take a step closer, assessing the setup. "What do you mean? There's no true order. I put them where I have space."

"I see that," she says, her voice trailing. "You should order them by cockiness. Like this one, for example." She picks up the biggest rooster trinket of them all. "This is definitely the cockiest cock. It should go at the top." She moves it to the highest shelf.

"Are you sure that's the one?" I ask, a smirk tugging at my lips when her cheeks catch fire.

"Matt," Daphne calls from the top of the stairs. "Are we eating soon?"

"Once you've washed your face."

She grunts, then shuts the bathroom door with a little too much force.

Zoey's lips twitch. "Does she have a room here?"

I nod. "Upstairs. Next to mine."

"It's great that she has her own space."

"She's over here quite often. I think she prefers it."

Her face softens, her eyes so tender it melts my heart a little further. "Not hard to see why. You've made it so safe for her."

A lump forms in my throat. "I try. She needs it."

Upstairs, the bathroom door creaks open, followed by Daphne's quiet footsteps leading to her bedroom.

"Do you want to take a shower while I make dinner?" I force my voice to sound casual, though I'm not sure I'm pulling it off when the only thought of her naked in my house drives me out of my mind.

Her eyes widen. "You cook?"

"I suggest you get out of your dirty clothes, and that's what you focus on?"

With a tsk, she shakes her head, her hair brushing her shoulders. "Wow, calm down, sir. I kiss you once, and you think it's an open invitation?" She takes a step closer, laying her palm flat on my chest. "Where are your manners?"

I swallow hard. Fuck, I don't know if it's the "sir" or the way she's scolding me so sweetly that turns me on more, but I'm like a dog in front of a treat. I want more. It takes everything in me to keep my cool; her proximity is fucking with my head.

"Just being a good host," I say, voice low but miraculously steady.

Her touch on my chest doesn't help the overwhelming need surging through my extremities and all the way down to my balls. Yeah, I'm royally fucked.

Zoey raises an eyebrow, her mouth quirking at one corner. "I'll take you up on your offer if you don't mind, while you whip us up something fancy."

I blink. "Fancy, huh? And, uh, for educational purposes, what, uh… what do you consider 'fancy'?"

Her hand falls, and she looks up at me, a glint of mischief in her gaze. "You know, five-star Michelin meals. What I eat every day, of course. You *do* have a waiter, right?"

I cough, trying to appear confident, but the reality is, my shirt is probably drenched again, this time from sweat. "Okay, I have to come clean." I glance toward the kitchen. "I don't exactly cook, per se."

"I should have known you were hiding a red flag or two. Here I was thinking I'd finally found myself someone who could rescue me from my home delivery spiral."

Her words have a searing effect on my heart. As if she's marking me as hers in capital letters.

"In my defense, I can heat things up."

That gets the cutest laugh out of her. The sound emboldens me. I need to hear it again.

"My buddy Oliver hooks me up with meals every week. The food at his restaurant is incredible."

She crosses her arms, clearly holding back another laugh. "*Every week?* Okay, no. Second red flag."

"Hey! I'm busy," I say, my face burning. "Don't knock it till you try it." Recovering quickly, I spin and stride to the freezer. There, I pull out a bag and toss it onto the counter. "Dinner is served, milady."

She stifles a giggle, and I mentally high-five. *Another one.* I won't rest till I have them all.

"You're something else, Matt Becker." She walks to the counter. "So. What's on the menu? Microwaved lasagna? You're spoiling me."

I laugh, probably too loud, but I can't help it. That's what she does to me. She puts a fucking smile on my face until my cheeks hurt. God, I don't want it to end.

"Don't worry. It'll be fancy enough for ya." I rip open the bag and dump its contents into a baking dish. "Oliver would kill me if I messed it up. It's not *that* hard. All I have to do is add the ricotta at the end."

Zoey peers over my shoulder, her breath hot on my neck. A moan escapes her mouth, and everything—and I mean *everything*—in me clenches.

"Not to be dramatic," she says, her mouth so damn close to my ear, "but this is my favorite food in the whole universe. I'd die rather than live without it."

I survey the frozen stuffed shells and marinara sauce. "I think the chef does the pesto himself."

As she backs away, she mutters under her breath. The words are unintelligible, but I swear they sounded filthy.

"Let me jump in the shower quickly, then we can get started on those bad boys," she says, already headed for the stairs. Halfway up, she freezes, her teeth sinking into her bottom lip. "Wait, I don't have any spare clothes. Do you have something I can borrow?"

I blink, then internally curse myself for not thinking of that tiny but crucial detail.

Now that you offered her the opportunity to clean up, idiot, you can't unoffer *it.*

As if it's not hard enough keeping my mind from going places it shouldn't when I think about her in the shower.

"I, uh, I have... Let me check." I take the stairs two at a time, my blood running fast in my veins.

In my bedroom, I grab a clean towel, then find a worn T-shirt in the closet and a pair of sweatpants.

"Come here. I think we can work with this," I call.

A moment later, her footsteps echo softly upstairs. "It'll definitely be too big for you," I say when she appears in the doorway, "but it's all I have." Hoarseness coats my words as I toss the clothes onto my bed.

Zoey walks over to the bed, surveying the shirt and sweatpants. "I'm sure I can make it look good." She lifts the shirt to her chest, then turns to me, a teasing tilt of her head. "How do you think it'll look? On me?"

I swallow. Hard.

The image of her in my sweatpants and shirt hits me hard, but honestly, my imagination already went off the rails ten minutes ago when she mentioned wearing something of mine.

"I think it'll look... just right," I manage, my voice tight.

Lie. *Lie, lie, lie*.

She's gonna look fucking delectable. I'll have to tug on the invisible leash clasped to my collar all night to avoid playing out the naughty thoughts swarming me.

"Just right, uh?" she says, her smirk morphing into a full-on smile.

I'm clearly not a good liar and I don't care. Let her see how much I want her.

"I'll be quick." Winking, she turns and sashays into the bathroom.

I swear I'm about to combust from the sight of her swaying hips. I watch her walk away, and I just *know* she knows. She's got me wrapped around her finger.

Once the bathroom door clicks shut behind her, I slump back on my bed and close my eyes, exhaling shakily.

Pull yourself together, asshole. Daphne is right next door. She needs me to be at my best all the time. I can't let myself get swept away like that.

And yet I can't wait for Zoey to come out of the bathroom. I can't wait to see her with her hair wet from the shower. Can't wait to find out how good she'll look in my clothes.

I drag a hand down my face and rub at my clenched jaw. I'm so fucked.

Zoey wasn't lying about stuffed shells being her favorite. Goddamn, did this woman eat tonight. Even Daph, who is a sucker for Oli's food, has never cleaned her plate as well.

She also didn't lie about making my clothes look sinfully good on her. When she came out of the bathroom, barefoot, with my sweatpants rolled at the waist and the ankles, my shirt damp from the tips of her hair, I could have fallen to my knees.

It hit me like a brick to the chest. You'd think it'd be impossible for her to look more beautiful than when she's wearing her pantsuits and high heels, her makeup and hair done, ready to take on the world.

But no.

It's the sight of her in those ridiculously large sweaters that drives me over the edge. And her in *my* oversized shirt? I'm a goner. I'm honestly surprised I haven't burned holes in them with how often I've stared, secretly desperate to rip them off her body or slip my hands under the hem and roam her soft skin.

"Did you know that your name is also the name of a flower?" Daphne asks Zoey, snapping me out of my dangerous spiraling thoughts. She's been firing off questions the whole evening, and Zoey's answered every single one without showing an ounce of irritation.

"I did not," she says, leaning forward. "Which one?"

My sister's face lights up at the question. "Camano Zoe. They're one of the forty-nine species of the genus Dahlia. More specifically, part of the sixth group of dahlias called ball dahlias."

"Are they pretty?"

Daph nods vigorously. "Very. They could easily be confused with mini balls of clouds. And they're groundbreaking for diabetes research because of the high concentration of inulin in their tubers."

"That's fascinating," Zoey says, padding to the sink with her empty glass. "I'm impressed by how much you know about flowers." She smirks at me. "You're putting your brother to shame. You should be the one running his store."

Daphne breaks into a wide smile. "Maybe when he's too old, I can take over."

"Okay, okay." I snort. "Don't bury me yet."

"Is that why you're called Zoey, then?" Daphne asks, ignoring me completely. "Because of the flower?"

Zoey pauses to think. It's adorably cute. The way she so easily humors Daphne with her endless questions warms up a little abandoned corner of my chest. "Hmm, I don't think so, but that would've been fun. My mom is francophone. Do you know what that means?"

"Yes, of course." My sister straightens in her seat. "That she speaks French."

Zoey fills her glass with water. "Exactly. She's from Quebec. She grew up in the francophone part of Montreal. I was born in BC, so I went to English school, but my mom made sure I learned French. She gave me my name so I never forget my roots."

Zoey speaks French. *Cool, cool, cool, cool, cool*. Nothing super sexy about that new tidbit of information. I tuck it away. Later. This is a thought for later.

"Zoey doesn't sound very French." Daphne wrinkles her nose.

I hold back a laugh. She can be so blunt sometimes.

"You're right again," Zoey says as she returns to her seat. "That's because the true way of pronouncing my name is *Zoé*."

I snap my attention to her. "I'm sorry, what?"

"Why don't you pronounce it *Zoé*, then?" My sister frowns. She's not the only one confused as fuck.

"Can we focus for a minute on the fact that I've been calling you by the wrong name this entire time?"

"Calm down." Zoey—or Zoé? *Who knows now*—pats my arm. "It's not a huge deal. Only my mom calls me Zoé. It's not easy to pronounce for English-speaking folks because of the sound that doesn't exist in this language." She shrugs. "I tried to spell it Z-O-E, without an accent, but I ended up being called Zo most of the time. Zoey is easier for everybody."

I stare at her. "I can't believe I didn't know your real name."

She flips her hair off her shoulder, fighting a smile. "You're being dramatic. It's the same name, only pronounced *slightly* differently."

"Still," I mumble.

Daphne doesn't seem to notice my confusion. She's back on her flower tangent. "It would have been very cool if you were named after the Camano Zoe, but it's okay. French origins are pretty cool too."

She bounces in her seat a little. "I have this huge encyclopedia of all my favorite flowers in my room. It's super thick, with pictures and everything. It helps me keep track of them all." She looks at me, questioning, and I nod. She turns back to Zoey, eyes glittering with anticipation. "Wanna see it?"

"Of course," Zoey says, far too eager for someone about to go through a hundred pages of botanical jargon. "Bring it down."

Like a little tornado, my sister dashes upstairs.

I drop the dishes in the sink and round the table. When I get to Zoey, I swivel the stool she's seated on until she's facing me.

My heart is so full it's going to burst into tiny fragments if I don't open the valves at least a little. I run my fingers up her thighs, the cotton of the too-big sweatpants the only thing separating us, and when she parts her legs to make room for me, I let out a shaky breath. At her waist, I bunch the fabric of my shirt in my fists.

"Thank you," I whisper, dropping my forehead against hers. Some of the hair trapped behind my ear falls out and shrouds us in our own bubble.

With her hands on my forearms, she steadies herself against my hold. "Nothing to thank me for."

I twist the shirt in my fists a little more tightly, relishing the way earthy notes of my shampoo infiltrate my nose and spike my dopamine levels. She smells like me, stroking a primal chord deep in my gut. "Not true in the slightest, beautiful."

She shivers. "I love when you call me that."

The instant her admission is out, her breath catches, like she didn't mean to share that with me but the words couldn't be kept a secret any longer.

"It doesn't even come close to doing you justice."

She's just inches away. I could dip a fraction of an inch closer and my lips would be on hers, and—

Rushed footsteps on the stairs startle me, and I ease away from Zoey, putting a healthy distance between us.

"Wait till I show you what I've found on the Cosmos atrosanguineus," Daphne says as she drops the heavy book on the table. "It's gonna *blow* your mind."

For two hours, my sister gives Zoey a masterclass in flowers, their origins, and the symbolism associated with each one. She tells her how they've been used by different civilizations, which ones are becoming extinct, and which new species are emerging. Hell, Zoey is absolutely right. Even I don't know that much about them.

Zoey can't get a word in. At some point, she and I exchange glances. Silently, I ask, "Do you want me to come and save you? Do you need help?"

She responds by smiling in a "don't worry about it" way.

So I stay leaned against the kitchen sink, arms folded tight, like I'm holding myself together, and watch the two of them for the rest of the evening. Daph talks and talks, swaying at times, tapping her fingertips on the table at others.

I have to swallow hard. Once. Twice. Again. Anything to keep my emotions bottled up. Between Mom's unwillingness to understand her own daughter and Andie's insistence on casting her as the villain, it's been a long time since I've seen my sister so comfortable with someone she's just met. And here she is, glowing and laughing with Zoey like she's known her forever.

When Daphne is free to stim and share her passion so openly, without limits or restrictions, that's when she shines the brightest. I would fight the entire world to keep her this happy.

I swallow again, though at this rate, keeping myself under control is a losing battle.

Two weeks ago, I couldn't have imagined that this beautiful woman, who's from a reality so different from ours, would fit into my life so seamlessly.

A tear escapes and rolls down my cheek. Then another. As they melt into my beard, I tear my gaze away.

She has no idea the gift she's giving me tonight. And I don't have the first clue how to repay her. With every day spent with her, a small light grows brighter inside me, like a quiet voice telling me I wouldn't mind trying to do so for the rest of my life. But that feeling is still too fragile, flickering too wildly like a candle flame in the wind, for me to fully embrace just yet.

I sniffle back the tears, reining myself in. At the sound, Zoey looks up from the page Daphne is showing her and meets my eyes.

"You okay?" she mouths, her brows bunched together.

I nod and smile. Of course I'm okay.

I haven't been this okay in years.

Chapter Twenty-One

Zoey

With each passing kilometer, my bones pull inward, unwilling to leave Pine Falls behind.

I dread the moment we cross into Vancouver. Even more so, I dread seeing my dad and my colleagues. Getting sucked into the madness of a job I'm not convinced I want anymore.

But at least I'm not going alone. I've reminded myself the whole ride that this is for Matt, first and foremost.

This weekend, I'm fulfilling my side of the deal.

I've already scheduled a meeting with Corey and Nicole—the two people helping me run the Leading the Future—for this afternoon to discuss getting Daphne's Wildflowers into the mentorship program.

"What are you gonna do with the money if we bring you in?" I ask as we near the city.

Matt glances at Daphne in the mirror, his lips tipping up as he takes in her sleeping form. "Depends on the amount of the check you'll write to me."

He tilts his head toward me and smirks. Then, with one more peek into the mirror, he splays his hand on the curve of my leg. Its warmth radiates through the fabric of my jeans. It feels possessive, the way his big fingers graze my inner thigh, his thumb sweeping at a gentle pace while his attention remains focused on the road, a content smile gracing his lips.

His touch steals my train of thought. My sense of direction. Is this what life with him would be like? Being constantly aware of his need to lay his hands on me every time we're together? Of his craving to keep me close? Would he ever get tired of it?

I shake the thoughts away. "I'm very picky. You're gonna have to impress me."

He throws a devastating grin my way, dimples on full display. "Isn't that what I've been doing?"

"Your efforts have been noted," I say.

"I had to give up an investment opportunity to take care of my sister while my parents are on their anniversary trip," he finally answers, his face flattening out. "I've been working on plans to grow the business for a while now. Not only because I have ambition, but because it won't be sustainable like this for long." He sighs. "The other reason—and the main one—is that if I don't get a serious influx of money soon, I won't be able to pay for Daphne's school."

I gape at his profile. "*You're* paying for her school?"

"I am." His fingers flex around the wheel, his jaw clenched. "Mostly, anyway. My dad is helping, but he's retired. My mom doesn't believe Daphne needs the accommodations and support. The only way I could convince her to let Daph attend is if I promised I'd cover the costs."

A burning heat spreads across my chest, and I grit my teeth. "Your mom should pitch in too. I'm sure it's not easy since your dad is retired, but caring for your sister should be a group effort. You can't take it all on your shoulders."

I wish people didn't have to resort to paying astronomical fees for private school to get the support they need for their neurodivergent children. Where is our public funding? Our public resources?

"She's… trying. She really is." He glances in the mirror again and lowers his voice. "She's part of the generation that doesn't understand why 'kids these days' have all kinds of issues and diagnoses," he says, rolling his eyes.

"The typical 'in my time, they were fine, and now, they're all autistic, and have ADHD. It's called being a kid!' huh?"

Matt laughs softly at my poor imitation of a grandma's voice. "Exactly. She's attributing Daphne's behavior to her being an introverted teenager. A difficult kid who's too focused on the things she loves to care about anything else. She hasn't put any effort into reading about autism. If she had, she'd understand that it's not that, all of a sudden, there's this massive wave of autistic kids. It's about better awareness and recognition. Autism didn't appear out of nowhere like some people would have us believe, as if it's some sort of modern epidemic." He tsks, his fingers drumming on the wheel in an impatient rhythm. "It's always been there. We're only now starting to listen."

"Daphne has been diagnosed, right? She did the tests?"

"Yeah, five years ago. Because I pushed for it. Even though she didn't need to do them. I always had an inkling, but I needed concrete proof if I wanted our mom to believe me." He continues to sweep his thumb softly over my thigh, tethering me to him. Or maybe it's the other way around. Maybe he needs the connection more right now.

"But even when we received the results, she was in denial. She loves Daph—I don't have any doubt about it. But I think she's scared of what having a special needs child means for her and for her daughter. Of the stigma Daphne will face all her life and the difficulties she'll encounter. The inevitable discrimination." He shakes his head. "She thinks that if she acts like her autism doesn't exist, it'll go away. If she continues to treat Daphne as a 'normal' kid, then she won't have to deal with all of this."

I put my hand on top of his. The weight of this must be unbearable to carry alone.

"In a weird, twisted way," he says, his tone full of defeat, "I believe she's trying to protect her."

"Have you broached the topic with her?"

He nods. "My dad has tried too. Though it's been a while. Maybe she'd be more open to discussing it now."

"You know," I say as we cross the Iron Workers Memorial Bridge separating North Vancouver from the city, "when I was studying pediatric nursing, I got to spend an entire semester working with neurodivergent kids. From what I noticed, struggling to understand and accept a child's diagnosis is more common in parents than you might think. And yeah, it can be pretty isolating for kids, but your sister has something many others don't. A great brother like you, Matt. And she has your dad." I squeeze his fingers. "You're going above and beyond for her, and I don't need a fancy university degree to see that she's loved and happy because of you."

He glances at me, his eyes shining. "I wish I could kiss you right now," he whispers.

"I wish you could kiss me too," I murmur back, surprised by how easily the words come out.

In the back seat, Daphne stirs, and instantly, Matt slips out of my grasp and reaches for the steering wheel. The cold that seeps into me lingers in a way I didn't expect. It shouldn't bother me, his restraint around his sister, and yet, unease tugs at me. The logical part of my brain understands that whatever's going on between us isn't a forever thing and that his priority is to protect the person who matters most to him in the world. Daphne has been through enough.

I understand. *I do.* So why am I so butt hurt? Why does it bother me so much that he wants to keep me hidden in the dark?

"Are we almost there?" Daphne asks, her voice heavy with sleep.

"In ten minutes." Matt glances at me. "Are we heading straight to your office afterward?"

"The meeting is at three," I say, picking at my nails. "We have time to get settled first."

The thought of being at the head office makes my stomach churn.

Fingers drumming, he nods. "Good, good, good. Gives me a chance to make myself presentable."

I raise an eyebrow, momentarily forgetting my own worries. "Nervous?"

"A bit, yeah." He blows out a breath. "I'm not used to fancy meetings in fancy clothes in the big city. Not really my scene. You?"

"Yes," I exhale. My old life seems so distant now, and diving back into it is like jumping headfirst into cold water.

I want to reach for him, but I rein in the temptation. Instead, I offer him a smile, the kind he likes so much, hoping it'll ease a few taut muscles. "You're gonna do great. Corey and Nicole are super sweet. You'll see."

We rehearsed last night. I threw all sorts of questions at him. They were tougher than the ones Corey and Nicole will ask, but I want him to be prepared. I briefed him on our very tight interview process and grilled him on numbers and operational capabilities. We went over it for hours. By the time we finished, he could nail every answer and give me precise action items he'd implement.

I can confidently say that Daphne's Wildflowers will be a fantastic addition to our mentorship program.

"And you'll be staying with Daph the whole time?" he asks, his voice laced with concern.

"I'll introduce you to the team and make sure you have everything you need, and then yes. I booked a conference room with comfy couches and told Corey to stock it with the treats she likes."

I turn in my seat and look at Daphne. "We can continue to go over your encyclopedia while we eat chocolates."

"Maybe the South America section?" She asks with a wide grin.

"Absolutely," I reply with the same enthusiasm.

I twist back around and find Matt smiling at me.

If it were just the two of us, I'd cup his face, lean over the console, and kiss him softly on each of his cheeks, then his mouth. When I pulled back, I'd say, "I believe in you." I'd stroke his jaw, giving him back some of the strength he's imbued in me over the past weeks.

But we're not alone.

So I just say, "I believe in you."

And I hope it's enough to make up for all the things I can't do.

Chapter Twenty-Two

Matt

"From what I've heard, they were impressed," Zoey says when we step out onto the sidewalk.

As we walk in the direction of our hotel, I fidget with the tiny button that pinches the skin on my neck.

For fuck's sake. How do men put up with wearing shit like this all day, *every day*? I can't breathe.

"You okay?" Zoey asks, frowning.

"Yeah, sorry. These clothes are just... *so* uncomfortable."

With a frustrated sigh, I rip it off. There.

I can barely walk straight because of how tight the pants are, and the shirt is trying to suffocate me.

"I think you look great," Daphne chimes in behind me.

"Thanks, honey." I force the words out through the tension in my body.

"I agree," Zoey adds. "It brings out your... assets."

Okay, now I laugh. I loosen the tie holding my hair back and shake the strands free. I groan. So much better.

Next to me, Zoey lets out a small whimper.

My gaze darts to hers in time to catch her ogling me for an instant before she shoots her attention to the ground in front of us.

I hide my smirk. "Nicole and Corey were very nice. I think it went well, but they weren't ready to give me a final answer. Told me we'll talk more tonight, once we have drinks in front of us."

Zoey tenses next to me.

"Everything okay?" I ask.

"Yeah, yeah." She sighs. "Not looking forward to it, that's all. It's gonna be packed with people I have to play nice with. The shareholders I need to convince will be there." She hesitates, glancing at me. "It's the company's annual cocktail party, so... my dad will probably be in attendance too."

I swallow, doing my best not to let my hatred for the man show. "Are you gonna be okay?"

Her eyes flash, like she didn't expect my question. "Will you?"

I shrug. "I don't care about the guy."

She flinches, and my heart sinks.

"Sorry."

"I get it. Don't worry."

Things I forget when I'm with Zoey:

- That she is set to inherit one of the largest hotel conglomerates in the world.
- That she is Oscar's daughter.
- That I'm a fleeting moment in her life.

It hits me then, as we walk through the doors of our hotel.

This is her life. This is her world. Those sky-high buildings and busy sidewalks crawling with people and plastics are to her what the cottages and cobblestone streets of Pine Falls are to me.

One day, this thing between us will come to an end. The lodge will be built, and Zoey will leave Pine Falls and find her way back here.

The thought settles into the pit of my stomach and makes me nauseous. Until now, I haven't really considered the possibility of losing her. *Actually* losing her.

But now that I do, it petrifies me.

I was delusional to believe that in any world, this relationship could work long term. That we could date long-distance for a while. That she'd eventually realize she missed her life in Pine Falls too much and that Vancouver isn't where she belongs.

This place isn't right for her. But she doesn't see it.

Since we arrived this morning, she's been nothing but a tight bundle of nerves. Jumpy. Short. A permanent scowl on her face.

Why can't she see what I see? She's *miserable* here.

None of this makes sense, and it's partly my fault. I've been burying reality under layers of denial and delusion.

No matter how hard I try to protect my foolish heart, I always get swept up in my fantasies and give it away to people who are bound to break it.

I never learn.

"You have all you need for tonight?" I ask Daph as I slide my suit jacket on.

She's sprawled on her hotel bed, already in PJs, a bowl of popcorn tucked under her arm. "Yep."

"I'll have my phone with me the whole night, okay? I'm just downstairs."

A knock comes at the door, and on instinct, I peer over my shoulder.

"If you need anything," I say as I move toward the door, "you call me, okay?"

Leaving her alone in the room, even if I'm only several floors down, makes me nervous. I have gone over my mental checklist ten times already, ensuring I haven't forgotten anything (snacks, phone, PJs, heavy blanket), but still, anxiety swarms inside me like thousands of angry hornets. I don't want a repeat of the movie night at the park.

"Yes, Matt," she says, her tone laced with annoyance, her focus still locked on her favorite HGTV show.

With a roll of my eyes, I stride to the door. When I open it, my breath stops short.

"Ready?" Zoey asks, flashing me one of her most beautiful smiles, her lips painted a red I can only describe as sinful.

I take in her black dress. The strapless bodice clings to her skin, shaping her breasts into curves I know fit perfectly in my hands. The slit in the skirt shows off the length of one smooth leg, ending right where I'm dying to slip my fingers.

My throat tightens. I almost choke on my saliva at the sight. God, she's making it very hard right now. Like… *literally*.

She's fucking stunning. A creature from another world.

"You like it?" she says cheekily.

My gaze snaps to her face. "You're fucking beautiful."

She blushes hard. But as her focus drifts, she frowns. "You're not wearing your bow tie?"

"I spent ten minutes wrestling with it before I surrendered." I hold my palms up. "These hands are way too big for fancy stuff."

Her lips part as she studies them. "Does that make me off-limits, then?"

The corner of my mouth twitches. "Absolutely not. You're in a league of your own."

"Well," she rasps. "Let me help you."

I move away from the door to let her in, my eyes following every roll of her hips as she walks in.

"Hey Daphne," she says as she approaches one of the two beds in the room. "Wow, you seem cozy in there. Maybe I should join you instead of going to my boring party."

Daphne slowly turns her head to Zoey, tearing her attention away from the TV reluctantly. "No, thank you. You don't look very comfortable in that. My pajamas are better."

Laughing, Zoey glances at me. "I bet. But since I'm already dressed up, I suppose we should make an appearance. Come here, big boy."

My heart thumps against my sternum. Shit. She shouldn't say stuff like that. Not when it takes every ounce of my resolve not to kiss the lipstick off her lips. Thank god for Daphne. Otherwise, I don't think I would have had the strength to leave this room.

I stand in front of her and crouch a little. In her heels, she has no trouble slipping the bow tie around my neck. As she does, her breasts graze my shirt with the movement, and I clench my fist, grinding my jaw so hard I worry I'll break a tooth.

Don't look down, don't look down, don't look down.

I shoot my eyes up to the ceiling and draw in a sharp breath.

Zoey lifts the collar of my shirt and tucks the bow underneath, her fingers nimble as she twists the fabric, making knots that make no sense to my brain.

"There you go," she says softly as she smooths either side to even it out. She taps my chest with the tips of fingernails painted the same color as her lips. "You cleaned up well too."

"Thank you." I cover her lingering hand with mine and bring it to my mouth, placing a quick kiss on top of it.

I turn around to my sister, who's once again oblivious to everything but the TV. "Daph, we're going downstairs. I'll be back in the room before eleven. Call me if you need me."

She waves me off, popping a piece of popcorn into her mouth.

With a sigh, I grasp Zoey's hand and head for the door. "Come on, beautiful. We don't want to be late for Daddy's party."

From the moment we walked in, the hairs on my arms have prickled with disgust. I feel out of place, out of my depth, out of control.

The hall is swarming with suits and money, people who think they're more important than the rest of the world. Corporate laughs, fake pleasantries, selfish interest; there's nothing genuine about a soul in attendance. Nothing but greed and status. It kills me to have to play that game too.

I lean against the bar, bringing the obscenely expensive glass of champagne to my lips. Zoey is in deep discussion with a group of shareholders—the same people holding her fate in their hands. Would I be a jerk if I admitted that a small part of me hopes they'll vote against her nomination, just so she can finally be free from this hellhole?

Listen to yourself, Matt.

If I were certain this is what she wanted, I'd never stop her. I'd endure a hundred more of these and plaster on my most arrogant smile. But after spending two weeks with her in Pine Falls, I can't believe for a second that she's happy right now.

I check my phone. It's already ten p.m. No calls from Daphne. Did I tell her to lock the door? Shit, I can't remember. Yes. I did. I think I did. I drag a hand down my face. And she had her heavy blanket with her, right? Was her phone charged before we left?

With a sigh, I scold myself silently. She's fine. She'd text if she needed me. One more hour to go, and then we can wrap things up. Tomorrow, we'll be back in Pine Falls.

All night, we've made the rounds. Corey and Nicole bailed last minute—some emergency they had to deal with—which kicked my stress up another notch. They sent a quick apology, promising that they'd be in touch soon, but still. Feels like I came all the way here for nothing.

Between forced pleasantries and small talk, I've shaken more hands than I ever have in my life, and said "nice to meet you" more times than I actually meant it. I've spent 20 percent of my evening nodding and smiling, but the other 80 percent? I've been watching her.

Even now.

I can't take my eyes off her.

All I've wanted to do tonight is kiss her. To drag her into a dark corner of the room and smudge her lipstick with my beard. Get her all over me and not give a single fuck about it.

I tilt my glass against my lips again, downing the rest of the champagne as Zoey walks over to me. She leans against the bar, her arm brushing mine. "Dad incoming, ten o'clock." The words are rushed and whispered, and as they register in my brain, she turns, her spine zipping up straight.

"Hey, Dad!" Her voice is too joyful, too chipper, like it belongs to somebody else.

Oscar embraces her. "Hi, princess. How's the night going so far?"

"It's been a success."

She smiles, but I'm as tuned into her facial cues as I am to Daphne's moods by now. She's putting on a show. It fucking guts me that she can't be herself around her own father.

"Can I introduce you to Matt Becker?" she asks, that bright expression practically painted in place. "He's been helping me get the hotel off the ground in Pine Falls."

Oscar quirks a doubtful brow. "Has he now?"

I hold out my hand. "Your daughter is very good at getting what she wants," I say, hoping it'll give Zoey a break.

Eyes narrowed, he hums and shakes my hand. "Weren't you part of the group that fought against my hotel plans a few years back?"

"I—"

"He's actually working very hard to get the townsfolk on our side," Zoey cuts in. "A great business partner."

Oscar hums again, clearly not convinced.

My stomach sinks. Dammit. Why do I care what this asshole thinks?

"I spoke to Craig and Mark," he tells Zoey. "They said most of the shareholders are reassured about your ability to lead. You handled yourself well tonight, princess."

Her face lights up at her dad's words. I want to punch him for it so badly. She admires him with every fiber of her being, but I know his type. I witnessed him in action in Pine Falls for almost a year when he was trying to seal that resort deal. This interaction? I see it in a matter of seconds. He knows exactly how to keep her under his thumb. He uses praise when it benefits him. When he needs to reel her back in.

It disgusts me.

"Thanks," she says. "The vote is next week. I'm sure I'll have good news to share with you then."

"I don't doubt it." He glances over her shoulder. "Enjoy the rest of the evening, you deserve it. I have a couple more people I need to greet before we wrap this up." He side-eyes me. "It was nice to meet you, Matt. Careful with my daughter, okay?"

Zoey gasps. "Dad."

Oscar chuckles, but his threat still hangs in the air. "I'm joking, princess." He pats his daughter's arm and leans in close, though not close enough to keep his next words from reaching me. "I know you'd never stoop so low."

I take the punch without flinching.

Straightening, he gives me a dark grin. Then he's gone. Next to me, Zoey is frozen.

I wrap my hands around hers, massaging them. "Are you okay?"

She lifts her gaze to mine. "I am *so* sorry." She covers her face, head lowered. "I—I don't know why he said that. That was so insulting. I don't—"

"Hey, hey, Zoé. Listen to me." I grasp her wrists and bring them down gently so she's forced to meet my eye.

The surprise flashing on her face when the sound of her name registers swells my heart with pride.

After she told me I was butchering her name, I spent hours on Google Translate, listening and repeating it until I could pronounce it correctly.

"What your dad says, or what he thinks of me—of us— doesn't mean *anything* to me, you hear me?" I cup her cheeks, not caring for a second that people might see. That her dad might see. Let the fucker choke on his gasp.

"You are all that matters to me. Nobody else in this room. Do you understand?"

She nods between my hands, eyes brimming with a kind of vulnerability I've never seen in her before.

She inhales shakily, her bottom lip trembling. "I understand," she whispers, her voice breaking slightly. "If anything, I'm the one who doesn't deserve you."

The words cut so much deeper than the vicious ones her dad slung. I wish I could wipe away all the hurt, all her doubts. Shut down all the voices that have told her she isn't good enough and make the assholes who are too stupid to cherish her suffer for it.

"You do deserve me." I tuck a lock of hair behind her ear. "More than anyone ever will." Swallowing, I trace her cheekbone with my thumb. "God, I want to kiss you so bad, Zoé. Let me kiss you. Please. It's all I've been thinking about all night."

A tiny moan escapes her lips, and it takes all I have not to dive for her mouth right here and now. Her eyes dart around, scanning the crowd.

"I—" She sucks in a harsh breath. "Not here." Now she's the one gripping my wrists and removing my hands from her face. She laces her fingers with mine and tugs. "Come with me."

I don't blame her for not wanting her dad to see us, but the secrecy still carves a small ache in my chest.

Ignoring the sensation, I follow, letting her guide me through the crowd. There's a new urgency to her movements, a sizzling current running up my arm. Once we're out of the throng of people, she makes a left turn and leads me into a quieter hallway. She doesn't stop until we're standing next to a cleaning cart stationed by the reception desk.

She snags an "out of order" sign from the cart, then drags me along again.

"What are you—"

"Shh." She walks briskly down the corridor, and I trail behind eagerly. She could be bringing me to hell for all I know, and I would gladly follow her through the fire.

She pushes through a door to the left.

"The bathrooms?"

Zoé releases me, and peeks into a few stalls, checking if we've got company. When she finds none, she opens the door and places the sign in front of it.

"There." Grasping the front of my suit jacket, she yanks me flush against her, her back hitting the door, and I have to brace a forearm next to her head to keep from crushing her.

"Kiss me now." Her commanding tone sends a thrill down my spine.

"Yes, ma'am."

I hook my finger under her chin, tilt her face to me, and lean in.

No prelude. No teasing.

Just her need melding with mine.

When I finally touch her lips, I'm home.

She tastes like my favorite things: flowers and sunshine. Or maybe she is my new favorite thing. I claim her mouth, coaxing her lips apart until I can glide my tongue against hers in long, slow strokes.

I grasp her waist, digging my fingers into the fabric of her dress, holding her tight against me.

Nails scraping along the back of my neck, she sighs, melting into me. A shiver ripples through me at the sound, threatening to bring me to my knees.

Her leg bends, sliding against the front of my pants, and my eyes roll to the back of my head. She pushes, putting pressure there, and I grow impossibly harder, a groan escaping me.

Zoé grins into my mouth.

"You proud of yourself?" I ask with a teasing smile.

"Not yet."

She rubs against me again, and I suck in a sharp breath. "You have to stop doing that."

I dip my chin, parting her lips with my tongue.

"Why?" she pants between kisses.

"Because I'm already struggling to control myself," I rasp.

Pulling back, her eyes hooded with lust, she says, "Then don't."

My heart goes into V-fib at her words. Like a switch has been flipped in my brain, her permission releases all the cuffs on my urges.

I capture her mouth again, pinning her between my body and the door, and drag one hand from her hip to where her dress splits.

"This has been driving me mad all night," I breathe. "Do you have any idea how much those legs turn me on? So fucking long and smooth." I dip my head into the hollow of her neck, kissing her collarbone as I toy with the hem of her dress.

When I finally slip my fingers underneath, grazing the fabric of her *very* thin panties, she tilts her face back and lets out a soft, low moan.

"Fuck, Zoé."

She moves her hips, trying to force me to where she needs me the most.

I can't refuse her. I can barely hold myself together. So I sweep my thumb against her underwear. And when I'm met with dampness, I curse against her throat.

She shudders, nails raking my scalp. "Push it aside."

I'm way past that point. Fabric bunched at her hips, I yank hard, her gasp swallowing the sound.

"It was in the way." I slip the torn lace into my front pocket, then quickly find my way back to the precious spot between her legs. When I press my fingers against her center, I let out a strangled breath that ripples over her shoulder.

I forgot how perfect she feels.

The night I met her, I had to force myself to not linger on that feeling, to tune it out. That current in my veins that screamed at me that nothing had ever felt so good or so right.

I'm not resisting it anymore. I'm embracing it now.

With gentle fingers, I part her lips, and once they're coated with her wetness, I move to her clit and rub circles around it.

Head tipped back, she chokes on air and tugs at my hair as I play with the most sensitive part of her.

"I could do this all night, beautiful." I bite her shoulder, then lick the spot where I left my teeth marks. "Stroking you until you can't hold it any longer and come all over my hand." I inhale, kissing my way up her neck until I reach her ear. "I love when you make a mess on me."

She whimpers.

"That sound." I groan. "Do it again."

Fuck, I want more. I slide a finger inside her, then another, and curve them.

Her back arches off the door. "Please, Matt. *Please*."

She grasps my biceps, her nails digging into the fabric of my suit jacket.

"Please what?"

"Make me come," she breathes.

Fuck. I sink my fingers deeper, and she makes it again, that fucking sound that causes every muscle in my body to go taut.

I brush the hair out of her face with my free hand, then cup her jaw, forcing her to look at me.

When her eyelids flutter closed, I tsk.

"Open those eyes for me. I want to watch you when you fall apart."

She obeys, and I quicken my pace, adjusting each motion to the rhythm of her breath catching, to her body tensing against mine.

And then she's there.

She holds my gaze, brows furrowed, lips parted. It's the single hottest thing I've ever seen. With one more pump of my fingers, she grips me hard and soaks my hand, her body writhing under me.

"M-Matt!"

I lean in and cover her mouth with mine, swallowing her cry.

"This is not a soundproof bathroom, Zoé. You have to keep it down."

I kiss her again, softer this time, cushioning her landing as she comes down from the high she's been riding.

Zoé softens against me, her body yielding in my arms. I withdraw my fingers slowly, wet and trembling with her heat, and bring them to her mouth. She parts her lips without a word, and my heart slams against my ribs.

As she twirls her tongue around each of my fingers, sucking and licking them clean, she closes her eyes and hums.

Groaning, I drag the digits out of her mouth and lean in so I can taste her on her lips.

It's a goddamn rookie mistake.

I should have known that her taste would be my undoing.

Hot need coils at the base of my spine, and blood rushes to my cock.

I grit my teeth, inhaling through my nose as I push my orgasm down.

But shit, it's a losing battle.

"Are you okay?" Zoé asks, still panting.

"I can't hold it." I bury my face in her neck. "I'm sorry. I have to—"

The words get trapped in my throat as my balls tighten, begging for release.

I'm shrouded in her scent, her taste on my tongue, on my hand. She's everywhere, yet I still crave more.

Fingers shaking, I fumble with the button and zipper of my pants until I finally pull myself out. Then I reach into my pocket and snatch her underwear.

Wrapping it around my length, I give myself one long stroke. "Let me come, beautiful," I pant, pleading. "Tell me I can come. I can't hold it. I tried but I can't."

Chest heaving, she nods. "You can come, honey."

"Thank fuck." I pump myself twice, hard and fast, and spill everything into the fabric of her panties.

When the spots dotting my vision fade and the tension flees my body, I let out a heavy sigh. "I'm so sorry for those." My head falls against hers, as I use what's left of her underwear to clean up the mess I've made.

"I don't care." She grasps my hand, halting my movement. Inch by inch, she slides against the door until she's crouching in front of me.

"What are you—"

When she flicks out her tongue and licks me, I swallow a strangled sound.

"Fuck, Zoé. You can't—"

She bends lower, running her tongue from the base of my half-hard cock to the tip, where drops of cum remain.

I stifle a moan, already thickening again. "Zoé, s-stop I can't—"

It takes all my self-control to push against the temptation to fuck her right here.

I tear away from her teasing mouth and zip myself back into my pants. Shit, I want her so bad. "I can't fuck you against a bathroom door, beautiful."

She gets up, smoothing her dress around her hips. The move snags my attention, fanning the flames licking up my insides. "Why?"

I let out a humorless laugh. "Because I can't keep fucking you against doors and walls." I inch a step closer, wrapping my arm around her waist. "I want to take my time. I want to taste you properly. Savor everything you give me until I'm not starving anymore. I want to explore you until I can draw maps of your body from memory." I ghost my lips against hers. "Let me fuck you slow and deep for hours and then hold you while you sleep."

The kiss I press to her mouth is full of all the tenderness she deserves. She should always be kissed like this. Like she's someone's most precious treasure. And I would give anything for that someone to be me.

When we break apart, her expression is raw. Yeah, she felt it too. That invisible pull between us is more palpable than ever. That evident truth that I've fought back until now is too strong to be ignored any longer.

I stuff her underwear into my pocket again and survey the slit in her dress. "Are you… are you gonna go back out there like that?" I clear my throat. "I mean… without anything underneath?"

She gives me a grin that screams trouble. "Don't stare at my ass too much, and we should be fine."

"That's a promise I definitely cannot keep."

Chuckling, she brushes her hair back into place and smooths her dress. "How do I look?"

"Beautiful. Like you just had the most earth-shattering orgasm."

She rolls her eyes and swats my chest. "Shut up." She tucks a strand of my hair behind my ear, then adjusts my bow tie.

"How do I look?" I whisper.

"Like you've just had the best orgasm of your whole life."

She opens the door, and I follow her out, biting back a laugh.

Yeah. I really did.

Chapter Twenty-Three

Zoey

"Is this punishment for last weekend?"

Ahead of us, Carl leads the way through the woods, ten third-graders following behind him.

"I take you to the city for two days, and you pay me back with mud and plenty of roots to trip over?"

Matt peers over at me, a smile tugging on his lips. "I like how reasonable you're being about this beginner-friendly, two-hour hike only thirty minutes outside of Pine Falls with a bunch of eight-year-olds."

I hide my amusement in my turtleneck. The truth is, being back here feels right. Vancouver was almost… suffocating. We were gone just over forty-eight hours, and yet when we drove past the Pine Falls welcome sign, relief flooded my system.

I'd completely forgotten that Matt was set to replace Oliver on Carl's monthly hike with the Year threes of Pine Falls School, but when he asked me if I still wanted to tag along, I didn't even hesitate.

Which, first, weird, because hiking and I aren't the best of friends. More like we're total strangers. I've never hiked a day in my life, nor did I own hiking boots until Matt left a cute purple pair on my porch yesterday, along with a bouquet of wildflowers. And second, I've actually been looking forward to today, to being with the kids and Matt while he showed me more about the place he loves so much.

"Jury's still out on the two-hour thing." I jump over a big root running across the path. "My dad used to trick me with phony estimated times when I was younger. 'It won't be more than thirty minutes, princess,'" I say in a deep voice. "Yeah, sure. Then four hours later, I'd still be spinning in a conference chair with my legs and arms dangling."

He laughs softly. "I promise you, Zoé, we'll make it back to the bus in about..." He checks his watch. "An hour and thirty minutes. You'll see. And the view up there will be worth it."

Catching my wrist, he pulls me to him and presses his lips to mine. It's soft, and far too quick. I try to hold him against me a bit longer, but then the kids start to make noises around us.

"*Ew.*"

"Kissing is *so* gross."

"Later," Matt whispers the promise, then turns to the kids. "Get moving, you noisy little monsters."

We resume our walk, Matt never leaving more than a few inches of space between us. He makes it so easy to lose my bearings. To forget that I have responsibilities and a job to do. Every time he comes near me, my body becomes hyperaware of his presence, vibrating with anticipation. Will he touch me? In what way? Kiss me? Hold me close enough for me to feel just how much he'd like me closer? Will he be as desperate as he was in that hotel bathroom, begging me for his own release?

God, it was so hot I almost came a second time at the sound of his plea and a third at the taste of him on my tongue.

Ever since that night, I've been longing for a chance to be alone with him, but his schedule hasn't made it easy. When he's not working at the store, he's looking after his sister, which leaves little room for stolen moments together.

And tomorrow, the people of Pine Falls will vote on my proposal. My stomach twists into a knot. Every hour brings me closer to leaving this town and stepping into my legacy, like a ticking time bomb counting down to its final second.

Plans change. There is more than one way.

"What would happen to Emile's land if the hotel wasn't built?" I ask as we continue our climb.

"Not sure," Matt shrugs. "I haven't heard anything about other projects. Yours is the talk of the town."

My heart pounds in my throat. Words dance on my tongue. Words that have only ever lived in my head, exploring an idea I've never given more than ten seconds before I came here. Lately, though, they've been all I fixate on. They worm their way in without my permission, especially when I find myself dreaming about another life.

"Hypothetically," I say, my voice reedy, "what would you think about me going back to school?"

He arches a brow, assessing me.

I glance away, unable to bear his scrutiny, keeping my focus fixed on the kids trotting in front of us.

"Hypothetically… I think you can do whatever you set your mind to. If you want to go back to school, then that's what you should do."

At thirty-two. After spending most of my career forcing myself to fit the mold my dad shaped for me. Gosh, I feel so stupid for never standing up for myself.

"What about the hotel?" he says, cutting into my thoughts. "And your dad?"

"I don't want to give up on the project," I reply. "I still believe it'd benefit the town and especially the small businesses that would be affiliated. But after the assembly vote this weekend, if it's secured…" I sigh. "I'm not…"

"You're not sure you want to take your father's place," Matt finishes for me.

I nod, startled when his hand brushes mine.

"It's okay, Zoé." He laces our fingers. "You're allowed to want something different. To change your mind. To grow."

The climb is getting steeper, our breathing picking up, and the kids are slowing down.

"Come on, guys," Carl shouts from the front of our group. "We're almost there."

"Am I?" I ask, the words barely audible. "It's always been my father's plan to give me the reins, and he's been wanting to retire for years. I pushed and pushed the deadline until I had no choice but to tell him I was ready."

Matt jogs a couple of feet ahead and helps a girl with pigtails climb a rock in the middle of the path. When I reach him, he holds out his hand. I take it.

"If your father planned his whole retirement around the promise that you'd take over his company," he says, helping me up, "then he's a worse businessman than I thought."

He has the good sense not to add *And I already had a pretty low opinion of him*.

I give him a look and he smirks.

"What I mean is, I can't imagine he'd put all his eggs in your basket. He must have a backup plan. But even if he doesn't, this is *your* future, Zoé. Not his. You didn't choose any of this. If you said no, the company would be fine."

My stomach flips. He's right, but... "I doubt he would ever speak to me again if I gave up now."

Matt scoffs, his fingers tightening around mine. "If that's all it takes for him to shut his own daughter out, then I'm sorry, beautiful, but he doesn't deserve to have you in his life." He shakes his head. "It's a fucking privilege to get to share this life with you." That last part is muttered, but I hear the words perfectly, and my pulse spikes.

In front of us, the kids start shouting.

"We're here!"

"Oh my god, is that my house? It's so tiny from here."

"Matt, come and see!"

"I'll be right there," he calls back.

We climb the few feet left separating us from the rest of the group, and once we're at the top, the sight comes into focus, stealing the air from my lungs.

The thick forest surrounding us throughout the hike clears, leaving us with a breathtaking view of Pine Falls.

I swallow, my eyes stinging from the gusts of wind and the desperate pang growing deep inside me.

It's so obvious to me now. I exhale sharply, angry with myself, drinking in the panorama in front of me.

It's so obvious. The words pound in my head.

And still, it sneaks up on me so fast, as I survey the town from here. It's so small and so peaceful, shrouded in pines and maple trees, tucked away on the mountainside like a beating heart in a sheltering embrace.

This is the place I want to call home.

I've never called anywhere home.

That knowledge sits on my chest, heavier than a rock at the bottom of the ocean.

What am I supposed to do now? Give up what I've spent years working so hard for, sacrificing love, friendships, hobbies, and pieces of myself along the way? Slam the door in my dad's face and turn my back on him, knowing there's a good chance he'll cut me out of his life?

I take a deep breath, the fresh scent of pine and earth filling my lungs and easing my clouded mind. "The University of British Columbia offers some interesting programs," I say, my tone low.

Matt's gaze is riveted on me. Intrigued, scared, wishful. "Yeah?"

Impatient too, by the sound of his voice.

"There's a pediatric nursing graduate course. Half online, half in residence in the hospital of the student's choosing."

The hum vibrating under my skin during the three years I spent studying pediatric nursing has never completely gone away. That rush of fulfillment that welled up inside me every day because I knew I could make a difference in someone's life.

It was all I wanted. Until my father decided otherwise.

But with each day spent in Pine Falls, that humming has been singing louder than ever. I feel it everywhere. Awakening and brewing in places I long ago sealed shut.

Matt's throat works hard, his gaze fixed on Pine Falls beneath us. "Online, huh?"

"Yep." I force my attention to the town too.

"That's... that's good." In my periphery, he nods. He throws a glance my way, but I can't bring myself to look at him. "If that's what you wanna do, I support you. Always."

Finally, I peel my eyes off the view and take him in. The wayward strands of hair floating around his face, the sweat that coats his skin shimmering in the daylight, that easy, lopsided smile that draws me in every time.

But it's his eyes that make my knees do a shaky little dance. The way he's watching me like I just gave him the world. Like I belong to him and nobody else.

My chest warms with tingling sparks.

I like it. I like it a lot.

Matt takes a step closer, twirling a lock of my hair around his finger. "Hypothetically," he whispers. His face softens and my heart follows. "How hypothetical is all of this?"

My eyes flutter shut. "I don't know. I—I'm thinking. I've been doing a lot of that. My head is a mess, Matt. I've never felt pulled in two directions like this before."

Like a tug-of-war between my heart and my mind.

"We'll talk tonight." He scans our surroundings, taking in the kids playing on rocks and running, having sword fights with sticks they've found along the rail. "When it's just the two of us."

I raise an eyebrow. "The two of us?"

"It's Saturday night. Daph is at a friend's house for her weekly sleepover. I thought maybe you could spend the night at my—"

"*Yes.*"

His gaze heats up, and a wry smile dances across his lips. "I can't wait to have you all to myself."

I want that too. In all the ways he can't even picture. The soft ways and the hard ones. I want the vulnerable moments and the unguarded truths. The simple, unfiltered trinkets of our lives woven together.

I want to be his. And that fucking terrifies me.

Chapter Twenty-Four

Zoey

"Will I be treated to your superior defrosting skills again tonight?" I ask, standing in front of his place.

Matt slides the key in the lock. "If reheating food was a sport, I'd be the best and you wouldn't be so smug." The door clicks open, and he turns to me. "Wait here."

Before I have time to ask why, the door shuts in my face. "Okay?"

This is definitely not how I thought the night would start. Though within thirty seconds, Matt is back, one arm behind him.

"Close your eyes," he says as he guides me into the house.

"Why?"

"Zoé."

"Okay, okay," I laugh and obey.

A rustling sound follows as he shifts and places something between us. "Now open them."

The lavender scent hits me before his words do. When I open my eyes, I'm met with a bouquet in the most gorgeous shades of pink. Butterflies flutter in my stomach.

"I've never received this many flowers, except from my mom," I whisper, dipping my nose and inhaling slowly. I don't know what I'm savoring more: the beauty of what this man created, the perfect accord of scents, or the way he always manages to make me feel like I matter more than anybody else.

"My fingers have been itching to make bouquets for you since the day you set foot in my store," he admits. "You get my creative spark going."

I nod to the flowers. "And what do these mean?"

"Roses are the most obvious." He takes a step closer, rotating the bouquet. "They're a sign of affection. Lavender is a promise to always be there to calm you down when you need it. And daisies, my personal favorite..." He removes one stem from the arrangement and sets it gently on the ground. Then he snaps the stalk short and, softly pushing the hair away from my ear, slides the pink flower behind it. "They symbolize new beginnings."

He lingers there, and on instinct, I lean in.

"Is that what we are?" I grip the sides of his shirt, fingers curling into the fabric.

"New beginnings?" He draws me closer.

"Yes," I murmur.

Matt's gaze flickers from my lips to my eyes. He's so close I can feel the warmth radiating from him, the steady beat of his heart, almost in sync with mine.

"You've been my new beginning for longer than you know." His voice is a breath against my skin, sending a shiver down my spine. "I think I was just waiting for the right moment to let myself believe it."

Hands tightening, I tilt my head slightly, drawing him in a little more.

So it's not just me. He feels it too.

That ache stirring deep inside me that roars every time he gets close, every time he touches me, every time he smiles. Hell, even when he looks at me with that smoldering gaze of his. That longing in my bones I cannot shake anymore.

That feeling that he's forever etched into me and me into him.

"You're mine too." The confession tumbles out before I can stop it.

His eyes darken, and the next thing I know, his mouth crashes into mine.

This isn't just a kiss—it never is with him. It's all the hunger we've been holding back, all the words we've been afraid to say.

Every sweep of his tongue is laced with desperation and urgency, as though we've both been holding our breath for too long. Every kiss is a spark, every touch a blaze, kindling a fire deep within me that I can't ignore anymore.

With his hands on my waist, he pulls me flush against him. The world narrows until there's nothing left but the heat of him, the taste of him, the way he fits against me like we were always meant to be this close.

I melt like wax on a flame.

Head tipped farther, I open more. How can I not want more of him at every turn? How can I resist when his mouth moves with a need that matches my own—wild, untamed, as though he's been starving for this, for us?

Heat rushes through me as my fingers entangle in his hair of their own accord. I can't think, can't breathe. There's only him, the pressure of his mouth on mine, the weight of his body, desperate and hungry.

When we finally break apart, our chests heaving, Matt rests his forehead against mine, a steady, teasing smile on his lips. "What do you say we skip dinner and jump straight to dessert?"

I laugh. "That's my favorite part anyway."

"Mine too." His hands flex on my waist. "Come on."

He bends down and picks up the bouquet, then drags me upstairs. In his bedroom, he releases me and fumbles with a small pile of clothing lying on the edge of his bed.

"Sorry about the mess." He throws them onto the chair in one corner.

"I told you already—it's fine." I survey his otherwise very neat room. "Plus, I always expect worse when I date younger boys," I say with a smirk.

"Oh, younger boys, huh? You're two years older, Zoé." He's in front of me in two strides, loose strands of hair framing his beautiful face. His eyes drop to my mouth. "Let's see if you still call me that after you've screamed my name all night."

He presses a thumb to my lips, parting them, his attention locked there. He lingers, not moving an inch, not even taking a breath. He just stares.

"Matt?"

With a jolt, he pulls away. He scrubs a hand down his beard. "I need a minute."

My chest tightens. "What's wrong?"

When he meets my gaze again, his eyes are full of undiluted want. "I can't tell you how many times I've thought about you with me." He nods toward his bed. "It's been a while since I brought a woman up here, and I can't tell you the last time it was a woman I—" He stops short, his features tense.

What was he going to say? *A woman I what?*

"It's a bit overwhelming." He exhales, the sound raw and pained. "I don't know where to start." He takes me in from head to toe. "I always want it all when it comes to you."

I swallow roughly, blood racing in my veins. "We've done this before."

Matt shakes his head. "Not like this. Not with—" He lets out a shuddering breath.

Not with all these feelings that shouldn't exist. I know this one. Because it doesn't make any sense to me either.

"It's okay." I take a step closer, pressing my palm to his torso.

He covers my hand with his, threading our fingers together, before bringing my arm to rest around his neck. "This was never supposed to happen," he murmurs. "You were never supposed to be more than a one-time thing. A business arrangement and then back to our separate lives." He cups my cheek with a tenderness that makes my chest pull tight. "Why did you have to become so damn important to me?"

I rise onto my tiptoes. "Why did you have to be everything I never knew I needed?"

Without another second's hesitation, I kiss him.

And in the instant it takes me to knot my fingers around his neck, his hands are on me, exactly where they should have been all along.

"Get me out of these clothes."

"Gladly."

He doesn't stop kissing me as he pops the button of my pants and shimmies the fabric down my hips. My top goes next. Standing in my bra and underwear, I fumble with the buttons on his shirt. I pull hard on them, trying to force them to snap, but nothing gives.

Impatiently. Matt grasps either side and yanks, sending them flying. "There. Is that what you were trying to do?"

A thrill zips up my spine. "Yes."

With shaky fingers, I slide the fabric down his arms, revealing the defined lines of his biceps, the taut ropes of his forearms, his chiseled frame.

I don't remember lingering long on his chest the first time—not that I had time before he shoved me up against the closest wall—and maybe that wasn't such a bad thing. If I'd gotten this kind of look at the glorious specimen before me, I would have spent weeks daydreaming about his solid arms alone, imagining him out in the forest, chopping wood. The perfect size to encompass me easily. And god, I'm ready for him to do just that.

I drag my focus lower, lingering at his navel. Fuck. I guarantee I would have daydreamed about that path of hair disappearing under his belt too.

"There's no chance I'll last if you continue to eye fuck me like that." His voice is low and ragged, dragging heat up my spine.

He takes his fill, his eyes roaming my body. Every of my nerve ending is begging for him to touch, to stroke, to consume me.

When he finally unhooks my bra and tosses it unceremoniously onto the floor, I moan in relief.

Before the sound has time to die, he cups my breast, full and heavy, in his palm and squeezes. Face buried in my neck, he drops hot kisses below my ear, on my collarbone, my shoulder, until he's right there. He hovers over my hard nipple, his warm breath sending goose bumps rippling over my skin. For a moment, he stays there. As if the bond tugging between us is too much for him, as if he, too, feels the tipping of this unstoppable moment. A before and an after.

But then his mouth is on me, and my mind goes silent.

Back arched, I press myself into his mouth. *More, more, more.*

"I know, beautiful. Fuck, I know."

I'm too lost in the flick of his tongue to even question whether I begged him out loud.

His free hand finds my other breast. He rolls my sensitive peak tight between his fingers, then pinches. I gasp, dizzy.

"Fuck, I want to take my time, but I can't." He slides against my body, kissing his way down my sternum to my belly, until he's on his knees before me. "I fucking can't. Look at you."

Fingers hooked in the waistband of my panties, he gazes up at me in a silent plea. I'm so wound tight, all I can do is nod.

Slowly, he drags my underwear down my legs, his knuckles brushing against me while his mouth creates a path from my thighs to my knees, then my calves.

Once I'm completely naked, he lets out a ragged breath. "Is this real life? How are you real?"

His hands cup the back of my calves and slide up, his calluses rasping against my skin until he grabs a handful of my ass.

On instinct, I sink my fingers into the softness of his hair.

"All I've been thinking about since Vancouver," he says, grazing the tip of his nose against my center, "is how the hell can I get your taste on my tongue again? One taste. That's all it took. One taste and I'm fucking addicted." He opens his mouth and licks me without parting my lips, his tongue flat against me.

I dig my nails deeper into his shoulder, tug harder on his hair. *Fuck.*

"Matt, please."

"I want more," he groans, the guttural sound rumbling from his chest as he forces himself up and sits on the end of the bed.

He spins me between his legs and guides me so I'm straddling him. Cool air grazes my bare skin as I hover a few inches over him.

"What are you doing?" he asks when I don't lower myself to his lap.

"I don't want to stain your pants."

His hold around my waist tightens, and he pushes me down onto his bulge.

A whimper escapes me when I feel the pressure of him between my legs.

"I told you," he grits out. "The messier the better."

Cupping my neck, he closes the distance. His lips are warm and soft against mine, setting a slow, torturous rhythm, one that tells me he would fuck me just like this too.

Meeting his movements, I lose myself in him again, in his taste and in his scent, everything that he is and has become to me.

"Sit on my face," he pants between two flicks of his tongue.

Breath stuttering, I angle back. "What?"

"Sit on my face."

"I—I've never done that," I confess, my cheeks heating.

His eyes soften, though his pupils stay wide with need. With his lips swollen and his hair falling over his shoulders, he looks like a vision pulled straight from my most feverish dreams.

"I'll guide you."

I squirm on his lap, and he stifles a groan.

"Okay," I whisper.

Lying back, he brackets my thighs with his strong hands. "Slide up to me."

I obey. As I shift my way up his body, he clutches my ass, adjusting me as he wiggles further down, positioning himself under me. "Now lower yourself."

"But I'm going to suffocate you."

He grins. "Really hoping you do. Now sit."

His command is clear and sharp, but his voice is the complete opposite. So soft that it loosens all my insecurities and hesitancies.

When I make contact with his beard, his name slips past my lips. At the first brush of his tongue, I forget my own.

It's too much and not enough. It's torture and sweet oblivion. He's in no rush, dragging long, purposeful sweeps over my clit, the pressure swirling and twirling, building like waves low in my belly.

It's embarrassing how close I am already. Instinctively, I start to rock my hips. Small, tentative movements at first, and, *oh fuck*, that feels good.

Matt groans against my flesh, the sound pulsing through my inner thighs, making my muscles clench around him. He digs his fingertips into the globes of my ass, holding me flush against his mouth as he licks and sucks until my legs begin to shake. Gripping a fistful of his hair, I tip my head back and grind against his face, using him to get right where I need to.

A few thrusts of my hips and I'm there. I cry out his name, riding the high on his tongue as he takes every drop I give him.

He eases me off him gently and lays me on my back. "Fuck. I can't get enough of you." He licks his lips as he shifts, then plants kisses on my stomach, on my breasts, on my neck until he hovers over me, need gushing from his gaze. "Can I fuck you now?"

"*Please.*"

He chuckles and brushes hair out of my face. "Give me a sec to grab a condom."

Standing, he unbuttons his pants and shucks them. His boxers and socks too. Far too casually, he saunters to his dresser, like there's nothing more natural to him than being naked while I'm sprawled out on his bed, his sheets around me. The moment is so familiar, so comfortable, yet intimate in a way I always believed only couples who'd been together for years could be. It pulls on all the strings he attached to my heart, the ones that are tightly wrapped around his.

This could be us in twenty years.

"Shit."

I rise up on my elbows. "What?"

He turns to me, holding up a small box. "I might have used the last one when I came to your place the first night you were here."

I groan, falling back against the bed. This can't be happening. I need him inside me. Now.

"I have an IUD. And, uh…" Gosh, I can't believe I'm telling him this. "I've never had sex without a condom. Jake was paranoid and refused to go without one. Still got tested after he and I split, but… yeah. I'm clear."

"Are you…?" Matt rubs a hand down his face and swallows tightly. "Zoé, wait." He drops the empty box and scrambles onto the bed. "Are you sure?"

Heart hammering, I nod. "I need you, Matt. *Please.* I've never needed anybody so much in my life." I can't help but zero in on where he's big and hard and so ready to push into me. "Please, honey."

He exhales a sharp breath. "Fuck, you make me so weak when you beg. I haven't been with anybody in a while either, and I did all the tests at my last check-up, so I'm good."

"Perfect, then." I wind my arms around his neck and bring him over me, moaning when the weight of his body crushes into mine.

With one hand wrapped around his length, he guides himself to my entrance.

"Shit, Zoé," he pants into my neck as he eases into me in small pushes, giving me time to adjust between them. "You feel too fucking good."

As the last word leaves him, he sinks deeper, filling every inch of me.

I choke out a gasp.

He stills above me and pulls back a fraction. "Are you okay?"

"Don't stop." I roll my hips, desperate to relieve the ache building in my lower belly.

I'm so full, and yet he's not close enough. It's like we've never fucked before. Like *I've* never fucked. In so many ways, this feels brand new.

Matt moves above me in a lazy rhythm, pushing slow and deep with each thrust. He murmurs sweet things against my lips, words he's never said out loud before—*I need you, stay with me, you're perfect for me.* Does he realize the secrets he's revealing so openly? Either way, I tuck them somewhere safe, collecting them like rare treasures for when I'll need them again.

His back-and-forth motion intensifies, his thighs nudging mine wider apart as he works himself to the hilt, hitting that perfect spot deep inside me.

"I'm so close, honey," I whimper, planting my nails in his arms.

Breathing ragged, he grasps my hips with more force, pressing into me, faster, harder. "I'm right there with you. Let me feel it. Let me have it."

The sound of his voice, so raw, so desperate, brings me even closer to the precipice, and I tighten around him.

He lets out a grunt, his movements rougher. "Give me one more, beautiful. I know you can give me one more."

Head lowered, he covers my nipple with his wet mouth and sucks hard.

I don't stand a chance. Pleasure slams into me, stealing the air in my lungs as I'm pushed over the edge. I arch into him, into his mouth still clamped around my breast, into his hands as he holds me tightly to him, until my orgasm rolls over me in endless, delicious waves.

As my body goes limp, Matt's movements grow jerkier, taut and short and so fucking perfect, sending my pleasure soaring again. He spills himself inside me with a shuddering groan that feeds my wildest fantasies. I'll replay that sound over and over in my mind for years to come.

With a sigh, his shoulders relax, and he rolls onto his side, tugging me with him.

"We're a mess," I say, plucking away a strand of hair sticking to his cheek.

"Just how I like it," he breathes, lowering his lips to mine. Even in this moment, he can't help himself.

What starts as a soft, gentle kiss turns electric. He moves his hand to my neck, pressing his thumb beneath my chin and sliding his tongue along mine in a burning, irresistible demand.

"Maybe we should get something to eat," I chuckle.

"Good call. I'm still hungry."

He crawls back over me, and I tangle my fingers in his hair, elation bubbling up inside me. "Not like that. A *real* meal."

"Fine." He flops back next to me in defeat. "I can offer you frozen pizza or frozen meatballs."

"A man of many talents."

He pinches my side, and I buckle my knees to my chest, giggling.

His face turns from amused to adoring between one heartbeat and the next. "That sound. Your laugh might be my favorite sound in the entire world. That should say a lot, considering you came twice tonight, both times with my name on your lips." He wraps a hand around my waist and drags me on top of him. "Do you know why?"

I rest my chin on his chest, peering up at him. "Why?"

"Because you reserve those just for me. Every time you laugh like that, I feel like the luckiest guy on earth." He pokes at the dimple in my cheek with one finger. "You put up a front for the rest of the world. You don't show them how extraordinary you are. The real you. But for some reason, you let me see it all." He strokes my cheek with his thumb, his other hand splayed over the small of my back. "The most tender sides of you. The most vulnerable ones. And those fucking beautiful smiles. I don't know what I did to deserve it, why you chose me of all people to open up to like this, but I swear to you, beautiful, I will never take this for granted. Not for one second. I'll spend every waking moment working to earn more of that laughter."

My heart picks up its pace, matching the way his thuds against my arms. "You talk like we have an infinite number of days ahead of us," I whisper.

"Don't we? Come on, Zoé—" He scrambles to sit up without releasing me. "Don't we?" he asks again as he guides me to straddle him. "Tell me you're not thinking of staying. Tell me I'm wrong." His fingers tighten on my waist on the last word, as if he can't accept the opposite. Can't bear to consider it.

His eyes search mine, pleading and full of hope. Yet, he knows the answer.

I tuck his hair behind his ear, then scrape my nails against his scalp lightly, relishing the way he twitches between my legs.

"Of course I'm thinking about it. I picture myself here every minute of every day." I tilt his face to mine. "But I have so much resting on my shoulders. And I don't know how to deal with all of it."

He presses a hand to my heart. "What does it say here?"

I bite my lip, knowing how much he will hate my next words. "My heart isn't the problem."

Or maybe it is, because without it, I wouldn't be in this mess.

His brow furrows. "What about that program you brought up today? Isn't it something you want to explore?"

I roll off his lap and wrap myself in his sheets, covering my body and my fears.

This is all too much. I feel backed into a corner, like a stray cat that's spent too many years roaming the streets to understand what's best for its own good. That's the downside of letting someone in, isn't it? I've given him the power to force me to face my truths.

"It's a possibility. I'd love to do it. I just don't know how to work it out with the company. With my dad."

I'm fucking scared. I need you to understand, please. This is a risk I never thought I'd consider taking before I met you. You make me want to be myself, and the consequences terrify me.

"You'll always be caught in the middle, Zoé," he says, voice thick. "And I can't put my heart on the line for someone who isn't sure whether she wants to stay."

"Why do you care so much?" I burst out.

A flicker of shock crosses his face. I can't blame him. My words catch me off guard too.

I lower my head. "Why does it matter so much if I stay or if I go back to my old life?"

He reels back, and instantly, my stomach sinks.

It was such a stupid thing to say. I didn't mean any of it, yet I used his insecurities against him. Played on his trauma, stomped on the tidbits of his heart he shared with me, hoping I'd keep them safe.

He looks down, a frustrated sigh escaping him. "How does it not matter to you? How can it *not*? Is it all in my head?" His words are like shrapnel, each one tearing through me. "Am I the only one who can't sleep at night because I toss and turn, thinking of you? Unable to focus because you consume me? Am I the only one whose pulse picks up every time a text notification comes through, who smiles like an idiot at every message? I care so fucking much if you go back because if you do, you're not here. With me. Making my life brighter in a thousand different ways. Because if you go, some piece of my heart goes with you, and it'll be so much harder to live. Because I—I—"

He stumbles over the words, surprise flickering on his face. Then he clamps his mouth shut, his eyes following closely behind, and sighs.

My heart lurches. *Because I what? Tell me. Tell me something I've never felt before. Something I've dreamed you might feel for me.*

"You what?" I plead.

He holds my gaze. "I… like you."

I scoff, his answer landing with a thud. "I told you I have a lot of baggage," I manage, though my voice wavers. "I told you my job was my life."

"Everybody has baggage, Zoé," he says, barely getting the words out. "It's called *living.* You think I don't have my own? Of course I do. Doesn't mean you have to shut yourself off from the person *begging* to help shoulder the load."

"I don't know how to do that," I breathe out.

"Let me show you." He cups my face with desperate fingers, forcing me to look at him. "Let me be here for you. *Please.*"

I swallow, restlessness growing inside me. I don't know how to do that. I want to scream, because the only person who's been here for me my entire life is *me.* I don't know how to let anyone else do that.

I don't know what it means. I don't know where to start. I don't—

I don't know.

"Zoé, hey." Matt grasps my fists, loosening my fingers. "Breathe. Come here."

He wraps one arm around my waist and tugs me to him, his front flush with my back.

"You're okay," he murmurs, brushing my hair in a way that soothes my very soul. Without releasing me, he draws the covers over us, tucking us away from the rest of the world, and curls around me until all of him is pressed against all of me.

"I'm terrified I'll lose everything," I confess into the crook of his arm. The life I've built, my career, my dad. *Him*. I don't know how to articulate all of it without having a full meltdown.

His hold on me tightens. "I get it. You're scared. But I'm here, and that will never change." For a moment, he's silent. Just as I consider breaking the tension, he speaks again. "Do you know when people say 'If you have no fans, it means I'm dead'?"

"Yeah?"

"Same sentiment applies here." He kisses the slope of my neck. "If you've lost everything, it means I'm dead."

I melt further into his embrace. The words settle my heart and clear my mind. Each sweep of his thumb across my belly quiets my frazzled nerves a little more.

We stay silent like this for minutes and then maybe hours. I lose count. His breathing slows and grows deeper, steadier.

When I'm certain he's asleep, I shift and face him, softly brushing the tip of my finger over the lines of his cheekbone. The ridge of his nose, the contour of his mouth, the sharp edges of his jaw.

Bravery overtakes me. Or maybe waiting until he's asleep makes me a coward. Either way, I lick my lips and whisper, "I've been alone for so long. It seems impossible sometimes to picture a life where I'm not. Where I'm happy. Where I do what I love. Where I can truly be myself. The price always seemed too high to pay." I press a featherlight kiss on his lips. "It isn't with you. Losing you would be so much worse."

His breath hitches, and for a second, I hold mine, heart pounding in my ribcage. One, two, three seconds pass. The rise and fall of his chest steadies.

With a relieved sigh, I nuzzle into him and close my eyes.

But then he presses his mouth against my forehead.

"You're not alone anymore, beautiful. I'm your support system now."

Chapter Twenty-Five

Zoey

Convincing, charming, engaging, striking deals. All the effort I've put into the past three weeks boils down to this. The assembly vote.

Don't forget all the kissing and fucking too.

I flush hard as I tuck a cream knit sweater into a black suede miniskirt, peering at the closed bathroom door where Matt is showering.

Daphne called to ask Matt if she could go to the botanical garden with her friend today. It took approximately half a second for him to agree and organize plans to pick her up tonight instead of this morning. Then the man was back between my legs just in time for breakfast.

By noon, he was actually starving for real food, so we took a break to visit Rosie at the café and check in on the town before tonight's vote. I left feeling more optimistic than I have since I arrived, though I have a suspicion it has a lot to do with the tall, long-haired guy who never let go of my hand as we strolled through town.

The afternoon was filled with activities similar to those of our morning. Matt took it slow, his movements unhurried as he mapped my body with his tongue. Then he dragged me to his shower and pinned me against the tiled wall. Before he left to pick up Daphne, he brewed a pot of coffee and sipped his while I went down on my knees for a treat.

Overall, a very busy day.

"I don't need to dress up, right?" he calls from the bathroom. "Can I stick to a shirt and jeans? Nobody will be looking at me anyway. You're the star tonight."

"Why are you asking me? It's your town."

He comes out, a towel wrapped around his waist, his chest still dripping wet.

I stare. I might even drool a little.

He rounds me, dropping a kiss to the slope of my neck. "Just making sure you weren't expecting me to look as good as you do. Because that's impossible." He takes my hand and retreats a step, giving me a little spin, making my skirt lift softly around me. "Fuck me, you're a goddamn dream."

He pulls me to him, or maybe he's pulling me in. I'm not sure anymore. Sometimes I can't tell where his craving ends and mine begins.

With a hand molded to my waist, his mouth moves over mine. I might have protested and pushed him away if I'd already applied lipstick, but something told me to wait until the last minute to do that.

"Matt." I dig my nails into his biceps, trying to extricate myself.

He only kisses me harder, tipping me back as he slips his fingers under my miniskirt and grazes my ass.

When he flattens both hands on my cheeks and squeezes, I bite my bottom lip to keep from moaning.

"Honey, hold on," I force out, each word breathy.

The phrase sounded much more firm in my mind.

God, I'm so weak.

"I really like that skirt."

I could have guessed by the way he grows hard against my belly.

"Your sister could walk in on us at any time. And we have to go."

With a groan, he gives my ass a cheeky slap. Then he takes an exaggerated step back. "You're not playing fair. At all."

"I was told I should charm the people of this town."

He steps into his underwear and slides them up. "You can cross that off your list. You've got everybody wrapped around your finger."

I roll out my lipstick and shuffle to the mirror so I can apply it. "We'll see."

"Damn, the place is full." I scan the faces in the crowd. So many are now familiar to me, which is a weird concept, considering that after ten years, I still don't know my own neighbors in Vancouver. "Daph, you might want to put your headphones on now."

I wipe the sweat off my hands. If Matt gave me my water bottle right now, it would slip straight to the floor.

Matt waves at Mia, who's twisted in her seat next to Rosie, wearing a wide grin. I can't decide whether her smile soothes or spikes my nerves. The expectation shining there settles heavy in my gut.

"Is that a good sign?" I ask, voice tight.

Matt lifts an eyebrow, his mouth kicking upward. "It's a lot of people, but if they're here, it means they're interested, right?"

"Or they strongly oppose the project and are ready to riot," I mumble.

"I swear I didn't put them up to it this time," he says, wiggling his eyebrows.

It takes everything in me not to roll my eyes. "You think it's smart to remind me right now that you're the one who started this?"

He angles in, his lips brushing my ear. "Anything to get you to relax."

As he straightens, a dark-haired woman with tattoos covering her right arm appears behind him.

"Hey, Lols."

Oh, right. His friend Lola, from the bookstore. The one who gave me the smutty book that had me wishing Matt would do to me what Jason did to Delia in chapter fourteen.

"Where have you been?" She hugs him, then Daphne, before pulling me close too. "You disappeared from the face of the earth."

"That might have been my fault." Cringing, I raise a hand. "I took him to Vancouver for a weekend, and I've been keeping him busy since."

Lola's eyes dance, and I wish the floor would open up and swallow me whole. I did *not* mean to make it sound as racy as it did.

"I'm glad my book recommendations gave you a few ideas." She waves her fingers in front of us. "Whatever this is, I ship."

"God, Lols, shut up," Matt groans. "Where is James?"

She nods to her left. "Over there. Saved you a seat." She turns to me. "Knock them dead, okay?"

"Thanks," I say, lips stretching into a tight smile, nerves once again overtaking me.

"Give me two minutes," Matt tells her. "I'll be right over." He nudges his sister, who's now wearing her headphones. "Daph, go sit with Lola and James."

With a wave, they're off.

Matt waits until his sister has her nose buried in her book before he turns to me and takes my hands. "Your palms are sweaty."

"I *know*. I hate it." Leg bouncing, I slip out of his grasp.

With a tsk, he snatches my hands again, this time holding them tighter. "You know a little wetness doesn't bother me, beautiful." He smirks. "Quite the opposite, actually."

I make a face. "If you're trying to turn me on *right now*, it's not working."

That's a lie. Only because it reminds me of how he made me soak his sheets using two fingers this morning.

I fill my lungs with air and exhale shakily, focusing on the way he massages the back of my hands with his thumbs.

I can do this. I will succeed. And my dad will finally be able to say how proud he is of his only daughter.

"Don't overthink it, Zoé," Matt says softly, a phantom caress against my heart. "And if you feel yourself slipping, remember: whatever the outcome, you did your best, and that's all that matters."

I nod.

He and my dad couldn't be more different. All my life, I've been pushed to do more. No matter how well I do, my best has never been good enough. What matters to him is winning. Being on top. Losing is for those who don't put in the hard work.

But Matt sees me for who I am first. In his eyes, my successes and failures don't define me. To him, they're experiences that help me grow.

"I needed this more than you know."

"Are you sure? You don't have a lot of secrets to hide from me anymore."

My next words barrel through me at the speed of a bullet, and there's nothing I can do to stop them. "I like you a lot, Matt."

His eyes shine, full of warmth. "I like you more."

"If you'd all take your seats," Rob says into the mic, startling us. "We'll start the meeting."

There's a low hum in the room as people grab snacks and drinks and get settled.

"Good luck." Matt bends and places a soft kiss on my cheek that makes me wish for a hundred more.

Then he's gone, taking his seat next to his sister.

"First item on the agenda: Emile's land," Rob says. "In accordance with his will, we'll need a majority vote to determine the use of this plot." He motions for me to come over. "As of tonight, only one proposal has been submitted. Miss Delacroix, whom I'm sure you all know by now, presented her lodge project three weeks ago. Zoey, you're welcome to say a few words before we move on to the vote."

I square my shoulders, releasing a sharp breath, then walk to the podium. These folks aren't strangers now. They're my neighbors, my friends, people I've come to know and care about. And yet, as I step onto the stage, their scrutiny is palpable, and the pressure reaches a fever pitch.

Not because of the uncertainty of the votes. No, the anxiety stems from the fear of disappointing them.

"Thanks, Robert." I adjust the mic. "Hi, everyone. Thank you so much for coming in such large numbers this evening."

A man cheers loudly. I recognize the voice immediately. As I home in on him, Matt straightens in his seat, beaming from ear to ear.

"Thank you for the enthusiasm, Matt." I bite back a smile.

As a chuckle rolls over the room, I unfold a piece of paper with trembling fingers and work to decipher the notes I scribbled messily on it.

"The uniqueness of Pine Falls must be maintained and highlighted, not altered or torn down. How can a hotel blend into your way of doing things while also serving you? How can we leverage your town's appeal in a way that not only works for you but also benefits you, while providing a new experience for tourists?"

Cooper sneaks into the room and winks at me as he slips into one of the few remaining seats beside Carl and his wife.

I scan the notes I jotted down a few weeks ago in preparation for the night, my throat tightening. It doesn't feel right anymore. Those people deserve better than an empty speech I put together before I knew any of them.

I fold the paper and slide it into my skirt pocket, then lean on the stand, inhaling deeply.

"Forget my big talk. By now, you've all probably made your decision. The reality is, I've spent the last three weeks getting to know most of you. With Matt, I've kinda had a crash course in all things Pine Falls. I've seen what makes this town so special, and I recognize the preciousness of its way of life. When I first came here, I had every intention of doing things differently from my father, but I don't think I understood how far off the mark he was."

I glance at Rosie and Mia in the front row, nerves stirring in my belly.

"You're doing great," Rosie mouths.

"I've grown attached to this town, its people." I can't help but look at Matt, a flutter rising in my chest. "I like everything about it. Your generosity, your kindness, your patience. Your steadfast support. It's changed me for the better. You've swept me away with your intensity and passion, and you've made me feel *so good*."

Matt's eyebrows shoot up, his lips curving into that signature half smile that never fails to send a rush of heat to my cheeks.

My pulse skips.

Wait, what?

I replay the last part of that statement, and the blood drains from my face.

A low murmur erupts, spreading through the rows like ripples on water. People shift, glancing at each other, then at Matt.

"No, I—I didn't mean… that's not—" *Stop stuttering, you idiot, and focus.*

I clear my throat, locking in on the doors at the far end of the room, my whole body burning in an inferno of embarrassment. "*People* have been so welcoming to me, and I'm in good hands. That's what I meant."

A man in the back says, "Yeah, you are," while another shouts, "Score, Matt!" Then, like cascading dominoes, the entire room bursts into laughter.

My cheeks burn. What I'd give to crawl beneath the floorboards and disappear forever.

Not on my to-do list today? Telling the whole town how well Matt gets me off.

"All right," Rob says, coming up beside me. "Decorum, please." He offers me a sympathetic smile. "Thanks, Zoey. That was very… informative."

I rush down the stairs and take a seat next to the stage.

"As usual," he continues, "raise your hand if you're in favor of the hotel project. Keep your hand down if you're against it."

My heart hammers in my chest, drowning out all the noise. "All in favor?"

I close my eyes. I can't look.

"All against?"

I hold my breath.

"All right. With forty-six *yes*es and three *no*s, the hotel project on Emile's land is approved."

My heart drops to the floor.

I did it. I can't believe I fucking did it.

Strong arms lift me, and I'm yanked into a hard chest. I'd recognize his scent anywhere.

"I *knew* you'd pull it off," Matt says, his voice muffled by my hair. "I'm so proud of you, beautiful."

I cling to him. I can't find it in myself to care that his sister, his friends, and just about every member of this community are watching us. Not when the clarity that washes over me as he cups my face and tilts me to him is more powerful than any rational reasons.

It doesn't sneak up on me this time. Deep down, I always knew we'd end up there. Instead, it slowly settles into my bones, taking root in my chest and spreading like vines everywhere his mouth has touched, his fingers have skimmed, his body has embraced, blooming quietly beneath my skin until I can't deny the truth any longer.

"I don't want to leave." I grip his shirt like it's the only thing keeping me upright. "I don't want to leave."

"Then don't," he breathes. "Fucking stay with me. Do I need to get on my knees and beg?" He cradles my face, his thumb pushing my lips open. "Because I will do it right here if that's what it'll take." His eyes travel between mine, agony dawning in them as the seconds tick by. "Do you need me to say it now, Zoé? Are we finally at the point where we stop lying to ourselves and to each other?"

The words burst out of me. "*I love you.*"

Relief softens his whole face. "Fuck, I love you too."

His mouth crashes into mine, kissing, nipping, licking, his tongue slipping in to taste me. My hand flattens on his lower back, fingers splaying in a possessive touch as I draw him closer.

My heart races like it's trying to catch up with his.

He loves me.

Kissing him eases an ache inside me but ignites everything else. It sets me on fire after the relief of his touch. It's a never-ending, soothing, scorching pleasure. One I'm perfectly content to endure for the rest of my life.

He loves me.

He releases me, panting and laughing breathlessly. I want to capture his magnetic joy so I can show him how easy it is to love him. Keep some for myself when I need brighter days.

"See? That's the intensity I was talking about earlier," I tease. "In case you weren't sure, I was talking about you up there."

He rests his forehead on mine, a smug grin plastered on his face. "Oh, it was *very* clear. For everybody. Thank you for the ego boost, by the way."

"Don't let it go to your head."

"Too late for that." He slips his hands into his pockets and rocks back on his heels. "Patty already stopped me on my way to you and made a move."

I roll my eyes. "Of course she did. What did you say?"

He leans in, his nose scraping my cheek. "Told her I was taken by the smoke show over here."

"That's right." I wind my fingers in his hair and brush my lips against his.

When he lets out a strangled groan in response, I beam with satisfaction.

"Matt?"

Matt freezes against me, his body going rigid.

Dread washes over me instantly. What. What is it?

He turns toward the feminine voice, his face falling. "*Mom?*"

"Dad broke his foot while you were on a stopover in Anchorage, and you had to be flown back to Vancouver?" Matt summarizes his mother's long story as he places cups of coffee in front of his parents.

"Does it hurt?" Daphne asks.

"It's better now that the doctors have given me a brace," Mr. Becker replies, pulling up his pant leg to show his daughter.

Matt's mother—she told me to call her Deb—hasn't taken her eyes off me since we left the town hall. Her scrutiny is palpable, and I get it. I was glued to her son's face when she met me for the first time. Great way to introduce myself, that's for sure.

Hi. Yes, Mrs. Becker, just a second. Let me remove my tongue from your son's mouth. There. Very nice to meet you.

"You finally listened to your mother, I see," his mom says.

Matt drawls out a low "*Mom.*"

"What? I'm glad you met someone." She turns to me, her smile pleasant. "It's been so long since his last girlfriend. I thought I'd never get grandkids."

Mr. Becker coughs into his coffee cup.

Oh, shit. Okay. No "What is it that you do?" or "How did you guys meet?" or even "What's your name?" Straight to my uterus and assessing my procreation capabilities, I see.

"Whoa, Mom, hey. This is inappropriate on so many levels. Please don't say stuff like that."

"It's fine." I lay a hand on Matt's arm—to his mom's utter delight. "Although we're nowhere near that, Deborah."

"I told you, it's Deb. And this is Paul."

Matt's dad gives me a playful salute, and I chuckle.

"So how was it, Daph, with your brother?" Paul asks. "Do you want to come back with us, or is it better at his place?"

"It was cool. But Matt is my brother, not my parents, and most of my stuff is here."

Paul smiles softly. "I know, sweetie. I was teasing you."

"Oh." She blinks. "Well, you know…"

Her voice fades into the background. All of them do.

Being at Matt's parents', in his childhood home, is so strange. But even stranger? Being surrounded by a family in the truest sense of the word.

I watch them as they laugh and talk, Matt and Daphne filling their parents in on the new school, their parents sharing vacation stories. There's such a familiarity between them, an easiness that makes *me* uneasy. It's Deb laying a hand on Matt's bicep as he tells her about Cooper's fundraiser and the show he gave on stage. It's Matt wrapping his arm around his sister's shoulder as she explains her latest art project in school to their dad.

The love they have for each other is potent, almost tangible. I feel it in the way Paul angles his body toward his daughter because he missed her and in how Matt constantly glances at his mom, ensuring he's right beside her if she needs any help.

And I stand there, on the outside looking in, as the fantasy plays out. A life I've never lived myself but always craved, one foot grazing the threshold of the door.

"Zoé?"

Matt's voice pulls me back to the kitchen. "Hmm?"

"I'm gonna help my dad get their things out of the car. You okay here?" He rubs my upper arms in a reassuring pattern.

I smile. "Yes. Don't worry about me."

He glances at his mom, then ducks in close to me. "Call me if you need me, okay?"

"I'll be fine," I insist, patting his arm before he strides away. "Where is Daphne?" I ask Deb as I sit down on one of the kitchen chairs.

"Oh, she went back to her room," she says, waving vaguely toward the hallway. "She's such an introverted kid. I can't keep her here with me for more than five minutes."

"She's been away from home for a while now. I'm sure she missed her space and needs a moment to get her bearings."

Deb shakes her head, her curls bouncing. Her hair is the same shade as Matt's, though time has threaded hers with silver. With a sigh, she drops into the chair next to me. "I wish she wasn't so difficult to handle. I'd worry less."

Rather than let her words rankle me, I pause, collecting myself, remembering all the times Matt has mentioned this type of comment from her. "For what it's worth," I start gently, "Daphne was an absolute gem while you guys were gone."

Would Matt be upset if I went down that road? It's none of my business, really. But she's giving me the perfect opportunity. And I can't ignore it, right? It's for Daphne's well-being. Matt would do the same.

"We even took her to Vancouver for a weekend."

Deb lifts her brows. "Really? And she didn't make a fuss?"

I shake my head. "She handled it like a champ. Autism is a spectrum, and for Daph, what helps most is consistency. Reassurance. From what I've witnessed, she thrives when she knows what to expect, whether it's bringing the things she loves or talking through the plan ahead of time so she can prepare. Mentally, emotionally. Physically. They're small gestures, but they can make all the difference."

Deborah stays silent for a while, sipping her coffee, her gaze distant. "How do you know all this?" she asks, her focus suddenly sharp and pinned on me. The stare reminds me of someone else's. The same eyes, with the same intensity.

"I studied it. A long time ago," I say, and her brows go up again. "It was the most meaningful moment of my life. Neurodivergent people are the best of us. Sometimes I wish we could see the world the way they do."

She hums, unconvinced. "What do you do now if you don't work in that field?"

"I work for my dad in hotel management. Although… it's a bit complicated right now."

I'm not about to unpack my existential crisis on this poor woman's lap. I've traumatized her enough for one day.

She peers toward the hallway.

"I don't understand my own kid," she says, though her voice carries a quiet hope, as if she wishes she knew how. "Matt is angry with me because of it."

My heart breaks a little. She looks tired and out of her depth. When Daphne was diagnosed, her parents weren't handed an instruction booklet or given the tools they need to understand her. Sometimes, ignorant people close themselves off. They activate their defense mechanisms when faced with situations they've never encountered. It's not fair for Daphne at all. Deborah should be doing the work. But maybe she needs that extra push.

"Start by listening to her," I say softly. "Not just to what she says, but to how she moves through the world. Her cues, her rhythms. You won't be perfect the first time, and you *will* make mistakes. But Daph will see that you're trying. And she'll love you even more for it, for choosing to understand her, even when it's hard."

I place my hand on top of hers, my stomach churning. Am I overdoing it? Maybe, but now that I've begun, it'd be silly to stop here.

"She doesn't need you to change the world for her. People will be mean and unfair. It's as inevitable as the sunrise. But you can help her navigate it."

Footsteps come from the hallway, garnering our attention.

As Matt bursts into the kitchen, massaging his pinkie finger, I retrieve my hand. Beside me, Deborah blinks her emotions away.

"Mom, your fucking demon bit me ag—" Matt looks from me to his mom and back again. "You guys good? Did I miss something?"

I get up from my seat. "Nope, everything's good. I was telling your mom about our trip to Vancouver."

He sidles up beside me and wraps his arm around my waist, bringing me to him, like it doesn't bother him one bit that his parents are right there, watching us with every ounce of hope in their eyes. "Are you ready to head out?"

"Whenever you want," I say.

He grins down at me. "Let's go, then. I have to stop at the store, and then we can go home."

Home.

The word sinks into my heart with a softness that makes me dizzy. That single word feels so right. And it has nothing to do with his place.

It's him.

He's my home.

Home is his steady heartbeat and his warm hands on my skin.

It's the slow mornings wrapped in blankets and the cozy nights bundled next to him on the couch.

It's the scent of his shirt that soothes me after an exhausting day, and the rhythm of his breathing as he sleeps beside me.

It's his name on my lips as I come undone in his arms.

As he leads me toward the door, his hand on the small of my back, he has no idea how my world just reoriented itself around his.

"Daph, we're leaving!" Matt shouts.

His sister runs down the stairs and throws herself at him. He sways but cushions the impact with an *oof* and holds her tight.

"I'll see you Wednesday for the parent-teacher conference at school, okay? Be good for Mom and Dad. I'm gonna miss you."

"Can I stay with you a little bit longer?" She buries her face in his neck.

Matt tightens his arms around her for another moment, then gently extricates himself from her hold. "Mom and Dad are back, kiddo. You should spend some time with them."

"But I want to stay with *you*," she says louder.

Matt glances at his mom, who nods her agreement, then at me. He sighs.

"I can't bring you back tonight because Zoé and I have plans. But I can pick you up after school tomorrow, and you can stay another week. Then it's back to Mom and Dad, okay?"

We have plans?

"Okay. See you tomorrow. Bye, Zoey!"

Without a backward look, she darts back up the stairs.

"Be careful with that foot," Matt tells his dad as he gives him a quick hug.

As we walk to the car, Deb calls his name. "Maybe I can come with you and Daphne on Wednesday. To the school. Meet her teacher and see how it is."

Matt sucks in a sharp breath. "Uh, y-yeah, sure. Of course. You can come anytime. I'll text you the details."

I hide my smile beneath the collar of my jacket.

Looks like the winds of change are sweeping over Pine Falls.

Chapter Twenty-Six

Matt

Blinds cover the windows of my store, giving me the perfect chance to surprise Zoé. She's waiting in my truck while I finish setting up the last touches, thinking I had to run in to check on a few things I didn't have time to do before the town hall this afternoon.

I can't wait to have her all to myself tonight. This is long overdue. No sister, no friends, no parents.

Just her and me.

The woman I love.

Fuck.

I love her so damn much.

And based on my mom's interest in visiting Daph's school, the two of them must have had quite the conversation when I was out helping my dad with the luggage. That makes me love her even more, if that's even possible.

I tried to needle the information out of her on the drive here, but she insisted all they talked about was the trip to Vancouver. I could tell by the way she stayed vague that she was hiding something from me, but I didn't press her on it. She doesn't have to tell me everything. My mom offering to join us on Wednesday is already the biggest step forward I could have dreamed of.

I'm not used to having an ally when it comes to protecting my sister, and the feeling is fucking intoxicating.

I open the shop door and slip outside. When I approach the truck, she's staring down at her phone. "Can you help me out with something real quick?"

"Me?" She snaps her head up. "With what?"

"No, not you," I deadpan, opening the passenger door. "Of course you. Come on."

She takes the hand I offer and follows me back to the store. "Should I tell you that you're way—"

I open the door and usher her in, and the words die in her throat.

Hands on her shoulders, I lean in. "I owed you a dinner and flowers. Remember?"

The whole shop is suffused with the soft light of hundreds of candles I've arranged around vases and flowers. In the middle of the space, cushions and blankets are piled together. And next to them is a pair of glasses and a bottle of wine, along with stuffed pasta shells.

She turns to me, the wheels in her brain racing. "How did you… When did you…"

Then she gasps. "Your flowers are gonna catch fire with all those candles!"

Chuckling, I caress her arms. "They're fake, don't worry. Do you like it?"

"I—I don't know what to say." She spins slowly, taking it all in. "I don't think I've ever seen something so beautiful in my life."

It's true that the store looks like a vision out of a fairy tale, with all the greenery and lights dancing like fireflies.

But the woman standing in the middle makes it downright magical. Enchanting.

"When did you find the time to do all of this?" she breathes.

"Lola and James helped me put it together this afternoon."

I didn't know my parents would be back in town today, but it worked out well in the end. It gave James and Lols a few more hours to finish setting up. I owe them big time.

"Come on. Sit with me." I lace our fingers and lead her to the cozy setup.

Once she's settled, I open the bottle and fill our glasses.

"To you," I say, tapping mine against hers. "And your vision for our town. Thank you for making us so much better."

Her eyes go wide, her mouth forming the cutest O. "*Our* town?"

"If you want it to be."

"I do." Though her words are clear, shadows drift across her face. "I need to talk to my dad first. Tell him I'm signing the papers for the hotel and that..." She exhales sharply. "That I don't want to take over."

It's the first time she's spoken those words to me. That she's acknowledged that she wants something different, that she *is* someone different from the person she was when she arrived.

I wasn't prepared for how my heart would race in return. Like a lock unfastening its hold on my hopes and desires.

"I have something to tell you too," I say, just above a whisper. "Corey texted me while I was at the car with my dad. I'm in. I'm starting the program in two weeks."

With a squeal, she throws her arms around my neck, coming flush against me.

I drag her onto my lap and hold her tight, whiffs of her shampoo tingling my nose.

"I'm so proud of you," she says. "You've worked so hard. You deserve it."

"Thank you." I close my eyes, breathing her in deeply, and rub circles on her back. I want to keep her here forever. Give her all the love she's missed out on for all thirty-two years of existence. Show her that she deserves to be loved the way she needs.

We sit in silence for several minutes, tangled in each other. Eventually, she pulls back and rests her forehead on mine.

"You make me feel more alive than I've ever been," she whispers, her breath warm on my lips.

I brush my mouth against hers. "I was living my life in the dark until you showed up and switched all the lights on so bright."

"I'm still scared," she confesses.

My heart thuds heavily. "Me too. We can be scared together."

She nods, her fingers weaving through the hair at my nape. "I love you."

"I love you so much, beautiful."

I press my mouth to hers, kissing her until I'm gasping for air. As soon as she opens and I slide my tongue in, my body goes unbearably tight with need.

The wild effect she has on me should be studied by scientists around the world.

Hands roaming, hungry and desperate, I fumble at the hem of her shirt, aching to feel her skin instead of the fabric. I peel off all the layers she was bundled in. Then it's my turn. In a heartbeat, we're both naked in the middle of my store, our clothes discarded on the floor.

"Hold still," she tells me.

Her demand scrapes on my skin like her nails on my spine, sharp and deliberate, and my toes curl with pleasure.

God, I like when she gets bossy.

She gets off my lap and kneels before me, her breasts swaying.

My balls tighten at the sight.

She wets her lip, positioning herself between my spread legs. "I love when you fuck my mouth, honey."

With a groan, I take my length in my hand and guide myself to her lips. "Open up, then."

She glides her fingers up my thighs, never taking her eyes off me, even as she lowers her head and welcomes me.

Though not completely. Rather than put me out of my misery, she swirls her tongue over the tip.

"Fuck, you're such a tease, Zoé," I hiss, tightening my grip around my cock.

She traces her tongue along my length, lingering like she's memorizing each vein, and then she pushes my hand away, replacing it with hers, and engulfs me in the heat of her wet mouth. Head dropped back between my shoulders, I groan, trying to stifle the pleasure surging through every part of my body.

She sucks hard, as if knowing how tortured I already am, and I turn feral. The pressure snaps at my primal instincts. Everything in me roars, urging me to give in.

I gather her hair in a tight fist and hold her still over me.

She lifts her eyes to me, her lips glistening and damp, swollen from her effort, her gaze full of want. "Please."

"Fuck. Don't move."

She obeys, only opening wide. Spine tingling, I shift my hips up and down, her hair wrapped securely around my fist.

In just a few thrusts, I'm there, tension coiling tight at the base of my spine. My thighs lock, but I don't slow, pumping in and out of her warmth, going as deep as she allows me. Praise falls from my lips between curses and shallow gasps.

You take me so well. Fuck, I love you. So gorgeous with your lips stretched around my cock. Wider, beautiful. That's it. Fuck.

My movements stutter, my balls tighten, my head swells against her tongue.

That's the moment I love the most. When I'm on the brink of spilling my release. When every strained muscle in my body is begging to relax. That fine line between pain and pure bliss.

I ride it till the last second. Till beads of precum form at the tip and she whimpers in response to the taste.

"Okay, enough." I tear her mouth away from me before I can come, then bring her flush to my chest, sealing her lips to mine. "Turn around."

Without giving her a second to follow my command, I do it for her. I spin her around, pulling a sharp gasp from her, and press her back tightly against my chest, my thighs bracketing hers.

Hand sliding between her legs, I bring my mouth to her ear. "You liked that, didn't you?"

"Yes," she breathes as my fingers play in her wetness, circling her clit already engorged with need.

I bite the tip of her ear. "I was ready to come in your mouth."

Zoé hums, rocking her hips against my hand. "Why didn't you?"

I press my palm against her pussy, nudging her closer to me. "Because I want to fill you again."

I grip my cock and sink into her. Her walls flutter as she stretches to accommodate me, and as I move inside her, the mind-blowing need to feel her clench around me levels out.

"Don't go too fast," she moans, her head falling back on my shoulder.

I press an open-mouthed kiss against her sweaty neck, reveling in the way her breasts bounce with every roll of my hips.

God, I love feeling her like this, with every inch of her molding around every inch of me, keeping the pace slow and deep until I'm slick with her need.

I palm her breast in one hand, teasing her clit with the other, fingers slipping lower, relishing the way I disappear inside her.

Body and mind.

"Take what you need from me, beautiful." I slide a finger in too, so snug and so perfect, and she shudders on my lap.

I sink my teeth right where her neck meets her shoulder and suck on the spot.

Her body goes slack against mine.

It's okay, I got her. I'll always have her.

Mine to hold.

Mine to pleasure.

Mine to love.

"Matt, p-please. I—"

She chokes on my name, my release climbing closer to the surface.

"Are you gonna say my name when you come all over me?" I pump into her faster, my finger stroking inside her with the same rhythm.

"*Yes.*"

"Say it." I pinch her nipple. "Say it, Zoé, because I'm so close."

Too close.

Hot need floods my body. I grit my teeth, thrusting my hips in hard, sharp movements, my thighs slapping against her ass.

"*Say it.*"

She clenches around me so tight my vision goes dark.

"*Matt.*"

Fuck.

Her body writhes as her pussy grips me hard.

I follow her off the edge. My release barrels through me fast and loud, and I spill myself inside her in thick, hot, sputtering bursts, crying out her name as I fill her with every drop of my orgasm.

Only when we've both stopped spasming do I remove my finger.

Cradled in my arms, she's breathless, warm and sweaty, red splotches scattered over her body from her climax. This might be my favorite version of her. The only one I want to keep for myself.

"I don't think I have enough energy left to go back to your place." She sighs as I roll her off my lap.

We lie on our sides, face to face, our knees tucked up against each other.

"It's okay." I brush away the hair stuck to her damp skin. "We can stay here as long as you want."

"Can we never leave?" She glances around the room, at the flickering of the plastic lights dancing on the walls. "You made it so cozy and warm. And safe."

With a chuckle, I pull her close, my nose brushing hers. "I'll always keep you safe. No matter where we are. Even if I'm not next to you. I'll always keep you safe."

She clutches my neck, holding my gaze, staring into my soul. "You're the best decision I'll ever make in my life."

My heart trips over itself. And I lay myself bare for her.

I hold eye contact, letting her see that she dragged me out of a dark hole I didn't know I was in until she blitzed through it, bright and warm. I wait for her to realize she was the one who stitched back together the cracks in my heart. One day at a time, with her care and her smiles. I let her feel the weight I used to carry alone and how light I am now that she's by my side.

Humming, I kiss the tip of her nose. "I think you and I were meant to meet at this exact moment in our lives. Neither of us would have been ready for such a profound change if it had come a few years ago." I swallow, a steady current running through me. "You altered my brain chemistry. My body responds to you in a way I've never known. You were meant to happen to me at this very moment. To prove to me that I could trust someone with my heart again. That I have the right to be happy. And I was meant to happen to you now too. To show you that you deserve a love that's honest and unconditional."

I lean in and kiss her.

I don't know how long it lasts, but at some point, our kiss becomes sloppy and need takes over once more. And just like that, the store is filled with moans and labored breaths, her name on my lips and whispered *I love you*s.

Until we plunge into oblivion again.

We do this all night.

Around five a.m., when early morning light filters through the curtains, Zoé finally falls asleep in my arms.

Chapter Twenty-Seven

Zoey

Matt woke me up this morning at ten.

Ten.

As in, I had already skipped two work meetings, and my dad had been harassing me for three hours before I was conscious.

Twenty-three missed calls.

He must think I've been kidnapped or that I'm lost in the woods. I'm half scared to turn the TV on and discover there's already an ongoing investigation into my disappearance.

But by some miracle, the familiar knot in my stomach doesn't tighten at the sight of the (twenty-three) missed calls. I'm not picking my nails, and my leg isn't bouncing. I'm not hung up on fears about what could have gone wrong or how long I have to fix it. I'm not rushing to call him back either.

I'm just… doing one thing at a time.

First: drink the coffee Matt poured for me. He cleaned up, rejecting my offers to help as he gathered all the candles and blankets. And my lacy bra stuck in one of the rose pots.

This man literally opened his store late to let me sleep.

Yes, I'm keeping him.

Then, he fed me the pastries he picked up from Mia's, convinced I would forget to eat for the rest of the day and insisting he wouldn't let me leave with an empty stomach.

I left Daphne's Wildflowers around eleven and headed straight to the mayor's office to sign the sale agreement. Heart pounding, I scrawled my name on the dotted line as if I was accepting the rights to the beginning of the rest of my life.

Once that was done, I drove back to the cabin, showered, and attended a one-p.m. meeting with Corey.

Dad hasn't tried to call me since this morning. And I have only one thing left to do before I call him back.

I scroll through the University of British Columbia website and navigate to the admissions page.

Okay, so I'm really doing this.

Deep breath. The sky won't fall on my head and the floor won't open up under my feet.

I click on the link for the pediatric nursing specialty and fill out the required fields. The program is set to start this winter, which gives me a few months to get my things in order. Talk it through with my dad and find a replacement.

I inhale and hold the air in my lungs, then force it out sharply. I don't even know how to approach this conversation. Probably with a ten-foot pole. Full-on knight gear, definitely.

Maybe I could be as brave as a man who's trying to get out of a situationship and text him *I quit.*

With a heavy sigh, I rub my eyes. As complicated as my relationship with my dad is, as flawed as he is, he's still my father, and I love him. The last thing I want is to shut him out of my life.

I fumble in my bag, and once I've found my phone, I snap a photo of my screen.

Zoey

> Look what I'm doing

Not two minutes later, his response comes through.

Matt

> I was just thinking about you. Someone walked into the store wearing ridiculous shoes. It's October, for fuck's sake.

> I'm so proud of you, beautiful. Are you feeling okay? Do you want to call me?

I'm your support system now. His words echo in my mind, wrapping me in his safety, as though he's standing next to me.

Zoey

I'm okay. A bit scared,
but mostly excited.

Matt

It's okay to be scared, but I'm
excited for you too. I can't wait to
see you tonight and celebrate.

I frown.

Zoey

Celebrate?

Matt

Your application. That's a big
step. You deserve to highlight it
properly. With frozen pizza and
hot sex for dessert. And by
dessert, I mean you. On my face.
So basically, a celebration for me.

Laughing, I type my message.

Zoey

Don't you have your sister
tonight?

Matt

> I'm dropping her off at my parents' for a few hours. I want to help you move your stuff to the hotel too. Are you sure you're okay with this?

Ah, yes. I need to pack my suitcases today. Charlee and Oliver will be back from their trip tomorrow. Initially, I planned to stay at Matt's, but now that Daph is spending another week at his place, it makes more sense for me to sleep at the Butterfly Inn. He doesn't want her to be uncomfortable, and I agree that taking it step by step is the most sensible option. It'll be easier for Daphne to get used to me living with her brother once she's not living with him too. And once I figure out what my next few months are gonna look like.

Zoey

> I'm absolutely okay with it. You guys should have your space. Looking forward to finally bonding with Ruth.

Thirty minutes later, the application is filled out and the fees are paid, and I have one thing left to do.

"Here we go." Heart in my throat, I hit the *submit* button. "Holy shit."

I rise from my chair and pace the room, shaking out my hands. *"Holy shit, I did it."*

It's only when I walk past the mirror in the hallway that I realize I'm grinning from ear to ear.

At three p.m., I finally pick up the phone. I tap on my father's contact, and on the second ring, he answers.

"What took you so long?"

Oh, he's very much grumpy. Great.

"Sorry, the day slipped away from me. I've got good news, though."

He grunts a flat "What?"

"I signed the land agreement this morning. We secured the lot for the hotel."

"That's great news, princess," he says, his tone only mildly more friendly. "So everything is in order? They can't back out of it again, right?"

Wow, that failed deal really traumatized him, didn't it?

"No, it's signed now. I sent it to our lawyers a couple of hours ago so we can get the ball rolling with our accountants and tax people."

"Perfect. The shareholders' meeting is next month. I'll shoot them an email today to let them know you closed the deal. Great job, princess. I don't want to get ahead of myself, but this should sway the votes in your favor. Jeff is gonna be thrilled. He's been pestering me about his golf course for two years."

I swallow, my throat like sandpaper. Maybe it's not the right time to tell him I don't want to—wait. *Golf course?*

"What golf course?"

"Attached to the hotel. The land is next to a small patch of woods, right? If we take those trees down, we can even out the ground and put in a golf course."

"There's no golf course in my proposal, Dad."

My voice comes out short. Tired. Confused.

He hums. "I know there isn't. We won't be moving forward with your project. I'll be sending you the new proposal tonight."

My legs wobble, and I almost go down. But I manage to remain upright until I throw myself into the nearest chair. "This is not what we agreed on. I convinced these people and won the town's vote based on the project I presented. They'll never accept something else."

He chuckles, the sound skittering over me like tiny spiders. "They don't have to. The land has been secured. The deal is done. All is good, princess. Sometimes, plans change. That's business, you know that. Why do you care anyway? You got what you wanted. The job will be yours. I'm proud of my daughter today."

A sharp, cold chill sinks into my chest.

The words I've been craving to hear for so long ring in my ears with a strident echo, their meaning completely hollow.

They don't have the impact I thought they'd have. There's no warmth to them. No sense of accomplishment washing over me. They feel wrong.

I should have known he'd choose this moment to say them for the first time. That he'd twist the kind of praise that's held such power over me for years and weaponize it against me.

I feel dirty. Like I've been complicit all along.

My stomach churns, nausea rising in my throat, bitterness coating my tongue.

"Dad, I gotta go. I'll call you back."

Without waiting for a response, I hang up, my breath coming out ragged.

He wouldn't really do this to me, would he? He wouldn't use me so blatantly. And for what? A couple more millions in his and his buddies' already overinflated bank accounts?

Hand shaking, I snag my computer and open my emails.

I need to come up with something. Shut down whatever this ridiculous plan is and find a way to stick to the original one, the one the people of Pine Falls agreed on.

Fuck, *the people*.

I close my eyes, pinching the bridge of my nose.

If I can't stand up to my father, if I can't convince the shareholders to back off…

Then I might as well say goodbye to Pine Falls. And everybody in it.

Dad sent over his disgusting proposal at five, and my head has been buried in it since, trying to make sense of how I could've been so blind.

Trying to come to terms with the truth: that he's been planning this for weeks, if not months. There's no way he would have whipped up something so outlined, so detailed, in a few days, let alone hours.

No, this was premeditated.

And there's a nagging voice in my mind that's planting the idea that maybe, the night I came over, the TV was on the Discovery Channel on purpose.

My own father has manipulated me. Moved me like a pawn when I thought I was his right-hand woman.

This is the last fucking straw.

I'm so lost in my thoughts, so consumed by this profound betrayal, that I don't even realize what time it is.

I don't hear Matt when he comes in. Don't notice his presence until he's standing behind me, his giant hands pressed on my upper arms.

"Hi, beautiful."

I startle and slam the laptop shut. "Hi," I heave. "You scared me."

Matt watches me, one brow raised. "Are you okay?" He rounds the chair and hooks a finger under my chin, forcing my gaze to meet his. "Zoé, tell me. What's going on?"

His eyes search mine, a scowl spreading across his face. I hate that I can't hide anything from him, that he takes one look at me and knows right away that I'm on the verge of crumbling.

"It's been a long day, that's all."

I free myself from his hold, the weight of his gaze too much to bear. But he doesn't let me get away with it.

Crouching in front of me, he gives me a tender look. "Talk to me. What's got you so worked up?" He nods toward my laptop. "What's on there?"

Tension builds in my throat. I don't want to hide it from him. I can't. But every part of me whispers that the moment I open that laptop, I'll lose him.

My eyes fill with tears at the thought. By tonight, my dad will truly have ruined all aspects of my life.

"Zoé, you're scaring me." He grips my thighs. "Please talk to me, beautiful."

I wish I could, but my throat is so tight, it's impossible to speak. So I open my computer, where my dad's mega hotel complex on Emile's land glares on the screen.

He scans the text, and I hold my breath. His frown deepens, the crease between his brows sharpening as he reads. He leans back slightly, confusion tugging at his features.

Then I see it. The way his jaw ticks. The way it locks tight.

"That fucking bastard," he seethes. "I knew it. I *knew* he'd pull something like that."

My stomach free-falls. "Matt, I'm so sorry. I didn't know he'd do that. I feel so awful. I swear to you I didn't know. I would never—"

"Zoé, hey, hey." He presses his hands to my face, sweeping his thumbs across my wet cheeks. "It's okay. Breathe. I'm not mad at you, honey."

I exhale shakily, rubbing my palms on my pants, the pounding in my chest relentless. "You're not?"

"Of course not. Have you not heard a word I've said for the past month? I know who you are, and you're not a heartless monster." He pulls a chair in front of me and sits. "Tell me what happened."

It takes a minute to compose myself, but eventually, I straighten and wipe my face with the back of my hand.

"I called my dad today to update him on the land," I croak out. "He told me he's taking over. The board doesn't want my lodge idea. They never did. My dad only wanted to secure the land." I choke out a sob. "He used me."

He blows out a breath, raking a hand down his face. "Okay, this is bad. Really bad."

He pushes himself to his feet and paces to the other side of the room. I follow his every move, my heart thundering in my ears at the same pace as the pulse in his neck.

"I've been looking for a loophole since I found out, but I haven't had any luck."

I'm not helpless anymore. I'm not scared or intimidated by my own father. Matt gave me the tools to fight back, and I intend to use them now.

"There's gotta be *something*."

"I've tried to call him, but he isn't picking up."

He runs his hand through his hair, the same path my fingers followed last night. "I don't mean to be blunt, Zoé, but your dad isn't open for negotiations."

"I don't think I am either. This is *my* project." My thoughts are reeling at a speed I can't keep up with. I can't think properly, can't focus clearly. "I…I'll check with my team, dig into the legal stuff a bit. Maybe there's something that'd make him back off."

He sits on the couch, his elbows on his thighs, and sighs with defeat. "We'll figure it out. But we have to do it fast. Because the minute this gets out—"

His phone rings. He picks up.

"Yes?" He rubs his jaw, his knee bouncing. A low *fuck* escapes his lips. "Now?" A pause. "Okay. We'll be right over."

"What is it?" I ask, my heart in my throat.

"Emergency town hall meeting."

"Why did you come?" Matt grits out between his teeth when his parents arrive with Daphne.

"Rob texted that it was an emergency meeting. We had to be here," his mom says. "What's the big deal?"

Matt pinches the bridge of his nose, exhaling. "I wish Daph would have stayed home, that's all."

The ride here was filled with silence and buzzing nerves; both of us were lost in our thoughts. Matt whispered, "It's gonna be fine" as he squeezed my fingers again and again, and I'm not sure if that was meant for me or to reassure himself.

"Do you know what it's about?" his dad asks.

His eyes dart to me. "Not sure."

I swallow. The tightness in my chest hasn't gone away since the email landed in my inbox, but now it's spread to every part of my body. It takes everything I have to push my feet forward.

When we get in, the place is packed, familiar faces greeting us with warm smiles and friendly waves as we find seats.

Rob walks to the podium, his features unreadable. Behind him, a white screen I haven't seen before has been set up.

"Thank you all for coming on such short notice," he starts, voice grave. "I had a very interesting call this afternoon, to say the least." He finds me in the crowd, his expression cold and harsh. That's when I know that this is the end for me. "And since this was a decision we made together as a community, I believe it's your right to know." His knuckles are white where he grips the podium. "The hotel project Ms. Delacroix presented was nothing but smoke and mirrors. The representative from Imperial Excellence I spoke to this afternoon confirmed that this"—he picks up a little clicker, and my father's mega complex proposal appears on the screen behind him—"is what we can expect a year from now."

The gasps across the room are loud and sharp, suffocating the air with a tension so thick it wraps around my throat. In every direction, people turn to me, their faces confused, betrayed. Sad.

"You're okay," Matt whispers. His words are meant to be soothing, though his own body is a wall of nerves. He laces his fingers with mine, and I focus on the warmth of his skin.

"What does this mean?" Patty, who's in the front row, breaks the agitated hum of the crowd.

"It means that Ms. Delacroix has led us on with her lodge project."

I shoot up. "I did *not*. My father took over without my knowledge."

"That's not what your colleague said when we spoke," Rob accuses. "It was his understanding that you knew all along."

"These are *lies*," I yell, my face hot. "I only received the proposal a few hours ago. Probably at the same time you did. Before that, I wasn't aware of any resort project."

"And we're supposed to believe you now? You betrayed us," Ruth shouts from the other end of the room.

Others pipe up, demanding answers and hurling accusations, each comment as harsh as the last. I slump in my seat, head down, my breath coming in small puffs of air.

"The bastard set you up," Matt seethes through his teeth, his hand gripping mine. "I'm gonna fucking…"

He continues to spew his anger, but I tune out all the noise. This is a repeat of my first town hall, only ten times worse. These are my people.

People I've grown to love and care for.

And they're all looking at me like they really believe I played a sick, twisted puppet game with them. Rosie, a storm raging in her eyes. Carl, shaking his head in disappointment. Cooper, his arms crossed, his stare cold.

"She's a liar," Patty shrieks. "She used us."

The crowd erupts like a wildfire, pointing their fingers at me, throwing their hands up in desperation.

The world blurs, moving in slow motion. Their faces twisted with rage, their mouths deformed by their fury, their scowls marring their features as they shout and demand I explain myself.

But I can't. I can't breathe. I can't move. I'm being pushed underwater, my father's hand the one holding my head down.

And then a high-pitched voice rises above all the others. "Zoey is not like that! She's kind! She's my friend!"

Daphne.

No, no, no, no, no.

My heart shatters at my feet as her voice climbs a few octaves, flooded with hurt and confusion. *"Stop being mean to her! Stop it!"*

Deb tries to settle her, to reel her back into her seat, but her efforts are in vain. Instead, she gets more worked up. Her plea turns ferocious as she screams her last words over and over again.

"Can somebody make her stop?" Patty asks loudly.

Matt is on his feet in an instant, his finger pointed at her. *"Fuck you, Patty."*

He rushes toward his sister and scoops her up in his arms without a second thought, shielding her from the noise, then strides through the door and disappears from my sight.

I exhale a tiny breath, knowing he's taking care of her.

But as thankful as I am that she's got him, he's no longer anchoring me. This time, when the current pulls me under, he's not here to bring me back up.

My breaths turn shallow, my blood roaring in my ears as my hands shake.

"Everybody, please. Let's settle down," Rob shouts.

It's pointless. Nobody listens.

My face is burning, my mind is reeling, my throat is closing.

"I have to go," I whisper, then louder. "I have to go. I'm sorry, I have to go."

I stand and wade through the crowd, dodging unhappy cries until I'm stumbling outside, gasping for air.

Matt is there, crouched in front of Daphne, rubbing her arms. His eyes snap to mine.

"Zoé?"

"I'm fine," I say, staggering toward my car. "Stay there. Take care of Daph."

He stands and takes a step toward me, but I hold my hand up, as if to push him away. "Daphne, Matt. She needs you."

He calls me again, but I'm already in my car, driving away.

Chapter Twenty-Eight

Matt

The past week has been rough.

I haven't heard from Zoé in seven days, except for her brief response to the twenty texts I sent asking where the hell she was. "At the Butterfly Inn, as planned," she said, but then asked for space to figure things out, telling me to focus on my sister.

Which I've been doing. But her silence has me worried sick.

The evenings are the hardest. She's always on my mind. What is she up to? Does she miss me as much as I miss her? I can't count the number of times I've driven to the hotel, only to turn around, respecting her demand.

Daphne has been asking me where Zoé is—why she's not coming for dinner, why I look so damn sad—and I don't have any fucking answer for her.

"Matt?"

I glance up at Lola, who's watching me, her lips tugged down in a frown. "Sorry, what?"

"Where did you go?"

I tilt my beer to my mouth, sinking deeper into the Adirondack chair. "I'm here," I mumble.

She gives me a kick.

"*Ow!*"

"Can you at least pretend like you're happy to see your friends? We haven't had a Friday night dinner in forever."

Since Oli has been traveling so much with Charlee lately, working on their next docuseries, we've done a shit job of keeping up with the tradition we started a decade ago. So tonight, I dropped my sister off with my parents and took the night for myself. But my head hasn't been in it.

I tighten my hold on my beer. "No, I'm glad to see you guys. I'm a bit distracted, that's all. Sorry."

Oliver watches me with narrowed eyes, his hair tousled by the light breeze. "So I've heard. Wanna fill us in?"

Brow cocked, I nod at Lola and James. "These two haven't told you everything already?"

He shrugs. "The basics. How you guys met and the whole… fake dating stuff for Emile's land. And last week's town hall…"

"I can't believe I wasn't here to see you pretend to date someone." Charlee breaks into a smile, adjusting her position on Oli's lap. "The *one time* you do something wild, and I miss it."

"Thank god you weren't," I mutter. The teasing would never have ended.

"So… did she lie?" Oliver hedges. "About the project?"

I snap my gaze to him, anger flooding my veins. "Of course not. Don't you know what an asshole her dad is?"

"We all do," James says, rubbing the back of his neck.

With a sigh, I shake my head. "He set her up real good. His own fucking daughter. And the whole community lost it on her last week."

Leaving me with an impossible choice: my sister or Zoé. In the end, she made it for me, but it's the decision I would've made myself. And knowing she understands that only makes me love her more.

My head falls. "Daph defended her in front of everybody. I've never seen her like that, and it broke my heart. She had a meltdown, and while I was calming her down outside, Zoé left. You have no idea how much I want to pay a visit to her dad."

Charlee bundles herself closer to Oli. "That man is the scum of the earth."

Lola and Char clink their bottles in agreement.

"Where did she go?" James asks.

I take another swig of my beer, staring out at the horizon, where the sun has finally set on the lake. "She's at the Butterfly Inn. She asked me to give her some time. Told me to focus on Daph. She's probably moving heaven and earth to find a way out."

"And you listened to her? You didn't insist on being with her and helping her through it?" Oli looks at Charlee. "What is it that you say all the time, sweetheart? That Matt is—"

"A hot piece of ass."

That pulls a laugh from me, at least. The first in a week.

"No, not that," he mumbles. "The other one."

She leans in and kisses his cheek. "Oh. An idiot."

With a grin, Oli snaps his fingers. "Exactly that. What are you doing, man? Go fucking get your girl. She needs you now more than ever."

Guilt eats at me, twisting my gut. "But she said she needs space. That she wants to fix this alone. I *have to* respect her wishes, don't I?" I rub my temples, feeling the weight of it all. "And what if she's mad? I did choose to comfort Daphne rather than stand beside her. I left her to face the town's fury all by herself. Maybe she's done with me."

"Matt." Lola dips her chin, her expression flat. "The woman's working her ass off for the town that all but strung her up a week ago, for god's sake. You think she's staying because she liked it? She told you she loved you."

"She *what*?" Oliver and Char scream at the same time. They look at each other and burst into laughter, Oli brushing his lips on her cheek in a faint kiss.

"Did you say it back?" Charlee scoots to the edge of Oli's lap, her expression full of anticipation.

I rub a hand down my face. "Yes."

She mumbles something that sounds like "What a hot-ass idiot." Louder, she adds, "Then, go!"

Oli rests his chin on her shoulder. "I can't believe you're still here talking to us. You really are an idiot."

Chest constricting, I glance at James.

He raises his eyebrows and tips his beer to his lips as if to say, "I told you so."

"Go!" Charlee insists.

"Fuck it." I get up and head straight for my truck.

"Bring her back here," Oli shouts from the deck. "Maybe we can help."

If she wants to talk to me, then yes, I'll bring her back here. I'll introduce her to everybody.

She'll be part of the family. A real one, for once.

"Oh, Matt, wait." Charlee scrambles off Oliver's lap and runs toward me. "I have something for you. Here." She digs in her pocket and pulls out a keychain with a rooster dangling from it, flashing me a smile. "For the cocklection."

I swing by the store and throw together a bouquet of her favorite flowers. The whole time, my heart doesn't stop racing.

At the Butterfly Inn, I jog inside and head straight for the front desk.

"Hey, Ruth." The owner of the Inn, a petite woman in her sixties, sits in a large armchair, knitting needles in her hands. "Can you tell me which room Zoey Delacroix is staying in, please?"

She peers at me over the pink glasses perched at the tip of her nose before she looks back at the cardigan she's working on. "Guest information is confidential."

"Ruth, please." I bounce on my toes, literally shaking. With a frustrated groan, I pluck a pink rose from the bouquet and thrust it at her. "*Please.*"

She puts her needles down, sighs, and takes the offered flower. "Fine. Room 203."

"Thank you."

I dash down the dim hallway and fly up the stairs, taking them two at a time. When I get to her door on the second floor, I rap twice on the wood.

There's some clattering on the other side and then the faint brush of the peephole cover against the surface. After a moment's pause, the lock rattles, and finally, Zoé appears in front of me.

"Hi," I croak.

"What are you doing here?" Her voice is soft, fragile. Like she might break if she speaks louder.

"I got a new cock, and I need help fitting it into your cockiness order," I blurt out in one breath.

Her eyes widen, and then she bursts into a laugh. "*What?*"

"My cock!" I yank my new keychain out with a little too much force.

"*Oh,*" she whispers, a hint of a smile playing on her lips. She leans in, squinting. "Definitely not very cocky."

I exhale a sharp laugh, but it dies when I take in her bloodshot eyes. Her rumpled shirt. Her oversized sweatpants. *My* sweatpants.

She's wearing them.

I swallow tightly and settle on her face again, the wrinkles at the corners of her eyes, the hair she's crammed into a sad bun on top of her head.

She looks like she's barely slept since I last saw her.

Fuck.

I scan what I can see of the room. The twin beds that have been pushed together. The piles of papers, the discarded clothes, the leftover food.

Fuck, it kills me that I let her go through all of this alone.

"Can I come in?" I ask.

With a nod, she moves out of the way.

"Ruth gave me the worst room," she says. "Though at first, she refused to let me stay at all, so it's a win, I guess."

My stomach drops. I can't believe she's been living like this for a week.

"These are for you," I say a bit hoarsely, handing her the bouquet, then sit on the edge of the bed, wincing when it creaks under my weight.

"Thank you." She takes the flowers and inhales deeply, then sets them on the other bed.

My legs jiggle relentlessly, my pulse hammering in my ears like it's desperate to reach her. I don't know why I thought I could sit down for this. I get up, raking a hand through my hair.

I'm about to speak, but she beats me to the punch. "Matt, I—"

"Please, let me go first," I cut in, urgency in my tone, despite my best efforts to stay calm.

Her lips stretch into a ghost of a smile, and she nods. "Go ahead."

"I'm sorry for not running after you after the town hall. I should have picked up Daphne and followed you to Oli's. We've been miserable without you. We miss you so much."

Zoé takes a step closer and lays her hand on my forearm. "You have nothing to be sorry for. I asked you for space, and you gave it to me. He's *my* dad, and he tricked *me*." Her voice wavers on that last part. "I needed to figure this out myself."

I deflate, some of the anxiety flooding out of me. My fingers ache to curl around her face and bring her to me.

"You did. But you needed me, and I know how easy it is for you to clam up. I should have done more to keep you safe. I should have at least fought for you that night."

Her eyes fill with tears, and I brush them away as they crest her lashes.

"I'm sorry too," she says, her voice shaking. "For putting us in this situation. I should have known he'd pull shit like that. And for hurting Daphne. God, her screams still haunts me. Is she okay?"

I tangle my fingers in the softness of her hair, pushing it away from her face. She leans into my touch. "She will be once you come back home, honey. She misses you."

She smiles, finally, then tilts her chin to the side, pressing her lips to my palm.

I exhale at the touch, my body going slack with relief. With my free hand, I bunch her rumpled shirt and tug her flush against me. The hitch of her breath lands softly on my chest and triggers a wave of shivers all the way to my toes. "I just want to know if you're okay."

"I'm better now that you're here." She worries her lip, her eyes big and full of warmth. Then, she places her hand above my heart like she knows exactly who it belongs to. "I didn't know how much I needed to see you."

"The past week has been rough," I say, still stroking her hair. "I hated not being with you, being kept in the dark, not being able to help when I *knew* you were struggling. You have no idea what I'd do for you. No idea how much I love you." I whisper the words, our mouths only inches apart. "No idea. And that's my fault. I failed to make it clear to you before, so let me try now."

I lean in, brushing my lips against hers with all the reverence she deserves.

"You made me love you so much that the life I had before you now feels so depressing. You've ruined me in the most exquisite way."

Tears well in her eyes again. I swear, if she starts to sob, I'll forget how to stand. I cradle her face like she's the most fragile, sacred thing I've ever held.

"You made me love you so much," I murmur, my voice breaking under the torrent of my emotions, "that nothing matters if you're not by my side. I don't want to exist in a world where you're not mine. I don't want space. I want you snug against me all the time. Come back to me. We'll figure this all out together. You and me. Let me love you every damn day until we're old and gray, swearing at kids who run through our yard and mess up the flowers I just planted."

A teary laugh escapes her, her hands balling into fists over my chest, clutching my shirt. "Can we fast forward to that part?"

I respond with a kiss to the tip of her nose before I bury my face in her neck, inhaling her scent that I missed so much.

"When I left that night," she adds, more serious now. "I told myself that I *needed* to do this alone, that it was all on me to fix because it was my mess. It would have gutted me if the rest of the town thought badly of you because you were involved with me. Better they blame the outsider, you know."

I lace my fingers with hers, squeezing some strength into her.

"But taking space from you might have been one of the hardest things I've ever had to do," she continues. "Do you know how many times I picked up the phone to call you? How many times I almost drove to your place and banged on your door?" She sniffles back more tears. "I kept myself busy, but everything reminded me of you. Flowers I saw when I took a walk to get some fresh air. The slice of pizza I microwaved in the hotel lobby downstairs one evening. Even freaking *chickens* in a field yesterday made me a sobbing mess."

"It's roosters," I whisper.

Why the hell are you even correcting her?

"Whatever," she laughs. "You've been haunting me for seven days. Even the silence was a constant reminder that you weren't here." Her fingers slide through my hair. "I love you, Matt Becker. I love you so much, I don't even remember who I was before you. And I don't want to, because that person wasn't me. You peeled away the stubborn layers I'd grown comfortable hiding behind and forced me to discover who I truly was. And I never want to go back. I want you in every way you'll let me. I want to live the kind of love that leaves me breathless. And honey, I can never catch my breath with you."

She draws back, her eyes shining with tears.

"Growing old together sounds like a dream I never thought I could have. We'll be the couple who always messes up our grandkids' names and still holds hands in grocery stores." She rises on her tiptoes. "Let's never do space again."

It takes all I have in me not to fall to my knees. I close the rest of the distance and brush my lips over hers, soft, light, steady. A promise woven in every caress. A vow that if she needed us to stay in this moment forever, I'd make time stand still. I wouldn't move. I'd remain rooted until kissing her became the reason I breathed.

My name escapes her lips in a sigh, her mouth opening, giving me access. I continue my slow exploration. I let go of her hair, my hands drifting to her waist, then her ass, where I squeeze tightly.

She whimpers. "I have one very important disclosure: I'm in a very gross state right now."

"Now that's a very tempting offer," I say, nibbling the lobe of her ear, pressing myself against her.

Sighing, she drops her head against my bicep. "It really is, but I have to kill the mood and tell you something."

I press a kiss to her crown. "What is it?"

"I've had my head buried in legal documents and our archives for the past week, and I've been in contact with my team to find a way out of this mess," she says, her voice bordering on defeat. "Unfortunately, the sale agreement I signed in the name of Imperial Excellence Group is airtight."

Dread washes over me. I sit on the bed, forearms on my knees, lacing my fingers.

Zoé gathers a small pile of paperwork, then sits next to me. "*But* I think I'm onto something..." She riffles through the pages of legal jargon I don't know a thing about. "I was wondering if I could maybe talk to your friends. Charlee, specifically. About what happened in Pine Falls with my dad's deal."

I straighten, sucking in a breath. "What do you mean 'what happened'? You don't know?"

She shakes her head. "He's always been vague about it. And I can't find any traces of it in our archives. Something's missing. From the beginning, it felt like he didn't want to tell me. I brushed it off, assuming it was his massive ego. Until he took over last week, and my raised flags began flashing red. Something is not adding up, and your friends might have the information I need."

"I thought you knew," I whisper.

She gasps. "*You know*? You know what went down?"

I scoot closer. "I do. But it's not my story to tell. The gang and I usually have dinner on Friday nights, and I actually came from there to get you. Oliver and Charlee will fill you in and answer all the questions you have." I get up and turn in a circle, surveying the room. "Let's start by packing your stuff. Time for you to come back home. Then we're heading to Oliver's. If we put our brains together, I'm sure we'll build a solid case against your dad."

Panic flashes in her eyes, and I press my lips in a firm line.

"I'm sorry, beautiful. I know this is not what you wanted."

"It is what it is. He dug his own grave." She gets up and stares down at her clothes. "I can't go to dinner with your friends like this."

I draw her to me until not an inch of space separates my body from hers. "They don't care what you look like, but if you need any reassurance of how hot you are in my sweatpants, I'm sure you can feel the effect you have on me." I press myself closer, and the sound that comes out of her mouth makes me even harder.

"Still," she murmurs. "Let me at least change."

Smirking, I release her. "Fine. I won't be able to think straight anyway, with you in those. And we need to focus. So you go change. I'll gather your stuff and load it in my truck."

I place a quick kiss on her lips, then spin her around.

"Meet me in the lobby in ten."

Chapter Twenty-Nine

Zoey

"So you haven't spoken to your dad at all?" Matt asks as we drive the familiar route that leads to Oliver's place.

"I haven't heard anything back, no. I tried to call him, but he's not picking up. According to his assistant, he flew to Europe last week to do some damage control with investors."

Matt hums, his gaze fixed on the road. "I'm surprised. The issue over there must be very important for him to stay silent." He glances at me. "Do you know what's going on?"

"No." I shake my head, fingers laced together in my lap. "We're a huge organization. There are always investors who need coddling, hands to shake. It never ends."

He hums again. "I think Charlee will have a lot to tell you."

I hope so. I'm so close to finding the last piece of the puzzle and having the complete picture. And with any luck, Charlee can lead me to it.

When we get there, his friends are all sitting on logs arranged around a crackling bonfire.

Nervousness sweeps across my body as we approach.

These are Matt's people. His family.

I don't want to mess it up.

As if he can sense my hesitation, Matt rounds the truck and circles his arms around my waist. "You're gonna be fine. I love you, so they'll love you too." With that, he guides me toward his friends.

"Hey guys," he throws out when we get there. "This is Zoé."

"Finally!" A woman with auburn hair jumps out of a man's lap.

I recognize her immediately.

"You're Charlee, right?" I ask, cradling my laptop to my chest.

She raises her eyebrows, a smirk stretching on her lips. "Matt talked about me?"

I chuckle. "No. I mean, yes, but that's not where I heard of you first. I saw one of your documentaries on TV." My cheeks heat. "Your passion for this town is contagious."

Her face lights up in the glow of the fire. "There's no better place in the world. This is Oliver, by the way," she says, settling back on his lap. He waves, drawing her closer to him.

I offer him a smile as Matt motions for me to sit on one of the logs, James and Lola scooting over to leave us some room.

"It's nice to see you again, Zoey," Lola says as she gives me a beer.

Matt snags it before I can grab it and twists the top off, hitting me with a grin that makes his dimple pop.

"So what do we do?" He asks, diving straight into it. "How do we put a stop to Oscar's plan?"

I garner my nerve and sit a little taller. "I need to know what happened here with his deal two years ago." I scan the group. "We don't have any record of the attempted project, which is weird. We typically keep copies of everything, even if proposals fall through. There's something he doesn't want me to know, but I think you all do. Tell me what happened."

Charlee watches me, the light of the fire dancing on her face. "Of course he doesn't. Oscar's shady as fuck." She glances at Oliver, who nods for her to go ahead. "Your dad wanted to tear down a historical building and put his resort in its place. When we realized it was against our bylaws, he still tried to convince our mayor to look the other way. Offered him money for it."

My stomach drops.

I knew it.

How many times can my father betray me? How many secrets will unfold before the man I thought I knew better than anyone turns out to be a total stranger?

"I think we should do some digging. Tonight," I say.

Eyes glinting, she rests her elbows on her thighs. "Because if he could do this to us…"

"Then how many other towns like Pine Falls are out there?" I conclude, nodding.

"How come you never realized what he was doing?" James asks, his tone marked with skepticism. "Aren't you the head of business development?"

"I am," I say, tearing my gaze away from Charlee. "But it doesn't mean I know everything my father does." Although I thought we were honest and transparent with each other. "I oversee a big team that scouts potential locations, identifying places we can expand or transform. My dad does his own thing. Clearly."

Matt rubs circles on my back. "I'm sorry, beautiful."

"Do you have access to the company's files?" Lola asks, nodding toward my laptop.

"I do."

I open it, connect to my phone's hotspot, and log in to Imperial Excellence's servers.

"So we find other examples, then we build a case against the company," Charlee says. "That should do the trick, shouldn't it?"

I swallow. "That's the plan."

My dad betrayed, lied to, used, and humiliated me. By all accounts, I should *relish* the thought of ripping his legacy to shreds. I should crave the satisfaction of watching it all burn to the ground. But we're talking about bringing the whole corporation down. His life's work. I can't shake the sticky feeling crawling up my spine at the idea. I won't back down. But Imperial Excellence is all I've ever known.

"We don't have to do this," Matt whispers, his gaze fixed on where my fingers hover above the keyboard. "We can find another way."

"I don't—" Charlee starts.

"We can find another way." Matt cuts her off sharply, punctuating every word.

I shake my head. "No, she's right." I blow out a deep breath, opening our acquisition data. "This is our best shot."

All I have left is this town. These people. And I'll do everything I can to protect them from Oscar Marchiatto.

Turns out, good old Dad has a lot of skeletons and shady business deals in his closet.

Questionable expropriations, construction on wetlands, last-minute changes to plans without approval from our architectural firm. We discovered at least five projects in the last ten years that raised my eyebrows.

In the past two weeks, with the help of Matt's friends, we've put together a solid case against Imperial Excellence, one concrete enough to present to the authorities. During those two weeks, we called mayors and contractors, gathered information, and asked for evidence. And bit by bit, we built an irrefutable record.

I leave my rental car in the company's underground parking and turn off the engine. Matt offered to come with me—insisted is more like it—but this is something I have to do on my own.

It's *my* dad to confront, *my* mess to clean, *my* future to build.

My inner child to heal.

As I'm striding for the elevators, my phone rings.

"Hi, handsome."

"Did you make it there okay?" Matt's voice is tinny and a little choppy down here under the building.

"Just parked." I press the elevator button with a shaky finger, my heart thumping against my breastbone. "Heading for his office now."

"How do you feel?"

I heave out a sigh. "Ready for it to be over."

He hums. "I understand. When you get home tonight, Daph and I will be ready to welcome you back with ice cream and a movie. Right, Daph?"

"Zoey can have the ice cream," she calls in the background. "I want the popcorn."

"Okay." I can't help but smile at the sound of her voice. "I'm going up," I say as the elevator doors whoosh open. "Wish me luck."

"You don't need it. Give him hell. I love you."

"I love you."

All the way up, my eyes remain fixed on the floor numbers as they scroll by.

Three. The number of weeks it took me to realize I was my dad's puppet.

Five. The people that I now call family.

Eight. How many times I've cried from sadness and rage over the past two weeks.

Twelve. The age I was when I understood my dad didn't really care about me.

Fifteen. The number of days it took me to bring this company down.

Ding.

The doors open on the twentieth floor, and I walk straight into my father's office, heart in my throat.

He watches me from his chair behind his desk, the Vancouver Harbour in the background.

"Finally back in the city, I see." He doesn't bother to stand and greet me. "I'm glad you came to your senses, princess."

"I'm not staying long," I say, holding his gaze.

He frowns, his mouth following the downward path I'm so familiar with. "Where are you going, then?"

Swallowing past the lump in my throat, I drop the envelope on his desk. "This is my official resignation letter. Today is my last day. I quit." I exhale sharply. "*God*, it feels good to say those fucking words to you."

He stares at the envelope like I've just tossed a bag full of trash, then sighs. "You never went through a rebellious phase as a teenager, so I guess I should have expected an early midlife crisis." He finally hauls himself out of his chair, then holds his hands out. "What do you want me to do, princess? Tell you I'm sorry I had to keep you in the dark with this project? I can't, because I'm not. It had to be done this way. You know why?"

He takes a step toward me, but I don't budge.

"It's because I know that heart of yours. You're tough on the outside but not so tough in here." He pats his chest. "The second I saw you with that man, I knew I'd made the right call. The faster you get over it, the faster we can move on."

His words glide over me like water on a pane of glass.

"In two minutes," I say, my tone stronger than I feel, "the police will barge through those doors and seize every document in this building. An investigation into the hotel group will be triggered. You will be arrested for fraudulent operations involving hush money, multiple law violations, and abuse of power. And me? I'll be cooperating with them in every way I can."

I take my own step forward, my voice as cold as steel. "I'll be the good little girl you taught me to be and burn your goddamn legacy to the ground."

He's too stunned to speak, his eyes full of horror and shock.

I don't linger.

I turn around and press the elevator button. When the doors open, I'm met with half a dozen police officers.

"He's over there," I say, my throat working hard. This time, I let myself look. I take in the face of the man who betrayed and hurt me in so many ways. The man who, despite it all, is, down to his bones, still my father. And then I step into the elevator and let the doors close on my past.

Matt and Daphne are waiting for me on the porch, Daph holding out a bowl of half-melted ice cream.

"I told you we would be ready to welcome you back with ice cream." Matt hits me with his trademark smile.

"We started the movie because I really wanted to watch it," Daph says.

The sight of their beaming faces lights up my whole heart, and the weight of the past few months evaporates from my shoulders like smoke in the wind. For the first time in thirty-two years, it feels as though I have something to come home to.

The realization wells up in my chest too quickly, too big to hold in, and as I hit the top step, I burst into tears, my legs turning to jelly.

Matt catches me before I fall to the ground, worry clouding his features.

"Whoa, Zoé, honey. What's wrong?" He cradles me in one arm, brushing away the hot tears rolling down my cheeks.

I bury my face in his chest, clinging to him.

"We can go back to the beginning of the movie," Daphne says, her tone a little panicked. "You don't have to be sad."

I laugh through the tears. "No, sweetie, it's not that. I'm sad, but I'm also relieved. It's a bit complicated. Come here."

I step away from Matt and pull her into a tight hug.

"Why are you crying if you're relieved?" she asks, her voice muffled in my hair.

I look up at Matt, whose eyes glisten under the porch's light. He swallows hard and sniffles, a comforting hand rubbing circles on my back.

"People cry for lots of reasons," I explain, keeping her snug against me. "When they're sad, when they're happy, when they're angry. And I guess I'm feeling a bit of it all right now. I had to say goodbye to someone important to me, so I was sad. But mostly, I'm relieved. And happy."

She pulls away, still holding my... well, at this point it's more cream than ice cream. "Why are you happy?"

I smile, my eyes filling again. "Because I get to stay with you guys."

Her legs start to bounce. "*You do?* Perfect. Do you like anime?" Before I have time to answer, she says, "We're watching *Mary and The Witch's Flower*. I can tell you what happened already if you want."

"Why don't you go back inside?" Matt says. "We'll join you in a minute, okay?"

"Okay! I won't restart the movie until you come back!"

And she's off.

I chuckle. "I love her so much." I sniffle, my gaze lingering until she vanishes inside.

Matt wraps his arms around me and pulls me close. "She loves you too. I love you too." He brings his forehead to mine. "Are you okay? Everything went… well? As well as it could go, anyway."

I thread my fingers through his hair. I still can't believe he's mine. My new beginning.

"It's done. I'm sure it'll be all over the news in the coming days, and the investigators will likely have lots of questions for me. But I also have so much to do here. I need to mend things with Rob and the town and explain that the company is probably going under, and that the hotel will not happen. But I have an idea I want to float to Ruth for the Butterfly Inn. If"— I grimace—"she'll speak to me. While I stayed there, it got me thinking. We could develop something great there. Since she voted against the project in the first place, I imagine she'll be happy when she finds out the deal is imploding, and anyway, I want to keep the promises I've made and—"

"Hey, hey, hey. Shh." Matt presses his lips on mine. "Take a breath, beautiful."

I laugh and then I do. I breathe him in, firewood and daisies, that scent of his I've come to crave. It curls around my heart like a cooling relief, settling the beat in my chest and slowing the pulse in my veins.

He clutches my waist, drawing me to him until there's not an inch of space between us.

"I know a lot of things are up in the air right now. Lots of things we need to tackle. Lots of loose ends to tie up. But not tonight. Just for a while, the rest of the world can wait." He cups my face, tilting me to him. "Tonight, I want to savor the happiness of finally having you all to myself. Of being able to think about tomorrow without fighting the fear that you won't be there. I want to take my time and love you all night, knowing that there are countless more ahead of us."

He kisses me, sealing his words on my lips like treasures he wants to keep. Unable to resist him, I tug on his hair, pulling him closer. Always closer.

His groan drowns out my own when our tongues brush. I have to force myself not to get carried away, because waiting for us inside is the other love of his life.

After a few minutes, we break apart, both a little out of breath.

Inside, we spend the rest of the evening with Daph on the couch, watching the movie and eating ice cream with popcorn sprinkled on top.

When she falls asleep halfway through, Matt carries her upstairs and tucks her into her bed before we slip into ours.

He keeps his promise.

All night, I lose myself in him, in his love, in his warmth, in the kisses he presses against my hipbone and thighs and all my secret places. Over and over, he tells me things that make me shake with pleasure. "I love you so much," hushed into the shell of my ear. "I want you again," groaned between my legs. Until we eventually fall asleep, drunk on all this love we've finally found.

And tomorrow, we'll go back to square one with Pine Falls, with my life, with his business, and everything else that comes our way.

But I'll never have to do any of it alone ever again.

Epilogue

Zoey

A Year Later

"*Y*ou know I have a zero percent chance of getting anything done when you come home in that outfit," Matt says, his hands roaming over my ass.

I roll my eyes, even though, secretly, I'm not the least bit annoyed by it. "And by outfit, you mean my scrubs."

"Yes." He slips his fingers under the hem of my top. "I told you, don't say scrubs. It's a *uniform*."

He kisses my neck, whispering my name, his grip tightening with painful pleasure. It almost makes me forget that I should stop him before he gets too wild.

Horny Matt is always my favorite to come home to after a long shift.

Studying pediatric nursing and doing my residency at the local hospital leaves me exhausted most of the time.

So when I get home, it's easy to give in. Most of the time, he insists on taking care of me, helping me out of my clothes, washing my hair, and doing all sorts of wicked things to my body. Then he feeds me frozen meals, and I fall asleep against him on the couch.

But not tonight. We have somewhere to be.

"I should let you know that a kid threw up on me today."

His hold on me loosens, and he buries his face in my neck with a sigh. "Well, that was an instant turnoff."

"I know," I chuckle, raking my nails through his hair. "It was the goal. We can't be late for the town meeting. Lola said it's an important one."

"Then let's get in the shower. We'll multitask." With a smirk, he tugs on the drawstring of my pants.

"I thought you said you took one already," I laugh when he bites my neck playfully.

"I'm covered in vomit by proxy. I need to wash this off." He lifts my top over my head, and when his attention lands on my breasts, his eyes go feral. "Yes. I feel very dirty. Shower. Now."

He picks me up roughly, pulling a yelp from me. As he strides to the bathroom, I cling to him, my legs encircling his waist and my arms draped around his neck.

The water is barely warm when he hauls me into the shower. "You've got two minutes, honey," I pant into the hollow of his throat.

Under the spray, he lines himself up with my entrance, smooth and hard. "Oh, don't worry. It's gonna take way less than that."

He pushes inside me, and like every time, I need a couple of seconds to adjust to his fullness. But when I'm ready, when I squirm and beg him to move, he doesn't hesitate. He fucks me hard and fast, hands clutching my hips, gliding me up and down his cock until I'm writhing against him and my legs clench tightly around his waist.

He follows me right after, moaning my name as he spills inside me.

When my vision has returned, he eases me to my feet and kisses me with aching softness. "I love you."

I smile against his mouth. "I love you more. Now get ready or we're gonna be truly late."

"Yes, ma'am."

Saying that the last year has been busy would be the understatement of the century. Busy would mean studying and doing my residency, driving an hour each way, and enjoying a few days off every other week.

That'd be the easy version. My year has been unbreathable.

After the investigation into my father's company, the hotel project on Emile's land was put on hold, and with it, all the promises I had made to the local small businesses and the people I've come to care so much for.

It took a lot of work to earn their trust again. Eventually, though, most apologized for their outbursts that dreadful night. Patty, naturally, did not. But after the town buried their hatchet, life reverted to the way it used to be. Before my residency, my days consisted of coffee at Rosie's and croissants at Mia's. Lounging in Lola's bookstore, devouring all the smut she recommended, then heading to Coop for a late afternoon beer.

After long talks with Ruth, I finally convinced her to let me invest in her hotel. My funds would allow her to renovate, expand, and upgrade her outdated booking system, as well as establish the partnerships I had always planned for.

Once school started, I had to get creative with my time. When I wasn't at the hospital or following my classes online, I was checking in on Justin's construction crew and helping Matt grow his business through the mentorship program—which, thankfully, was not legally tied to my dad's company. This year, he hired his second employee, and with the store running full speed, he was able to fund his sister's school without breaking a sweat.

Every minute available after that, I've devoted to Matt and Daphne.

And finally, *finally*, three months ago, just in time for the tourist season, the new and improved Butterfly Inn opened its doors. Bookings have reached a record high. Carl's expedition trips are sold out until next year, the microbrewery tours we've organized with Cooper are a must-hit on the Pine Falls itinerary, and Mia and Rosie are the official breakfast suppliers.

The town has been thriving, and the best part is that the locals are reaping the rewards of all that hard work.

"What are you thinking about?" Matt asks as we walk hand in hand into the room.

"How far everybody has come this year. It feels like a whole new town. Don't you think?"

He squeezes my hand. "It does, and you have everything to do with it."

I smile, accepting the compliment, knowing he won't allow the brush-off on the tip of my tongue.

"Why do you think Rob called this emergency meeting?" James asks when we get to our group of friends.

"It has to be about Emile's land," Oliver says. "It's been sitting on the town's books for too long. They have to decide what to do with it."

"Hopefully someone will propose something soon," I mutter as Matt guides me into a chair.

"How's school going?" Charlee asks, leaning forward to peer around Oliver.

"Good," I say. "Saving every penny I can to eventually open my own practice in town one day."

Matt hums next to me, his arm resting on the back of my chair. His support over the past few months has been unwavering.

Opening a practice here in Pine Falls. That's the new dream. But between the money I poured into the program for Matt's store and the renovations at the Butterfly Inn, my bank account is running low.

Mom offered to help me, but she already lives on a relatively tight budget. Having her by my side, supporting me at every turn, means more to me than any amount of money could.

When I broke down and told her about the Pine Falls saga, we spent hours on the phone, the two of us fighting to catch our breath between sobs.

Despite its loads of challenges, this year has been transformative in so many ways. The most important change of them all was the shift in my career and aspirations. It took me a while to find the specialty that was right for me and even longer to figure out what I want to achieve after I finish school.

All my life, others have made choices for me. Then, last year, I suddenly found myself standing in front of a blank canvas, and the sheer number of options was overwhelming. But with Matt and my mom acting like my own personal cheerleaders, celebrating victories as ridiculous as when I passed my first exam, I'm no longer afraid.

It'll take time, but I'll get my practice up and running. And once I do, it'll be the most reputable pediatric practice in all of BC. I'll make sure of it.

"Everyone, please grab a seat. This won't take long," Rob says into the mic, his tone official. "Thank you. The matter on the table tonight is a vote on a project for Emile's land, as I'm sure everybody knows."

Frowning, I tilt closer to Matt. "Did you know?"

"No."

"Matt," Rob calls. "Would you join me up here, please?"

Twisting to face him head-on, I blink.

Matt only grins, a slow, teasing expression that suddenly makes my stomach flip.

"Okay, maybe I knew a little bit." He drops a quick kiss on my cheek. "Okay, bye."

Then he's gone. Up and out of his seat before I can string a single thought together.

My heart takes off at a sprint as he joins Rob at the podium. What is happening?

I glance at Lola, and when she spots me, a mysterious smirk tugs at the corner of her mouth. Charlee catches my eye and winks. *Winks.*

What is going on?

"Thank you all for coming tonight," Matt says into the mic. His voice moves over me like a caress. "As we all know, we welcomed a new member into the Pine Falls family last year." His eyes find me. He always finds me. "She arrived in ridiculous shoes and yelled at me for almost running her over while her head was buried in her phone. Remember that, honey?"

As laughter bubbles up around me, I manage a dazed nod.

"What are you doing?" I mouth.

His grin widens. "I believe everyone here has met Zoé," he continues. "And therefore, you all know she's one of the most selfless souls you'll ever encounter. She gives everything she has to the people she loves, and, lucky for us, we are those people. For the past year, she's poured her heart and energy into making good on a promise that fell apart through no fault of her own. And somehow, she still delivered. For every single one of us."

My throat tightens, and heat pricks at the backs of my eyes.

Lola scoots over, taking Matt's chair, and slides her hand in mine.

"What is he doing?" I whisper, voice cracking.

She nods to him. "Just listen."

"I won't make this a big speech. You already know why I'm here. But Zoé, honey, you don't. So let me skip to the part that matters. Tonight, I am officially submitting plans for a project on Emile's land. My proposal grants Zoé the land for her future pediatric nursing practice. The practice will be built with the help of every willing citizen in Pine Falls, through any service they can offer and materials they can donate, or simply through time and a little bit of love. All in favor, please raise your hand."

There's no holding back my tears. One by one, people around me lift their hands. Next to me, Lola beams and releases me so she can raise hers high.

"Patty, don't be a jerk. Come on," Matt adds playfully.

Patty groans, but she puts her hand in the air too.

"There you go." Matt chuckles. "In a unanimous vote, the project is adopted." He leans toward the mic, his voice dipping low, full of tenderness. "Honey, everybody in this room has rallied for you. This is how loved you are."

I break. A full-on tears-streaming, heart-bursting mess. The room erupts, the air swelling with cheers. But my brain can't keep up with the avalanche of joy and disbelief crashing over me.

When I wipe at my eyes, clearing my vision, I find Matt standing at the podium, waiting for me with a steady smile, his gaze never leaving mine. My world narrows to him. To us.

Lola nudges me, startling me back to reality. "Go," she whispers, teary-eyed too.

It takes a second to get my legs moving and to wipe away another wave of tears, but then I'm weaving through the crowd full of people I consider family, heading straight for the podium.

Matt reaches for me, sliding his arm around my waist and dragging me to him in one smooth movement. I bury my face in his shoulder and laugh through the hot tears staining his shirt.

"What the hell just happened?" I whisper into his chest.

He bends down, his lips brushing my hair. "After all these years, Zoé, you finally get everything you deserve." He pulls back a fraction, zeroing in on something behind me. "There's one more thing missing. Wait for me."

He lets go of me and jogs to the back of the room, where his parents and Daphne are standing. He crouches and takes something from his sister's hands before leaning in for a hug. Then he darts back.

"Now," he says, his mouth at my ear, the words just for me. "For this part, I only need one vote."

He kneels, holding a beautiful oval-shaped ring between his thumb and index finger.

The crowd lets out a collective gasp. My breath catches too, my knees ready to give out.

I don't fight it. I go down and meet him there, crying again.

"Are you serious right now?" I choke.

He swallows hard, his voice trembling like he's battling to keep himself from falling apart right along with me. "Zoé, the moment you showed up, you turned my life on its head, and I've never been the same. I know it's fucking cliché, but I'll roll with it."

He lets out a wet chuckle.

"You came here with the wild notion that you were not worth loving, but honey, letting me love you is the greatest gift you could ever give me. Every day, I wake up to find the love of my life sleeping soundly next to me, and I go to bed every night with the overwhelming knowledge that you'll fall asleep in my arms. It's a heady thing, the realization that this could be my life until I take my last breath. I don't want to wait any longer to make it official."

His eyes shine as they lock with mine.

"So what do you say? Will you marry me?"

The world stills. My heart stops. And even though I'm crying, and laughing, and probably in shock, the answer comes to me so clearly.

"Yes," I breathe. Then, louder, with everything I have, I say it again. "*Yes!*"

I throw myself into his arms, and he catches me like he always does, steady and sure, kissing me like no one's watching, even as the room bursts into applause.

He draws back, his face lit up with pure joy. "I love you so much," he says as he slides the diamond onto my finger with a shaking hand.

I say it back again and again as I pepper him with kisses, my tears melding with his, our hearts pounding in sync.

Somewhere in the room, Charlee's shouts ring out over the chaos, and then there's a pop. Champagne flows, and just like that, we're pulled into hugs and laughter and well wishes. Through it all, Matt never lets go of my hand, the one he put a ring on.

The party goes on all night. Music blasts through speakers, and the center of the room transforms into a dance floor that has Matt swaying his hips against mine.

Hours later, we're back home, tired but grinning from ear to ear. Side by side on the porch, we look up at a sky starting to soften into the pink of dawn, my head resting on his shoulder.

I hold my hand out in front of me, admiring the way the diamond catches the morning light. The sight fills me with pride and tugs at my heart at the same time.

"Everything okay, beautiful?" Matt murmurs.

I nod against him, smiling. "This is gonna be a happy life."

He slides his arm around my waist, nestling me deeper into him. "I agree. Forever has a nice ring to it."

Acknowledgments

My first thanks go to Grace. Thank you so much for being an incredible beta and sensitivity reader. You took FaceTime calls during a road trip to Nashville, offered thoughtful feedback, and guided me through the nuances of autism representation with care and honesty. Jack was in my thoughts the entire time I wrote this book, and I truly hope I've made both him and you proud. On a side note, Horny Matt is for you.

Thank you as well to Paul, Grace's husband, who generously shared his own experiences—as both a man and a father—to help me better understand what it really means to care for a child on the spectrum. Your insight made the book better, and I'm deeply grateful.

To Sara and Tyla. Thank you for being awesome sensitivity readers and for helping me fine-tune the autism representation. Your comments were thoughtful and incredibly valuable.

To Lety. Thank you for holding my hand throughout the process of writing this book, and really, through life. For beta reading, offering advice, chatting with me, reassuring me, brainstorming with me when I didn't have a lot of confidence in the story, and being an amazing friend all around. Your steadfast support this past year has meant the world to me, and I'm so incredibly grateful to have you in my life. I'm so glad we made it through. I love you.

To Leni, for once again creating the most beautiful cover I've ever seen. I love that you took a chance on using watercolor brushes. The result is breathtaking. We've been doing this together for four years now, and I consider myself incredibly lucky. I adore you.

To Jess and Payton. Thank you for being the best beta readers! Your excitement, feedback, and constant support made writing this book so much more fun. I'm so happy I can count on you to always be on my team.

To Gen. A big thank you for staying on the phone with me for hours to untangle a plot that truly went through hell and back. The cocklection would not exist without you. I hope you see that as the best legacy you could ever leave on this earth. I'd be proud. Also, you championed me to write Matt's story, and I'm so glad you did. It wasn't easy, but your excitement for it made me push through. I love you.

To Valkyrie. Thank you for being there for me throughout this writing process and waiting patiently until I was out of my writing cave. I'm never the best of friends during those times, but you still stood by me. I love you.

To Beth, the best editor there is! Thank you for working hours on the manuscript. The book is endlessly better because of all the hard work you did. I know working with a nonnative English speaker isn't always easy, and I deeply appreciate the care and effort you brought to all three editing rounds.

To the indie bookstores I've had the pleasure of partnering with over the past year, thank you for carrying my books, doing pre-orders with me, and being the best advocates for indie authors. If I had the money for a tour, I'd do it in a heartbeat to thank you all in person.

A huge thank you to the real, human artists I've had the privilege of working with to create art for this book (@kidovna and @kf1n3), especially Anna. Thank you for working so quickly to meet my deadline. I fear the world isn't ready for the day we meet in person. It's gonna be fireworks.

To Jess, my PA extraordinaire! Thank you for creating social media posts for me and helping me out with marketing. If I sell more books, it's because you rock.

To Emily, Kelley, and Emily. Your support since day one has meant the world to me. You each hold a special place in my heart, and I'm so grateful to have met you through this little corner of the internet. Every book I write, I have you guys on my mind, and I just want to make you so proud.

To my Katie. Thank you for being the best of friends. For coming with me to every convention, for endless FaceTime calls, for feeding into my Taylor Swift delusion, and always being there for me. I love you to the moon and to Saturn.

To David. I love you so much. Your joy is contagious, and the way you support me every chance you get makes my heart swell tenfold. You're my most fervent champion, and I'm so lucky to do life with you (now go read my books, though).

And finally, to my readers. Thank you, thank you, *thank you*. Every year, more of you join the "Elodie's Readers Club," and it fills my heart to see this little community grow. I truly couldn't do this without you. Your passion for my books, your reviews, your posts, your likes, your messages, your support, and all the love you've shown me over the past four years mean everything.

I want to keep writing books you're proud to hold in your hands and display on your shelves. I hope Matt and Zoey's story will be as dear to you as it is to me.

About the author

Elodie Colliard is a Canadian and French romance author based in Montreal, where she lives with her two very needy cats and her romance-worthy partner. Though she now calls Canada home, her heart is never far from the Alps where she grew up.

An avid reader (and dreamer) since childhood, she never gets tired of watching people fall in love. After all, she's a Cancer through and through, and emotions are her specialty.

When she's not immersed in reading or working her other full-time job in politics, you can find Elodie crocheting, cuddling with her cats, or behind her keyboard, creating the heartfelt, empowering love stories everyone can dream of.

Follow her on

Instagram/Threads @elosreadingcorner
Tiktok @authorelodiecolliard
www.authorelodiecolliard.com